The Green Viper

by

Rob Sinclair

CW00953659

Also By Rob Sinclair

The James Ryker Series

The Red Cobra (Book 1)
The Black Hornet (Book 2)
The Silver Wolf (Book 3)

Stand Alone

Dark Fragments

The Enemy Series

Dance With The Enemy (Book 1)
Rise of The Enemy (Book 2)
Hunt For The Enemy (Book 3)

Sleeper 13

Praise For Rob Sinclair

The Silver Wolf offers everything you could need in a thriller, it's dark and heavy hitting which gives it an edge, there's suspense but plenty of action for the adrenaline junkies, twists all over and I can't stress enough how amazing the overall plot is. – ***David's Book Blurg***

OMG what a story….. Once again the author draws you in straight from the start and doesn't let you go until the very last page. – ***Chelle's Book Reviews***

The Silver Wolf is an exciting and thrilling read that sent my heart racing. If a gripping story line with bags of action isn't enough to tempt you then believe me when I say The Silver Wolf himself will. – ***By The Letter Book Reviews***

Fast paced, action packed and absolutely bloody brilliant!! – ***The Quiet Knitter***

It has everything you'd want in an espionage thriller – a tight twisty plot, great characters, horrible villains and surprise twists. – ***Between the Lines Book Blog***

For Lynne and Les

Prologue

He was almost numb to the pain now, his mind and his body both spent. There was the unmistakable metallic taste of blood on his tongue. It coated his mouth, filled his throat. He swallowed, no longer able to muster the strength to spit the thick liquid out. Seconds later more blood was already pooling.

The skin on his face was stiff from the dried blood caked on his cheeks, but more blood was still fresh, coming from his nose, which must be broken he thought, and from the gash above his eye. His head throbbed and with each pulse a new wave of liquid oozed down his face.

He remained upright, but only because of the two men holding him. Without their support, he surely wouldn't be able to stand.

They shoved him another step forward, closer to the edge, their grips like industrial vices. Both men were tall. Taller than he was, and heftier too. Despite this, he wanted desperately to fight back, wanted to hurt them. Yet his body wouldn't allow it. His head and mind felt disconnected from the rest of him.

His thoughts wandered. He tried to remember how he'd come to be *here*.

Of course, he knew the answer in a physical sense – out on the balcony on the top floor of the apartment block. The two men had dragged him out, each one wrenching an arm firmly behind his back, twisting his wrists so that his elbows, his shoulders, were at breaking point.

What he struggled to answer was how his life had brought him to this point. When did it all go so wrong?

Throughout the ordeal, the two men hadn't spoken a word to him. But then they hadn't needed to.

He knew why *they* were there.

Another step and they reached the balcony edge. His head dangled forward and he could see the outline of the thick concrete slabs far below. The blood stopped pooling in his mouth, the droplets instead spilling into the emptiness beneath him. He felt a chilling wind against his face.

He blinked, then opened his eyes wide. Thought he saw the ground moving – coming toward him, it seemed.

He thought again, *How did I get here?*

And then he thought about *her*.

Chapter one

Mid-June, central London. At 9am the sun was already blazing in the deep-blue sky. People were out and about in their droves, those lucky enough not to be heading to the office dressed as if they were already at the beach. Who could blame them? The city was sweltering. The heatwave was three days old, though in typical UK fashion thunderstorms would likely wipe away any trace of summer before the end of the week, and the city would abruptly return to its normal drizzle. For a short while, though, London could just have well been in the subtropics.

James Ryker couldn't stand it.

To him the heat was nothing but an aggravation and an inconvenience. He'd barely slept in the night, again. With no air con in his modest second-floor apartment, a few hundred yards from the southern edge of Hampstead Heath, he'd been forced to leave the windows open all night. Which wasn't exactly a quiet experience with traffic noise and late-night revelry continuing through until dawn and beyond.

This perhaps explained, even despite the lack of sleep, why Ryker was up and out so early, and why he was in such a bad mood as he jostled past pedestrians on his way to Hampstead Underground. Wearing a pair of jeans and a plain grey polo shirt, he wasn't exactly dressed for the occasion either and sweat droplets were forming all over his skin.

He paused outside the entrance to the red-brick Edwardian station. Just looking at the throngs of commuters hustling to get inside and knowing how unbearable the heat would be down there was enough to make Ryker's head spin.

No. He'd rather walk.

A little over an hour later – and a good deal sweatier, having strode at pace – he finally arrived outside the entrance to Carter & Blake's, an exclusive private bank which had only two branches in the world; one in London, the other in Zurich. Housed in a wide-fronted neoclassical sandstone building on a street full of high-end boutique offices, the bank was as discreet as they came – no colourful signage, no ATM, no posters in the windows advertising mortgages or savings account interest rates. The only indication at all of the nature of the business occupying the building was the brass nameplate bolted to the rendered stonework by the entrance.

Ryker wiped his brow with his arm and drained the rest of the bottled water he'd picked up on the walk, then headed up the three steps to the glossy black double doors. He pressed the intercom button. Stooped slightly so that his face, at the top of his six feet three inch frame, was within view of the camera. He'd tidied himself up that morning, was clean-shaven. His green eyes sparkled, his mousy-brown hair still neatly trimmed from the day before, though his casual attire was almost certainly far removed from that of the bank's usual clientele. At this establishment looks really didn't matter. If your name was on the list, you were coming in… so to speak.

'Good morning, sir,' came a tinny male voice through the intercom speaker. 'May I help you?'

'John Burrows,' Ryker said, using one of his many assumed identities from another life. 'Here to access my box.'

'Your thumb on the reader please.'

Beneath the intercom box, a small plastic cover, flush with the wall, slid out of sight, revealing the thumbprint scanner beneath. Ryker pushed his right thumb onto the pad. Waited a few seconds. As ever there was no green light or ding or any other indication as to whether the scanner had accepted his thumbprint. Ryker looked up to the camera again.

'Okay, thank you, Mr Burrows. Please come in.'

There was a clunk as the locks on the front doors released. Ryker glanced over his shoulder – habit more than anything else – then headed inside.

***

Ten minutes later Ryker was standing in the basement underneath Carter & Blake's, in a small booth, five feet by five feet square. Behind him a thick maroon curtain was pulled across to give him privacy from the vault manager stationed across the room beyond. In front of Ryker, on top of a polished wooden desk attached to the wall, was the dull grey metal safe deposit box that had lain untouched in the vault for so long.

More than two years, Ryker had figured, but how long was it exactly? Perhaps more than three years even. He'd never been a fan of using regular high street banks, much preferring to keep his assets in hard form. He'd long made use of safe deposit boxes and the like for keeping his monetary wealth, and other crucial possessions, secure. Over the last few months he'd slowly been working around the houses, heading back to old haunts in the UK and beyond, dipping into his cash reserves as and when needed. Despite the continued offers and requests for his services, from one man in particular, Ryker was still enjoying a well-earned break.

Well, perhaps *enjoying* wasn't exactly the right word. But he wasn't quite ready – mentally – to return to action just yet, and until that point came, he'd have to continue to use the not insignificant cash he'd built up over the years.

Ryker lifted the lid on the box and looked inside. Several bundles of sterling notes, totalling well over six figures. Some euros, dollars. Two passports. He flipped through them quickly. A flood of memories crashed through his mind. He put the passports back. Had no need for those right now. In many ways he hoped he never would again.

He picked up one of the bundles of sterling and stuffed it into his jeans pocket. Was about to close the lid when a small object partly hidden at the back of the box caught his eye. He stuck his hand in and lifted it out. A small, plain cardboard box. Inside was a mobile phone and charger.

He frowned. It took his brain a few seconds to recall when he'd left that and why. He rarely used a phone for more than a few weeks at a time, simply picking up cheap prepaid handsets and discarding them when the money ran out. So why had he kept this one?

The memory hit him, and he suddenly recalled exactly when he'd last been to Carter & Blake's. He'd had that phone before heading off to Russia for an assignment that went wrong. Very wrong. How his life had changed since then…

He pushed the power button on the phone. No juice. The device had been left untouched for more than two years after all. He pulled out the charger and plugged it into the socket underneath the desk. It took a couple of minutes before the green screen of the cheap and out-of-date handset came to life. Ryker stared at the top-left corner. No signal. He lifted the handset up, searching. Got a single bar, though it only lasted a few seconds. Shaking his head, he pulled the phone down and scrolled through. No call history. No messages. Not a surprise.

The phone vibrated in his hand. Ryker's eyes flicked to the top again and he saw the single bar disappear once more. But the intermittent signal was sufficient for the message to get through. Ryker, big thumbs on too small keys, clumsily tapped away to open up the text. Focused on the date initially. The message had been waiting in the ether for more than a month. Ryker stared at the content. Not even a whole word, just two letters and a number.

HP2

He frowned. He knew what the message meant. But it was impossible.

He stared at the sender's number. Was absolutely sure he didn't recognise it. He made a mental note of the digits, then quickly stuffed the phone and charger into his pocket, picked up the deposit box, turned and pulled the curtain across.

Over the other side of the room the immaculately groomed vault manager was still sitting quietly behind his desk. He looked up expectantly.

'Mr Burrows, you're finished?'

'Yes.'

'You got what you needed?'

'And more.'

***

Ryker stepped out into the sunshine and squinted, bringing his hand up to shield his eyes. Not only was it impossibly bright compared to the bank's basement, but it felt like the temperature had risen several degrees in the few minutes he'd been inside the cool interior. With his eyes and his body still adjusting, he headed on down the steps and made his way on foot east toward Hyde Park, the grumble of petrol and diesel engines, the whoosh of tyres and the honking of horns from the traffic on the busy city roads filling his ears. He soon arrived at Marble Arch, and stepped across the jam-packed tarmac along with the hordes of tourists and locals aiming for the park, past the multitude of black cabs waiting at the lights.

He moved into the park through a wrought-iron gate by the looming white marble ceremonial arch, then purposefully along twisting paths until he reached the shimmering Serpentine Lake. The scorched grassy fields to his side were already packed with sunbathers enjoying the weather. Rubbish bins overflowed with remnants of the night before, the orange-jacketed park staff struggling to keep up with the mess of the masses – like Ryker, the park workers probably couldn't wait for the rain to arrive.

Seeing the park so busy, Ryker thought about leaving and coming back another time, earlier in the day, or at night, or at least once the weather had returned to normal when the park would be much quieter. But then sometimes the more crowded an area, the easier it was to become congruous with the surroundings.

Keeping his head low, Ryker continued along the edge of the lake that was crammed with blue pedalos slowly bobbing about. He moved on past the boat-hire centre and spotted the bench he was looking for further in the distance. An elderly couple were sitting there together, their hands entwined on the man's lap. Ryker carried on up to them and took the small space to the man's right at the edge of the bench.

None of the three said a word. Ryker kept his eyes on the water in front of him though he sensed the man and lady shuffling uncomfortably at his presence. Two long minutes later the couple got to their feet. The man mumbled something under his breath. Ryker looked up and smiled at the man who frowned before turning and plodding off with the woman.

Sometimes it paid to be quietly mysterious.

Ryker quickly glanced around him again, then slipped the small multitool from his trouser pocket and flicked out the two-inch-long knife. He pushed the tip of the blade behind the small plaque screwed to the top wooden panel at the back of the bench and carefully pushed down. He moved the knife back and forth a couple of times… sure enough, the yellowed edges of a piece of paper poked out from underneath the plaque. Ryker pushed down further then carefully prised the paper away. He put the knife back in his pocket and glanced about again to satisfy himself no one was giving him the eye. All clear.

He stared down at the small piece of paper, mangled by weeks of weathering. Carefully unfolded it. The note was handwritten.

I need your help. Call me.

No sign off, just a phone number he didn't recognise. His face gave away no reaction, yet his brain was swimming as to who the message was from and what it meant. One thing he did know was who it *wasn't* from.

Only two people knew of Ryker's drop points, and of the deliberately old school methods of communication adopted in order to send messages – instructions – via those avenues. Ryker was one of those two people. The other was Charles McCabe, Mackie, Ryker's ex-boss at the clandestine Joint Intelligence Agency. But the message wasn't from Mackie. It couldn't be. After all, when this message was left here, Mackie was already long dead.

Chapter two

The South Greenwich Hospital was a private clinic in an ominous-looking blue-brick Victorian building that to Ryker looked like it could have been an asylum from a horror film, had it not been kept in such good condition. A new wing on the eastern side of the building built out of aluminium and seven feet high panes of glass showed the relative wealth both of the company who operated the clinic and of the people who could afford to use it.

Ryker sat on a bench among the sycamore trees in the open gardens at the front of the facility. He checked his watch. Ten minutes late. He spotted movement off to his right and looked up to see Peter Winter shuffling toward him. Winter, a similar age to Ryker, still carried a youthful appearance with a thin, wrinkle-free face and full head of light-brown hair, yet he walked like he was thirty years older. A result of the bomb blast that had nearly killed him and everyone else inside the offices of the JIA the last time Ryker had worked an assignment for them.

'How's the leg?' Ryker asked, not getting up from the bench.

'The leg's not too bad. My hip? That's another story, but I won't bore you with the details.'

Winter turned, took his left foot off the floor, outstretched the leg, then more or less fell backward into the seat, grimacing as he did so.

'So here we are. Again,' Winter said a couple of heavy breaths later, a pained look still on his face.

'Here we are.'

'I wondered how long it would take for you to get bored living a life of nothingness.'

'I've been plenty busy,' Ryker lied.

'Sure you have.'

Ryker glared over at Winter. Noticed the thick bags under his eyes. He wondered what case the Commander was working. There was no doubt Ryker was intrigued about life within the JIA, now that he was no longer a part of it, even if he wouldn't admit it to anyone. And he certainly wouldn't ask about it.

'I was here not too long ago, actually,' Winter said.

He slipped his hand into his pocket, brought out a battered brown leather wallet. He rummaged inside and took out a small square photo of a bald-headed blue-eyed baby.

'Jessica. Six months old. She was born here.' He nodded over to the clinic. So perhaps his newborn child, rather than a gruelling case, explained the bags under his eyes.

'You didn't trust the NHS?' Ryker said.

Winter shrugged, smiled. 'There are *some* benefits to what I do.'

'Congratulations,' Ryker said, doing a good job of hiding his bitterness, though he had no ill feelings toward Winter. He was only jealous of how his own life was so empty in comparison, even though he could never imagine settling down and having children.

'Thanks, but believe me, it's no walk in the park. You might see me as nothing more than a desk jockey, but still, the JIA and babies are not a sleep-filled mix, that's for sure.'

'I can imagine.'

'But enough of that. Why don't you explain properly what's brought us here?'

'Mackie.'

Winter huffed. 'Yeah, you said that on the phone. Someone's been using your old drop points.'

'Someone who doesn't know shit about drop points.'

Winter raised an eyebrow but Ryker didn't bother to explain. The issue was, the drop points were a means of communicating only if Ryker or Mackie had somehow been compromised. As such any message sent by that means would include pre-designated code words, both to show the message as genuine but also to alert the other party to any particular threat. There was no such coding on the message left for Ryker. Yet someone had still known about the drop point. Someone who had a number for Ryker that was more than two years old. A phone he'd used in the few weeks before heading off to Russia. An assignment that saw Mackie killed and Ryker's life turned upside down…

'I can't believe Mackie would have been so stupid to let slip–'

'Not stupid,' Ryker said. 'Careful. And caring. What would you do to protect your family?'

Winter sighed and looked over to the hospital again. 'I understand she's not in a good way,' he said. 'But the doctors have agreed you can see her.'

'Thank you.'

'Do you want me to come too? I already have a fair idea what this might be about.'

'You do?'

Winter held Ryker's eye for a minute but didn't elaborate.

'No. I'll see her alone. You wait here for me if you like.'

Another sigh. Winter checked his watch. 'Yeah.'

***

The inside of the hospital was clean and modern, at odds with the gloomy gothic appearance of the outside. A young male nurse called Lehman escorted Ryker through the wide and bright corridors, past numerous closed doors, most with blinds pulled down. There were no open wards here; every patient had their own private space. They eventually came to a stop and Lehman knocked on the door then slowly pushed it open and stuck his head inside. He muttered something then stepped in, closing the door behind him.

Ryker remained standing outside, straining to hear. A few seconds later came the scrape and rustle as curtains were drawn open along their runners. Lehman's head poked out of the door again.

'She's just woken up, but she wants to see you.'

Ryker nodded and Lehman opened the door fully and stepped to the side. Ryker headed in. His eyes fell upon the frail woman sunken into the bed. Her lined face was almost as pale as the sheets that covered her body. Her hair had lost nearly all of its colour and was thin and wispy. She looked over at Ryker. She was breathing heavily, wheezing, her chest rising and falling several inches with each constricted breath. A tube ran out of each nostril to the ventilator machine by her side.

'Carl,' she said. Carl. Another name. Another life.

'Janet.'

Janet Campbell. Charles McCabe's widow. She'd never taken his surname. His decision. Protection for her, for the family – a degree of separation from him, given the clandestine and often dangerous nature of Mackie's work.

Today was the first time Ryker had seen Janet since… No, he tried not to think about that.

Her eyes welled up as he approached. Despite himself, his own eyes filled and he had to fight hard to hold off the tears.

Ryker crouched down beside her. Thought about taking her hand, but that was a step too far. They weren't that close. Never had been.

'I'm sorry,' he said. 'I–'

'You don't need to say anything about that. It wasn't your fault. And you got the people who killed him.'

'He was like a father to me,' Ryker said, hanging his head.

'And you were like a son to him.'

Ryker clenched his fists in anger at all of the shit that had pervaded his life. Losing Mackie, and the circumstances surrounding his death, remained one of his most raw experiences.

'But you weren't his son,' Janet said, a certain coldness in her words.

The change of mood helped to bring Ryker's focus back. He looked up. Saw the hardened look on her face.

'You weren't his son,' she said again. 'But you can help his son. Please, Carl, you have to help my son.'

11

Chapter three

Scott Campbell was dressed in his best suit, a navy-blue tailored outfit from Savile Row – though by far one of the cheaper options from the renowned London street. Unsure of exactly what to expect from the day ahead, he had decided to treat it like he would have done any other day six months ago when he still had a client-facing role for Berwin Moore's, the London-based accountancy firm. Not that Henry Green was a client, nor was Campbell an employee of Berwin Moore's anymore. That ship had sailed. Was Green the answer to Campbell's problems now? Maybe, maybe not. Regardless, he'd taken a shine to Campbell since the younger man had arrived in New York, and now Green had made Campbell a proposition. Whether through curiosity, naivety, or a combination of both, Campbell had agreed. Green wasn't the type of man to say no to.

He stood outside the banged-up doors to the Evolve nightclub and looked around. At ten to nine in the morning the club, which took up a large corner plot in the Meatpacking District of Manhattan, looked grotty in the daylight. Paint peeled off window frames surrounding blacked-out panes of glass, render on the walls was cracked and bubbling, and all manner of trash from the previous night's revelry lay strewn across the street.

Campbell knew though that come the evening, and darkness, Evolve remained one of the hottest spots in New York City, with its over one thousand capacity regularly filled. Although that knowledge wasn't from first-hand experience. In fact, today was the first time Campbell had ever been to the club. He knew it was Green's main base. Every day he was getting closer to the inner circle, it seemed.

He brought his hand up to shield his eyes and looked up and down the street. Took two steps to the left so he was shaded from the rising sun in the sky to the east that created long spindly shadows across the street and surrounding buildings. Sirens in the distance caught his attention. He saw no flashing lights, and the sound of the sirens soon faded away behind the growl of the traffic nearby.

He watched the cars heading past. Myriad yellow cabs, Priuses, a multitude of SUVs that were entirely impractical in the city. Finally he spotted the gleaming black S-Class Mercedes stopping at the lights in the near distance. He knew that was his ride even before the car pulled to a stop right by him. The tinted back window glided down and Henry Green's pockmarked face poked out.

'Well come on then,' he said, his voice a barely disguised growl as normal.

Campbell said nothing; he scooted around to the other side, opened the door and sank into the plush leather interior.

***

Campbell tried his hardest to keep his manner calm as they emerged from the Lincoln Tunnel into industrial New Jersey, en route to the Port Newark–Elizabeth Marine Terminal a few miles away. There was no doubt his nerves were building. As confident as he was, Green just had that effect on him.

'A bit of privacy please,' Green barked to the driver, who Campbell hadn't met before and had been introduced only as Alvaro – though he looked like a stereotypical chauffeur in his black suit and black tie. The only other person in the car was a South African man mountain called Eric Steinhauser, sitting up front with the driver. Campbell had met him before but had never exchanged more than a couple of words with the beast. Perhaps he didn't talk. Just kept his mouth shut and did as he was told. Perhaps that was the best way to act around Green.

Alvaro glanced in the rear-view mirror and nodded and a second later a blacked-out glass divider rose effortlessly to seal the back cabin from the front.

'Today could be the start of something,' Green said, turning to face Campbell. 'You've already shown me you've got a good head on you, and I'm not just talking about that accountancy training.'

Campbell grimaced. He'd never seen himself as the professional accountancy type, despite his parents' best efforts. Which perhaps explained why that career had seemingly come crashing down around him not long ago. He'd never fitted into that life, had never wanted it. If anything, he was hoping that Green could see past his professional background, but maybe that wasn't going to be the case.

'I'll always have work for someone like you,' Green added.

'Happy to help,' Campbell said, feeling somewhat lame that he didn't have anything better to say.

Green sucked in a breath through his teeth like he often did. Campbell wasn't sure what that meant, though the way it twisted Green's lips made him think it was a sign of displeasure. He played with the thick gold signet ring on his finger that was engraved with his initials: HG. Campbell glanced up to the collar of Green's open-necked shirt where the thick band of a chain was just visible. Overt was Green's natural style, no doubt about it.

'How's Kate doing?' Green asked.

'She's great.'

'Tell her to call me more often. She's always too busy doing something or other.'

Campbell smiled. 'Yeah, don't worry. I'm in the same boat as you on that one.'

That same sucking noise again. It made Campbell flinch. He looked out of his window. As they moved onwards through Newark, the largely industrial buildings outside were a stark contrast to the glitz and glass skyscrapers they'd left behind in Manhattan, still visible in the distance out of Green's window. Having only been in the US for a week shy of three months, Campbell had never before ventured to this side of the Hudson.

Perhaps he shouldn't have done so today either. The voices of his parents echoed in his mind, their warnings as clear as they were relentless. He pushed them into the deepest recess.

'You know when I was your age I'd already made my first million,' Green said, matter-of-factly. 'How about that? Twenty-five and I was a millionaire. And that was when millionaire meant something. Hell, I was too young to even know what to do with it back then. Splashed out on all sorts of nonsense – expensive cars, gold watches. No thoughts about the future. But that was because I was sure there would be more of it. And there was – a helluva lot more in fact. Especially since I left London for here. But it was those first few years that made me the man I am today. It's those years that determined where I was going in life. You've got to take the opportunities when they arrive. You never know if you'll get another one or not.'

Campbell stared intently at Green as he spoke. Although the two men were far from close, Campbell already knew that Green loved to brag like this, to build himself up like he was the big cheese. Yet the point Green was making still resonated. If Campbell hadn't taken the opportunities presented to him he would never have moved to London after finishing uni. Would never have met Kate. Wouldn't have moved with her to New York after being booted out of Berwin Moore's, or be sitting where he was now. Campbell was undoubtedly content with some aspects of his life – Kate in particular – but he also couldn't face the prospect of living with regrets, which was the main reason, he kept telling himself, why he was intent on getting closer to Green.

Looking at it another way, though – what had Green sacrificed to get to where he was? Who he was?

'Did you look through the numbers I gave you?' Green asked, snapping Campbell from his thoughts.

By 'numbers' Campbell assumed Green was referring to the detailed books and records he'd been given the day before for the shipping business in New Jersey they were about to visit.

'Yeah,' Campbell said, his mood sinking slightly. Here it was again. Scott Campbell the numbers guy. Could he ever be more than that?

'And?'

'It depends what you're after here. What do you want to know?'

Green looked out of his window. 'I've got a deal in the pipeline. I want to buy up some warehousing near the docks. I've decided to start holding my own inventory for the clubs, cut out the middleman.'

'So you're looking to buy Albert Reynolds's business?'

Green looked back, a snide smirk on his face. 'You could say that. Me and him go way back. Technically I already own five percent. He's got an ideal location. I'm not bothered about the business, I just want the property. He's agreed to sell up but his price is too high. He wants five million for it!' Green threw his hands in the air for effect. 'It's only a damn warehouse, the land and the building can't be worth more than two, and there's no way his business is good enough to make up the difference.'

'I agree,' Campbell said.

'Yeah?'

Campbell, more enthused, rummaged in his satchel and pulled out some papers with his handwritten calculations. He passed them across to Green who stared at the contents as though they were in a foreign language.

'When I first looked at his books, I thought he'd over-egged the valuation. I mean, he hasn't made a decent profit in years according to those records. The profit projections to get to a five million valuation would have to be much higher than he's ever recorded.'

'So? What are you trying to say?'

'I think Reynolds has been a bit clever with his numbers. He's cooked his books.'

'He's been screwing me?' Green said, eyes narrowing.

Campbell felt his heart lurch as thoughts of the possible consequences of his answer flashed in his mind. 'I honestly don't know. I'd have to compare the books to what he's paid you in profits. My best guess is he's been skimming cash out of the business, creating the appearance that he's only break-even, when in fact he's making a decent amount of money. Probably to avoid paying too much tax.'

Green was silent for a few moments and Campbell could almost see the cogs moving as Green processed the information.

'So what's it really worth?' Green asked, with just a hint of anger.

'Could be what he's asking for, as much as five million, if you take into account the true numbers. But the accounts he's prepared for the taxman show a different story. By supporting the numbers in his valuation he'd basically be admitting he's lied to the IRS. If he doesn't want to do that, then he'll have to go with a valuation more in line with the much smaller profit he's been declaring.'

'Which would be what?'

'Maybe a million, one point two at most.'

Green looked away again, deep in thought, and Campbell realised his heart was racing. What he'd uncovered was a small-scale fraud. For a few more months he remained a paid-up member of a professional accountancy body back in England and had an obligation to report what he'd found, yet instead he was giving Green the means to screw Albert Reynolds over it. Was he really so determined to impress this man?

'You've done good,' Green said, returning his focus to Campbell. He gave a half-smile, revealing a mouth of overly white teeth that was at odds with his heavily weathered, hard face. 'I'll make sure you get a decent wedge for this.'

Campbell said nothing to that. Was Green's offer called remuneration or simple bribery?

Whatever the answer, Campbell didn't mind too much. Feeling a wave of satisfaction, he sat back and let out a contented sigh.

Chapter four

The Port Newark–Elizabeth Marine Terminal was the East Coast's largest container ship facility with hundreds of warehouses lining the area immediately around the docks. Albert Reynolds's warehouse was a large corrugated iron structure with a tall pitched roof on a grotty road containing numerous other grotty warehouses and small factory buildings.

Although Reynolds's building was clearly in use, it was by no means modern – the iron was heavily rusted, with new patches bolted sporadically around the structure like bandages covering a grazed knee. The grounds around it were little more than a large gravel pit with potholes deep enough to lose a tyre, and were flanked by a high chain-link fence with rusted barbed wire on top. The fence too was ageing and Campbell guessed it probably wouldn't pose much of a threat if someone actually wanted to get over it, or even through it.

The main gates to the premises were open and they drove straight through toward the loading doors to the main building, the tyres of the Mercedes crunching on the gravel surface and throwing up stones in all directions. A large faded sign at the front of the warehouse displayed the name of the proud occupant as J.B. Reynolds & Son, suggesting the man they were there to see was in fact the second-generation owner of the business.

'What do you want this place for anyway?' Campbell asked. 'It looks like it's on its last legs.'

The sharp look Green returned him suggested he should have kept his mouth shut.

'Strategy,' Green said. 'It's all about strategy.'

Alvaro shut the engine off and Green grabbed his black leather briefcase from the footwell and put his hand on the door. He and Campbell and Steinhauser got out – Alvaro remained behind the wheel.

The three men traipsed across the yard, Campbell feeling like a child next to Steinhauser. The big man was six five, maybe six six, and despite his size – in all directions – it was clear even with his suit on that there wasn't an ounce of fat on him, the fabric of his suit stretching out at the chest and shoulders, his thick neck overflowing from his collared shirt. Steinhauser looked down and caught Campbell's eye. Campbell held it for a second before Steinhauser smirked and looked away.

They carried on through the main door, to the side of the loading area. The inside of the warehouse appeared largely unused, with some shelving and boxes and a few crates cluttered toward one half, but most of the other side was empty. Quite how Reynolds made any money at all, Campbell really didn't know.

Campbell followed in line with Green and Steinhauser as they moved over to the small office area in one corner which was built with thin partition walls. Reynolds and another man were sitting inside waiting for them behind a cheap pine desk. Reynolds looked at least in his early sixties, possibly older, with thin wiry white hair and a droopy face. The man next to him was in his thirties with bright red cheeks and a face as round as his belly.

'Morning, gents,' Green said, approaching Reynolds. The two men shook hands. He turned to Campbell. 'This is Scott Campbell, my new accountant.'

Campbell looked to Green, not sure how to react to the introduction, but he quickly composed himself.

'And this is my accountant, Lynden Spector,' Reynolds said.

More handshakes before Reynolds motioned for Green and Campbell to sit. Steinhauser remained on his feet, arms folded, by the side of the desk. Reynolds gave him a wary glance but said nothing.

Spector handed over a bundle of bound papers, a few pages thick. 'Mr Green, I've prepared a detailed report for you showing how we arrived at the valuation,' he said. His accent was a broad New Jersey drawl, unlike Reynolds's much more clipped tones. 'And you'll see from the calculations that this is at the low end of the scale, but Mr Reynolds says you're an old buddy and he wants to get the deal done quickly.'

'How much?' Green asked.

'Five million,' Spector said.

'Five million!' Green feigned shock. 'Come on, Albert, are you taking the piss?'

'I'm sorry, Henry, that's what it's worth,' Reynolds said. 'I've been in charge here more than twenty-five years. I've made a profit every year but three.'

Green sighed and sat back in his chair.

'Yeah, about that,' he said. 'That's not quite the whole picture is it?'

A slight shuffle from Reynolds.

Green looked to Campbell, then to Spector. 'Why don't you two step out for a minute? Let us old friends talk this over like gentlemen.'

Reynolds glanced at Spector and nodded. Campbell got to his feet. Moved to the door. Steinhauser opened it but remained on the inside. When Spector and Campbell stepped out Steinhauser shut and locked the door.

'What the hell?' Spector tried the handle. 'What's going on?' He glared at Campbell who shrugged, though his heart rate was rapidly building and he sensed what was to come. What he was torn over was what he should do himself.

A moment later there was muffled shouting from the inside. Loud banging. A groan.

'Jesus, what the fuck!' Spector shouted. He banged on the door. No answer. He moved around the side where a wide grimy window looked out from the office to the warehouse floor.

Campbell followed him. Flinched when he looked inside and saw Green with a hammer in his hand…

Steinhauser was behind Reynolds, one thick arm around the old man's throat, pinning him in place. Reynolds's face was contorted and twisted and looked like it was about to burst.

It happened in little more than a second.

With his free hand, Steinhauser pinned Reynolds's hand to the desk.

Green hurled the hammer down.

Reynolds screamed in pain as the flesh in his hand was torn, the bones crushed, and spatters of blood flew across the desk.

Both Spector and Campbell reeled back in shock.

'No fucking way,' Spector said, his whole body shaking. He pulled a phone from his pocket. Campbell reached out and grabbed Spector's shoulder.

'Get the hell off me!'

Spector threw him off and stepped away. Campbell moved up to him.

'Put the phone down,' Campbell said.

Spector lashed out, trying to shove Campbell away. The back of his hand caught Campbell across the cheek.

Campbell clenched his teeth. Glared as Spector pulled the phone to his ear.

'I said put it down.'

Campbell launched himself forward. Grabbed Spector's arm with force. The phone went flying. Spector tried to wriggle free, his arms flailed. Campbell, instinct and anger taking over, balled his fist and launched it into Spector's flabby side. Before he recovered Campbell twisted around and wrapped his arm around Spector's neck, squeezing hard.

'Get... off... me!' Spector croaked.

Campbell thumped him again. Grunted as he dragged Spector over to the window. He pushed his face up against the glass.

'You want that to be you!' Campbell shouted through gritted teeth. Spector said nothing. Just squirmed. 'Well do you?'

Spector made a noise. It sounded a little like 'no'.

Campbell loosened his grip. His eyes fell on the hapless Reynolds beyond the glass and he quickly looked away again. 'Good.'

Panting heavy breaths, Campbell pulled Spector away from the window and released his grip. Spector kept his eyes on the floor as he smoothed down his suit and adjusted his shirt and tie. He was shaking with fear. Campbell was shaking with anger – and nerves – and was trying his best to contain it.

Another clattering bang from inside, together with a loud shout of pain. Spector held his head in his hands. With the adrenaline subsiding, Campbell's insides churned. How far would Green go?

The door opened and Campbell caught Steinhauser's eye. Felt his legs go weak.

Green turned around, a mangled smile on his face which broadened when he saw the state Spector was in: a line of blood was coming from his fat lip.

'Gentlemen. I think we're ready for you,' Green said.

Spector shuffled back inside. Campbell stared at Reynolds as he walked back in. The older man's tie was pulled loose, his shirt was torn and dotted with blood that was dripping from his nose and from a gash above his eye. He cradled his smashed hand to his chest. The bloodstained hammer remained on the desk.

'No... No!' Spector yelled and Campbell sensed he was about to turn and run and readied himself to grab him again.

'Sit... down,' Reynolds stammered. 'Please... Just sit down.'

Spector, trembling, did as he was told and Campbell followed suit. Steinhauser stood guard by the door.

'We've agreed a price, gentlemen,' Green said with a wry smile. 'We just need you two to witness the transaction.'

Green blotted a speck of blood on the document in front of him then pushed the papers over to Spector. The accountant took one glance at the front page and his face twisted in disgust.

'One hundred thousand dollars! You gotta be–'

Reynolds held up his unbroken hand to cut him off. He looked defeated. A different man to the one who'd been sitting there minutes earlier. 'Just sign it. Please.'

Campbell stared blankly at Green who caught his eye. Said nothing. Just winked. The gesture sent a chill right through Campbell's core.

Spector signed, then the document was passed to Campbell who scrawled his signature without pause. Green smiled and got to his feet. Grabbed the briefcase from the floor and plonked it on the table. He opened it up and Campbell saw the bundles of cash inside.

'It's all there. One hundred thousand, as promised,' Green said. 'So are we done?'

Reynolds looked up from the money. His whole body was shaking, and he was sweating, beads running down his face, but Campbell also thought he could see tears. Tears from a lifetime building his own business which had come crashing down on him in just a few minutes.

'Yes, Henry, we're done.'

'Fantastic. Pleasure doing business with you, Albert,' Green beamed. 'As ever.'

Green held out his hand to Reynolds. 'Ah, no need.' Green smirked again and took his hand back. 'You might want someone to look at that.'

Reynolds slowly got to his feet. Spector stayed in his seat looking bewildered.

'What are you waiting for?' Green said. 'Off you go. Both of you.'

Reynolds nodded. Closed the briefcase with his good hand. Spector gingerly got to his feet and shuffled out of the door behind his boss. Through the murky window of the office, Campbell watched the old man and his accountant walk across the warehouse floor and out through the open loading doors.

'You already had the hundred thousand ready,' Campbell said. He wasn't sure if it was a question or a statement, nor whether he was impressed or horrified by what had just happened. 'You were only ever going to give him a hundred thousand? It didn't matter what I had found.'

Green turned to look at Campbell, the smile gone now.

'Scott, you've still got a lot to learn, but you did good here, and I'm glad to see you've got some balls too.' By which Campbell believed he was referring to how he'd dealt with Spector. But why had Campbell done that? Why had that reaction come so naturally to him?

Green reached into his jacket pocket and came out with a small brown envelope which he held out. 'Here's your cut.'

Campbell hesitated for a moment before taking the envelope. He didn't look inside. Green gave him a slap on the back like they were old friends.

'Come on, let's get out of here. This place is a dive.'

Campbell didn't say anything. He put the envelope inside his jacket, unopened. He didn't know what to think; the conflict in his mind grew stronger, causing a stabbing that blurred his vision for a few seconds.

'Kid, I said come on,' Green said, wrenching Campbell back to reality. Green was already a few steps away.

Campbell moved after him, trying to push the fog in his mind into that recess that was already crammed full. This time it didn't really work.

Still, he would feel a fair amount better later that day when he finally opened the envelope to find it filled with twenty thousand dollars.

Chapter five

Three days after his visit to South Greenwich Hospital, Ryker arrived at Heathrow with just under two hours to go before his flight. As ever the place was heaving, and even though the temperature outside had dropped over the last couple of days, the huge glass-fronted Terminal 5 building felt stuffy and claustrophobic despite the powerful air-conditioning system working overtime.

After checking in with his cabin bag, all that he needed for his trip of undetermined length, Ryker grabbed an overpriced bottle of sparkling water and downed some as he headed off to the queue for security. He didn't make it that far. Spotted Peter Winter a mile off. Winter was standing beside a newspaper stand, his stare burning into Ryker like he had lasers coming from his eyeballs.

'Fancy meeting you here,' Ryker said, coming to a stop and taking a look around. Winter seemed to be alone. No lurkers who could be security guards or undercover agents waiting to whisk Ryker off somewhere. A good first sign.

'You don't seem surprised to see me.'

'What can I say?'

Ryker hadn't spoken to Winter since he'd visited Janet Campbell in the hospital. The Commander had already scarpered by the time Ryker had finished inside. He'd thought it strange at the time that Winter hadn't wanted to know what the deal was. Perhaps he'd had Janet's room bugged and knew everything anyway. Or perhaps it was Ryker who was bugged and Winter had been following his every move for the last three days. Not that Ryker was particularly worried about that. He'd done nothing wrong.

'So?' Winter asked.

Ryker didn't say anything.

'You know it doesn't take a genius to figure out what this might be about. I was close to Mackie too. Close to all of them. And I know what's been happening with their son.' Ryker kept his mouth shut, though he did wonder exactly which part of the story Winter was referring to. 'Don't forget who I am, Ryker. I've done my due diligence before coming here today.'

The same thought of Winter's surveillance reach flashed in Ryker's mind. The truth was, he'd be seriously pissed off if Winter had been snooping on him, though he wasn't about to show that to the Commander today.

'If you already know the answers, then why bother to ask me the questions?' Ryker said.

'Because I'd rather talk to you about this. About what you *think* you know. But more importantly about what you're planning to do next, and what kind of mayhem will follow.'

'Mayhem?'

'Chaos. Destruction. The normal result of you going on a rampage.'

'That's not what mayhem means.'

'No?'

'Comes from the verb maim. Originally meant the intentional removal of a body part, a limb or an eye most usually. To stop someone defending themselves in combat.'

'So you've been memorising the dictionary in your time off?'

Ryker glared at Winter but didn't respond.

'The point is, if I really wanted to, I could stop you going.'

Ryker raised an eyebrow. 'Why would you do that?'

'Because for some reason I give a shit about your well-being.'

'I'll be fine.'

'Yet it's not just you I'm concerned about. I can and will help you if–'

'Seriously, Winter, I don't need your help for this one.'

'Says you. Though I wouldn't put any money on it given your track record.'

They fell silent for a few moments. Ryker's mind churned with what he'd found out at the hospital three days ago, what he'd found out through his own research since, and what he needed to do next.

'When will you realise I'm someone you can trust?' Winter said, and Ryker thought he could sense a hint of hurt in the man's tone.

'I already know that. But when will you realise that sometimes the less you know about what I'm doing, the safer it is for you?'

'So now it's you looking out for me?'

Ryker looked away, over to the security queue that was in a momentary lull, then back to Winter.

'I'll see you around,' he said.

Winter shook his head. 'Let's hope so.'

Ryker turned and headed away.

**

Later that afternoon, as the British Airways Boeing 787 Dreamliner touched down at Newark Airport, the jostle as the wheels screeched onto the tarmac surface was enough to rouse Ryker from his light sleep. It took more than two hours for the couple of hundred non-US citizens on board to pass through immigration, Ryker toward the very back end of the long queue. He felt only the slightest trepidation when it was his turn to approach the border guard for his paperwork to be scrutinised. Winter's words sloshed in his mind again – but then the JIA Commander hadn't put in place any measures to stop Ryker leaving the UK, so why would he have done so at the US end to prevent him entering the US?

Winter wasn't Ryker's only concern though. The last two times Ryker had set foot on US soil he'd ending up shooting people. He'd killed people. Not good people, but still… he wouldn't exactly expect the US authorities to take kindly to his reappearance if they figured out who he was. Especially as this latest trip wasn't even remotely official business.

It turned out Ryker needn't have worried. When it was finally his turn the weary border guard took less than two minutes to look over Ryker's documents before stamping his passport – in the name of John Burrows – and waving him through.

Another hour later and Ryker was driving out of the airport in a rented Toyota Corolla that was about the dullest thing he'd ever driven. Still, he was in the US on his own expense so he figured there was no need to waste money.

The skyscrapers across the Hudson sparkled in the distance and drew him in as Ryker made his way toward New York City. The temperature indicator on the car's dashboard slowly crept up from 76 °F to 90 °F, even hotter than London a few days ago. Ryker had never been to the Big Apple in summer and already wondered if he was about to regret this impromptu trip. At least the tiny-engined car had decent air con…

Arriving in the city not long after 5pm, Ryker battled traffic, traffic lights, tourists walking around here, there and everywhere with their eyes glued to the sky, and the more wily local pedestrians as he headed north in Manhattan, his first port of call the cheap boutique hotel he'd booked on Amsterdam Avenue in the Upper West Side. Once checked in he set about finding some food before making a stop at an electronics store on West 72nd Street.

Re-energised with pasta and meatballs from a local Italian joint and with a backpack slung over his shoulder holding his supplies, he next made his way on foot the few blocks to an apartment building off West 78th Street. At nearly 6pm the roads and pavements were busy with both commuters and people heading out for the evening. There were few tourists in this mostly residential area of the city that was crammed full of traditional brownstone residences on the west to east streets, and larger stone high-rises on the wider avenues. Street sellers on every other corner had large cool boxes, their handwritten placards indicating that today they were selling bottles of chilled water – for varying prices, depending on the relative wealth of the streets they were on. Whatever the weather, the street sellers always stocked what was needed; water, umbrellas, hats or scarves depending. Ryker bought two bottles as he headed along.

Every now and then the ground he walked on rumbled as the subway passed by underneath. At least he wasn't stuck down there, and with the sun slowly heading down in the west, the tall buildings all around gave plenty of shade. Still, with the high humidity to add to the general climatic discomfort, Ryker's shirt was wet and clinging to him when he arrived outside an Irish bar across the street from his target location.

Ryker took a seat outside with a cold beer, and grabbed the camera phone he'd purchased at Heathrow earlier in the day from his pocket. Phone in hand, he discreetly snapped a few photos of the building on the corner of 78th as he worked his way through the pint. It was far from his usual drink, but he wanted something long-lasting that meant he could sit quietly for some time.

Just shy of an hour later, with his eyes busy on the street in front of him and the building across the way, Ryker's gaze fell on a gleaming black S-Class Mercedes. The luxury car pulled up directly outside the apartment building. The back door on Ryker's side opened and a man climbed out – in his twenties, tall and slim, wearing a tight-fitting navy-blue suit and looking somewhat jittery.

It had been many years since Ryker had last seen Scott Campbell; Campbell had been barely a teenager. Would he recognise or remember anything about Ryker at all?

A few words were exchanged between Campbell and whoever was still inside on the back seat. Ryker tilted his head a few inches to the side to try and get a glimpse. Had his thumb on the white button on his phone screen as he looked, clicking away taking pictures.

The young man briefly glanced in Ryker's direction before looking away. There were a good dozen people outside the bar on such a balmy evening and Ryker was sure he hadn't been spotted.

Campbell shut the car door then headed around toward the apartment building. Seconds later the Mercedes pulled back into traffic and Campbell moved through the security doors into the building's foyer and out of sight.

Ryker looked at his watch. Finished up his drink. He counted up fourteen floors of the apartment building and focused on the glass there. Sure enough, not too long after he saw the slats on the blinds on one of the windows twisting around. Then nothing.

Ryker surveyed his options. Checked his watch again. It was only early in the evening in New York City but it was nearly midnight back in England, and he was jet-lagged. He could head back to his hotel and quite happily crash out until the morning. On the other hand, he was here now...

Making his mind up, Ryker got up and went inside for another drink. A coffee, he decided. It could be a long night ahead.

Chapter six

About an hour after Campbell had returned home from work, he and his girlfriend, Kate, headed out of the apartment, hand in hand. Her in a light summer dress, him in chino shorts and a sky-blue shirt, Ryker guessed they were off out for dinner or drinks. Either way, he had a bit of time to himself.

Ryker stayed where he was outside the bar a while longer as it slowly got busier and busier. By the time he got up from his seat, the sun was making its last appearance of the day across the water of the Hudson a few blocks away. The streets and pavements on the Upper West Side were quieter than they had been when Ryker had first arrived in the city a few hours before, but the many street-front terraces of cafes, bars and restaurants were now heaving.

As Ryker headed across the street to the building where Campbell and Kate lived, the opportunity he needed appeared right in front of him. The young man in a blue and grey shirt and matching baseball cap uniform stepped from his moped and looked up at the gleaming glass-fronted building. All of five eight, tall and scrawny, he had olive skin that was peppered with zits.

Ryker strode up to him, his eyes fixed on the bright-red pizza delivery bag in his hands. And the delivery slip pressed between the kid's spindly fingers and the thermal fabric.

'For 8D, right?' Ryker said. The young man flicked his gaze up to Ryker and took a half step back before his eyes darted to the delivery slip as he processed the question.

'Yeah?'

'For DeMarco?' Ryker asked.

'Yeah, how–'

'How much do I owe you?'

Ryker was already pulling notes from his wallet before he got a response.

'Twenty-one eighty-five.'

'Keep the change,' Ryker said, handing him thirty.

'Thanks,' the guy said, somewhat surprised as Ryker gently wrestled the pizzas out of the bag.

'How much for the cap?' Ryker asked.

'What?' The kid reached up and brushed the rim as if checking he was indeed wearing the cap still.

'A souvenir of my time in New York. I'll give you another twenty for it.'

Before the guy had a chance to respond Ryker reached up and lifted the cap from his head, and as the kid took another half step back Ryker palmed him another twenty.

'Thanks,' Ryker said.

Without waiting for a response he turned on his heel and strode toward the apartment building doors with the two pizza boxes. He pressed on the intercom for 8D. Turned to see the still bemused delivery man shaking his head as he climbed back onto his moped.

'I've got your pizzas,' Ryker said to the female who answered the intercom. The outer security doors buzzed open and Ryker walked into an airy and cool foyer. Off to his left was a polished wooden reception desk behind which sat an overweight man in his fifties – half concierge, half security guard, he didn't seem particularly interested in Ryker's presence.

'Evening,' Ryker said.

He nodded to the guy and the guy nodded back but said nothing. Ryker carried on to the lifts and was soon heading up to the eighth floor. He emerged onto a carpeted corridor and moved on down to 8D. The young lady who'd answered the intercom was already standing by her open door. She gave Ryker a questioning look but said nothing of his appearance.

'How much?'

'Twenty-one eighty-five,' Ryker said.

A raised eyebrow at his accent but again no question about it. She gave him twenty-five and thanked him then shut the door.

At least he'd made some of his money back. He kept the cap on and his head down as he moved back along the corridor which he'd seen was covered by CCTV. Whether or not the guy downstairs was reviewing live coverage or not, Ryker wasn't sure. The unknown answer wasn't about to deter him now. He headed on up to the fourteenth floor in the lift and was soon standing outside the door to 14C where Campbell and Kate lived.

Ryker glanced up and down the hallway. Apart from him, it was empty. He took out his pocket multitool and a small torsion wrench then worked the pin tumbler lock for the front door. Given the security doors and guard at the front of the building, Ryker was banking on the security at this end, so high up, being lax. And he was right. It took him less than thirty seconds to pick the lock and as he slowly swung the door open and held his breath he heard no beeps and saw no other indication – a panel on the wall, PIR sensors – that the apartment was alarmed.

Ryker stepped inside and shut the door behind him. He slipped the backpack from his shoulders, unzipped it and then took out the four tiny wireless cameras he'd purchased earlier. He set off to find a suitable home for each.

Chapter seven

After showering and changing, Campbell and Kate headed out toward Green's brownstone on the Upper East Side, a block from Central Park. As a celebration for his earlier business 'deal' – the second that Campbell had been involved in that week – Green was having a BBQ with a few friends. Campbell was quietly pleased about being put in that bracket.

In the days since the violence at Albert Reynolds's warehouse, Campbell had remained conflicted both about what he'd become embroiled in, but also his own actions. Yet he'd barely hesitated at Green's subsequent request for assistance. Was Green finally a man who 'got' Campbell and saw his true potential? Plus, undoubtedly Green was able to give Campbell something that he desired: money. He didn't crave it, it wasn't the be-all and end-all, but he certainly desired it.

So Green wasn't a straight-edged businessman – Campbell wasn't so naive as to not see that – but then how many successful men really were? How many of them had led squeaky-clean existences where they had never cut corners, never tried to get one over on someone else just to make themselves that little bit richer? Campbell didn't fully condone Green's approach exactly, but he had to be realistic about the world.

Earlier that day, with Campbell's assistance, Green had concluded a deal to sell two of his inner-city bars, and a recently refurbished apartment block in Brooklyn, to an Irish guy called Shaun Doherty. From what Campbell had gathered, Green and his half-brother Charlie Ward had spent a long weekend in Ireland a few weeks back as Doherty's guests, and hadn't fared too well either at poker or at Lingfield Park races. Green didn't tell Campbell how much his debt to Doherty was, but he presumed it was well into seven figures given the discount Doherty was given on the properties.

For his efforts Green had handed Campbell an even larger and thicker envelope than before, containing forty thousand dollars in bundles of crisp hundreds. That envelope, like the others he'd received since *helping* Green, remained at the bottom of Campbell's bedside drawer. Out of sight, but not quite out of mind.

'You okay, Scott?' Kate said, tugging on his arm as they walked hand in hand across 5th Avenue.

'Yeah. Just a busy day.'

She said nothing to that. For weeks she'd been encouraging him to seek a new job. She knew Green had been giving him errands, but did she have any inkling exactly what they'd been up to? Would she be pleased for him?

No, the answer was she'd be horrified, which was why he'd downplayed the whole thing as much as he could.

'We don't have to stay long if you're tired,' she said.

'I'll be fine with some food and some booze inside me.'

She gave a meek smile. Soon after they arrived outside the Greens' home – a townhouse in a plush row on East 93rd Street, just around the corner from Madison Avenue. Although the properties on the street had all been built originally for individual families, in recent years many had been carved up into separate apartments and studios. The Greens, however, retained one of the original full townhouses. Four storeys of affluence.

To Campbell it was like walking into an antiques shop. The downstairs had decades-old wooden flooring, beautifully restored, with pristine rugs placed strategically around, and the place was cluttered with paintings, vases, mounted plates, chandeliers and other expensive fittings. Campbell had been inside once before, but this time found himself even more nervous he might knock over and break some priceless inanimate object. What would Green do to him?

Campbell and Kate walked through the house to the backyard that, at thirty feet long, twenty wide, was a pretty damn big outside space given the inner-city location. Green was in the far corner on a decking area, standing by his monstrous gas-powered barbecue, armed with a foot-long pair of tongs and donning a faded dark-blue apron with big white lettering indicating that the proud owner was the 'World's Best Dad'.

'Hi, kids,' Green bellowed.

They walked over to him and Kate gave her dad a hug. The two men shook hands.

'Where's Mum?' Kate asked.

'She forgot to get salad. Not sure who's going to eat that stuff, but she insisted. Should be back any minute. Help yourselves to a drink, there's plenty going.' Green pointed to the large table at the far end of the garden, packed with beer cans, wine, soft drinks bottles and glasses.

'Nice apron,' Campbell said, then wished he hadn't when he saw a sneer flash across Green's face.

Green looked to his daughter and smiled. 'Kate bought this for me, what, about fifteen years ago? Never cook without it.'

'He's not kidding. Wears it every time. How embarrassing can you get?'

'I'm a proud dad, that's all.'

A moment's awkward silence ensued before Kate grabbed Campbell by the arm and whisked him away to get a drink. Although they'd dated for more than a year, Campbell hadn't quite worked out the relationship between Kate and her dad. Whenever they were together it was like they were the perfect father and daughter, all hugs and kisses and reminiscing of good times past. But Campbell knew things weren't anywhere near as rosy as that. There were definitely unspoken grievances between the two of them. Though he sensed it was more on Kate's part really; Green generally seemed oblivious to anything but himself. Not that Kate had ever divulged her true thoughts about her dad or his business empire to Campbell, nor had he really asked.

Drink in hand, Kate began mingling and socialising the way she did – so natural at engaging with people whether she knew them or not. Campbell tagged along by her side, somewhat lamely, as she introduced him to people he'd never met, mostly family friends, couples, some with their small children. Most of the guests were older than Kate and Campbell, and the conversation reflected this – babies, schools, trust funds. Nothing of interest to Campbell. He found it hard to focus his attention on any of it, particularly as he had one eye on Green the whole time. Was that because he admired Green and his infectious confidence, or because he was so wary of him and what he was capable of?

Green didn't speak to the guests much – too busy tending to the cooking – but every now and then he would catch Campbell's eye. Eventually, Campbell politely excused himself from the latest conversation between Kate and some couple whose names he'd already forgotten, and headed over.

'You back for more?' Green said, flipping a burger.

'I wouldn't say no.'

'Best get one of these before they go. After this batch I'm done. Too much cooking, not enough drinking.'

A wave of raucous laughter came from a group of guests standing around the drinks table.

'I don't think anyone else is having the same problem,' Campbell said, looking over at them.

'Have you told Kate what you've been helping me with?'

Campbell wasn't sure from Green's tone whether he should have done or not, but Kate didn't know any details about what had happened at Reynolds's warehouse, nor of the subsequent work Campbell had been involved in, and she certainly didn't yet know about the money.

'No, I didn't tell her.'

Green took his attention away from the cooking. 'And why would you not tell her?' he asked, clearly agitated. Campbell was sure he heard conversations around them hush slightly.

'I don't know. I mean… it just hasn't come up.'

'Hasn't come up? I've given you sixty thousand dollars this week alone. Is that not something you would normally tell Kate about? You've been looking for a job since you got here.'

'Yeah, of course. It's just… you're right, I'll tell her.'

Green glared for a few seconds. 'I don't want you keeping secrets from my daughter.'

'It's not a secret.'

Green huffed before focusing back on the meat. 'There's nothing wrong with working for me, is there?'

'Not at all.'

'Good, so you'll tell her next time.'

'Next time?'

'I have another deal coming up. I could do with your help again. You good with that?'

Campbell opened his mouth but before he could speak Kate appeared and threw her arms around him.

'Hi boys, what are you two talking about?'

'Oh… I…'

'We were just discussing the baseball from the other night,' Green said, jumping to Campbell's rescue. Green gave Campbell a look. He knew what the look meant. Green was bailing him out. Everyone became indebted to Green, one way or another.

'Baseball?' Kate said, looking at Campbell quizzically. 'Since when have you watched baseball?'

'Well that's the problem, isn't it?' Green said. 'This lad needs to get out and experience the local culture a bit more. How long have you two been here now?'

Kate gave her father a questioning look but didn't bother to answer. 'Baseball will have to wait. I'm going to have to steal you away, Scott, for a few minutes. My friend Karen wants to talk to you about Exeter; she went to uni there as well.'

'No problem,' Green said. 'Just remember what I said, Scott.'

Campbell held Green's hard stare for a second before he was dragged away.

***

When Campbell and Kate arrived back at their apartment on the Upper West Side, at a few minutes past 1am, Green's words were still swimming in Campbell's mind. He and Kate, both seriously tipsy, got ready for bed, neither saying much to each other, and Campbell could sense Kate getting more and more tense with his silence.

Minutes later they were lying on opposite sides of the bed as though there was an invisible barrier between them.

'Are you going to tell me what's up or am I going to have to beat it out of you?' Kate asked with a wry smile.

Campbell didn't find her words in the least funny.

'I know there's something going on, Scott, so just tell me.'

He turned over to face her and brushed some loose strands of hair from her face.

'Actually it's good news,' he said, trying his best to sound upbeat. 'No need to carry on the job search.'

Her face lit up. She sat upright.

'You're kidding? Which one? PwC? You really wanted that one.'

No, you wanted it, Campbell thought.

'Not exactly. You know I've been helping your dad.' Her face dropped, but it was too late to turn back. 'I think he wants me to work for him full-time.'

The bombshell hit her. She began crying. 'What? Why?'

He tried to put his arm around her but she shrugged him off.

'Come on, Kate, it's not a bad thing.'

'Not a bad thing? Are you stupid?'

He frowned, went on the defensive. 'I thought you'd be pleased.'

'Pleased? We didn't come here for you to work for *him*. We came to get away from London, start fresh, get your career back on track.'

'Which is what I'm doing. We've been getting on great, and if this week's anything to go by he's going to pay me a small fortune.'

'What? Of course he'll bloody pay you well! That's what he does best, using money to buy people.' She made no effort to hide the hostility and contempt in her voice.

'He's not buying me, Kate. I want this.'

'Scott. He's my dad and I love him, but you're not like him. You're just a normal guy.'

'What the hell is that supposed to mean? What, I'm just an accountant? You know, you sound just like *her*.'

Kate's face soured further. 'You don't get it, do you? You're better than he is. A better man. I chose you *because* you're so different to him.'

Campbell huffed, really not sure what to make of her words. Was he really so different to Green? Or was it Kate and his mum who had a seriously wrong impression of who he was, seeing only what they wanted and not reality? Campbell had tried to live up to that image, he really had tried, but it wasn't him. He didn't *want* it to be him.

But then Campbell's mind took him back to the warehouse, and what had happened that day. Of course he'd heard rumours about Green and his brother's business empire ever since he'd first started dating Kate, though the two of them had never talked about it. She had surely heard those rumours too, but what did she really know about her dad?

And if Campbell continued down that road, where would it all end?

One thing he wouldn't risk was losing Kate. He reached out and took her hand. She didn't shake him off this time. 'What do you want me to do, Kate? If you don't want me to work for him, then I'll tell him that.'

'No, Scott, you can't stop now.' She stared into his eyes, a very serious look on her face. 'He wouldn't let you quit now, even if you wanted to.'

Chapter eight

Ryker woke at 7am the next morning when his laptop pinged to tell him the motion-sensitive camera in Campbell's lounge had spotted movement. Ryker watched the feed for a couple of minutes, observing Campbell and Kate getting breakfast and preparing themselves for a day's work. The picture quality from the wireless cameras wedged into nooks and crannies in furniture and air vents was good, though the sound quality was only average. Still, there was little to see or hear of real interest, Ryker quickly decided, noticing there was a certain distance between the two of them following the awkward conversation the night before about Campbell now working for Henry Green. Campbell's closeness to his girlfriend's father was the very reason Ryker was in New York, though him being a fully paid-up member of Green's crew was a new development, and not a good one, as far as Ryker was concerned.

He closed his eyes again to try and catch some more much-needed sleep.

No use. Even though it was early in New York and he'd had all of five hours sleep, his body clock was screwed and his mind was too wired. He got out of bed, fixed himself a strong coffee, showered then headed out.

At a little after 8am Manhattan was already stuffy and sticky. Another baking hot day was in store, to Ryker's annoyance. He had several spots in the city he wanted to scope out that day, and although he had the Toyota it would be far quicker to use the subway. Ryker sucked it up and decided efficiency trumped comfort.

He spent most of the morning trailing around Soho, Greenwich and the Lower East Side before moving over to Midtown and the Meatpacking District, a name given to the west-side area as a result of the abundance of slaughterhouses that dominated the neighbourhood in the early-twentieth century. Other than the many sprawling redbrick buildings previously used to process meat, little remained of that past, and the neighbourhood was quickly becoming more residential and, in some places, trendy.

It was in the Meatpacking District that Ryker saw the same black Mercedes as had escorted Campbell home the night before pull up outside a nightclub called Evolve. Both Green and Campbell got out of the car and headed into the club together.

Was Evolve Green's main base?

Either way, Green and Campbell certainly appeared quite the team, and Ryker was deep in thought about his next move. He'd come to New York City on a personal mission. Not for vengeance or justice, which had been his primary driving forces for so many missions, over many years, but for loyalty. He owed Mackie. And by extension he owed his widow, Janet. But Campbell was a grown man. What exactly was Ryker looking to achieve here? Of course, a simple man-on-man chat with Campbell to straighten him out and try and make him see sense wasn't what Janet was looking for by way of help for her son – that much was clear. Otherwise why would she have reached out to someone like Ryker?

But then although Janet had been dismayed by her son's continued obstinance and bad life choices, his sacking from his solid job in London for gross misconduct, and the fact that his girlfriend's father was a suspected criminal kingpin, she hadn't known Campbell was actually working for Green.

Yet what *could* Ryker do to help this situation?

The fact he didn't yet have a clear answer to that was the very reason he'd decided to play the long game, why rather than heading from the airport straight to Campbell's apartment to have it out with him the day before, Ryker had instead decided to spend some time spying – learning not just about Campbell and the mess he was getting involved in, but about the people around him too. Henry Green in particular.

Ryker knew little about Green as a person so far. What he did know, he didn't like. Ryker had met plenty of men like Green. Arrogant and wealthy, and prepared to go to great lengths to preserve their status, they were men you couldn't reason with. And in Ryker's experience there was usually only one way to deal with them. You had to defeat them entirely.

Intent on doing the rounds, Ryker carried on his reconnaissance and by mid-afternoon he was riding the inferno of a subway northwards, beyond Central Park and up into the Bronx. An area Ryker was unacquainted with.

With a population approaching one and a half million, the Bronx could well have been a large city in its own right. Although undoubtedly poorer on the whole than neighbouring Manhattan, it was clear even within a few minutes of Ryker's first visit that the borough had plenty more upmarket spots, pockets of wealth highlighted by modern redevelopment, and, for the most part, a relaxed and neighbourly residential air about it.

Ryker also sensed, though, that the wrong turn down the wrong street could quite quickly lead a stranger to a place of deep regret.

He felt suspicious eyes on him as he walked up from the newly developed area around the Yankee Stadium, the outside of which reminded Ryker of a gladiatorial amphitheatre, and he was soon standing underneath the raised subway tracks looking over to the corner of East 170th Street to a traditional-looking Irish bar called Malloy's.

With Victorian style red-painted wood panelling around the entrance doors, sash windows with glazed panels, and the Irish flag and green shamrocks all over, the large single-storey bar wouldn't have looked out of place in Dublin.

What was noticeably different about this place, though, compared to the other premises Ryker had already scoped out that day, were the two men standing outside. Not bouncers as such – there was no officiality to their look – but they were definitely security. Like you'd expect to find outside a mafioso-run restaurant across the city in Little Italy.

One of the men was short, maybe five seven or eight, but he was wide and had a rounded face with an angry snarl. He wore jeans, a scratched-up black leather jacket and a grey flat cap. The taller man on the other side of the doorway looked like he could have been his big brother, minus the cap.

How either could stand to wear their thick jackets, given the weather... well, there was only one reason to do so: they were carrying weapons.

Before now Ryker had been intent on only scoping the outside of the various properties he'd identified from his research into Green. But, other than Evolve, where Green and Campbell were still encamped when Ryker had left earlier, this was the first property from his list that had looked even slightly intriguing.

Ryker pulled away from the metal pillar he was standing by and waited for a break in the heavy traffic. He darted out after a run of yellow taxis and then casually walked up the street, making a beeline for the Malloy's entrance.

The smaller of the two men – the bulldog – nudged his companion in the side and the two shared words as they both locked their glares on Ryker.

'Afternoon, lads,' Ryker said, with as pleasant a smile as he could muster.

Another shared look between the two. Perhaps slightly flummoxed by Ryker's English accent.

'We're closed,' the bulldog said.

Ryker indicated the sign behind him with the opening times.

'I don't speak Gaelic but I'm pretty sure the word for closed isn't spelled O-P-E-N.'

A raised eyebrow.

'I heard this place does the best Guinness this side of the Atlantic,' Ryker added.

'Now who told you a thing like that?' the bulldog said in his thick Dublin drawl. 'Might as well be piss water.'

'Nothing like back home, right? Still, this place was recommended. Can I?'

Ryker nodded to the door. The men glanced at each other again before both took a half step to the side to give Ryker enough space to head on in.

Ryker stepped inside the gloomy interior that was filled with dark-wood furniture to match the walls and bar. The many tables and booths were almost entirely empty save for two middle-aged men quietly drinking pints together in a corner. Ryker took a stool by the bar and glanced into the mirror that covered the wall in front of him. Saw the big man from the door was now on the inside, propped up against the wall by the doorway, his death glare fixed on the back of Ryker's head.

'What can I do for you, fella?' said the barman. Another Irish native, though with a younger and kinder and ever so slightly cheerier face. His tight-fitting vest to show off his many tattoos together with his thick beard and carefully cropped hair painted quite a different image to the two at the door. Hipster, Ryker believed the look was called.

'Pint of Guinness, please,' Ryker said.

The barman went about pouring the drink. 'You're a bit far from home,' he said.

'Yeah. Aren't we all.'

'What brings you over here?'

To the Bronx or to Malloy's? Ryker thought but didn't ask.

'Just visiting.'

'Did you forget to get off the train? Not much to see up here.'

'I can see why you're a barman and not a salesman.'

A bit of a smile from Hipster though it was hard to tell with the thick beard covering his mouth.

In the mirror Ryker noted the big man take a couple of steps closer to lean against a pole. The two other drinkers looked over then quickly drained their glasses and got to their feet.

'Have a good day, gentlemen,' the barman called as the two men strode purposefully for the door, heads down.

'Bit quiet in here,' Ryker said.

'New management.' The barman put the creamy-topped pint down in front of Ryker. 'Might take a while to get things moving.'

Ryker took a long sip of the drink. It didn't taste half bad even if it wasn't exactly his favoured tipple.

'Probably doesn't help having those two lumps standing outside the door.'

Ryker noticed the barman look over to where the big man was standing, a slightly sheepish look on his face, but he didn't respond to the quip. Ryker turned his focus to the TV behind the bar which was showing a horse racing meet. He was taking a long drag of his Guinness when he heard loud chatter and then an eruption of laughter from some unseen corner of the bar. He looked over and noticed the curtains drawn across an archway at the far end of the main room. A VIP lounge, if the dive bar could be afforded such a title for its most exclusive spot.

When Ryker looked back the barman was staring at him. More nervous than anything else. A second later the curtains twitched. A man poked his head out to look around. Gave the barman a disapproving look.

'We're due to close in five minutes,' the barman said to Ryker. 'Need to get ready for the evening shift.'

Ryker glanced back to the curtain. The man had retreated to the inside again. In the mirror Ryker noticed the big guy take two more steps in his direction.

Ryker was intrigued, that was for sure, but the barman was right. Time to call this one quits.

After draining another couple of inches of his pint, Ryker got to his feet.

'Not bad,' he said to the barman. 'See you around.'

The barman said nothing.

Ryker headed toward the doors. The big lump had his steely glare fixed on Ryker the whole way. He stepped backward in line with him to reach the door first and pulled it open.

'You have a good day,' he said.

Ryker smiled at him. 'I already am.'

He stepped out into the oppressive sunshine and strode away. Walked a full square around the block until he came back to the spot where he'd been standing under the subway tracks not long before. Not completely hidden from view, but a safe distance at least.

The bulldog remained outside but there was no sign of the big guy now. Soon a black BMW X5 came rocking to a halt directly outside the bar's double doors, partly obscuring the entrance from Ryker's view. He could just about make out the tops of heads as the doors to both the bar and the X5 opened. Three men came out of the bar and climbed into the SUV before it pulled away at speed.

Ryker was left staring at the doors to Malloy's once more. The same two leather-jacketed men were standing outside again. After a few moments the big one headed on inside. The bulldog scanned the streets for a second and seemed to lock eyes with Ryker. He didn't bother to move. Just stood his ground. After a few beats the bulldog turned too and pushed through the doors.

Ryker gave it a couple more minutes, but whatever excitement had taken place inside Malloy's was already over. He moved off, back toward the nearest subway station, his brain firing with questions and theories.

From what Ryker had gathered from his own intel, Malloy's was just one of several bars owned by Henry Green and his half-brother Charlie Ward. But both of those men were cockneys. Ryker had seen nothing in the intel he had so far of a clan of dubious-looking Irishmen within the mix. So who the hell had been behind that curtain? Who were the men shepherded into the X5 with an armed detail alongside them?

Questions Ryker was sure he'd find the answers to sooner rather than later.

Chapter nine

It was after 9pm and Ryker was sat drinking at the same bar he'd been to on Broadway the previous day. He wasn't there to spy this time though. Not yet anyway. Later in his hotel room he'd catch up on the footage from the cameras in Campbell's and Kate's apartment but for now it was time to relax a little, even though tiredness was quickly setting in once again.

The modern and bright bar was a stark contrast to Malloy's, not just in decor and ambience but in clientele. The place was swarming with well-groomed young professionals mingling after a hard day's work in the city. Ryker wasn't sure which of the two bars he fitted into most comfortably.

He ordered another bourbon from the barmaid and a glass of water to go with it. His second and final alcoholic drink of the night, he decided.

The couple on the two stools next to Ryker put down some dollar bills for the barmaid then headed off toward the exit. The seat next to Ryker wasn't empty long. A young woman sat down and ordered a white wine. Ryker carried on looking into the mirror behind the bar, people watching, and noticed the woman next to him glancing at him every now and then as she sipped from her glass. He sensed she was going to try and speak to him – quite a turn-up given his natural stand-offish manner.

'I saw you here last night too,' the woman said. Ryker didn't react. 'My name's Jane,' she added.

Ryker turned to look at her then. He took in her flowing silky black hair, her smart business wear – a blouse and suit trousers – and the wide and inviting smile on her face. She was holding her hand out to him. He took it and gave a gentle shake.

'John,' he said.

Her smile widened. Yet another reaction to his accent? Even just one word was a big giveaway.

'Ha, our names are both Js then,' she said.

'I guess they are.'

'You're from England?' she asked.

'Yeah.'

'On holiday?'

'Yeah.'

'On your own?'

'What you see is what you get.'

'Huh.'

Ryker faced back to the bar. A few moments of silence. Not awkward for Ryker, but he could sense that Jane wasn't overly enamoured by his lack of conversational skills.

'I love England,' she said. 'I was there last year.'

'It's nice. Apart from the weather. And some of the people.'

'It rained every day.'

'Tell me about it. Though I'm not sure the heat here is anymore bearable.'

'If it carries on the city will be dead. Everyone heads out in the middle of summer when it gets like this.'

'Not a bad idea.'

More silence.

'Not much of a talker, are you?' she said, her tone harsher, as though becoming perturbed at the stilted conversation.

'I didn't ask you to come over, did I?' Ryker said, sounding more abrupt than he'd intended.

'Jesus, there's no need to be such a dick.'

She turned and was about to get up from her stool.

'Okay, I'm sorry,' he said. 'It's just been a long day.'

He downed his whisky and indicated for another. Sod it.

'You want anything?' he asked Jane.

She turned back around on the stool, a sullen look on her face. 'I'm good.'

'Sorry,' Ryker said. 'Let's start over.'

'It's okay. Aloof is the British thing. Plenty of American girls are into that.'

Aloof. Not something Ryker had been called before. Perhaps it was a compliment.

'So you're a native New Yorker,' Ryker said – more of a statement than a question.

'Born and raised in Queens. How long are you in town for?'

'Haven't decided yet.'

'You're a hard guy to read. What do you do? For a living?'

'I'm retired.'

'You don't look that old.'

'*That* old,' Ryker said, smiling.

'Retired from what?'

'This and that.'

'You don't say. You're a big guy. Hard face. Army vet, perhaps?'

Ryker sighed, looked her square in the eyes. 'Look, Jane, I was trying to be nice here. Thought maybe I'd read the situation wrong when you initially took that seat. I was prepared to give it a chance. You never know. But I didn't get it wrong, did I? So if you've got something on your mind just spit it out so we can dispense with the pointless chit-chat.'

Jane flinched at his words. The sullen look returned to her face. A moment later though she straightened up, shoulders tight, and her face hardened – an air of confidence and control about her that she'd kept hidden before when playing the role.

'You're right,' she said, with a hint of a smile. She got up from the stool and reached into her handbag. 'I wouldn't exactly say it was a pleasure talking with you, John, but if you do want to do this again, you've got my details.'

She placed the small white business card on the bar in front of him. He took one glance at it then stuffed it into his pocket.

'Nice to meet you, Agent Chan,' he said.

'And nice to meet you, John…?'

'John Burrows.'

'See you around.'

She turned and moved off toward the doors. Ryker watched her the whole way, ever so slightly disappointed that he'd read the situation for exactly what it was, rather than it genuinely being someone interested in him. The problem was he'd met enough police and law enforcement agents in his time, the world over. Hell, he'd been married to Lisa, an FBI agent. He could spot them a mile off. Yet he was still angered both by the manner in which she'd approached him, but more so by the fact that she'd approached him at all.

At some point over the last day and a half, Chan or someone else from the FBI had had eyes on Ryker. They'd been spying on him as he did his own spying. That meant some or all of Green, Campbell and the Irish clan were themselves under surveillance. Which was far from ideal. Ryker would have to be ultra-cautious from now until he figured out what the hell was happening.

Ryker drank his third whisky slowly as he pondered. When he'd finished that and his water he thanked the barmaid and headed out into the night.

At this relatively early hour the streets were far from deserted but the atmosphere felt edgier to Ryker than it had before. As he headed across West 77th Street toward Amsterdam Avenue, his senses heightened; it didn't take him long to decide he wasn't alone. Two people were on his tail. Chan's cronies? Or was Ryker now within the sights of Green or the Irish mob, following his earlier trip around New York?

Time to find out.

Rather than heading to the hotel Ryker decided to lead the lurkers away. No point in making things easy for them. Without being too obvious, it was hard for Ryker to make out much of the two people following him, other than they were there, and not going away.

Ryker carried on walking, taking lefts until he was eventually heading back west across Broadway and toward West End Avenue. The thin strip of darkness of Riverside Park lay ahead of him, and the inky black of the Hudson beyond. He could lure them into the park, but it was a large and unfamiliar area and for all he knew the place was already crawling with reprobates doing drugs or whatever – no need to go looking for trouble.

Instead, Ryker spotted an opportunity right across the street. He checked behind him and saw a van coming his way. He listened to the engine noise getting louder by the second and when the vehicle was just a few yards from him he darted into the road and sped across to the other side and into an alley between two tall red-brick apartment buildings.

Ryker strode a few yards down the narrow, darkened space then turned to look back to the street. Would they follow or just carry on? Their choice now would tell him a lot about who they were.

Seconds later two men appeared at the foot of the alley, their hooded figures silhouetted by the streetlights behind them. Ryker still had no clear read on who they were, but the hoods and the fact they had now shown themselves suggested they were unlikely to be undercover police or Chan's FBI colleagues. Which meant they were a more imminent problem.

As the men swaggered forward one of them reached into his pocket and the metallic clink when he drew his hand out told Ryker he was carrying a flick knife. Not good. Ryker didn't like knives. They were the most personal of weapons. He didn't like guns much either – they were ruthless and unforgiving – but in many ways shooting someone was easy. It was usually done from a distance, so you didn't have to see the damage, to *hear* the damage, to *feel* the damage, that the bullet inflicted. Pushing a blade into someone's body was completely different. It was a horrible sensation, to feel the flesh as it was torn open.

Light seeping out from a side window one floor up caused the blade to glisten and cast a glow on the men's faces for a split second as they moved forward. Ryker didn't recognise either of them. They were young. Teenagers or in their early twenties with cocky swaggers picked up from watching wannabe gangsters in hip-hop videos.

'You got five seconds to empty your pockets,' the one with the knife said, lifting the blade up.

The two men were about five yards from Ryker, who stood motionless, weighing up his options. He would rather have avoided trouble altogether if he could, but that didn't look possible anymore. The one with the knife sauntered closer, put his face right up to Ryker's.

'You gonna give me your money or 'm I gonna have to break your face?'

The guy was about two inches taller than Ryker, but he was scrawny, and without the knife he wouldn't have bothered Ryker at all. But the weapon did make a difference. With just one attacker, Ryker would have been comfortable, but two made things more tricky. Any move he made could leave him exposed to an attack from the second guy. Maybe he had a knife too. Maybe even a gun. But that was assuming these two actually had it in them to stand and fight at all.

'I said gimme your fuckin money,' the lanky kid said, swishing the knife in front of Ryker's eyes. He reeked of marijuana.

Ryker didn't bat an eyelid. Then he sprang into action.

He grabbed the guy's knife hand with his left arm, twisted and pushed the wrist to bursting point. Screeching, the guy released the weapon, and in one movement Ryker grabbed it and spun him around into a headlock, using him as cover from his friend – just in case. He pulled the knife up to the man's throat. Jabbed the blade into his flesh. The second guy was now holding a blade too, Ryker realised, but he was flummoxed, standing at the ready but with no clue what to do.

'Drop the knife,' Ryker said through gritted teeth. It clanked to the floor. 'Now, you give me *your* fucking money.'

The second guy shook his head, confused. Ryker pressed the tip of the blade further and the man he was holding struggled and groaned.

'Do it!' he shouted to his friend.

'Empty your pockets,' Ryker said.

The guy did as he was told.

'Put the cash on the ground.'

Not that he was going to take that for himself. He'd hand it to a homeless person on the way out. This was simply a lesson for the two thieves. Hopefully one they'd learn something from.

The companion soon finished and straightened up.

'Now piss off.'

The friend turned and ran for the street.

'You too,' Ryker said. He released his grip on the man he was holding and drove his heel into his back to send him scuttling away.

Ryker watched them for a second before moving forward and grabbing the money from the ground. He strode for the exit. The guy in front of him was just about to head out of sight when blue and red strobes of light pierced the darkness.

'Stop! Police!' came the shouts from out on the street.

Ryker cursed his bad luck, slowed and crept toward the end of the alley. There was no other way out. The mugger didn't heed the warning. Burst into a sprint and darted out onto the street, heading in the opposite direction to the lights. There was a chorus of shouts and calls. A police officer raced across the alley entrance, heading after the would-be mugger.

A moment later two uniformed officers appeared in front of Ryker, crouched low, guns drawn.

'Stop right there!' one of them shouted to him.

Ryker did so. He wasn't about to fight the cops.

But it wasn't just the cops he had to worry about.

A plain-clothed female stepped out of the darkness behind the policemen. Caught in the streetlight, she was tall and slim with a light-coloured blouse and long dark hair that gleamed even in the thin illumination.

'John Burrows,' Agent Chan of the FBI said with a knowing smile. 'We meet again so soon.'

Chapter ten

After he'd come clean the previous night, neither Campbell nor Kate had said anything more about him working for Green that morning. He hadn't yet told Kate exactly how much money her father had given him, and she hadn't asked. Campbell had thought about putting the growing pile of green paper into a bank account but he was too scared to do so. Surely someone walking into a bank with that much cash would raise suspicions? So for now he decided he'd spend it when he wanted, and the rest he would sit on.

Still, wherever he kept it, the money was a wedge between them, and in thinking over that he realised the solution may well lie in the problem. In an effort to show his devotion to Kate, Campbell had used ten thousand dollars from Green to buy an engagement ring. A 1.25 carat diamond solitaire, set in platinum, that he purchased from one of the renowned diamond dealers on West 47th Street. He'd been mulling over proposing to her for some time anyway. However much she was disappointed about him working for Green, she remained the woman he wanted to spend the rest of his life with. He just hoped she wouldn't question the timing.

After finishing his business with Green, Campbell had rushed home to give the apartment a once-over and to prepare the surprise candlelit meal. He lay tea lights out all across the open plan lounge-diner and drew the curtains to block out the daylight and heighten the candlelight.

Kate arrived home not long after seven, looking tired and slightly dishevelled, but when she walked into the lounge and saw the effort Campbell had gone to, her face lit up. For a few seconds at least, before a look of suspicion took over.

'Don't say anything,' Campbell said, moving up to her and putting a finger to her lips. He took her hands and pecked her on the cheek. 'What's your tipple? Champagne okay?'

'Have I ever said no?'

Let's hope things stay that way, Campbell thought.

They settled down to eat, though Campbell's appetite deserted him with his mind too focused on the task ahead. His chat was about as lame, and he could sense Kate becoming more questioning of his manner, though she didn't say anything. When he'd cleared the plates away after their steak main, he finally built up the courage and dropped down onto one knee. No big speech. Just keeping it simple.

'Kate, I love you more than the world. I want to spend the rest of my life with you. Will you marry me?'

She cupped her hands to her mouth. Her eyes welled with tears.

'Oh my God, look at the ring! Of course I'll marry you, Scott Campbell.'

Somewhat in shock, he grabbed her hand and pushed the ring into place. She eyed the jewel for a second, twisting her finger to showcase the sparkle of the diamond in the candlelight. Then she leaped from the table on top of him, almost sending the settings onto the floor. She straddled him on the thick carpet, kissing him passionately, entwining her tongue with his. She pushed herself closer to him, murmuring when she felt how aroused he was. He moved his hand under her blouse, up toward her breast. She moaned in pleasure. Then, as quickly as she'd jumped on him, she sprang off and ran to the other side of the room to pick up her phone.

'Mum is going to go crazy when I tell her!' she squealed. 'Mum. You are *not* going to *believe* what Scott just gave me!'

And so the conversation went on, howls and yelps for a further ten minutes, before she was handed over to her father to tell him the news. A few more minutes of the same before finally she was done. Campbell decided to make himself useful in the intervening period and by the time she was finished he was back at the table with dessert and a second bottle of champagne ready and waiting.

'They're so excited, Scott, they want us to get married at St. Matthews. That's okay with you, isn't it?'

'Kate, for you, anything.'

It sounded cheesy, but he really did mean it.

***

Not unexpectedly, Campbell awoke to a horrendous hangover the next morning, having followed the two bottles of champagne with a few whiskies. Kate fared slightly better in the hangover stakes, at least managing to eat some breakfast, which she brought into the bed, but Campbell was a mess. His mouth felt so dry it was like he'd chewed sand all night. His head throbbed and his stomach ached. Yet when he woke that morning he was happy. Truly happy.

'Jesus!' Kate said as she kissed Campbell on the lips. 'You need mouthwash. Lots of mouthwash. It's like kissing a distillery'

Campbell managed a half-smile before shutting his eyes again.

'Dad's messaged you,' Kate said.

Campbell was suddenly more alert. He sat up in the bed and Kate handed him the phone. A text message. Sent just after eleven the night before.

'What's he got planned for you this time?' she said, her initial morning happiness on the wane.

Campbell said nothing. No need to spoil the mood.

'Well?'

'It's fine, babe. Honestly. It's just a job.'

She rolled her eyes and groaned. Grabbed some clothes from the wardrobe and padded out the room.

***

An hour later Campbell was standing outside their apartment building in the sunshine, baking in his suit, when Green turned up in the S-Class. Campbell climbed into the back.

'Congratulations,' Green said, with little warmth.

'Thanks,' Campbell said.

The car pulled away. The middle divider was already up. Campbell wondered who was driving and whether anyone was up front in the passenger seat today.

'You should have asked for my permission though,' Green said.

Campbell looked over and saw the glower on Green's face and the creases on his forehead.

'How do you mean?' Campbell responded.

'You should have asked me for my permission to marry my daughter.'

Campbell's heart skipped a few beats. Was Green joking? Slowly the icy manner melted away and Green's face broke out into a wide smile.

'I'm just pulling ya leg, ya daft sod. I'm glad you're gonna be family. Just don't you ever hurt her, you hear me?'

'I'm not going to hurt her,' Campbell said.

Green's face flicked back to ice in a flash.

'You hurt her and I'll kill you.'

Green let the threat hang for a few seconds. Campbell didn't say a word, just waited until Green's face once again relaxed. What the hell was this guy on?

'I can tell she really loves you.'

'I love her too.'

'You're a good kid.'

Green reached over and slapped Campbell on the back of his head. Was that supposed to be a sign of affection?

'Given you're going to be family, I've decided to give you a proper role you can call your own. No more odds and sods. What do you say?'

Campbell said the only thing he could say. 'Yeah. If that's what you want.'

They arrived at Evolve nightclub shortly after. As on the previous occasions Campbell had been there, from the outside the club looked grotty and somewhat unkempt. He was actually intrigued as to whether it would be any different on an evening.

He'd suggested going plenty of times with Kate but she hated the idea, claiming she could never relax for a night out knowing her dad or his colleagues could be watching her every move. Campbell preferred low-key bars anyway.

Campbell and Green stepped from the car and headed for the entrance door, which was already ajar. Inside the dim interior a team of workers were cleaning up from the night before. Campbell followed Green across the part carpet, part laminate flooring that was sticky from drinks spilled by last night's revellers. The club had a myriad of different rooms, each with its own style of décor. The building had once been a theatre, and the layout of the past remained evident with the various areas of the club – side rooms, VIP lounge, seating areas – on different levels.

Green headed to the highest point of the club where his personal office with a large glass front looked out over the main dance floor, up in the gods section of the original theatre. Steinhauser was standing at the top of the staircase, next to a door with a 'Private' plaque affixed to it. Steinhauser nodded to Green.

'Morning, boss.'

Green nodded back but said nothing. Steinhauser opened the door and Green and Campbell headed inside. The office space was large and rectangular, with a thick maroon carpet. Mahogany wood shelving ran along one long side, the window on the other. Green's large dark-wood desk sat pride of place at the far end, before a metal filing cabinet, and a sofa and a meeting table were arranged at the end toward the door.

'You know this is my main office,' Green said. He walked around to the big leather chair at the far side of the desk and sat down. 'And you can see why. Pretty nice, isn't it?'

'Yeah. It is,' Campbell said, looking around, though really he thought it was gaudy and overly flash.

'You can help me run things from here.'

Green paused, eyes fixed on him. Was Campbell supposed to say something to that?

'This is your office now too. I'll even get you a desk.'

'Thanks, I'm... I... thanks, Henry.'

Green raised an eyebrow before he got back on track.

'From now on, you're in charge of all of the books.'

Campbell cringed inwardly. So there it was – he was still just an accountant. Though what more had he expected? At least being Green's accountant was a world away from his old life, he guessed. There was certainly little about it that was *normal.*

'First up, I want you to take a look through everything. See what you think about the state of things here. How we're recording everything, whether we can make any improvements. You think you can do that?'

'How long have I got?' Campbell said, half-joking. The task could in theory take days, weeks, depending on exactly what Green was after.

'I've got a few meetings this morning, but I should be back at some point this afternoon. Sound good?'

'Er, but I–'

'As you know, I've now got the nine bars and clubs after giving Malloy's and the others to Doherty. Charlie directly manages five of them, and I manage four, including this one. Each of the clubs has a day-to-day manager who does most of the legwork, collecting the cash, paying the staff, restocking the drinks, sorting DJs and all that. There're also fifteen investment properties in the city which are straightforward rental income.'

Green pushed himself on his chair across to the filing cabinet behind him. 'Files for each club and property are here. Annual accounts, tax returns, cash records. You'll figure it out.'

He looked at his watch and got to his feet. 'You need anything, give Steinhauser a nudge.'

On cue, Steinhauser opened the door from the other side. 'They're waiting for you downstairs,' he said.

'See you later, kid,' Green said. He winked at Campbell who opened his mouth to say something but he was too dumbstruck and couldn't manage a word.

Green walked out. Steinhauser gave Campbell an amused smirk before he shut the door, leaving Campbell alone in the room, brain whirring.

As he watched Green heading down through the club, back toward the main entrance, Campbell soon snapped himself out of it, and moved over to the desk and sat down on Green's plush chair. He stayed there for a few moments. Looked around. Swivelled the chair this way and that. He had to admit, it was a position he could get used to.

But what the hell was he supposed to be doing? For minutes he didn't move. He didn't know where to start. But Green had shown faith in him, and was clearly expecting something of Campbell. He couldn't just sit there.

Leaning down from the chair he pulled open each of the desk drawers. The top right drawer was locked. No sign of a key. The other drawers contained stationery and various papers, not much of interest to Campbell. He looked over to the filing cabinet and decided to examine that next. The unit was five drawers high, two wide, and each drawer was crammed with files and papers; invoices, receipts, ledgers, bank statements, tax returns. It was obvious from the mishmash nature of the records that there hadn't been any kind of qualified accountant looking through them in an age. The records were a disorganised minefield.

Not really knowing where to focus first, he decided to just start looking in order, from top to bottom. As he scanned through he tried to piece together in his mind what all the categories of documents were. How would a club actually work?

Just think logically, he told himself. How does money come in and how does it go out?

He started to fit together in his head how it should all look. Before he knew it, he was deep into the ins and outs of Green's financial records, taking only a couple of short breaks to fix himself coffees from the expensive-looking machine in the far corner. The clock on the wall had wound past noon when

Campbell first spotted a transaction that appeared out of place. He was scanning a ledger which he thought was a cashbook for Evolve, highlighting the cash coming into and out of the club; door receipts, till receipts from the bars, wages, DJ costs. An old ledger, going by the dates; the transactions were at least a couple of years ago.

He frowned, flipped a few pages, spotted another similar transaction. Then another. The cogs in his mind ground.

Campbell went back to the cabinet and found another similar file for Evolve, but for more recent dates. Started to look through. Saw exactly the same pattern, the transactions at regular intervals.

Picking one date to focus on, he then went back to other records, trying to piece together all of the transactions that had occurred that day to try and identify the source of the anomaly. If he could eliminate what the transactions weren't, that might tell him what they were.

Campbell nearly jumped out of his skin when the door to the office suddenly burst open.

'Scott, boy, how you getting on?' Green bellowed, walking in through the open door. Steinhauser followed on his heels, glaring at Campbell.

'Everything okay?' Green asked, feigning concern at Campbell's startled reaction.

'Yeah. Of course.'

'So how're things looking?'

'Good. But… well, to be honest, Henry, I can see whoever's been keeping this stuff was no accountant.'

Green looked less than impressed. But was he unimpressed with Campbell or with whoever had done such a poor job on the accounts? Green slumped down onto the sofa. Steinhauser remained on his feet.

'No disrespect,' said Campbell, 'but this is a mess. It'd take me ages to put all this together properly and make sense of it.'

Green sighed. 'That's what I thought. Sounds like you're in the thick of it. I'll leave you to it.'

Green went to get up from the sofa. Campbell's mind raced, debating whether or not to raise a question over the curious transactions. Either Green knew what they were and could give a simple answer – was perhaps even expecting Campbell to ask – or he didn't know about them at all, which meant that he would probably want to know about them.

'Actually, I did find something.'

Green stopped, sat back down. 'Go on.'

'It's just… these transactions here. In the cashbook.' Campbell got up and took a file over to Green, pointed at one of the examples from just a few weeks before. 'I haven't been through everything, but these transactions, they appear every few days. I don't know what they're for. They show cash coming into the club but it's not clear where from. Certainly not anything obvious like the takings from the door or the bar.'

'So what are you telling me, Scott? What do you think they are?'

Campbell had no sensible answer to that. He had got as far as deciding what they weren't, but not what they were.

'I don't know. It's definitely money coming in, but maybe from something other than the clubs.'

Green smiled – a look of satisfaction? The reaction made Campbell all the more nervous.

'You got it in one, kid. That's exactly what they are. You were right about the state of our records. How long has it taken you to spot these transactions?'

'A few hours, but they stick out like a–'

'Enough said. Come on, there's something I want you to see.'

Green put the file back on the desk and headed for the door. Campbell remained rooted to the spot. Green turned and waved him over, then opened the door.

'You're coming too,' Green said to Steinhauser.

'Where to?' the big man asked.

'You know where,' Green said, looking back to Campbell with a glint in his eye. 'It's time for Scott's induction.'

Chapter eleven

The inside of the car was quiet as they made their way out of the city. Green had been less than explicit about what he wanted to show Campbell, but nonetheless he felt he knew. The penny was finally dropping. The most obvious explanation for the extra cash was that Green was laundering money through his clubs, and in all likelihood there was only a short list of sources for such money.

Was this really the life he wanted for himself? Campbell wondered, not for the first time.

'I realise we never properly discussed your ongoing remuneration,' Green said not long after they'd emerged from the Lincoln Tunnel in New Jersey. Bound for Albert Reynolds's warehouse again, Campbell realised. 'Remember what I told you the last time we were headed down here?'

Campbell could. He could remember virtually every second of that day. He didn't bother to answer the question though. He was sure it was rhetorical anyway.

'I never had it easy in New York. I'm an outsider. An immigrant, in the eyes of the natives. But the whole city, the whole bloody country, was built by immigrants. It's in everyone's blood, just a generation or two back. You've heard of Michael Bloomberg, right?'

'Of course.'

'One of the richest men in the world. Intrinsically linked with New York. His grandfathers were from Russia and Belarus, yet everyone thinks of him as a true American icon, whatever the hell that means. Same for almost everyone else you've heard of who matters.'

Green paused. Campbell wondered about the relevance of any of the patter.

'The point is,' Green continued, 'anyone can make it here. You might not get any help, but if you fight for it, it's yours. The land of opportunity, but bollocks to that land of the free bullshit. Money makes this country tick. Now I've got plenty. I have the houses, the cars, all of it.'

He leaned closer to Campbell, eyes gleaming. 'I want you to be part of this too, Scott, and I'm not just saying that because you're marrying my daughter. I've seen you're good at what you do, and I have a need for what you're good at. But you're not just a numbers man. I see that. I see that you're so much more.'

'Damn right,' Campbell blurted without thinking.

Green smiled. 'I never had a son. But you… we're gonna be family, and if you play this right, we can make a lot of money together. Isn't that what you want?'

'Yeah. It is.'

Green took a sip of his bottled water and placed it back in the cup holder on the wide central armrest.

'You know, this car cost me a hundred grand. I've got two of them. Both the same. You want to know why? Because I can. That's it. Simple as that. I don't need two, but who cares? That could be you in a few years.'

Green broke the eye contact for a few seconds, looking out of his window, before turning back to Campbell. 'How much were you making in that old gig of yours back in London?'

Campbell snorted. He'd hated every aspect of that job, even if it had paid relatively well. 'It wasn't bad. About sixty a year,' he said.

'Sixty grand?' Green smirked. 'A year? Fucking hell, kid. They took you for a ride.'

Tell me about it, Campbell thought.

'Let me put it like this. You're going to get paid more for your new job with me. A lot more. I'll more than quadruple your previous salary, give you four hundred grand a year. Sound fair?'

Campbell didn't answer. He couldn't. His mind was in overdrive, the nagging voices of his parents growing louder by the second.

You choose this path, you're no son of mine...

'But,' said Green, and he paused, as if gathering his thoughts – or perhaps just for dramatic effect. 'But you need to understand that I'm paying you – generously – for two things. First, I'm paying you to do the numbers for me. Do it properly, get everything in shape and looking good. That's your main job and it's why I brought you in.

'But the second part of your job is the most important. For you, for Kate, for me, and everyone else. That part is you keeping your fucking mouth shut. About what you do, about what you see, about what you hear.'

Green stared into Campbell's eyes, and neither of them blinked for a few seconds – a game of chicken as to who would look away first. Finally, Green resumed talking and Campbell felt he could break the eye contact without losing face.

'I'll pay you well, and when I say keep quiet, I mean not a fucking word. You talk to no one, understand? That includes my daughter. Tell her you work for me, but nothing more.'

Green smiled, as though he was doing Campbell a favour by bringing him into his dirty world. Then he leaned closer.

'If you can't keep this deal, then Scott, we have a problem.'

Campbell tried his best to appear calm and in acquiescence but inside, his head was in bits and his heart thumped in his chest as he tried to convince himself this was what he wanted. It was, wasn't it?

The car rolled to a stop. Campbell had been so consumed he'd had no idea they were so close.

'Come on, we're here. Follow me.'

Green got out of the car and walked toward the warehouse entrance. Campbell stepped out and around in surprise. In just a few days the place had been transformed. The grounds looked neat and tidy, with a pristine-looking resurfaced blacktop and not a single weed in sight, and the chain-link fencing had been mended. Campbell turned as he walked after Green and noticed that the small wooden security booth at the entrance gate had been re-established and a uniformed guard sat inside, manning the red and white barrier to get onto the property.

Strangely, he also noticed that all of Albert Reynolds's signage remained, though it was newly repainted.

Two uniformed security guards stood watch at the main loading doors to the warehouse. Both were big and wide like nightclub bouncers. It was like Green had a steady supply of these guys.

As he walked into the warehouse, Campbell saw even bigger changes on the inside. The same shelving area remained toward one side of the building but was now about half-filled with boxes. Some were plain, others had logos of various alcohol brands. Stock for the clubs and bars, no doubt.

The biggest change, however, was the other side of the warehouse. About half of the area was now walled off with a partition ten feet high. There were just two doors in the partition and no windows. Each of the doors was guarded by another burly man, like those stationed outside.

Except each of these men held an automatic weapon.

Campbell stopped in his tracks when he saw the guns. His heart faltered. Other than on a police officer, he'd never even seen a gun up close before. Had never thought how he would react to being in a situation like the one he was now in. He was shocked, a little scared even, yet in a way he was also mesmerised, almost in awe.

'This is where we're going to be basing our main operations now,' Green said, oblivious to Campbell's moment. 'Like I told you before, I'm using this place for storage, but I'm also using it to manage our merchandise. First lot is arriving today which is why my men are already here.'

Green headed toward the nearest of the doors in the partition wall. Campbell followed, doing his best to avert his eyes from the armed men, as if one wrong glance might set them off on a deadly shooting spree.

Campbell followed Green past the guard and through the door. There were no windows on the inside. The room was lit by strip lighting in the panel ceiling, and there was a single connecting door on the far side, which Campbell presumed went through to the room being guarded by the other armed man.

The area had cheap wooden workbenches along two walls and in the middle. A variety of laboratory equipment and weighing scales sat sporadically around the surfaces. Other than the equipment, the floors and tabletops were spotless, everything brand new and in pristine condition.

'This is where the good stuff happens, where the money is made. Extracting, cutting and repacking. The other room as well. Two smaller rooms makes it easier to keep guard over who is touching what.'

Green stopped walking and turned to Campbell. 'I'm sure you've probably twigged by now, Scott.'

Of course he had. Green didn't need to say it. Drugs.

'What you see here is a multi-million dollar business.'

Campbell didn't know how to react, what to say or what to do. He simply nodded his head, trying to act like this was any other day – no big deal.

'I've been doing this for years. I've got good market coverage in New York City but also in New Jersey. The gear comes in from other states and from overseas. Both via the water and in the air. This is where the money is. I use my own network of dealers, and most of the profit comes directly from the bars and clubs. If you attract the right clientele, you can make a killing. Much better than out on the street.'

'The transactions in the books…' Campbell said.

'Not all of it goes through the books. What does go there gets washed in the bank accounts, but I keep a lot of it in cash too. Clubs are a high-cash business. Drugs are a high-cash business. Everything fits together perfectly. To the outsider, I just run some very profitable bars. Your job is to make sure those transactions are properly hidden. Create some scheme that won't crack under scrutiny. Can you do that?'

Campbell couldn't believe how open Green was about the operation. The man was a drug dealer. Not just a dealer, but a dealer to dealers. Yet here he was chatting away like it was nothing.

'Look, Scott,' Green said, sounding as angry as he now looked, perhaps because of Campbell's lack of meaningful response. 'You're a big boy. I thought you could handle this, but–'

'I can handle it. I *want* to handle it.'

'Good. Because this shit happens, with or without you, and with or without me. This is what people want, and it pays. Get your head sorted because this is you now.'

Green reached into his jacket and pulled out an envelope – even thicker than the last two he'd given Campbell. He threw it over to Campbell who clumsily tried to catch it. The envelope evaded his grasp and fell to the floor. Campbell bent down to pick it up. Green's frown deepened further.

'Your signing-on bonus. Don't spend it all at once.'

Green turned and walked back out to the main warehouse, leaving Campbell standing there bemused, the envelope clutched to his chest.

***

Campbell arrived home before Kate that evening. Several hours after the trip with Green, he still felt numb. No emotion. The voices in his head had subsided. Had he gotten rid of them for good? He wasn't sure whether that was a good thing or not.

He sat down on the sofa, still clutching the envelope. He opened it up and tipped the contents onto the table in front of him. The bundles of cash fell out into an untidy heap. He reached out and grabbed some loose notes, felt the texture of the money with his fingers, put the paper to his face and smelled it. An unmistakable smell. A scent that haunted and lured people in equal measure.

Campbell put the notes down and stared at the pile. Smiled. Then frowned. He just didn't know how he *should* feel.

Each small bundle in front of him had a small paper band around it with printed lettering stating that it contained ten thousand dollars. There were five in total. He sat back on the sofa, not taking his eyes off the money.

'Hey, babe,' Kate shouted as she came through the front door. Although startled by the noise, Campbell didn't move. Moments later she appeared in the lounge doorway. Her eyes fell on the money still strewn across the coffee table. Her face turned sour.

'What the hell, Scott?'

Campbell spoke almost as if he were in a trance. 'It's my bonus. Off–'

She held up her hand to stop him. 'No. Don't say anything. I really don't want to know. Just get it out of my sight. Please.'

She walked back out the room, slammed the door shut.

That was fine by Campbell. She didn't want to talk about it, and neither did he.

Chapter twelve

After arresting him in the alleyway, the police had manhandled Ryker into the back of a waiting NYPD squad car and driven a couple of blocks to the 20th Precinct, a grim-looking three-storey slab of concrete near the corner of Columbus Avenue. At the desk Ryker had kept his answers to the duty officer's questions to the point, and minutes later he was shepherded to a holding cell.

Although pissed off, he wasn't in the least worried about the arrest. For starters, he'd done nothing wrong. He'd been attacked by two thugs. He hadn't yet tried to explain that to the NYPD officers for one very good reason: FBI agent Jane Chan.

In Ryker's eyes it was more than a little convenient that minutes after she'd approached him in the bar, he was being hustled down a grimy back alley by two young hoodlums – and lo and behold, who should be waiting around the corner but the NYPD and said FBI agent.

Whatever. If the FBI or the police were looking to play games with him, he'd go along and see where it went.

The cell in the 20th Precinct smelled like shit. Still, however basic and downtrodden it was, it remained a damn sight better than many of the other places in which Ryker had been locked up in recent years.

After seemingly endless hours, the cell door clunked open and Ryker was ushered out by a uniformed officer and taken down a bland corridor to an equally bland interview room – a perfect square with a lino floor, one-way glass on one wall, a CCTV camera in the corner, a single strip light overhead and a Formica table with three chairs. One of the chairs was already occupied – by Jane Chan.

'Don't you ever sleep?' Ryker asked her, noting the clock on the wall. He hadn't seen the time since he'd been stuffed in the cell – it was now nearly 9pm, around twenty-four hours since he'd been brought in.

'Only when I have to.'

'I'm guessing this isn't one of your regular hang-outs?'

The officer plonked Ryker down on the chair at the opposite side of the desk to Chan then headed out, shutting and locking the door behind him. Chan seemed confused by Ryker's comment. He decided to help her out.

'I mean I didn't think your lot and their lot got on too well.'

'You mean the FBI and the NYPD?'

'I mean the FBI and any police force.'

'Perhaps you've been watching too many movies.'

'I wish.'

'We have a very positive working relationship with the NYPD. But your concern is noted.'

'So what can I do for you?' Ryker asked.

Chan raised an eyebrow. Perhaps she hadn't expected Ryker to be so chatty. But what did he have to lose? Or to hide?

'Last night you were arrested on suspicion of aggravated assault.'

'But I'm guessing I won't be formally charged with that.'

'You think?'

'I do.'

Chan shifted in her chair a little. 'And why do you think that?'

'Do you have a victim for this alleged assault?'

'Me personally?'

'The NYPD or the FBI or the CIA or the ATF or whoever.'

A sigh from Chan. The first sign of exasperation, or just an answer to his question.

'Perhaps we should start over,' she said.

'Sure. For starters, you can tell me why I'm really here.'

'I just did.'

'No. Tell me why I'm *really* here. And why *you're* here. Aggravated assault certainly isn't a federal offence.'

'You're an expert on US federal law now?'

'Perhaps I watch too many movies.'

A slight smile from Chan? It didn't last.

'Let's get this back on track. And please, don't interrupt me. I have got other things to do tonight.'

'Heading back to the bar?'

Chan sighed. 'No. I'm already three hours late for my babysitter. If I keep doing this every night I'll be blacklisted by every sitter in Queens.'

Now Ryker finally did feel bad for Chan. But only a little bit.

'Sorry,' he said, holding his hands up. 'Go ahead.'

'You've been arrested on suspicion of aggravated assault. You're correct, that is not a federal offence, and quite frankly the FBI have no interest in how that case works out. *But* your arrest happens to have direct crossover with an ongoing federal investigation in this city. An investigation I'm leading, and as of right now I have you listed as a person of interest in that investigation.'

Ryker folded his arms. 'What does that mean?'

'It means my presence in this city has been signed off by people way higher in law enforcement than the Commanding Officer of 20th Precinct.'

'You can get me out of jail?'

'This time I can. The question is do I want to?'

Ryker thought again about the two thugs in the alley. Would Chan and the FBI really have the audacity to have set the whole charade up in order to get a hold over Ryker? Of course they *would* have the audacity, Ryker knew, but could they have set up such a sting in the short time he'd been in the US? More importantly, why would they want to?

Plus, if they wanted dirt on him to get him onside, they'd have been better off tailing him properly and having him arrested for breaking and entering, surely?

'So? Do you want to?' Ryker asked when Chan's question was left dangling.

'That's up to you now.'

She turned over the top two sheets of the small bundle of papers on the desk in front of her. A printed profile of a British national named James Ryker. She pushed the sheets over the table.

'This is you? James William Ryker? Born June 5 1980?'

'That's me,' Ryker said.

His brain was now whirring. Of course he'd given his name to Chan as John Burrows the previous night. They'd most likely got hold of his immigration records in that name from when he'd landed a few days before, and through checking his facial features and his fingerprints and whatever else they could had managed to match him to his 'real' identity.

James Ryker, although itself a concocted identity, appeared bona fide, and to anyone with base-level access to records it was just another name. Yet Ryker's profile was marked. He was a former asset of the JIA, which meant any access to his profile – or even searches for his name either across records held by British authorities, or in databases held by countless governments and agencies of allied countries across the world – would trigger an alert back to the JIA. Back to Peter Winter.

Which meant the Commander would by now know of Ryker's arrest in NYC. What would his response be?

'Please can you tell me the purpose of your visit to the United States of America?'

'Leisure,' Ryker said.

'Leisure? That's it? That's a pretty wide category.'

Ryker shrugged. 'There's only two categories; business, leisure.'

An unimpressed look from Chan.

'Do you know this man?' she asked. She turned over a photo for Ryker to see. Campbell.

'No,' Ryker said.

'You're sure about that?'

'I don't know him.'

'Do you know his name?'

'No.'

'He's called Scott Campbell.'

'Well now I know his name.'

Chan sighed. 'Do you know his mother and father?'

'No.'

'So you're telling me you don't know Janet Campbell? That's Scott Campbell's mother.'

'I don't know her.'

'What about Scott Campbell's late father, Charles McCabe?'

Ryker shrugged. 'I've only been in the US for a few days. I haven't met many people yet.'

'Fair point. But each of the people I've mentioned is a British national, not American.'

'Still, I don't know them.'

He could tell Chan's patience was wearing thin. Yes, he was lying. Was it blatant to her? He couldn't care less, but he certainly wasn't about to open up about what he did and didn't know about Mackie and his family.

'How about this female? Another British national.'

Another picture. This one of Kate Green.

'Never met her in my life,' Ryker said. A truth finally, not that his answer brought anymore of a positive reaction from Chan. 'What have you got against British people anyway?' Ryker asked. 'I thought we were all friends.'

'I've got nothing against British people. If they come here lawfully and undertake lawful activities while here. So you don't know this woman either?'

'I already gave my answer.'

'Her name is Kate Green. She's the only daughter of Henry Green and his wife Jackie.'

'Don't know any of them,' Ryker said, shrugging.

'This is Henry Green,' Chan said, revealing yet another picture.

Ryker sighed. 'You do realise I might be British but I don't actually know every other British person? It's quite a big place really.'

'Very cute, Mr Ryker. And this one?'

A face Ryker really didn't recognise now.

'Shaun Doherty,' Chan said. 'He's actually Irish.'

'Never been to Ireland.'

A long sigh from Chan. 'You see, the trouble is, if you were prepared to help me here, tell me why you're really here, under a bogus identity, and what you know of these people, then I could help *you*. Seems to me you're in need of it more than I am.'

'Seems the opposite to me, to be honest.'

'Really?'

'I'm not going to be in here much longer, am I? And you seem to have quite an investigation on your hands with all these people, who you seem to be intimating are involved in unlawful activities–'

'Some of them, not all of them.'

'Fair enough, but with so many *persons of interest*, as you put it, maybe you should get some more staff rather than recruits off the streets like me.'

'Thanks for the advice.'

'So is that it?'

'Unless you're prepared to talk to me properly, I guess it is.'

There were a few moments of silence. Then Chan looked down and shuffled the papers and photos back into a neat pile. Her jaw was clenched and a vein throbbed at the side of her head. She was fuming but trying to keep it contained.

'I'm sure we'll see each other again soon,' Chan said, getting up from the chair.

'Back at the bar, perhaps?'

A look of incredulity from Chan, but then the tiniest smile.

'Good luck with the boys in blue.'

Ryker said nothing to that. Just turned and watched as Chan headed for the door. She knocked and waited for it to be opened from the other side. A moment later she stepped out into the corridor and was out of sight. The door was slammed shut and the lock turned.

Chapter thirteen

Having eventually arrived home not far off midnight, and then spending another twenty minutes pleading with the babysitter not to strike her off for good, Jane Chan seriously struggled to get herself moving the following morning. After tearing around her apartment and unsuccessfully trying to whip her three kids into shape, she just about managed to get them to their school breakfast club on time. Then she hot-footed it across Queens to Manhattan and onwards to the Civic Center area near Tribeca and 26 Federal Plaza – a looming forty-one-storey glass and concrete block that housed the FBI's field office in New York City, a stone's throw from New York City Hall.

She'd been due to debrief her boss, William McKinley, on progress in the Henry Green investigation at eight thirty, but it was nearly nine when she exited the lift on the twenty-third floor, the back of her blouse sopping wet from the commute on the furnace-like subway. The baking weather was becoming as persistent and monotonous as her boss. A storm was needed to clear the air outside. She sensed a storm was likely what would greet her that morning.

Chan knocked on the meeting room door and McKinley shouted for her to enter. She opened the door and stepped into the drab room that, like much of the floor, was like an office from a different era: thin panelled walls, grey metal venetian blinds on the windows, worn out carpet-tile flooring. It looked like it had barely been touched since the building opened in the sixties.

'Morning, sir,' Chan said, nodding to McKinley, who was sitting at the other side of the round table in the middle of the cramped room. He had only a slightly sour look on his face – result.

She did a double take when she realised he wasn't alone. Next to him was Assistant Director Margaret Ennis, the top dog in the city and a rising star frequently tipped for a top position at Quantico in the future.

Chan had never spoken to Ennis in a social situation. Could only recall one other time when Ennis had spoken to her directly about an active case. Even so, Chan had already decided she hated her. Ennis was a stuck-up cow who cared only about one thing: her career. She was so uptight it was like she ate bars of lead for breakfast every morning and she had unmoving facial features to match. McKinley, as dogged and belligerent as he often was, at least had a human side to him. Occasionally.

'Ma'am,' Chan said, nodding to Ennis. A touch of a nod in return from Ennis but her face remained absolutely rigid. Most likely her presence was bad news, Chan decided.

'Please, take a seat, Jane,' McKinley said.

Chan did so. Ennis checked her watch.

'Sorry I'm late, sir,' Chan said to McKinley. 'It was–'

'It's fine, really. I know you're dealing with the kids, and I know you more than make up the hours.'

Ennis made a little noise in her throat. A scoff? What the hell was that about? *She* certainly had no idea what it was like fighting the constant battle between being a single parent and an FBI field agent.

McKinley on the other hand, despite his fiery side, was generally supportive of Chan's commitments outside work. Like he said, it wasn't as though she didn't put the hours in.

'I prepared an update for you…' Chan said, digging into her bag for the two-page printout, 'but I hadn't realised we'd have company. I've only got one copy.'

She held it up in the air.

'No need,' McKinley said, waving it away. 'We need to detour slightly anyway. Which is why Assistant Director Ennis asked to be here this morning.'

'Though I do have to head off for a nine thirty, so we need to keep this to the point.'

'Of course,' Chan said, trying her best to sound amenable. 'Is there a problem?'

'There was, but we've now resolved it,' Ennis said.

'Okay?'

'From now on you're to refrain from any and all contact with John Burrows, aka James Ryker.'

'What the hell are you talking about?' Chan's face twisted in both surprise and disgust. The fact there were micro-movements in Ennis's facial muscles suggested she was less than impressed with Chan's reaction.

'Is there a problem here?' McKinley asked Chan, his tone now hard.

'Yeah. I think there is. You're gonna have to tell me what's going on,' Chan said. 'I already told you about this Ryker guy yesterday. He's involved with Green and Campbell somehow. You must see that from what I've shown you? The surveillance?'

McKinley waved this away then looked to Ennis.

'Agent Chan,' said Ennis, 'I can't tell you why, but you need to listen to this. James Ryker is not part of your investigation.'

'Is he still at 20th?'

'They released him a couple of hours ago,' McKinley said, unable to meet Chan's eye now.

'Under whose authority?'

'It doesn't matter whose. NYPD had no grounds to hold him, and like I just said, Ryker is not part of our investigation so we have no grounds to hold him either.'

'No grounds, then what about–'

'Have I made myself clear, Agent Chan?' Ennis said, her voice now raised.

'Not really.'

Ennis glanced to McKinley who gave her an apologetic look.

'Ryker is up to no good,' Chan said. 'How much longer are we gonna let our city be overrun by foreign gangsters?'

'We're hardly talking about the Sicilian Mafia here,' Ennis said nonchalantly, as though Chan's case was an irrelevance.

'Says who?' Chan said, well prepared to stand her ground to the big dog. 'At the very least we should put Ryker on the next plane home.'

'What happens to James Ryker is not of your concern. Agent Chan, you simply need to listen to this and accept it. You have been warned.'

Chan huffed and shook her head but decided against anymore debate – what was the point?

Ennis checked her watch and got up from the seat. 'I'll need to speak to you again later,' she said to McKinley.

He didn't look too eager at that prospect. 'Yeah, sure.'

'Have a good day, Agent Chan. Keep up the good work.'

'Thank you, ma'am,' Chan said through gritted teeth.

Ennis marched toward the door the way she did, with as little movement in her limbs and torso as possible. Everything about her was so robotic.

Chan remained where she was, her eyes fixed on McKinley until the door opened and then closed behind the assistant director.

'What the hell?' Chan said.

McKinley raised his hands and shrugged.

'Who is this Ryker guy?'

'It doesn't matter who he is. You need to drop it.'

'This is bullshit.'

'Chan, watch your damn tone with me. I've got your back here but not if you're going to burn me too. Just forget about Ryker. You've got plenty else to go on.'

Silence. Chan could tell from the look on McKinley's face that he wasn't exactly filled with joy by the turn of events, but he'd made the decision to suck it up and accept the command of his superiors. Perhaps she should do the same. Or perhaps not.

'Now, what have you got for me?' McKinley said.

Chan slapped the update paper on the desk. 'Read it yourself.' She got up from her seat.

'Sit down!' McKinley bellowed.

Chan paused, but then did as she was told.

'Sorry,' she said. 'It's just…'

She didn't know how to finish the sentence. She knew McKinley wasn't the enemy here, and there was no need for her to ruffle his feathers unnecessarily. In all likelihood Ennis wasn't the enemy either. The truth was Chan was simply frustrated that she'd made so little progress in the last few weeks. She'd hoped James Ryker's sudden and mysterious appearance might be a step in the right direction, but that door had been closed almost the second it'd opened. So now what?

McKinley scanned the update paper for a few seconds. 'Just give it to me straight. Where do we go from here?'

'I thought we had a way in with Ryker, but I guess that's gone now. So Campbell remains the option.'

'As you've been telling me. But other than sleeping with Green's daughter, I'm not sure what he can give you.'

'You're wrong. That kid's role is growing by the day. I think Green has finally taken him into the family business.'

McKinley raised an eyebrow. Looked again at the paper.

'You're gonna need something on him to get leverage.'

'That's what I'm working on. But it could take time.'

A long sigh from McKinley. 'How much time?'

'I don't know, but… it'll work.'

It has to, she thought, but didn't say.

The fact was, Campbell was their perfect target. From what they understood, he'd led a straight-edged life back in England. Until he'd got into an altercation with a co-worker which resulted in said co-worker receiving a broken jaw and Campbell receiving a police caution and his marching orders from his cushy city job. And now he was in New York and edging closer and closer to Henry Green. His relationship with Kate put him in a position of trust with her father, and it seemed Campbell's future father-in-law had taken a liking to the guy. But Campbell wasn't one of them. Not really. Most likely he'd be petrified of going down, of losing his woman, so chances were he wouldn't turn down an advance from the FBI, if only they had some leverage…

They needed dirt on Campbell. Or at the very least, they needed to convince Campbell they had dirt on him. Was that the better move? Just bluff it and hope for the best? It was the quickest solution but it also carried the big risk of permanently closing the door, and potentially even tipping off Green to everything.

McKinley sighed. Again. Sat back in his chair.

'Is there anyone else?' he asked.

'There's Shaun Doherty.'

'The Irishman.'

'He's an old acquaintance of Green. We discussed this last time, but I get the feeling there's more to that relationship we're not seeing.'

'In what way?'

'Doherty's sudden presence here means something. He's not just here for a brief visit. I think he's building his own business.'

'With Green or without him?'

'Good question.'

She saw a now-familiar look on McKinley's face. 'Please tell me you're not going to warn me off Doherty too?'

'No. Not at all. Far from it. You're right about him. Doherty is bad news. Keep on top of it.'

'I always do.'

A nod from McKinley, then a sly glance at the clock on the wall. 'Is there anything else I should know about?'

Chan thought for a moment. She wanted to bring Ryker's name up again but thought better of it. Not yet, anyway. 'No, I'm done.'

'Good. I'll catch up with you later then.'

McKinley got to his feet and headed on out. Chan stayed in her seat, her brain firing.

Who on earth was James Ryker to have gotten an assistant director at the FBI so uptight? And why the hell hadn't Ennis and McKinley simply been straight with her about the whole thing?

Whoever James Ryker was, Chan decided one thing; she wouldn't drop it. Whether he was a good guy or yet another of the bad ones, Ryker had a story, and he had a reason for being in New York. Chan was certain that reason had something to do with Green, Campbell or Doherty.

She didn't yet have many answers, but she'd damn well find some one way or another.

Chapter fourteen

A police officer opened the doors and Ryker stepped out on West 82nd Street, squinting in the bright sunlight. He turned back to look at the 20th Precinct building then glanced up and down the street. The leafy green of Central Park was just a block away eastwards. As inviting as it was after all those hours in a cell, he turned and headed the opposite way down 82nd, back toward his hotel just a few minutes' walk away.

No explanation had been given as to why he'd been let out. He'd simply been told, 'It's time for you to go.'

An officer had handed Ryker the few possessions he'd had on him when he was arrested and sent him on his way. No indication that any follow-up was needed in relation to the attempted robbery or assault, no warning about his future behaviour, no threat of deportation. Not much of anything really.

The most obvious answer was that Peter Winter or someone else at the JIA had pulled some strings to get the flimsy case against Ryker dropped. If that was the case he was grateful, though he didn't owe them because of it.

The other possibility was that Agent Chan was the one pulling the strings. Was she playing him?

However it had come to be that Ryker was out walking in the morning sunshine, he was sure of two things. One, he was staying put in New York until he succeeded in helping Mackie's son. Two, he hadn't seen or heard the last of Agent Chan. He'd have to do his best to keep his nose clean from now on, and be extra vigilant in his own activities. Every move needed to be above board, or at least out of sight, as far as that was possible.

Having grabbed a strong black coffee and filled bagel from Zabar's, an extensive Jewish delicatessen on the corner of Broadway and West 80th, Ryker made his way back to his hotel room. He'd managed a couple of hours sleep on the rock-hard bunk at 20th Precinct and that'd keep him going for now. He had a busy few hours ahead, scouring the surveillance his cameras had been recording.

As he pushed the key card against the pad on the door handle to his hotel room, he heard the click and went to push the handle down. An image flashed through his mind of what lay beyond – the room torn apart and all of his possessions missing. Would the FBI do that?

He needn't have worried. As he opened the door, he saw everything remained in place, untouched. Though that didn't stop Ryker spending the next hour poring over every nook and cranny of the room for any hint that someone had been there, either snooping or to leave eavesdropping or tracking equipment.

Everything was clear. Ryker was actually pleasantly surprised by that. Yet it wasn't a good feeling, he eventually decided. It all felt too convenient, like he'd missed something.

Some time later, with his belly rumbling once more and another trip to the deli around the corner on the cards, he was still flicking through the surveillance footage he'd gathered when the hotel room phone rang.

Ryker got up from the armchair and strode over to the bedside table to answer it.

'Mr Ryker, I have a call from England for you.'

Ryker already knew who it'd be. At least that told him how he'd got out of jail.

'Thank you,' Ryker said. There was a click as the call was connected. 'Morning.'

'Afternoon, actually,' Peter Winter responded.

'Before you ask, I didn't do it.'

A sarcastic laugh from Winter. 'Didn't do what?'

'Whatever the NYPD say I did.'

'You getting the feeling yet that perhaps you should pack your bags and come home?'

'Just because of a little bit of trouble? And this from the man who's been badgering me for months to come and work for him.'

'Exactly. Work for me. On official investigations.'

'Official? That's not how I remember the JIA.'

'You know what I mean. And you know I'll look out for you if I can, Ryker.'

'I appreciate it.'

'I wasn't finished. I have to say, I am disturbed at how after just a few short days in the US you've got yourself on the wrong side of not just the police but the FBI too.'

'Force of habit.'

'Something like that.'

'In all seriousness, Ryker, don't take this too far. This isn't a game and if you get yourself in serious hot water, I may not be able to stick my toe in after you. My involvement becomes a lot more complicated.'

Ryker had wondered how long it would be before the niceties wore off. He was surprised it had taken so long.

'Whatever you say.'

'I'm serious. Think of this one as a personal favour to help you out with a misdemeanour. But you carry on, and eventually you'll be in too deep for me to pull you out. Believe me, the FBI don't like being told what to do, and they won't forget your name. James Ryker is the identity I helped to give you. Tarnish it through recklessness like you did the identities that went before it and I won't help get you another one.'

Ryker gritted his teeth. He got the message loud and clear. But he hadn't asked for Winter's help in giving him a new identity, just like he hadn't asked for the JIA to spring him from jail. The NYPD and FBI didn't have grounds to charge him anyway. All the JIA had achieved was to buy him an early release by a few hours and to make the FBI even more suspicious of his presence.

'Ryker, I know you're still there,' Winter said after a long silence. 'And I know this isn't the first time we've had to have a conversation like this one… but it will be the last.'

'I got it.'

'I really hope you'll consider coming home. We can talk properly about what you're trying to achieve over there. If the FBI are already all over this then why not let them deal with it?'

'I'm sorry. I'm grateful for you helping me, but that's not going to happen.'

Winter sighed. 'Then this time you're on your own from here.'

The phone line went dead. As calmly as he could, Ryker placed the handset on its cradle. He looked back to the laptop, at the flickering images of Campbell and Kate on the screen.

Winter had made his point, but Ryker wasn't backing down now. He was only just getting started. And Winter was dead wrong about one thing; Ryker wasn't alone. Not by far. In a city as big as New York, there were eyes and ears everywhere, he mused, then headed on over to his computer.

Chapter fifteen

Shaun Doherty sat in the expansive morning room of the Georgian-style Long Island mansion. The property, which he was renting from a close friend, was grand but not excessively big with six bedrooms, a separate two-bed guest annex and two acres of land. Plenty good enough for now – he'd only been in the US for a few weeks after all.

At fifty years old Doherty considered himself to be in the prime of his life, both physically and mentally. Immaculately dressed, as always, in linen trousers and a tailored powder-blue shirt, Doherty had soft facial features that belied both his age and his domineering personality. Clean shaven, with his hair slicked back, and a few buttons of his shirt undone, he looked every bit the eighties Miami playboy.

Doherty sat back on the brown leather sofa, legs crossed, and sipped the treacly coffee. Not bad. He stared at the men in front of him. The room was silent except for shallow breathing.

One of Doherty's goons – Victor – was across the room by the door which opened out onto a sprawling central hallway with marble floors, crystal chandeliers and a large gallery staircase. Victor was big and had Herculean strength, in contrast to his pea-sized brain. Danny, much shorter, but twice as vicious and more than twice as clever and cunning, was positioned directly behind the sofa opposite Doherty, upon which sat the dishevelled figure of Jamie Carter.

The ever-useless Carter, Doherty thought.

Doherty had first sent Carter to New York five years ago to manage and help expand Doherty's business interests there. But that first foray had been less than successful and Carter had come skulking back to Ireland a year later. Doherty wasn't normally the type to forgive such a failure, but he had known Carter for a long time and decided to give the man a second chance. That was two years ago. Carter had been bumbling along ever since, and Doherty had finally decided it was time to take control.

You want a job done properly, and all that.

Plus, given the businesses he'd recently acquired from Henry Green and his idiot brother Charlie Ward, Doherty felt now was the time to really make his presence in the Big Apple known. The city had long been a safe haven for the Irish. Doherty would show New York what the Celtic Tiger was really capable of.

But not with Carter in tow. The truth was that Carter wasn't up to the job and Doherty would be better off without him. Not only was he a poor entrepreneur, but he'd begun to attract unwanted attention: failing to buy off the police and failing to obtain the most profitable drug-dealing lines. In theory Doherty had an arrangement with Henry Green and Charlie Ward, and each week he had to pay them a share of *his* takings. Which left Doherty with virtually nothing. The time had come for change.

Carter looked around nervously at Danny, then at Victor. He fixed his gaze back on Doherty.

'Shaun, what can I say, I made a mistake. It won't happen again.'

Doherty took another sip of coffee then slowly and carefully placed the cup back onto the saucer on the glass coffee table, not making even the slightest sound. He sat back again and took a deep breath.

Victor took a step toward Carter.

Carter's expression turned from frightened to angry. There was still fight in him. But not much.

'Tell your thug to step back,' Carter said, glaring at Victor.

'Thug?' Doherty said. 'Victor's no thug. He's a warrior. If anyone in this room is a thug, it's me.'

Carter stared at Doherty, clearly confused by the statement.

Doherty sighed. 'Looks like I'll have to teach you. You know what *thug* means?'

No answer from Carter now.

'Thugs were professional robbers and assassins in India. Travelled across the sub-continent for six hundred years. By some accounts they killed millions in their time. God knows how much they stole. Thugs were clever. Conniving. They'd infiltrate roving bands of travellers, becoming part of the groups. Then launch deadly attacks when least expected.'

'Sounds like you, boss,' Danny said, with a wry smile.

Doherty glared at him. 'My point exactly.'

The description was certainly apt given his plans for New York.

'Please,' Carter said, his confidence now all gone. Doherty felt sure the man was about to clasp his hands together and start to beg. He really hoped his long-term acquaintance wouldn't degrade himself like that.

Events with Carter had come to a head as a result of a police raid the previous night at The Malibu – Doherty's longest-standing club in New York, in the Park Slope neighbourhood of Brooklyn. Carter had failed to pay off the right people within the NYPD, and the bastards had smashed the place up and scared off the hundreds of punters inside, possibly for good in many cases, and made only a small number of arrests for possession. Corruption among the local cops was rife, and from what Doherty could gather the raid was likely nothing more than a warning that they wanted more money in future.

Really the raid itself wasn't much more than a mild inconvenience to Doherty. But the fact the raid had taken place at all was going to piss off Green no end, given that he and his brother were the suppliers of the drugs and stood to lose the most if the police ever traced anything back to them.

Doherty had done business with Green and Ward for many years, but that didn't mean he felt a shred of loyalty toward them. Naturally, with Doherty being the man he was, he already had his greedy eyes on *acquiring* some more of their holdings. To a man like Doherty, friendship didn't really come into it. Anyone who stood in the way of him achieving money and power was fair game.

Carter wriggled uncomfortably in his seat. 'Shaun, what can I say? I messed up, but it won't happen again. You know you can count on me.'

No, the problem was Doherty couldn't count on him at all. Carter didn't see the bigger picture, and he didn't have the vision or the ambition that Doherty did.

With Doherty's continued silence, Carter became increasingly agitated, looking left and right to Danny and Victor. Yeah, it was only a matter of time before he started begging. Doherty wouldn't let that happen.

Doherty nodded to Danny who promptly shot forward and grabbed Carter around the neck, squeezing hard enough to control Carter but not so hard as to render him unconscious. Carter squirmed about pathetically, gasped for breath; his hands flailed, trying to loosen the grip around his neck. A pointless exercise. He had no chance. He tried to speak – more like croak – but Doherty wasn't listening.

Danny dragged Carter off the sofa. Carter's arms and legs continued to flail but he was quickly running out of steam. As if he was resigned to his fate and nothing he could do or say would change whatever it was that Doherty had planned.

Which was about right.

Danny kneeled and brought Carter down onto the Persian rug in the middle of the room. Carter was on his back, his head resting against Danny's bulbous thighs.

'Put your feet on the table,' Doherty ordered. 'Do it!'

Carter whimpered, and only did as Doherty instructed when Danny tightened the grip further. Sweat now poured down Carter's face.

A snide grin on his face, Victor came over and tied Carter's ankles together with rope, then secured the rope to the leg of the coffee table, leaving Carter's legs suspended in the air. Carter continued to squirm but he was going nowhere.

Victor walked behind Doherty and came back into view a moment later lugging a ten-pound sledgehammer. Carter's eyes widened with terror, and now he begged.

'No, Shaun. Please! Don't do this. I'll do anything!'

Carter truly was a sneaky fucking weasel, begging for his life like that, Doherty decided. He gave a stern glance to Victor, indicating for him to get on with it.

Victor lifted the sledgehammer above his head, grunting, his faced screwed in effort.

Carter yelled, 'No… please!'

He screamed as Victor slammed the hammer down. It impacted with his right knee, and there was a horrific crunch and squelch as the lump of metal shattered bones and tore through flesh. Carter's leg caved downward. He screeched as blood spurted out from his stricken limb and onto Danny and the expensive rug.

Danny flinched at the blood on his face and arms but strengthened his grip on Carter's neck, making it impossible for Carter to muster the breath to speak, let alone scream any further.

Another nod from Doherty. Victor brought the hammer down on the left knee. The blow was even more ferocious than the first and all but severed Carter's lower leg save for strands of skin and sinew. The hammer continued its trajectory and pummelled into the wood floor beneath the rug. Victor looked to Doherty as if questioning whether he was in trouble for the damage he'd just caused to the flooring. Doherty couldn't care less.

He nodded to Danny who let go of Carter. His body slumped onto the rug, his head lolling lightly from side to side. No sounds came from his lips.

'Finish him off then get rid of him,' Doherty snarled to the goons as he got to his feet. 'And call a decorator because there is no way I am letting my little girl play on that rug now.'

He turned and left Danny and Victor to their work. He had no interest in seeing how they'd finish the useless prick off. Although Doherty's words had been vague, Danny and Victor knew what to do. They would remove all of the main identifying features from the body – fingers, toes, teeth – before burning the body and burying the ashes. Doherty didn't want anyone finding Carter. This wasn't a message kill. This was getting rid of someone who was in his way.

Would anyone even miss Carter? Doherty doubted it.

Anyway, the job was done. One less problem to worry about. But plenty more still to sort.

Chapter sixteen

Following his 'induction', Campbell spent the next couple of days making the transition into the Green empire. His first task was ensuring he properly understood the ins and outs of the bars and clubs so he could better design a system for keeping on top of the financial affairs. These operations were highly profitable, even without the extra cash from Green's side business. Other than dealing with those transactions in the books, Campbell had decided he'd stay well away from that other business. He didn't plan on returning to the warehouse in New Jersey any time soon. The less he saw and thought about the drugs, the easier it was for him to justify working for Green. Ignorance was bliss. Hats full of money helped too, he realised.

Green had explained to Campbell exactly how he wanted the drug money dealt with. Half of it through the books, to be washed in the bank accounts. The other half for Green's cash stash, which was, to a large extent, unaccounted for. Though Campbell could already tell that if fifty percent of the money was being stored as cash then Green was sitting on a fortune. Not only was Campbell responsible for accounting for the money, he had to physically handle the cash, picking it up from each of the premises at regular intervals. Seeing the endless bundles was enough to make his eyes water.

Campbell had to admit that, in a perverse way, the operation that Green and his brother Charlie Ward had concocted impressed him. The inner workings of drug dealing was something he'd never given much thought to, yet the business was bigger, more complex, more intricate then he would have imagined, and in the main it was well organised. There were tens of people working for

Green and Ward, possibly hundreds of people if the clubs were included, and Green was on top of pretty much everything.

It made Campbell wonder how far Green could have gone as a legitimate businessman. The evidence suggested he would have been every bit as successful. So what had made a man like Green turn to crime? Had it been hard-wired in him from birth or was it the result of a series of events in his lifetime which led him in that direction?

Campbell thought about the same question for himself. Growing up he'd always been in conflict with his parents. His father's secretive role for the British government, and the fact that he was rarely around, together with his mother's high expectations and overbearing nature with her only son, had roused a disgruntlement and rebelliousness in Campbell even at a young age, and he'd long fought against the *norm* as a result. He had convinced himself that he'd had no choice but to work for Green, that he had been drawn to the seedy underworld through no fault of his own, but was that really the truth? Was it in him just like it was in Green?

Had Green had a choice all those years ago?

'I've made a few changes to how we account for the merchandise,' Campbell said to Green. They were sitting in the office at Evolve. Campbell tried his best not to use the word *drugs*; it was one of many denials he had in place to make him feel better about his role. But it was also for security reasons. While they didn't go as far as speaking in codes, they did try to keep conversations about the drugs and the associated money as bland as possible. You never knew who might be listening, Green had told him.

'It was too obvious that those receipts weren't related to the clubs. I've set up a system so that the merchandise money is scattered through the books, included in other legitimate entries, so it's added on to the door receipts, the till receipts etc., and it's spread among all the bars and clubs so that each entry is only for a relatively small amount of cash. That way, even if someone was looking for it, they'll have a much harder time trying to find it.'

Sometimes Campbell could barely believe the words that came out of his mouth. To think that only a few months ago he had been sat at his desk at Berwin Moore's preparing footnote binders – living his mother's dream.

He had thought a few times about the analogy of the man who sold his soul to the devil. He was already richer than he had ever been. But at what price? Yet he wasn't the one making or selling the drugs. He was just accounting for it. If he wasn't doing what he was doing, it wasn't as if the drug world would just disintegrate into nothingness. So why shouldn't he take advantage of it? Of the opportunity that he'd been given? Yes, he still had a soul. Boundaries. But perhaps those boundaries were moving: they were fluid, not rigid.

'Scott, this is exactly what I'm paying you for,' Green said, turning to Charlie Ward on the sofa by his side. 'What did I tell you?'

Campbell hadn't yet had much interaction with Ward. Green's half-brother looked nothing like him – a good ten years younger, he was tall and lanky with a large Roman nose and squirrelly eyes. But the brothers did share some commonalities; arrogance was one of them.

Ward glared at Campbell with disdain, as though he didn't yet feel he was worthy of being part of the family business.

'Yeah, not bad, kid,' Ward said in his gravelly voice, and Campbell would take that, even if the suspicious glower remained.

'We need to get out of here,' Green said, slapping his brother on the thigh. The two men got to their feet.

'Er. Actually, there is one other thing, Henry,' Campbell said. 'Yeah?'

'I've done some analysis of the performance of the clubs, looking back over the previous few months, and I've noticed that the merchandise money took a bit of a drop a few months back, and it hasn't quite recovered.'

Campbell stood up and showed the printed bar chart to Green. 'Maybe something happened in the way you were recording it, but there's a definite dip around February time. In percentage terms it's not that big, but it works out at about ten and twenty grand a week less than last year on average. I wasn't sure if I was missing something.'

Green screwed up his face. He looked to Ward, who looked equally unimpressed and just shrugged in response. They were angry but Campbell could also see that Green was deep in thought.

'Do you want me to do a bit more analysis?' Campbell said. 'Maybe the answer will come out.'

'No. What you've done is enough. I'll find the answer. You can be fucking sure about that.'

Green stormed out of the office, his brother in tow, who slammed the door shut behind them. Campbell was left standing at his desk, the paper flapping in his hand as he wondered what the hell he'd just started.

Chapter seventeen

The time had come to make his move, Ryker decided. He'd spent another day tailing Campbell around the city. One thing was clear: Campbell was well and truly on the inside with Green now. He was even driving around in one of Green's shiny black Mercedes. Newfound wealth – but at what cost?

It was clear from the apartment footage that Campbell's relationship with Kate was far from rosy. The two of them had barely spoken at night or in the morning before work the last couple of days, despite Campbell's marriage proposal. An added complication, for Ryker. He was in New York to pull Campbell away from the clutches of a life of crime, but that meant either pulling him away from Kate or getting her out too. Was she an innocent party in the whole thing? During Ryker's brief time in New York he'd only spent a few hours looking closely at her movements away from the apartment, but there was nothing to indicate she was part of the family business.

He'd think on that one some more. Regardless, now Ryker just needed to determine the best time to approach Campbell. He'd seen no further sign of surveillance by the FBI since his release from police custody. Were they really out en masse or had Chan just got lucky in spotting Ryker lurking? He didn't yet know, and the only thing holding him back from confronting Campbell now was the thought that perhaps the FBI would see the whole thing. He'd have to pick his moment, be absolutely sure.

With any luck, that chance would come sooner rather than later.

Yet Ryker had another party to contend with now. Shaun Doherty. He'd not seen the man's face until Chan had shown him the picture when he was at 20th Precinct. Doherty was surely the man he'd seen shepherded out of Malloy's a few days before. In some way, Doherty was linked to Green. But was he friend or foe?

One thing Ryker did know – he was bad news. He'd already had a contact back in England give him the lowdown on Doherty who had a long track record in the underworld: extortion, corruption, prostitution, drugs, weapons peddling and violence. His presence in New York intrigued Ryker. Having determined that Campbell was spending much of his days cooped up inside Evolve nightclub filling in spreadsheets, Ryker figured it was worth spending a bit more time figuring out Doherty's agenda.

Which was why today Ryker was once again in the Bronx, and once again spying on Malloy's.

It was with keen interest therefore that Ryker spotted a familiar-looking black Mercedes crawl past the pub and park up on the side street nearby. And he was even more interested when the man who stepped out of the Mercedes wasn't Henry Green, but Scott Campbell.

Chapter eighteen

Campbell hadn't heard a peep from his boss since he'd stormed out of the office the previous afternoon. Today Campbell was continuing his collections, heading to premises to collect the weekly profits, which included the drug money, and reconciling the cash stashes against till receipts – anything left over was the money from the 'merchandise'. As well as Green's own bars, Campbell also needed to visit Malloy's in the Bronx. Although Doherty now owned the bar, he was still using Green's dealers and the profits were to be split evenly between the two. Campbell had been told to meet a man named Carter there to go through the money.

Although it almost certainly would have been quicker to use public transport for the collections, it was simply impractical to expect Campbell to lug all that cash around the city. As such, Green had indefinitely leant him one of his humongous Mercedes. That certainly made travelling through the stifling city a whole lot cooler, and yet Campbell was hot under the collar. There were tens of thousands of dollars from each bar and by the end of the day he'd have a substantial amount of cash sitting in the boot of the car. What was he supposed to say if the police stopped him and found it? He was sure there must be a better way of organising the collections, but for now this was how Green wanted it to work.

He arrived at Malloy's mid-afternoon, not long before rush hour was due to kick in. He found a parking spot on the street alongside the bar and made his way to the front entrance. Malloy's wasn't the worst looking of Green's bars – or ex-bars – but having seen the takings history, Campbell could scarcely believe that such an ordinary-looking bar could generate so much.

Campbell paused mid-step when he spotted the two leather jacketed bouncers on the doors.

'Afternoon,' he said to them. Both gave him the evil eye. 'I'm Scott Campbell.'

'He's inside,' the taller one said before opening the door and ushering Campbell into the darkened interior.

The big man followed Campbell inside where a flashily dressed man in his forties or early fifties was sitting on a bar stool reading a newspaper. A heavily tattooed man stood behind the bar, wiping a pint glass. The place was otherwise empty.

'Are you Carter?' Campbell said, walking up to the man on the stool and extending his hand.

The guy looked up, his lips pinched in disdain. 'No I am fucking not,' he spat. 'I'm Shaun Doherty.'

Campbell's heart missed a beat. Doherty was basically Green's contemporary. The snarling look of offence on Doherty's face suggested Campbell wasn't off to the best start.

'Sorry, Mr Doherty. I was told to expect Carter.'

'Carter's not here. What do you want?'

Doherty placed his paper down. Picked up the smouldering cigarette from the ashtray on the bar and took a long drag. He got up from the stool and the big man went and hovered by his side.

'Henry sent me. I'm… here–'

Doherty broke out in a wide smile.

'I'm fucking with you, man.' Doherty held his hand out and Campbell shook it. 'Sit down. Can I get you a drink?'

Campbell sat on the edge of a stool, hoping this signalled he wouldn't be there for long. He just wanted to get the money and go. Not only because Doherty was giving him the creeps, but also because he had two other bars to get to before he was done for the day.

'No drink. I'm good thanks.'

'So you were saying? Henry sent you here? What for?'

'For the money.'

'What money?'

'The takings for the week… you know?'

Doherty pursed his lips and looked over to the big man who shook his head, then to the barman who did the same before turning away as though he didn't want any part of this.

'Don't know what you're on about. What takings?'

'Henry's share… from the merchandise?'

'Merchandise? This is a fucking pub. We sell beer not T-shirts. And it's *my* pub. There's no money here for Green or anyone else.'

Campbell didn't know what to say. Was Green playing with him sending him here like this? He thought about calling Doherty out. Smiling and laughing and hoping the others followed along. Yet the stern face on both Doherty and his henchman suggested they were deadly serious.

'So what are you saying?' Campbell asked, feeling lame that that was the best he could muster.

'Do you not speak English? There's nothing for you here. What don't you understand? Now either buy a drink or please, fuck off.'

'Does Henry know about this?'

Doherty's expression turned even grimmer. Campbell was sure he could see the big man clenching and unclenching his muscles as though readying for action.

'I don't give a crap what Henry Green knows. Now run along, pal, before you get yourself into trouble.'

The bouncer took a step forward. Campbell more or less fell from his stool onto his feet, and took two shaky steps backward.

'That's fine,' he said. 'No worries.'

Campbell had got the message. Without saying another word, he turned and strode for the exit. Just before he reached the door, he looked over his shoulder and saw the bouncer was following him. Campbell's heart pounded. He pushed the door open, nearly smashing it into the second guy still stationed outside who gave him a menacing glower. Campbell walked faster still, nearly a jog as he bounded away, glancing behind him every other step to make sure they hadn't followed him. He let out a sigh of relief when he reached the Mercedes and dove inside unscathed.

What the hell was going on with Doherty? And what the hell was he going to tell Green?

Campbell should have headed on from Malloy's to the remaining bars but he was too consumed. He tried calling Green but got no response and decided to head back to Evolve, hoping Green was there.

Apparently, he was in favour with the god of traffic lights, because Campbell made it back to the Meatpacking District in twenty minutes. He parked up and made his way to the club entrance with the two filled duffel bags. The doors were locked. Campbell had a key. He dropped the bags and opened the door and noticed the lights were on. He picked up the bags and headed inside.

'Hello!' he called out. No response.

He set off for the office. At the foot of the first set of stairs was one of Green's men – Campbell didn't know this one.

'I presume Henry's here?' Campbell said to the man.

'He's in the office. But he's busy,' the man replied.

Campbell wasn't sure if that meant he wasn't allowed to go up, but the guy didn't try to stop him as he walked past. As Campbell climbed the final steps he noticed another one of Green's heavies at the door to the office. He recognised this one. His name was Deontay. He was tall and bulky like the others, his suit jacket and trousers strained to bursting point from the muscles underneath. The door to the office behind him was closed.

'He's busy,' Deontay growled. An American accent – one of the Southern states. Green certainly wasn't afraid to take a multi-cultural approach to his empire. 'Why don't you come back later?'

'How long will he be? This is pretty urgent.'

'Didn't say. Just said he didn't want to be disturbed.'

'Could you let him know I'm here?' Campbell heard a howl from the other side of the door, then shouting, but he couldn't make out any words. He already had an idea what was going on in there – what worried him most was why.

Deontay said nothing as he chewed his gum and glared at Campbell.

'Look, I really need to speak to him.'

Campbell went toward the door. He managed to get within a yard of it before Deontay manoeuvred to block him, but Campbell still managed to knock on the wood loudly before his path was blocked and Deontay shoved him back.

'Don't fucking test me,' Deontay growled.

'Henry, it's me,' Campbell shouted, ignoring the threat. 'We need to talk.'

Deontay didn't say anything more, just glowered and took another step forward, forcing Campbell to back-step away from the door.

A few moments passed before the door was opened by Green. Just a few inches, enough to poke his head out.

'It's not the best timing, kid.'

'You need to hear this.'

Green paused then sighed. 'Very well. Come on in. This concerns you after all.'

Green opened the door and Campbell walked past Deontay who shook his head in disapproval. Inside the office Campbell's eyes were drawn to the forlorn figure sat in the middle of the room on a metal chair. He gulped and faltered in his step.

Each of the man's legs was bound to a chair leg. His hands were tied behind his back. He was naked and blood streaked his body from head to toe. Plastic sheeting covered the floor all around the chair. Steinhauser was standing behind the man, the plastic coveralls over his suit smeared with blood.

Campbell turned back to the door, a large part of him ready to take flight and run as far and fast as he could. Deontay was there. He placed himself in the middle of the doorway, blocking it.

'No,' was all Green said.

Campbell, shaking, turned around and looked at Green. The sleeves of his white shirt were rolled up to the elbows. Blood speckled his hands, arms and chest.

Green shrugged. 'You said you wanted to come in.'

'Jesus Christ, Henry,' Campbell said, horrified.

He glanced to the man on the chair but couldn't bear to look for more than a split second. What he'd witnessed at Reynolds's warehouse was one thing, but this? He'd never seen so much blood before. The guy was still alive but was mumbling incoherently, his head bowed.

'I don't need to see this.'

'No? But this is because of you.' Green glared at Campbell, then looked back to the man. 'This fuck has been stealing from me.'

Green walked over and threw a fist into the man's stomach. He yanked on the man's hair, pulling his head upright. His face had multiple lacerations; his left eye was completely closed up. The vague imprint of the letters HG blazed red on his cheek – from Green's favoured signet ring, Campbell realised.

'Isn't that right, Johnny boy?' Green said to the man then threw his head back down.

'I'm… sorry… Henry,' Johnny said in laboured breaths. 'Please. No more.' The words were slow and slurred.

'I think he's had enough,' Campbell said.

Green gritted his teeth. 'Not yet he hasn't.'

He threw his fist into Johnny's face again, followed by a flurry of punches to his body. The pendant on the thick chain around Green's neck slipped free from inside his shirt and jostled in the air with each strike.

Green paused, chest heaving from exertion. He noticed Campbell looking. He smiled. Seemed to relax a little. He gripped the pendant and looked to Campbell.

'It's a viper's head,' Green said entirely casually before dropping the pendant back into his shirt. 'Kate bought it me years ago.'

Campbell said nothing.

'I always thought it was apt, for me.' His eyes pinched and he turned back to face Johnny. 'Some people call vipers sluggish, but they're not. They're clever and cunning. They move slowly but surely, taking everything in, waiting for their moment. When the time comes… they're vicious, and when they strike you can be damn sure they strike fast.'

Green nodded to Steinhauser who pummelled Johnny's sides with his boulder-like fists. Each thump caused the man's body to jump and made Campbell's insides ache.

'Henry, please, if this is about the missing money–'

'Damn right it is. I've been asking around. Apparently this kid has been getting smart, skimming from me down at the warehouse.'

'What? No! It's not him. I think it's Doherty.'

At that, Green froze, and Steinhauser paused too, mid-punch.

'It's Doherty. It has to be,' Campbell said. He had no clue who Johnny was, or what he'd been up to, but he wasn't responsible for the missing money. At least not the money Campbell had identified. That money was related to the bars now under Doherty's control, and given Doherty's earlier attitude, it didn't take a genius to figure out what had happened. 'He's taken over those bars. He wouldn't give me *any* takings today. I think he's already been taking some of your cut for months.'

'That slimy fucking Irish prick!'

Green looked like he was about to explode. He turned his attention back to Steinhauser and Johnny but didn't speak.

'Boss?' Steinhauser said.

'Did I tell you to stop?!' Green screamed. 'Carry on 'til I fucking tell you to stop!'

'But, Henry, it wasn't him!' Campbell pleaded with Green.

'No one steals from me and gets away with it.'

'You can't just kill him!'

Green turned, grabbed Campbell around the throat and slammed him up against the wall, lifting him clean off his feet. Green squeezed hard and Campbell rasped for breath as his heart and head fired into an unrelenting panic.

'You don't tell me what to do! Ever. Got it?'

'Yes,' Campbell managed to choke out.

Green released his grip and Campbell slumped to his knees gasping for breath and nursing his neck. He looked up and saw Steinhauser with a baseball bat in his hands. He lifted it over Johnny's head.

'Don't,' Campbell whispered.

'No… please…' Johnny whimpered.

Steinhauser brought the bat crashing down onto Johnny's skull. Campbell flinched and there was an almighty crunch as wood hit bone. More blood splattered onto Steinhauser and the plastic sheets that lay all around. Steinhauser swung the bat up above his head and down again with even more ferocity. This time some of the blood splatter reached as far as the glass that looked out over the club below.

Campbell retched. A completely reflexive reaction.

'For Christ's sake! Get the fuck out of my sight, Campbell,' Green shouted, absolute disgust in his tone. 'I'll call you when I need you again.'

Campbell didn't need to be told twice. He turned and bolted out of the office, down the stairs and out of the club into the heat of the afternoon. Which hardly helped his nausea.

Outside he darted around the block, heading for the Mercedes. He couldn't get the image of the bat hitting Johnny's head out of his mind: the sound as Johnny's brain was pulverised, the blood and bone and pieces of flesh that flew across the room.

He stopped running when he reached the car, but with the grisly images still replaying in his head, he hunched over again, trying to hold his stomach in, his hand against a lamp post to hold himself up.

That was when he heard the voice.

'Dear, oh dear. What a mess, eh?'

Campbell looked up to see a man standing next to the curb. Campbell did a double take; his head was in such a mess he was unsure whether he'd seen him before.

'You're in deep shit, Scott Campbell,' the man said. 'Deep, deep shit.'

Chapter nineteen

Ryker looked down at Campbell, waiting for the eureka moment.

'Who the fuck are you?' Campbell said, his tone not as confident as his words. The guy looked a state, was white as a ghost.

'I said who are you?' Campbell took his hand off the lamp post, standing straight.

Ryker said nothing, just waited for it…

'What the… Carl Logan?'

'In another life.'

'What happened to you? You look…'

Campbell lost his train of thought. Ryker felt he knew what he'd been trying to say. The last time they'd met Ryker had been far more fresh-faced.

'Time takes its toll on us all,' Ryker said.

'What the hell are you doing here?'

'I was going to ask you the same question.'

Campbell pushed past Ryker and stormed away, making for his car. He took the remote from his pocket and there was a beep as the doors unlocked.

'Scott, wait.'

Campbell paused. Turned to Ryker. Gone was the shitting-himself-out-of-his-depth look, replaced with a confident anger.

'I've got nothing to say to you.'

'No? This is one problem you won't be able to run away from.'

'What problem? And I'm not running from anything.'

'Then let's go talk.'

'About what?'

'Your new employer, perhaps.'

That wiped away just a sliver of his confidence. Campbell looked nervously over Ryker's shoulder as though Green was there with his goons.

'She sent you here, didn't she?'

'It's not as simple as that. Why don't we talk?' Now Ryker looked over his shoulder. 'You probably don't want Green to see you with the likes of me.'

'You? Why? What are you?'

'Campbell, stop being a dick. You don't belong here, in this life with the likes of Green. But I can help you.'

Campbell looked incredulous. 'What are you talking about?' He put his hand out to the driver's door.

'What would Kate think about her man being banged up for the rest of his life?'

Campbell paused.

'Let's go somewhere to talk. We've got a lot of catching up to do.'

Campbell huffed. 'Fine. But not around here.'

'Okay then,' Ryker said, smiling. 'You're driving.'

Ryker scooted over to the passenger side of Campbell's car and jumped in.

Campbell drove them back to the Upper West Side and with each block they passed up Broadway a little more colour returned to his face. They were both silent, Ryker deliberately giving Campbell time to stew. Ryker knew some of the troubles Mackie and his wife had with Campbell when he was a youngster, in many ways their own making with matters not helped by Janet's overbearing nature toward her son, and Mackie's stressful and secretive life. Rebellion was just the start, though the way Ryker had always thought of it was that the kid was just lost in life, much like Ryker had been through his childhood and teen years, though his and Campbell's backgrounds couldn't have been more different.

Until Mackie had taken Ryker under his wing.

Perhaps Mackie's fatherly touch only worked when he was trying to mould teenagers into robotic killing machines, like he

had with Ryker. Campbell on the other hand, Mackie's own son…
Ryker truly believed Campbell's parents had wanted the best for
him. A normal life. For whatever reason Campbell wasn't the
man either parent had intended. Yet Ryker already sensed now
that Campbell was far from content with the position he'd found
himself in. He was in denial, out of sight from what was left of
his family in London. Maybe Ryker's appearance was the reality
check he needed.

With no chat, Ryker mulled over what had got Campbell so
worked up. When he'd seen Campbell arrive at Malloy's earlier
everything had seemed fine, but then Campbell had raced out of
there as though he was running for his life, and headed straight
back to Evolve. Minutes later he had raced out of there too and
looked like he was about to throw up.

What had he seen?

They stopped on West 65th Street, the gleaming double
towers of the Time Warner Center visible in the near distance
at the southwest corner of Central Park. Campbell, face sullen,
led the way to a 1950s-style diner on Broadway. A young blonde
waitress in a red and white dress showed them to a leather booth
in the far corner, well away from the few other punters. The smell
of grilled meat, eggs and grease filled the air. Ryker wondered if
the location was a wise choice given Campbell's near vomiting not
long ago. He ordered some coffee and eggs. Campbell ordered
only a sparkling water.

'A regular haunt of yours?' Ryker said as the waitress headed
away.

'Not really,' was Campbell's vague response.

A few moments of awkward silence. Awkward for Campbell
at least. Ryker could tell from the younger man's fidgeting that his
mind was in turmoil.

'It's been a long time,' Ryker said. 'Last time I saw you, you
must have been only twelve, thirteen.'

'I was fourteen, actually,' Campbell said. 'But I was always
small for my age.'

He wasn't wrong there. He'd been a short and scrawny teenager. Ryker had known he was bullied badly at the private school he'd attended. Back then Ryker had held a soft spot for his boss's son, had wanted to look out for him, offer advice on how to deal with the bullies and become more confident in himself. Maybe Campbell had taken that rebellious advice too far, given where he'd ended up.

'I thought you were dead,' Campbell said with no particular feeling.

'Yeah,' Ryker said. 'Clearly not. Though Carl Logan is a thing of the past. I'm James Ryker now.'

Campbell shook his head, a look somewhere close to disgust on his face. 'Jesus, it's a wonder I didn't end up even more fucked up than I am, growing up with so many secrets and lies around me.'

Ryker didn't know what to say to that. Campbell had a point.

'Your dad always wanted what was best for you.'

'What would you know? You just did whatever he told you. Probably killed for him. Didn't you?'

Ryker didn't answer.

'Of course you did. He never told me much about his job but it doesn't take a genius to figure it out.'

'He was a good man.'

'Maybe. But he was a shit dad.'

Ryker clenched his fists, trying his best to hold back a response. The last thing he needed was a slanging match over Mackie's parental skills.

Campbell half smiled, but the look was wiped away in a flash. 'I remember this time, we were asked to talk about what our parents did for a job. Everyone has to do that, right?'

Ryker said nothing. He was sure it was a common thing for kids in school to do, though he knew from his own experience how such a simple and well-intentioned subject could lead to all manner of problems for some less fortunate children.

'Anyway, I really didn't talk much. All I could say was my dad worked for the government. That was the stock response he always told me to give. *But what does he do for the government?* the teacher asked. I said he worked in an office. That was it. It doesn't sound much now but some of the boys thought it was hilarious that my dad did something so seemingly boring and indescribable. Took the piss out of me relentlessly. Until I grabbed one of them by the throat one lunchtime and told him my dad trained assassins and if he didn't shut up I'd send one of them after his family.' That half smile again. 'And you want to know something really funny?'

Funny? Not quite what Ryker was thinking.

'In my head it was you I was picturing, shooting that kid in the head. You see, I always knew what you were.'

'Why don't we move on–'

'I'm not finished. Naturally, after that I got the shit kicked out of me. Like I said, I wasn't a big kid. Those lads weren't scared of me in the slightest, even after what I'd said. I was a loser, plain and simple. I told my dad what happened. In tears I pleaded with him to do something about it. Find a way to punish those boys and teach them a lesson they'd never forget. He looked so disappointed in me... and do you know what he told me?'

Ryker shook his head.

'"We don't solve our problems with violence, Scott",' Campbell said in a mocking impression of Mackie. 'Can you fucking believe that? His whole life was about solving problems with violence. But apparently it's okay if you're a step removed and use trained assassins under the radar.'

Campbell went silent now. Ryker really didn't know what to say. On the one level he could understand why Campbell had struggled so much with the concept of what his father did for a living, but that still didn't justify what he was now doing to his own life.

'Sometimes I question whether my dad's really dead,' Campbell said, 'or if that's all some elaborate lie too.'

'No, he's dead.' Ryker looked down. 'He was shot right in front of me.'

'So I heard,' Campbell said, his eyes narrowing in distrust. 'You were wanted for his murder.'

Ryker held his tongue at that. It was true. Mackie's death was a set-up concocted by the Russian FSB to heap pressure on Ryker and get his own people to turn on him. It had worked. Until Ryker had gone on a bloody rampage to punish everyone involved in the deceit. Obviously that part of the story was a little less public. In the aftermath Ryker had been given a new identity by Peter Winter and what at the time seemed like a way out from his life working for the JIA. Somehow, though, he kept getting drawn back in at every turn.

'Quite honestly it made no difference to me that he was killed,' Campbell said bitterly.

'You don't mean that.'

'What would you know? He was a lousy dad. He cared more about the likes of you than he did me.'

Ryker shook his head but didn't otherwise react. He hadn't come all this way to argue the toss over Mackie. Yes, it was true Mackie had been a father figure in Ryker's life – and he'd certainly needed one – but that didn't mean he hadn't cared for his own son too.

The waitress came back over with the drinks and Ryker's food. He took a steaming pile of eggs on his fork. Some of the colour drained from Campbell's face again as he stared at the food.

'Let's get this back on track,' Ryker said after swallowing the mouthful. 'I'll help you, because I owe it to your mother and father to do so.'

'My mother? I've only ever been a disappointment to her. She probably only gives a toss now because she's on her deathbed and is finally regretting how she treated me.'

Ryker could only shake his head at that. He was startled by Campbell's lack of compassion given the state Janet Campbell was in. Clearly there was more to the story that he didn't know.

'Does she even bother to call me, or contact me directly? No, what she does is somehow finds you and sends you off after me to clear up the mess in your own special way. What, are you going to make me disappear if I don't go along with what she wants?'

'I'm here to help you.'

'And what if I don't want or need your help?'

'You need it. Whether you want it is a different question. But if you don't accept my help you'll likely end up in the hands of the FBI, the same as Green and the others. And it'll be sooner rather than later.'

At the mention of the FBI, Campbell's remaining confidence disintegrated. His eyes became rabbity as he stared around the place, as though he suddenly believed the Feds had eyes and ears on the conversation that very moment. Perhaps they did.

'That's bullshit… wait, you're not with–'

'Of course not. I'm here off my own back. But I've already had one run-in with the agent gunning for Green. The closer you get to him, the bigger the target you're painting on your own back.'

Campbell shuffled in his seat. For the first time in the conversation Ryker felt that he actually had his full attention.

'The FBI know all about Green and his brother Charlie. The clubs, the prostitutes, the drugs, the extortion…' Ryker was embellishing now, but he could tell by the look on Campbell's face that he was heading down the right track. 'Green and his gang are linked to about half a dozen murders.'

Ryker looked for any tells on Campbell's face or in his movements, but all of a sudden he was remarkably cool, no obvious sign of emotion. But then his lack of outrage at what Ryker had said was probably the biggest tell of all.

'How the hell would you even know what dirt the FBI have on Green? And if everything's so clear cut why hasn't he already been arrested?'

Ryker smiled. Campbell glowered, as though offended by Ryker's response. Then Campbell's phone chirped in his pocket. Ryker inwardly groaned. This was the escape from the awkward conversation that Campbell needed.

Campbell took the phone from his pocket and before Ryker could protest he'd answered it.

'Henry,' Campbell said. 'I... no, not at all, I was... no, I was just getting some food. You want me to come back?'

A few seconds later, Campbell pulled the phone away from his ear.

'I need to go.'

Campbell couldn't even look Ryker in the eye. He got up from the bench. Ryker grabbed his arm, pulled him close.

'I have to tell you, your poker face is really quite shocking,' Ryker said as Campbell squirmed. 'You didn't look surprised, shocked, outraged when I mentioned drugs. When I mentioned murders. Barely a flinch even. You didn't try to plead your innocence.'

Campbell's face dropped. For the first time he looked genuinely scared. Ryker had him absolutely pegged.

'You go running back to Green. But I'm not finished with you. See you around.'

Ryker let go and watched Campbell stride out of the diner.

Chapter twenty

Green had told Campbell to head back to the club, but he hadn't said why. As Campbell had sat in the diner on the Upper West Side with the man who now called himself James Ryker, Green's call had seemed like a lifeline, getting Campbell away from the unwanted conversation. Yet as he drove back to Evolve, that glimpse of relief soon faded. He was in a state of utter confusion. He really had no clue what he should do next.

Not long ago he'd witnessed Henry Green and his crony murder a man. Next up had come the shock of discovering Carl Logan aka James Ryker was on his tail. Campbell knew little about Ryker on a personal level, but he did know that Ryker was ruthless and dogged and had lived a life of violence. Whatever his agenda, he was the last person Campbell wanted on his case. And the mention of the FBI? Just what the fuck was he supposed to do now?

Of those three adversaries, he had no idea which he was better aligning himself with. Could Ryker get Campbell – and Kate – out from Green's criminal kingdom? He certainly hadn't been looking for a way out, if anything he'd been intent on getting himself further *in*. But wasn't what Ryker was offering a better scenario than the alternatives? Campbell couldn't go to jail. And anyway, he hadn't killed anyone. He hadn't bought or dealt drugs. Green was the bad apple, not him, so why should he have to suffer?

The biggest problem, though, was that Campbell did feel loyalty toward Green. The man was Kate's father after all, and he was the man paying Campbell a small fortune.

When Campbell arrived at Evolve, his brain still a confused mess, Green, Steinhauser and Deontay were standing at the bar by the empty main dance floor. Green had changed his clothes – he was now wearing jeans and a designer blue shirt ensemble that was more or less identical to before, but without the spatters of poor Johnny's blood. Campbell wondered what they'd done with the body. Was it still in the office where he spent most of his working week? How could he ever concentrate properly in there again now, knowing what had happened? He shivered at the thought, goose pimples erupting on his skin.

Campbell approached the three men and their hushed conversation stopped. Green turned around.

'Scott, where have you been?'

Campbell felt his legs wobble. What would Green do if he knew Campbell had just met with a government spy? That's essentially what Ryker was. Or what he had been at least. 'I told you, I went out for some food.'

Green glared, seemingly not buying Campbell's straightforward explanation, but he didn't push it. 'We're going to see Doherty. We need to sort this crap before it gets out of control.'

'You want me to come with you?' Campbell asked, surprised.

'It was you who came to me all in a fret, so yes. You can explain what's going on.' Green turned to Deontay. 'You stay here and clean up in the office. I want it useable again by the time we get back.'

Campbell cringed at Green's words. Deontay didn't look too impressed by the request either. Oh, the glamorous life of a henchman.

Green walked toward the doors of the club followed by Steinhauser and Campbell, who was starting to wonder how his day could possibly get any worse. Outside they climbed into the S-Class, Steinhauser in the driver's seat and Green and Campbell in the back.

'What you saw earlier, Scott,' Green said, after a couple of minutes of driving in silence. He turned to Campbell and gave him a hard stare. 'What you saw was necessary. You don't get to where I am by letting people take the piss out of you. You have to set an example.'

An example? How could he possibly justify killing a man in cold blood as setting an example? Campbell thought.

Campbell's eye fell down to Green's neck and the gold chain that was still visible. He could hear Green's earlier words about vipers echoing in his head.

'If I don't keep on top of things like that, people stealing from me, then it spirals,' Green said. 'I've seen it. Sooner or later Billy big bollocks wants to take a pop at me as he thinks he can take over. You need to remind them constantly who the boss is.'

'Yeah, well, there's no doubt you showed Johnny who's boss,' Campbell said, his contrary tone surprising himself as much as Green.

'Don't get smart with me, kid. All I ask for is loyalty. Without that…'

Green didn't need to finish the sentence. Campbell got the point.

'What will you do with the body?' Campbell asked. 'I mean, how on earth do you cover something like that up?'

Despite the distress and disgust that he felt, there was no doubt he had a morbid curiosity. Putting together Green's apparent ease and even eagerness to commit the act, with the devil-may-care attitude he was now exhibiting only a short time after, Campbell was convinced this man had killed before. Or at least had been instrumental in having people killed.

'Scott, sometimes I don't get you,' Green said, shaking his head. 'One minute you look like you're about to cry like a girl, the next you ask a question like that.'

Campbell looked away out of his window, ashamed.

'I prefer this side of you. This is the side that'll make you a survivor in this game. A winner.' Green clenched his fist in triumph as he spoke. 'Like I already said, Johnny is an example to others. We won't hide the body. I want people to know what happens if they fuck with me. The police won't tie him to me. He's a low life. They'll put his death down to gangland violence. They won't pursue it. It won't get any attention in the papers.'

That's what you think, thought Campbell. What would the FBI make of Johnny's demise?

They arrived in the Bronx not long after. The three of them headed up to the main doors of Malloy's and Steinhauser stepped forward and knocked. After a few seconds, one of the bouncers from earlier – the smaller one – opened the door, a snide grin on his face.

'Gents, come on in. Mr Doherty's expecting you.'

They filed in, Steinhauser in front, Campbell at the rear. Once again there were no patrons inside. Doherty was still sat at the bar, on the same stool as earlier. Had he moved at all? His newspaper was next to him on the scratched wood. His other henchman was sat at the table in front of Doherty. No sign of the tattooed barman now.

'Shaun, good to see you,' Green said, his face breaking out into a wide smile. The two men hugged and patted each other on the back as though they were best friends, despite the obvious tension in the room.

'Henry, sit down. My man'll fetch you all a drink. Victor, get the boys a drink,' Doherty said.

Victor, the taller and angrier of the two heavies, grumbled and went behind the bar. He gathered some tumblers and poured out generous measures of Irish whiskey. Doherty got off his stool and ushered Green and Campbell to one of the tables. Steinhauser remained standing, positioned behind Green. The smaller of Doherty's men stood behind his boss.

'Have you met my boys?' Doherty said. 'The big lad over there is Victor. The bulldog here is Danny.'

Green nodded in acknowledgement. 'Looks like you're making yourself at home here.'

Doherty shrugged. 'I've always fancied trying to conquer America. U2 did it, so why not me?'

Doherty smiled at his own quip, as did Danny and Victor. Campbell saw Green clench his fists, his knuckles turning white.

'I've sent Carter back home,' Doherty continued as Victor brought the drinks over on a tray. 'I'll run things here myself now. Like I told your boy earlier.' Doherty nodded to Campbell.

'I heard about that,' Green said.

Doherty now glared at Campbell as though any problem was his making. 'There seems to be some confusion. Your boy...' Doherty stopped, feigning that he was trying to remember Campbell's name.

'Scott,' said Green.

'Yeah, Scott, he thinks I owe him some money.'

'No, Shaun. You owe *me* money. You know our deal.'

'Except I'm getting the arse end of that deal. So there's two ways we can make this work. We renegotiate, or I go somewhere else.'

Doherty took a gulp of his drink. The cheer Green had initially expressed was quickly fading.

'Hey, I'm just a businessman looking for the best deal,' Doherty said with a casual shrug. 'If you're not offering me that then I'll look elsewhere.'

'So what are you asking for?'

'We split ninety–ten. A commission for you. After all, you're basically just an agent.'

'Are you taking the piss?'

'Come on, buddy, risk and reward and all that.'

Campbell's heart raced in his chest. He knew Green was incensed even if he was trying his best to appear calm. Campbell on the other hand was twitchy; he felt as though the room was about to erupt in violence at any second.

Doherty shrugged again. 'I could always start sourcing my own stuff. You know what? If the price is right I could even sell some to you.' He winked at Green.

'You little prick!'

Green jumped out of his seat and lunged toward Doherty. He took a swing with his right arm but Doherty leaned back in his chair just enough and Green's fist only grazed him. Green, off balance, collapsed onto Doherty and the two of them hit the floor.

Campbell shot up from his seat and back-stepped, trying to get to a safe distance. Steinhauser joined the melee, pulling Green up and away from Doherty, the big South African an unlikely peacemaker.

But the damage was already done. Campbell froze to the spot when he felt pressure on his temple. Something cold and hard.

He didn't need to look to see it was a handgun barrel pressed up against his skin. Victor.

Across the other side of the table Steinhauser and Green were back on their feet. Danny was a few feet away, his gun pointed at Green, whose chest was heaving with rage. Doherty clambered back to his feet. Bizarrely he appeared absolutely calm still.

'So what now? You're going to shoot me?' Green said. Not a trace of fear in his voice. Only anger.

Campbell was frozen. He daren't flinch, afraid that any movement would cause Victor to pull the trigger.

'There'll be no shooting here today,' Doherty said. On cue, Danny and Victor lowered their weapons. 'But the deal we had is over. I'll sort myself out from now on. You want to quarrel about that then you know where I am.'

'Fine. You stick with your shitty bars. But don't go getting any silly ideas about moving in on my business.'

Doherty didn't react at all to Green's veiled threat.

'Come on, boys.'

Green turned and stormed for the exit. Campbell scuttled after him. Outside Green paused, standing by the curb, hands on hips. When Steinhauser went up to him, Green turned and threw his fist into the big man's ribs. The shot caught him by surprise and he doubled over, winded. Green followed up with an arcing right hook that sent Steinhauser to the ground.

'Some fucking protection you are,' Green raged. 'You've got a gun; next time use it.' Steinhauser propped himself up on his knees. The blotchy outline of Green's signet ring was already visible on Steinhauser's cheek. Green hurled his shoe into his face and sent him back to the ground.

'And you,' Green sneered, as he turned to Campbell. 'Jesus, remind me not to bring you along again. About as much use as a… ah, fuck it.'

He lurched at Campbell, making him flinch. Green shook his head in disappointment and carried on to the car.

Chapter twenty-one

When Campbell arrived home that evening, he collapsed on the sofa in his apartment, exhausted. Outside the windows the setting sun lit up the skyscrapers of Midtown with warm orange light, but as he gazed out at the sight, Campbell shivered as Ryker's words once again echoed in his head.

The FBI were out there somewhere.

His head throbbing, Campbell got up and walked to the window. Looked at the glass of the buildings across the street for a few moments, not exactly sure what he expected to see. He saw nothing.

He closed the electric blinds, then slumped back down onto the sofa, the day's events repeating in his mind. The first run-in with Doherty. The murder of Johnny. The meeting with Ryker. And then another meeting with Doherty, and *a gun pointed at his head*. How could so much shit have happened in just one day?

Wasn't he out of his depth now?

What Campbell wanted more than anything was to talk to someone about what had happened, relieve the tension and anxiety that was almost bursting out of him. But who would he talk to? Not Kate, and that wasn't just because Green had told him to never speak to anyone about what he saw on the job. He didn't want to talk to Kate because he wanted to protect her. To protect the image she had of her father and future husband.

Campbell had never felt so alone.

Your father would be so disappointed...

'Shut up!' he screamed, the gesture immediately halting the continued voice of his mother in his mind. He put his head in his hands as his eyes filled with tears. One escaped, cascading down his face, and he quickly wiped it away when he heard the front door open. But he couldn't wipe away the thoughts in his head. He took a deep breath and tried to compose himself.

'Hi,' Kate said as she bounded into the lounge.

She was dressed in a tight white gym top and a white tennis skirt. Her face was red from exertion. She put her gym bag down and, looking over at Campbell, her expression turned to concern.

'Scott, what's the matter, babe?' She sat down next to him on the sofa, leaned into him and ran a hand through his hair.

'Nothing. Just been a long day. Where've you been?'

She took her hand back and bent down, fiddling with the laces on her shoes.

'I was playing squash with a friend from work. I've been meaning to for a while. It was really good fun actually.'

'Yeah? Who did you play with?'

'Oh, it was just Mark from the office.'

'Mark Powell?'

'Yeah,' she said, not looking up from her shoes.

'Since when have you been friends with that idiot?'

Kate looked up and gave him a cold stare. 'What does that mean?'

Campbell had met Powell before at a work party. He really didn't know much about him, just that he came across as a cocksure arsehole, and today really wasn't the day that he wanted to hear Kate had been spending time with another man, however innocent it was.

'Powell is a creep,' Campbell said.

'What, you're going to start telling me who I can and can't hang out with now? You're turning into him more and more every day.'

Campbell said nothing as Kate got to her feet, though his anger remained piqued. He'd never thought of himself as the jealous type but the thought of Powell spending time with Kate made his insides boil.

'Jesus, Scott, it was only a game of squash. I do have a life too, you know.'

She grabbed her gym bag and stomped off to the bathroom. After a few moments, with his head still brimming with unwelcome thoughts, Campbell got off the sofa and walked over to the sideboard. He poured himself a large Scotch. An expensive single malt Green had given him. Campbell had never really liked whisky – it wasn't exactly the drink of choice for a typical beer-guzzling twenty-something male – but he hoped it would take the edge off.

He took a large gulp, draining the glass, then poured himself another. He felt the effect of the alcohol, calming his senses, slowing his heart, the fog in his mind beginning to clear.

After downing his second glass, he headed off to the bedroom. As he walked in, Kate was standing in front of the mirrored fitted wardrobes, towelling her bronzed skin that was damp from the shower she'd just taken. He watched her, longingly and regretfully. There was no doubt he'd spent too much time recently embedding himself in Green's business rather than with his future wife.

He walked up behind her, took the towel from her and gently patted her back where her wet hair was dripping. After a few moments she turned to face him. She was a few inches shorter than him and she looked up into his eyes. She was still angry, but he could tell she was calming. He went to kiss her but she pulled back.

'Eurgh, you stink of whisky,' she said, playfully.

He dropped the towel, grabbed her and pulled her close and this time she didn't resist as he pressed his lips onto hers.

'I'm sorry,' he said.

He kissed her again and after a few seconds she murmured sweetly and pushed her body closer to his, and Campbell immediately became aroused. He wrapped his arms around her and she jumped up, sliding her legs around his body. He took her weight easily, moved to the bed and they collapsed onto the mattress still kissing, still entwined.

For the first time in days, Campbell was able to forget all about Henry Green.

Chapter twenty-two

Ryker parked the Toyota Corolla in the car park of a small convenience store a little over a mile from his destination and made the rest of his way there on foot. Ryker walked down the leafy street, eyeing the perfectly aligned slabs, pristine grass verges and high walls either side that shielded the expensive and sweeping residences beyond. He'd rarely been to a place which exuded such overt opulence as the Hamptons on the South Fork of Long Island.

The setting sun directly ahead of him as he moved, Ryker pulled his baseball cap low and kept his head down, the sound of crashing waves from the nearby Atlantic Ocean, just beyond the partially concealed mansions on his left, filling his ears. The street he was on was crammed with security cameras, both belonging to the homes but also those run by the local government of Suffolk County. On his short traipse Ryker also spotted not only a patrol car for the Suffolk County Police Department ambling past him, but also one of a private security company hired no doubt at the expense of the nearby homeowners.

He was only surprised nobody bothered to stop to talk to him.

Ryker soon reached his destination. Looked up and down the road. All quiet. He veered off the pavement and into the thick undergrowth that ran alongside the seven-feet-high, white-perimeter wall of the house beyond. He crept along the wall, out of view from the road, his senses primed. When he reached the edge of the undergrowth, where the wall was split by huge wooden entrance gates, he came to a stop. As expected the area in front of the gates was covered by two more cameras. No point in going in that way. On his walk along the wall he'd noted just one other camera on the inside, pointing toward the grounds beyond. There were surely other cameras on the inside too, but with such a large plot it was unlikely every inch was covered. The best bet was to go in directly under the camera he'd seen, dropping into its blackspot, and scope out the grounds from there.

Ryker turned and made his way back, then scuttled to the top of the wall and quickly lowered himself down into the thicket of hedges the other side, the camera directly above him.

In front, the hedges soon opened out into a huge expanse of manicured lawns, fountains, rose-beds and shaped box-hedges. It reminded Ryker of a typical garden of an English stately home, not to mention the Georgian-style house in the distance with its perfectly symmetrical proportions, large sash windows and grand columned entrance.

Ryker took just a few moments to fully capture the surroundings. Most importantly, he saw no one. No garden staff, no security and certainly not Shaun Doherty or his cronies. Were they still all out and about in the city?

But it did look like someone was home, somewhere, judging by the three vehicles – large and new – parked off to the side of the house by the separate garage unit.

Satisfied that he could make it to the house undercover, Ryker confidently moved forward, using the natural obstacles of the garden to shield him from view, and sticking to areas he believed were blackspots for the few cameras visible on the inside.

He soon found himself by the garages, the crashing of the waves directly beyond the house now louder than before. A quick dash across the yellow gravel and he was propped up against the side wall of the main mansion.

Ryker pulled the balaclava from the backpack and slipped it over his head. He wasn't here for a confrontation, and if someone saw him, he at least wanted to hide his face as he made his escape.

He slowly moved along the wall, heading for the back. Beyond another lawn, the garden gave way to small dunes and then white sand, the blue of the Atlantic Ocean trailing to the horizon. He spotted the gleaming white yacht moored a couple of hundred yards out, its paintwork glistening in the orange light of the low sun. Every now and then the sounds from the yacht carried to him: laughter, music, shouting. Some sort of party. Ryker couldn't see the faces clearly at a distance, but he could only guess Doherty was on the boat and acting as host.

Which gave Ryker the perfect opportunity to go snooping – exactly what he'd hoped to achieve from this trip. Doherty remained the one man in the mix who Ryker didn't yet know enough about, and Ryker was becoming increasingly intrigued by his role in Green's world, particularly after the two run-ins that had taken place at Malloy's that day. The latter of which had seen Henry Green flooring his bodyguard in anger.

Ryker held his breath for a few moments, preparing himself, but also listening for any sounds nearby, someone from inside the house perhaps. Then he made his move. He dashed across the back of the mansion and in through the open patio doors, pulling to a stop inside a brightly decorated lounge.

No one there. A camera in the corner of the room. He was inside now, and his face was covered. Too late to worry about cameras. He moved across the room for the doorway, which opened out into a marble-floored hall. He stopped again. Listened. Moved away and to the adjacent doorway. An office. On the polished wooden desk was a laptop computer, lid closed. On the coffee table nearer to him was an iPad.

That was where Ryker headed.

He slipped the backpack from his shoulders. Took out the USB connector cable and the thumb drive that he'd already pre-loaded with software for this exact purpose. He picked the iPad up and slipped the connector into the charging point. The iPad screen came to life. As expected a four-digit pin was required to unlock it. Not a problem. The software on the thumb drive would do its job in seconds. A four-digit pin had only ten thousand permutations. The software could crack codes with millions of permutations in mere minutes.

The screen unlocked. The green light on the thumb drive blinked. For the next phase it would take a full image of the machine's small hard drive. That too would take just a few minutes given the limited capacity of the tablet's memory.

While he waited Ryker's fingers danced on the screen. First he went into the email app. No password needed. He scanned through the first few emails. None jumped out at him. Back in his hotel later he'd do a full search of the data using keywords. The thumb drive blinked again. Imaging complete. Next up was the laptop, which would likely hold far more data.

Ryker pulled the thumb drive out then paused as he looked at the email on the screen. The title was *Persons of interest*.

He pressed the screen to open the email. Was left staring at a grainy picture of himself, taken from inside Malloy's bar. Ryker scrolled down the other pictures in the email. All of him and Scott Campbell. His heart beating faster, Ryker looked to the top again. The sender's name was simply *Eagerbeaver*. Who the hell was this? Attached to the email was a brief report. An ID profile of Scott Campbell… and James Ryker.

'What the hell?' Ryker whispered under his breath.

Ryker wasn't concerned that Doherty had found out his identify; what he was more bothered about was that Doherty had felt the need to do so. Why? And who was the mystery *Eagerbeaver*, someone able to gain access to such information?

A noise outside. Ryker crept closer to the window. Peered out.

'Shit.'

A small dinghy was powering its way across the darkening water from the yacht. About halfway back to shore, Ryker could now make out Doherty's face on-board. And that of one of his cronies from Malloy's. The big man.

Ryker went to put the iPad down. He was out of time.

But another email caught his attention and he couldn't let go.

Logistics update

Ryker looked out of the window again. He still had a few seconds. He opened the email. Saw it was a run-through about plans for… something. Discussion about new shell companies in the Cayman Islands, holding entities for assets now belonging to Doherty. Comments too on the identification of a 'drop point' in New Jersey that was perfect for their operation – a little used airstrip. Drugs?

What was this? What was Doherty planning?

A bang from outside the room. Ryker's eyes flicked to the window. The dinghy was still a few yards from shore and slowing. But someone was out in the hall.

Ryker exited the email app, quickly wiped the screen with his shirt sleeve, and put the iPad down. He crept to the doorway. Heard a toilet flushing not far away.

Hide and wait? No, the risk of Doherty landing and coming back inside were too great.

Ryker darted across the marble, trying to keep his feet as light as possible, aiming for the room directly across the hall – a kitchen? He was sure there was a door there that came out by the garage side of the house. He was only a few feet across the hall when he heard the shocked scream of a woman behind him.

He skidded to a stop. Turned. Saw the woman there, towel wrapped around her, hair dripping. From the boat party? Had there been two dinghies?

'Danny!' she screamed as Ryker stormed toward her.

She cowered back. Into the toilet. Ryker grabbed the door. Slammed it shut. Yanked up on the handle as hard as he could and felt the mechanism twist out of shape.

She wasn't going anywhere.

More footsteps upstairs.

Danny? Whoever that was. Ryker would rather not wait and find out.

He dashed back across the hall to the kitchen. Sped to the end. Crashed open the door there, then spun on his heel and back out into the hall, just as pounding footsteps approached both from outside and down the stairs. He slunk into a corner under the staircase. There was shouting all around him. Questions about who the intruder was – a burglar? – and where he'd gone.

The next moment he saw feet rushing past, into the kitchen.

'This way,' he heard a male voice call. Then more shouting as the men gave each other further instructions.

Ryker waited. The voices outside became more distant. He peeked out from his hiding place. A man was over by the toilet, trying to open the door. Short and stocky, wearing only beach shorts. One of the bouncers from Malloy's? Danny?

Ryker rushed for him. The guy didn't even sense Ryker's presence before Ryker clattered into him. The man's forehead cracked off the door and he collapsed to the ground.

Without looking to see what damage he'd done Ryker turned and sprinted for the lounge and the open patio doors beyond.

Not breaking stride, he burst out onto the back lawn. Looked left and right. Saw the outline of someone moving around the side of the house toward the garages. They were all looking in the wrong place.

Well, nearly all of them.

As Ryker raced across the grass, heading for the sand, he spotted the big man lurching toward him. The other bouncer from Malloy's. In shorts and an open shirt, his thick muscles rippled as he sped to cut Ryker off.

Ryker didn't bother to try and get away. He went straight for the guy. Shimmied at the last moment, sunk his body down and swivelled, his outstretched leg swiping the big man off his feet. Ryker threw his body down. Smashed his elbow into the guy's face. Ryker went to get up. Realised the guy, barely conscious, was grasping the strap of his backpack. Ryker launched his foot into the man's midriff, then yanked on the bag.

He didn't let go.

The strap snapped and Ryker fell backward into the long grass of the dunes. He was about to get up and grab for the bag again when he saw a figure coming into view at the side of the house. Chose instead to stay crouched low.

It wasn't clear if the big man in front of him was out for the count or not, but either way he still had tight hold of the backpack. With more figures congregating by the house, Ryker realised he couldn't afford to hang around. He made a snap decision. There was nothing of real value in the bag, nor anything that compromised him.

He'd lose the thumb drive, but he could live with that. Most important for him now was to get away cleanly.

Staying low, Ryker back-stepped through the long grass of the dunes, down the bank until he was at the edge of the sand, out of view from the house.

He turned and ran.

***

Nearly an hour later, Ryker finally made it back to his car, tired and parched and full of questions. He flopped down into the driver's seat. Fired up the engine.

He didn't drive off. First, there was a phone call he had to make.

It'd been a long day. He still had a lot of thinking to do, but he'd seen enough to know he needed some help. Ryker firmly believed Shaun Doherty was up to no good, and judging by what he'd seen on Doherty's iPad, both he and Campbell were on the Irishman's radar.

That didn't bode well for either of them.

The call was answered on the fourth ring.

'Agent Chan?' Ryker said.

A short pause. 'Yes. Who is this?'

'It's James Ryker.' More silence. 'I've got a proposition for you.'

Chapter twenty-three

It was nearly eleven thirty when Maloney called, and Chan's mind was still thinking over the day, and in particular the bizarre call she'd taken from James Ryker not long ago. She was fixing herself some supper at home – a two-bedroom apartment in Queens in a pre-war building that she'd lived in since she was first pregnant nearly ten years ago. How her life had changed since then.

'Maloney, please don't tell me you're still at work?' Chan said as she answered the phone.

'Er, yeah, I am actually. Sorry for calling you so late.'

Chan sighed and put the frozen meal into the microwave then set it on high for four minutes. It whirred away and she headed for the lounge, being quiet as she crept across the hallway so as to not wake the kids.

'Don't be silly. What have you got?'

Maloney was the agent she'd put in charge of surveillance on Green's premises. It had already been quite a day with various comings and goings across Green's empire, the most curious of which being Green's trip up to the Bronx which had ended with him beating up his own henchman out on the street.

Plus, there was that damn James Ryker, who'd first turned up at Evolve in the afternoon and met with Campbell, followed by Ryker's call to her earlier after apparently breaking and entering a home in Long Island occupied by Shaun Doherty. What was this guy James Ryker on?

Though his proposition…

No, she needed more time to dwell on that before she came to any conclusion.

'I spotted something unusual from the feeds on Evolve,' Maloney said. 'The club hadn't opened yet for the night but I saw a van pull up to the back doors. They were loading or unloading something but I couldn't see properly because of the angle.'

'It could just be a bog-standard delivery?'

'At 10pm? Plus, they normally get their main deliveries on a Thursday, before the weekend.'

'So what are you telling me?'

'Just what I saw. I thought it might be important.'

'Okay. Thanks for letting me know. Why don't you give it up for today? Let me know in the morning if anything else comes up.'

'Will do,' Maloney said before Chan hung up.

She shook her head. Over in the kitchen the microwave pinged and Chan's belly grumbled expectantly. She'd not eaten since lunch.

She really wasn't sure if what Maloney had seen was of any importance. Time would tell. Maybe it was nothing. But maybe it was everything.

***

Chan was rudely awakened the next morning at 6am, not by her kids, like most mornings, but by her vibrating phone. With her mind still busy when she'd got into bed just after midnight, she'd had all of three or four hours of sleep. Groggy and crotchety, she shoved the kids out of the door as they were still getting themselves dressed, palming them off on her neighbour who had become her saviour in recent days.

She arrived at the scene in the Bronx less than forty-five minutes later.

There was an ambulance parked up on the main road, across from the raised subway line, together with a number of NYPD cars. The alley, around the corner from the bar, was cordoned off with blue and white police tape.

Chan walked toward the cordon, the ground vibrating as a train rumbled past behind her. At the tape she took out her ID.

The uniformed officer there looked like he was about to debate her presence – the classic Feds versus police standoff – but then Detective Amanda Spencer of the NYPD came striding over and soon settled matters.

Spencer was a similar age to Chan, and had a similar level of seniority within her own organisation, though with a husband but no kids probably had quite the different life. Certainly she always seemed more happy and relaxed than Chan generally felt. Chan stooped under the tape and walked with Spencer down the alley where numerous other officers and CSIs in their white overalls were busy at work.

'I'm guessing you're the reason I got a rude awakening this morning,' Chan said.

The call had come in from her boss, but for now this was an NYPD murder case, and it was nothing more than good fortune that Spencer was assigned to it. She remained one of the few people in law enforcement in the city who Chan knew could see beyond battle lines and was willing to be open and honest with the FBI when it was likely a case was relevant to both organisations.

'Just doing my bit,' Spencer said as they came up to the dumpster behind Malloy's bar.

'So what have we got?'

'A deceased male. We were alerted by an anonymous call, a man claiming he'd seen the body. Call was traced to a phone booth not far from here. One of our locals came to check it out and found the body.'

'Have you ID'd him?'

'No. The deceased looks like he's been beaten to death – his head's cracked open like an egg – though we'll have to wait for the post-mortem to confirm the exact cause of death, and time. ID will be a problem because there was nothing on him and his fingers, toes and teeth are missing. And I'm not sure anyone is going to recognise his face, the shape it's in.'

Chan winced at the words.

'As I'm sure you guessed from the location, the bins belong to Malloy's, which is why you got the call. I figured it might be of interest to your investigation.'

'You're not wrong there, Detective,' Chan said.

Chapter twenty-four

Unfortunately, despite the previous night's love-making, Campbell didn't manage to keep Green out of his thoughts for long. First thing in the morning and he was headed back to Evolve. As usual, when he arrived, the cleaners were hard at work clearing up the debris of the night before. Had they any inkling of the mess that had been in the office just a few hours prior to their arrival?

Campbell walked through the club and up to the office. It was like any other day – all signs of yesterday's violence had been removed. Campbell wasn't surprised to see Green sat on the sofa reading a newspaper, a pot of coffee on the table in front of him.

'Morning, Henry.'

'Scott,' Green said, a smile breaking out on his face that made Campbell immediately suspicious. He'd expected Green to still be pissed off with him over the run-in with Doherty.

'You're looking pleased with yourself,' Campbell said as Green folded his paper and put it down on the coffee table.

'That I am, kid.'

'Are you going to tell me?'

'Let's just say our Irish friend will be enjoying some unwanted attention from the boys in blue.'

'Yeah?'

'Our friend Johnny turned up outside Malloy's last night. Police are swarming around the place this morning apparently. I would love to have seen Doherty's face.'

'You set him up?'

Green's face turned sour in a flash.

'Just putting some pressure on him. He needs to know who's in charge in this city.'

Campbell had to admit the thought of Doherty being hassled by the police over a crime he didn't commit was amusing. Green was a criminal thug but for some reason Campbell had plenty of respect for the man. He had no respect for Doherty. There was something not right about him, nothing but malice and contempt inside him.

Steinhauser came into the office and whispered into Green's ear. The big man's left eye was black and swollen from the beating Green had delivered outside Malloy's, but he seemed oblivious to the fact that the man who'd inflicted that upon him was the man he was now speaking to.

Campbell heard his mobile phone ring and reached into his pocket. The caller ID was withheld.

'Hello,' Campbell said.

'It's Ryker.'

'Oh… hey, how are you?' Campbell said, trying to be as calm as possible. What the hell was Ryker trying to do? Get him killed? Thankfully, Green was busy talking with Steinhauser.

'You with Green?'

'Yeah.'

'Okay. Just wanted to let you know there was a fascinating development this morning. The police have found a dead body down a back alley near Malloy's. I'm guessing you might know something about that. Perhaps you can tell me all about it next time we meet.'

'Yeah. The thing is, I'm a bit tied up today.'

'No you're not,' Ryker said. 'So let me rephrase that for you. I'll meet you at midday. Same spot as yesterday.'

'You mean by the lamp post, right?' Campbell said.

'Very funny, Scott. I'll see you there.'

Ryker hung up. Campbell lowered the phone and looked over to Green who was still deep in a hushed conversation with Steinhauser. Neither of them had noticed the beads of sweat which had formed on Campbell's brow.

Chapter twenty-five

'See you around, Detective,' Shaun Doherty called as Detective Spencer turned and headed for the door with her sullen colleague.

He got up from his chair and set about making a coffee behind the bar. Across the other side of the room Danny closed and locked the front door then came over.

'You want one?' Doherty asked.

'Whatever you're having. So what do you think?'

Doherty could see Danny was seething – his face was red and stuck in an angry snarl.

'This doesn't change a thing,' Doherty said. 'They've got nothing on me or any of us.'

'But do you think it was Green?'

'Of course it fucking was. But that prick will get what's coming to him.'

Danny grunted in acknowledgement.

Despite the unwelcome and unexpected visit from the NYPD, Doherty remained upbeat about progress. Everything was falling into place now. The perpetually useless Carter had failed twice to make a success of New York, and now here was Doherty, barely a few weeks in and already on his way to getting everything he wanted. Granted, his approach was considerably different to Carter's, but that just showed how small-minded Carter had been.

Following the run-in with Green the day before, Doherty had set in motion a plan that had been in the works for months, and the fruits of his labour were finally beginning to pay off. The dead body turning up by his bar was far from ideal, and he had to accept that the NYPD would have him on their radar now.

But Doherty had ways of dealing with the police – money, in the main – and for once, he really had done nothing wrong. He had a perfectly good alibi for the night before. He hadn't killed that guy, whoever he was, and neither had his men, so there couldn't possibly be any evidence to link him to the murder.

The bigger question was: why had Green killed the guy in the first place? Was it just to try and put some heat on Doherty? That seemed a bit of an extreme measure even for Green, yet Doherty wouldn't put it past him.

Regardless, Doherty wasn't the kind of man to take an attack lying down. He would have his revenge on Green, but he'd do it his way. If everything went as it should, Green would get what was coming to him.

Half an hour later, after two strong coffees and by which point Victor had confirmed the police had left the scene outside, there was a knock on the door to the bar. Doherty looked at his watch. Right on time. Victor walked over and opened the doors.

It was the contact.

'Shaun. So this is your new place then?' the man said as he walked in.

'You like it?'

'It's just like every other damn Irish joint in the city.'

Doherty didn't like the way he said it, but he'd let it slide.

'Tell me, where are we at?' Doherty said. He had no intention of friendly chat with this man.

'I'm in. Just as we planned. He's starting to talk. I don't think he'll ever give me everything he knows but that's not really important.'

'No. What's important is that he takes the bait.'

'I'm sure he will. If it's there.'

'Don't you worry about that. It's all set.'

This was the best part – a true masterstroke, Doherty believed. Green thought he was top dog in New York, but he was about to find out the hard way just how wrong he was. There were so many gullible people in the world. All he needed to do was to play the right ones the right way.

'Okay,' the contact said. 'I'll wait until I hear it from my man. Then I'll put it into play.'

'You do that. Any news on my intruder?'

'Nothing. You told me not to get involved with the local police and–'

'You shouldn't need to. It's a simple task I gave you.'

The contact shrugged. 'Most likely it was a would-be thief. A dumb thief, for sure, but there you go.'

Doherty snorted. He didn't buy that line for a second. 'What about the other information I need?'

'I'm working on it. As soon as I hear, I'll let you know.'

'Unless I get it soon, this whole thing will be for nothing.'

'I know. Like I said, I'm working on it.'

'No cock-ups. You're in too deep to ever go back.'

The contact glared at Doherty, clearly agitated, but he said nothing.

'I think we're done,' Doherty said.

The contact nodded then turned and headed on out. Victor closed and locked the door behind him.

'When this is all over,' Doherty said to Victor, 'remind me to kill that prick. I fucking hate the Feds.'

Chapter twenty-six

After the unwelcome call from Ryker, Campbell kept himself busy with paperwork for the first hour of the day, waiting for the rush-hour traffic to die down before he made his way to the other clubs to belatedly collect the previous week's money. He'd just managed it by the time the clock wound around to eleven thirty and he decided to head on to the diner on the Upper West Side to meet with Ryker.

But why was he even bothering? Who the hell was James Ryker to him anyway? Yes, his father had been fond of him at one time, for some reason, but so what? Neither had any loyalty to each other, or any hold over each other.

Campbell could remember the first time he'd met Ryker, or Logan as he'd been then. Still a teenager, and Campbell a young schoolboy, Logan was basically a dropout. Yet Campbell's father, working for an offshoot of MI6, as far as Campbell could gather, had moulded him for his own purpose into a combat-ready espionage machine.

That was always his father's thing. Making people do what he wanted them to. Largely the dirty work he couldn't or wouldn't do himself. It had never really worked like that with Campbell though. For most of his life it had felt like his father cared more about his work, and the grunts that he trained, than he did his own family. Perhaps that was why Campbell had tried so hard not to turn out like him, or the people who'd worked for him.

So why should Campbell now take advice from Ryker or anyone else of that ilk?

Yet Campbell also knew that Ryker was a man you were better off not being on the wrong side of. Most people who attempted that wound up dead.

Campbell arrived at the diner five minutes late, still agitated by the thoughts of the past coursing through his mind. He spotted Ryker at the same booth as the previous day, already drinking coffee. As Campbell approached, Ryker glanced about the place, as though checking Campbell was alone.

'You eating today?' Ryker said with a wry smile as Campbell took a seat.

'What are you having?'

'Waffles and bacon.'

'Sounds good.'

The same blonde-haired waitress as the day before came over with a wide smile and Campbell placed his order. Only when she was out of sight did Campbell lock eyes with Ryker.

'So what happened yesterday?' Ryker asked.

Campbell wondered which part of the shitstorm that was yesterday Ryker was referring to. How much did this guy know, and how? He'd talked about the FBI having eyes on Green's business, but this guy didn't seem to miss a trick.

'Looked like quite a lot of excitement outside Malloy's,' Ryker added.

'You were there?'

Ryker shrugged. 'Was just passing.'

Campbell scoffed. 'Of course you were. And what exactly do you think you saw?'

'I saw your boss beating the crap out of a guy twice his size. And I saw you looking like you wanted to wet yourself.'

Ryker smirked.

'You don't know the half of it.'

'So what was going on?'

'Exactly what does any of this have to do with you?'

'Nothing really. Except I hate scumbags. From what I know, Green is definitely one. Doherty too. I like to see men like them punished.'

'James Ryker, world police.'

'Something like that. But I know you're not like them.'

'Yeah, so you say. But you don't know anything about me really, do you? And what do you know about Green?'

Ryker shrugged. 'What about the dead body?'

Campbell's heart skipped a beat. He felt his cheeks flush a little and all of a sudden he struggled to hold Ryker's gaze. He scolded himself. What a childish reaction.

'Seriously, Scott, you need to work on that poker face. Worst I've seen. So tell me what you know.'

'I'm guessing you mean the body found outside Malloy's this morning?'

'Is there more than one?'

'What? No! And I've no idea who it was. I only saw it on the news this morning.'

'No you didn't. It's not been on the news.'

More flushing in his cheeks.

The waitress brought over their food orders.

'Looks good,' Ryker said, giving the waitress what Campbell took as a suggestive look.

'Enjoy,' the waitress said, returning the look before skipping back to the kitchen.

'Smooth,' Campbell said.

Ryker took a mouthful of bacon then looked at his watch for the umpteenth time, before glancing behind him toward the door. On cue it opened and a raven-haired woman in a grey trouser suit strolled in.

Ryker turned back to Campbell and beamed a knowing smile. Campbell didn't like it one bit. He looked over at the woman again, and saw she had her sights set on their table.

'What is this?' Campbell said, his nerves painfully evident in his voice.

Ryker got to his feet and shook hands with the woman.

'Scott Campbell, meet Special Agent Jane Chan of the FBI.'

Chapter twenty-seven

Campbell shot up from his chair. Ryker reached out and grabbed his arm.

'Sit down,' he said, with enough authority in his tone to get Campbell to take pause.

'You set me up?' Campbell said.

'I'm giving you a chance to do the right thing.'

'Please, Scott, sit down,' Chan said. 'Don't make a scene here.'

Campbell thought for a few seconds, his eyes darting this way and that. He had nowhere to go. He took his seat again. Chan sat down next to him, boxing him in. Campbell pushed his barely touched plate of food away.

'You're not hungry now?' Ryker asked.

'Just say what you've come to say,' Campbell said, to neither Chan or Ryker in particular.

'I want to help you, Scott,' Chan said. 'Ryker's explained to me who you are and why you're here in New York.'

Campbell glared at Ryker. 'And why's that?'

'Because of Kate Green.'

Nothing from Campbell now.

'You've got yourself into a world that's not you,' Chan said, her tone soft and sympathetic. 'I can help you, and I really want to.'

It had been a tough call for Ryker whether to involve Chan or not. On the one hand, he rarely worked well with law enforcement, always wary that they were too constrained by rules and regulations. But from the little he'd come to know of Campbell from these past few days in New York, he sensed that if Campbell was going to turn his back on his newfound life of crime, it was more likely he'd do it under the pressure of the likes of the FBI than from any threat Ryker could give him. And with the likes of Doherty in the mix too, and his as yet unknown agenda, Ryker would rather have the FBI on his side, if possible, rather than creating another enemy.

Perhaps this wasn't the solution that Campbell's mother had envisaged when she'd called upon Ryker's services, but in many ways Ryker really wasn't the man he used to be. If there was a lawful, and less violent way, to get Campbell away from Green, it had to be worth pursuing.

Luckily, although she remained seriously distrustful of Ryker, Chan had agreed to speak to Campbell.

'It's time to think smart, Scott,' Ryker added, with noticeably less sympathy than Chan. 'Why don't we start our conversation over for Agent Chan's benefit. What happened yesterday?'

Campbell glared at Ryker but didn't say a word.

'Please, Scott,' said Chan. 'I've taken a big risk being here today. The cat's well and truly out of the bag now, so to speak, in terms of our involvement, and this can only go one of two ways for you now. You help me, and I can get you out of this life, or you don't and when Green's kingdom comes crashing down, you'll still be on the inside.'

'You'll give me immunity?'

Chan squirmed in her seat. Ryker knew why. Campbell was asking for something that Chan couldn't give. Yet Campbell wasn't completely dumb, Ryker knew. Even though Campbell was out of his depth with Green, it was unlikely he'd divulge everything he knew just like that, without agreements in place, without legal representation. But the fact he was still sitting in the diner was a good start, and the fact he'd even mentioned immunity rather than laughing the whole situation off meant he would rather get out than keep his mouth shut and go down with Green and his other associates.

'Let's take things one step at a time,' Chan said.

Ryker stepped in. 'Like I said, tell us about yesterday. You have a meeting at Malloy's. After that, Green beats up one of his guys on the street. A few hours later, a dead body is found in a dumpster at the back of the bar.'

Silence. Ryker could tell Campbell was seething, but he couldn't care less. It was about time he stepped up and took responsibility for the shitty situation he'd put himself into.

'I get it,' Chan said. 'You've been drawn into this world under romantic pretences. Probably you've seen guys like Green in the movies. The gangster with a strong moral code. Noble, powerful, just. But that's crap and you know it. In Hollywood you never get to see the aftermath, the destruction of lives that crime brings. Men like Green are responsible for ruining countless lives. Wives, husbands, mothers and fathers and children all affected by drugs, or the violence that world brings with it.'

'I don't know anything about the dead guy,' Campbell said.

For once, his manner was calm and confident, and Ryker almost believed him. Almost.

'Why don't we take a step back?' Chan said. 'For my benefit. Tell me how you met Kate.'

'Seriously?'

'Seriously. Humour me.'

'I met Kate at work, when we were both in London. She was a PA, I was a graduate doing accountancy training.'

'When did you first meet Henry Green?'

'Only a few months ago. We moved to New York because Kate missed her family so much. We–'

'Seriously?' Ryker said.

Campbell glared daggers. 'Seriously what?'

'Why don't you tell us the real reason you ran away from London?'

'I didn't run away from anything.'

'No, I guess not. You were booted out. You beat the crap out of a co-worker. Who knows why? They sacked you and you were lucky to get away with a police caution, for what I've heard was a vicious and unprovoked assault.'

Ryker could tell Campbell was now clenching his jaw to hold back his anger. What lay underneath?

'So you came to New York for a fresh start, right?' Chan said, still calm and empathetic.

'Yes,' Campbell said.

'And then what?'

'I don't know really. It just happened… At first I thought I was just helping out my girlfriend's dad. Doing a bit extra on the side. I… Why would I have said no? Things just went from there… and then… Here we are now.'

'What is it you do for Green?' Chan asked.

'I'm his accountant. I keep the books for all of the nightclubs.'

'So you must know about the drug money, then,' Ryker said. 'Unless you're the world's most clueless accountant.'

Campbell shot Chan a look. 'Why exactly is he here?'

Chan sighed. 'Maybe step it down a notch, Ryker, yeah?'

Ryker raised an eyebrow but didn't protest.

'You can be open and honest with me, Scott,' Chan said.

'You know what? I think I want to go. I want a lawyer before I say anything more.'

'A lawyer?' Ryker said. 'Why, what have you done wrong?'

'It's my right.'

'You're not under arrest. We're just enjoying a spot of lunch.'

Ryker saw the look of concern on Chan's face now. If she followed protocol she had to leave it there, let Campbell walk out and get himself lawyered up. But Ryker didn't want to give Campbell an inch. He just hoped Chan would see it his way. The fact she was there at all suggested she wasn't averse to bending rules if it meant getting to the right conclusion.

'What was the meeting at Malloy's yesterday?' Chan asked, and Ryker was pleasantly surprised that she was willing to push on.

'We were just talking business,' Campbell said. 'Malloy's is owned by Shaun Doherty now.'

A flicker in Chan's eyes. What did she know of Doherty? So far she'd kept her cards clutched tight to her chest.

'How long has Doherty been the owner?' she asked.

'I've no idea. It's quite recent, I think.'

'And he and Green were arguing? That's why Green was so mad afterward?'

'They didn't see eye to eye.'

'On what, exactly?' Ryker asked. 'Drug money?'

'Enough with the drugs!' Campbell said. 'From what I know, Green sold Malloy's to Doherty, but on the condition that Doherty gave Green some of the takings. Doherty's now refusing to keep his end of the deal. That's it.'

'You must know more than that, Campbell. You do the numbers for Green and I'm pretty sure he doesn't give away his gear. So you must see the money.'

Campbell stared resolutely at Ryker. He clearly wasn't going to give anything like that away – certainly wasn't going to incriminate himself without some sort of deal with the FBI in place. So what? Ryker could see how rattled he was, which was Ryker's main intention in arranging the meeting.

'Do you know who the dead man is?' Chan asked.

'No,' Campbell said.

'Do you know who killed him?'

'No. But if the body was found outside Malloy's then surely it's the people at that bar you should be looking to for answers.'

Ryker laughed sarcastically. 'For starters, why would Doherty be stupid enough to leave the body there if he killed the guy? If I was a betting man I'd say it was Green who had that guy killed, whoever the hell he was. Maybe it was Doherty's man, or maybe Green just wanted to get Doherty in the shit. What do you think about that?'

Campbell shot Ryker an incredulous look. 'You really have quite an imagination.'

'Please, Scott,' Chan said. 'This is a serious matter. A man is dead. He was gruesomely murdered, his body mutilated to stop us ID'ing him. Right now we can't even inform his family he's dead. If this is the start of some gang war, we need to stop it escalating. We need to take action before anyone else is killed.'

The colour drained from Campbell's face, but he held firm. 'I'm sorry. I can't help you.'

Chan sighed.

'Are we done?' Campbell said. 'If not, I want a lawyer before answering anything else.'

Chan looked to Ryker, who shrugged.

'Yeah, I guess we're done,' she said.

Chapter twenty-eight

'I didn't upset you, did I?' Kitten asked with her usual sultry purr.

She slowly twirled the hairs on Charlie Ward's chest with an elongated fake fingernail as they lay naked in the bed, both covered in a thin film of perspiration from their endeavours.

'No, it's not you I'm pissed off with.'

It was the scheming Shaun Doherty who would soon get his comeuppance, if Ward had anything to do with it.

'I thought you'd want to know, that's all.'

'You're right. I did want to know. You did good.'

'Will he be in trouble with Henry now?'

Ward didn't answer that one. In trouble with Henry? Why was it everyone assumed Henry Green called all the shots? For the most part they were equal partners in their business ventures, yet Ward felt like he was forever in his half-brother's shadow.

Yes, Green was confident, headstrong, arrogant, and that had gotten him far in life – all in all he was a natural leader. But it wasn't as though Ward was an idiot. He'd made plenty of money from ventures he'd taken the initiative on; he ran some of the most exclusive nightclubs in the city, and managed two dozen of the most expensive escorts around, Kitten being one of them. Henry had nothing to do with the prostitute business – he wasn't interested, seeing it as low return for the amount of effort required. But then Henry was married, whereas Ward was a true bachelor.

Of all the escorts he managed, Kitten remained his firm favourite. In another life perhaps they would have been an item.

'Baby?' Kitten said.

Ward picked up her arm from his chest, shuffled out from underneath her and clambered to his feet at the side of the bed.

'When will I see you again?'

He looked down at her. With her slim frame, balloon-like breasts and heavily tanned skin, she resembled a human Barbie doll. Ward loved it. So did a lot of other men, which was why she was so sought after. But Ward didn't have to seek her out. He could have her whenever he wanted.

'I'll call you,' he said as he stepped into his boxer shorts. 'And if you hear anything else, you tell me straight away.'

'Of course. Anything for you.' She blew him a kiss.

Two minutes later Ward stepped out from Kitten's apartment building into the heat of the day on West End Avenue, and traipsed east, heading for the subway on Broadway.

Kudos to Kitten. She really did have a way of making men spill their hearts out to her. With sex as good as it was with her, she'd learned to be a master manipulator of men – and women. She considered it a talent, and wasn't averse to blackmailing the suckers if the information was juicy enough. Not this time though. She'd simply come straight out and told Ward what she'd heard of Doherty's plans to scupper Green's upcoming deal with the Colombians. She knew where her loyalties lay.

Ward needed to go and see Henry, tell him what he'd found out about that shitbag Shaun Doherty. But first, another call. Walking through the grounds of the sprawling Lincoln Center with the giant arched and columned blocks looming over him, he dialled the number from memory and listened to the dial tone as he scanned the area around him.

'Special Agent Trapp,' came the man's voice.

Ward cringed at hearing the title. 'It's me.'

'About time you called. Your brother has been a busy boy. You want to meet?'

'Can't right now. But I've got something for you.'

'Yeah?'

'That prick Doherty.'

'What about him?'

'Not so fast. I've got a proposition for you. I give you this, you help–'

Laughter on the line. Ward clenched his fist, trying to channel his anger away.

'I what? Forget that your brother is a drug-dealing, murderous scumbag?' Trapp said. 'How about you tell me what the fuck you're on about and then I'll tell you what I want you to do next. That's what you do now, Charlie Ward. You do what I tell you.'

Ward bit down on his lip to hold back the response he wanted to give. 'We need to meet face to face.'

'Where and when?'

'4pm. The usual.'

'I'll see you there. And you better make it worth my while this time.'

The line went dead. Ward felt like flinging the phone away and roaring with anger to release some of the tension consuming him. What he wanted more than anything was to tear Trapp's skin from his face. But for now, he would play along. Did Trapp really have it in for Green so bad that he'd pass up the opportunity to get Doherty? What was the difference to him as to which gangster he sent down?

The problem was, Trapp really was calling the shots. Ward remained in the FBI man's pocket. And if Green found out about Ward's deal with the Feds... It didn't matter that they had the same mother. Green would kill him, and it wouldn't be quick.

Not that Ward had been given any choice when the Feds had approached him. Now, though, perhaps he had a chance to move on. A way to save his own skin without snitching on his brother.

He was heading across Broadway when in the distance he spotted what he thought was Henry's gleaming black S-Class parked up on the road. Thoughts of his own deceit, and the fact that maybe his brother had just been watching him speak to an FBI agent, crashed through his mind. Was it a set-up?

But then he realised it wasn't Green's car after all. It was the S-Class he'd loaned to that weasel Campbell. What was he doing around here?

Campbell was so weak and pathetic it made Ward sick. The way he saw it, there was no need to have the kid around. Ward had run his clubs just fine before Campbell came on the scene. So Campbell was good with numbers. Who gave a flying fuck? Running a club was about more than counting numbers. Ward felt his brother was taking liberties with Campbell, just because the kid was banging his daughter. Perhaps it was Henry who was losing the plot.

Ward carried on across to the diner; the car was parked outside. Through the glass Charlie couldn't see any sign of Campbell. But he could see a tasty-looking blonde waitress. He pushed open the door and stepped inside and gave her his winning smile.

Then he spotted Campbell standing up from the booth in the far corner. He was with two other people Ward didn't recognise. One was a gruff-looking casually dressed man. The other was a svelte woman in a figure-hugging business suit.

He immediately pegged her for what she was.

'You little bastard,' Ward muttered under his breath.

He turned around and bolted for the door.

Chapter twenty-nine

Ryker stopped talking to Campbell to look up at the man who'd just walked into the diner. He immediately recognised him. Charlie Ward. Henry Green's no-good half-brother.

'Shit,' Ryker said, as Ward turned and ran outside. 'Stay there, Campbell.'

'Ryker, stop!' Chan shouted.

Ryker didn't heed her warning. He sprinted for the door, crashed it open and turned left when he got outside. Saw Ward already twenty yards ahead of him. Somehow Ward had figured out who Chan was. If Ryker didn't get to Ward, Campbell was dead.

Ward took another left up ahead and Ryker followed suit. The crowded streets around the Lincoln Center were less than ideal for a foot-chase. Pedestrians stopped and stared, dumbfounded, at the two men rather than getting out of their way, which meant they both barged into the sorry bystanders as they raced through the streets.

'Stop, FBI!' came the shout from behind Ryker. He didn't bother to look behind him. Could tell from the shout that Chan was a good distance further back. He wasn't letting Ward get away.

Ryker got lucky when Ward was forced to sidestep to avoid a young woman with a pram. He tumbled to the ground. Ryker closed a few yards before Ward was back on his feet.

They carried on, quickly moving away from the crowded streets of the Lincoln Center and on to quieter residential streets around West End Avenue, glimpses of the river visible in the near distance every now and then. No more shouts came from Chan. Had she lost them in the melee?

Ward turned down a side street. Ryker had already managed to close half the distance on him. He spotted Ward taking a right, ducking into another street at the last second, but as Ryker turned the corner he couldn't see Ward up ahead at all.

Chest heaving, Ryker stopped running. Looked left and right, up and down the deserted street in front of him. He spotted the entrance to an alley on his right. Headed that way, keeping close to the building on the opposite side. He wondered if Ward was carrying a weapon. Ryker wasn't. Too late to worry about that.

Ryker crept to within a yard of the alley and stopped. His heart beat quickly from the exertion of the chase. He took two heavy breaths, then burst forward into the alley and… stopped. Still no sign of Ward. The alley was about thirty yards long, with large bins on either side. Ryker took a few steps forward, sure that Ward was hiding behind one of the bins.

'Why don't we talk, Charlie?' Ryker shouted out. 'No need for you to get hurt here.'

Ryker took a few more slow half steps. Then heard sharp footsteps behind him. Too late. He couldn't react quickly enough and the blow to the back of his head sent him stumbling forward. Ryker lost his footing and fell onto one knee, momentarily dazed, his head pounding from the blow. He wasn't sure what had hit him, but given the force, it wasn't a fist.

As he attempted to turn, he spotted Ward, metal rod in his hands, swinging it toward Ryker's face. Ryker ducked, avoiding the blow, and grabbed hold of the rod. He lifted up, twisted and wrenched the rod away. He hurled it behind him and the metal clattered along the tarmac to a stop.

The two men squared off. Ward was angry and snarling. Ryker was calm and ready. He didn't want to fight. But he'd damn well not stand there if Ward was going to come at him again.

'Seriously. We should talk,' Ryker said. 'Or this won't end well for you.'

'Yeah?'

Ward was an equal match in size and height to Ryker, but Ryker wasn't in the least concerned about the position he found himself in. Not even when Ward took out a knife.

Why was it always a knife?

The blade, about four inches long, was a flick knife, easily concealable. Ward held it out toward Ryker, smiling grimly.

'Really?' Ryker said.

'I knew something was wrong with that little shit,' Ward sneered.

He lunged toward Ryker with a roar of rage. Ryker dodged the attack and moved behind Ward. He grabbed Ward's wrist and threw his other arm around Ward's neck. Squeezed hard.

Ward gasped for air and tried desperately to release the hand holding the knife, but Ryker's grip was too strong. So Ward used his free arm to try to punch and pummel Ryker, but from his position he was unable to connect with any great effect, his shots landing weakly on Ryker's upper legs and waist. Ryker tightened his hold further and Ward tried to claw at the arm around his neck.

'Drop the knife,' Ryker said, still calm and in control.

'You piece of shit!'

Ryker squeezed harder still, eliciting coughs and splutters from Ward, who was becoming weaker by the second.

Up ahead, Ryker spotted Chan careening around the corner, her gun drawn.

'Jesus, Charlie, drop the knife! And Ryker, let him go!'

Ryker thought about that one for a moment.

'I said let him go! Before I shoot you both.'

Ryker did as he was told. He unwrapped his arm from Ward's neck and used his foot to propel him forward and away. If the idiot wanted to come at Ryker again, with a gun pointed at his back, then so be it.

Ward rolled on the ground, knife still in his hand. He clambered to his feet.

'Drop the knife,' Chan shouted. 'Now!'

Ward was facing Chan. Ryker willed him to do the sensible thing. Why on earth didn't he…

Ward spun around and lunged for Ryker again. Ryker ducked to the side. Two gunshots boomed, echoing around the confined space. Ward plummeted to the ground, two small holes punched into the back of his shirt, the patches of red widening as his body lay crumpled.

Ryker looked over at Chan. Loose hair flapped around her face. Her cheeks were red; she was panting heavily. She lowered her weapon but kept a double grip on it as she stepped forward. Ryker moved over and kicked the knife from Ward's partially open hand. He kneeled down beside the man and pushed him onto his side. Ward was still breathing, but he was out of it.

'I need an ambulance!' Chan shouted into her phone before giving the address. 'I need it now!'

'Was it really worth it?' Ryker said to Ward.

He opened his mouth to speak. Blood bubbled out. Ryker looked at him with intent. He sensed, hoped, that Ward was about to say something worthwhile… A deathbed confession, perhaps?

'Fuck… you.'

No. Apparently Charlie Ward wasn't the type.

He let out a long, slow exhale, and then he went still.

Ryker looked up to Chan, who put her hands up to her head. 'He's dead?' she said.

'Yeah.'

Chapter thirty

'What the hell have you done this time, Chan?' McKinley said, walking into his office and slamming the door shut.

Chan was sat down in front of McKinley's desk. After more than two hours on the scene of Charlie Ward's death near West End Avenue, she'd headed straight to the office. She remained in a state of disbelief. Not so much because she'd taken the life of a man – she was able to justify that to herself, given that Ward had attacked Ryker – but because she didn't know why Ward had run in the first place. Nor why he'd then decided to ignore her warnings and try to stab Ryker despite knowing Chan had a gun pointed at his back.

Ryker. What the hell was she going to do about that now? He'd been way calmer than her in the immediate aftermath. Had quickly concocted a plan: that he would scarper and she'd claim she'd met with Campbell alone, had chased Charlie alone. What did that say about Ryker? That death and violence seemed to move him so little?

She had no clue whether his plan would wash. Surely, though, it was better than admitting to McKinley that rather than steering well clear of Ryker, as she'd been instructed, she'd actually made the decision to use him as an asset.

'Well?' McKinley asked.

'Well what?'

'Are you actually trying to screw this whole operation? Or maybe you've decided you've had enough of being an FBI agent?'

'No, sir. Neither of those.'

'Then what?'

'There was nothing else I could do. Ward gave me no choice. We need to think about the bigger picture. I think we have a way into Green's empire now.'

'Which is what? Green's dead brother?'

'No. Campbell.'

McKinley paused for a moment and Chan took that as a good sign.

'I was meeting with Campbell this afternoon. I was making good progress. Then Charlie Ward appeared…' Chan shook her head, bewildered by how the day had turned to shit so quickly.

'Why on earth would Charlie Ward run from you?'

'He must have realised I was FBI, or police maybe. I had to believe he was going to blow the whistle on Campbell.'

'Somehow I find that hard to believe.'

'But that's what happened! Why else did he run off like that?'

'Except Charlie Ward was already our informant!' McKinley blasted, and both his words and his bark halted any articulate response from Chan.

'What? No. But–'

'He was working for us, goddamn it. That was until you decided to gun him down in broad daylight.'

Chan's mouth opened but she was speechless. They'd had Charlie Ward and not told her about it?

'Why the hell wasn't I informed?' Chan asked.

'Because it was too big a catch. We had to keep it under wraps. You don't need to know everything that goes on here. You've got your job. I've got mine.'

'You should have told me. It could have changed things.'

'No. You've changed things. You've killed the best informant we had on this case. And what am I supposed to go to the public with? FBI agent shoots informant to death in city street battle? Our whole case against Green collapses if he realises what we've been up to, and if he knows we had anything to do with his brother's death.'

'What are you suggesting?' Chan asked, suspicious but also slightly relieved at what she was now hearing. Keeping the case against Green going had to be the biggest issue right now.

McKinley sighed. 'For now we cover up the death as best we can, but it's going to need a hell of a lot of sign-off from up above to do that. The main concern is that we don't jeopardise the investigation.'

Chan huffed. Agreement with McKinley's proposition? In many ways she was shocked the FBI would do such a thing, but it made absolute sense if it meant getting to the end goal.

They sat through a few moment's silence as Chan's brain whirred.

'How did we get Ward onside in the first place?'

'Probably better if you hear this from the man in the know.'

McKinley picked up his desk phone, gave the order, and thirty seconds later there was a knock on the door.

'Come in,' McKinley shouted.

The door opened and in walked Nate Trapp. Chan had noticed him at his desk earlier but hadn't spoken to him. The truth was they'd never got along. They were at the same level of seniority, but Trapp was one of those types whose main purpose in life seemed to be to get one over on his contemporaries. Like plonking himself into the middle of someone's investigation to undermine the other agents there. Plus Chan hated the fact that McKinley had long favoured Trapp over her. Mainly because he was almost a carbon copy of his boss. But in a more snide and creepy way.

Trapp – tall and slim and well groomed, with a handsome face marred by an almost-jeer – stayed on his feet next to Chan. No acknowledgement that she was there.

'Go ahead,' McKinley said to him.

'I've been working Charlie Ward for about three weeks.'

'How did you get in?' Chan asked.

Still Trapp wouldn't look at her. 'Maybe you know Ward had a thing for ladies. Prostitutes. Some of them are... how shall I put it, not very old.'

'He's been sleeping with underage girls?'

Trapp nodded.

'You were blackmailing him?'

'You make it sound sinister.'

'Charlie Ward put himself in that position,' McKinley said.

'Anyway, despite the dirt on him, we hadn't had much success. I got the feeling he was stringing us along, looking for a way out. But just today we had our first breakthrough. He came to talk to me. He had inside information on Shaun Doherty…'

Doherty again. Chan held her tongue, but the Irishman was involved in everything that was going wrong the last few days.

'Ward believed Doherty is making a substantial drugs purchase in a few days' time, under the nose of Green. It's due to take place at a disused airstrip in New Jersey. Ward didn't know the exact location, but I've managed to track it. There's only one airstrip that would be suitable in terms of size, location, availability.'

Chan had to admit that, if true, it sounded like a brilliant opportunity to catch Doherty in the act. It was exactly the sort of information she'd been desperately trying to uncover about Henry Green. And yet…

'How did Charlie Ward even know about this?' Chan asked. 'The impression I get is that Green and Doherty aren't exactly best buddies.'

'One of his whores told him apparently.'

'We're going to bring Doherty down at the deal,' McKinley said to Chan. 'The Henry Green investigation will carry on separately, but until we have Doherty, he is our priority.'

'I disagree… sir.'

The room fell silent. McKinley glared at Chan. Was she supposed to carry on?

'Whatever we announce publicly, Green is going to find out about Ward. It already looks like there's a tit-for-tat quarrel between Green and Doherty–'

'Based on what?' Trapp said.

'Based on what happened after Green went to see Doherty yesterday. Based on the dead body found outside Malloy's a few hours later.'

'What about that body?' McKinley asked. 'Do you know anymore?'

'Detective Spencer is still waiting on the forensics results so we don't know much. But you have to admit the MO points to gangland killing, the removal of identifying features–'

'At the moment that's entirely circumstantial,' Trapp interjected.

'Please can you stop interrupting me?' Chan said, shooting him a look. 'My point is that we could already be on the brink of a much bigger problem between Green and Doherty. And with Ward's death, which you've already said we need to try to cover up, who do you think Green is going to blame?'

'Doherty,' McKinley said.

'Exactly. We can't let an all-out drug war break out in Manhattan. We have to keep on top of Green. To do that we need to push on with Campbell.'

'We?' McKinley said.

'Yes. Well I…' Chan slumped, realising what McKinley meant by that. She looked to Trapp who appeared faintly amused.

'Trapp, give us a minute.'

Trapp gave Chan a knowing look as he turned and headed for the door.

'I'm off the case?' Chan asked, before biting her bottom lip to stop it shaking.

'You killed a man today. There has to be an investigation.'

'But I was so close with Campbell.'

McKinley sighed. Held her gaze for a few moments.

'I can't give you any guarantees, but I don't want to lose you, Chan. You just need to give me some time to try and clear this mess up. Go home for the rest of the day. Don't even think about touching this case until I tell you otherwise.'

Chan nodded. Got up from her chair. Under the circumstances it was probably about the best outcome she could hope for.

'But I do need your badge and your gun before you leave.'

Chan gulped, but handed them over. Then, head down, she made her way to the door.

Chapter thirty-one

Campbell had left the diner straight away when Ryker and Agent Chan galloped out of there after Charlie Ward, despite Ryker's instruction for him to stay put. He was scared.

He'd roamed the streets for more than two hours after that, thinking. What had happened to Ryker and Chan and Ward? Did Henry Green now know that Campbell had been talking to an FBI agent? Green would surely kill him if that was the case, regardless of the fact he was supposed to be marrying Green's daughter. He felt like a dead man walking. On his long traipse he'd walked right past the area where police tape cordoned off an alley near West End Avenue. He hadn't got the full details from the eager bystanders as to what had happened there, but it didn't take a genius to put the pieces together. Charlie Ward was dead.

What the hell had gone on between Ward and Chan and Ryker?

One thing Campbell was sure about: he wanted to keep well away from Henry Green for now. Just in case.

It was dark outside by the time Campbell built up the courage to head home. He found Kate curled up on the sofa, watching TV. She was tired and not particularly chatty, a growing problem between them recently. For the next hour or so he remained anxious, not knowing what to do with himself. He half expected a knock on the door any minute from Green, or one of Green's heavies, come to give him the same treatment that poor Johnny had received.

'Scott, just snap out of it!' Kate shouted finally, without taking her eyes off the seedy reality show she was watching. 'What's got into you?'

He slumped down on the sofa next to her.

'Sorry. Just got a lot on my mind.'

She moved across the sofa to him. Brushed up against him, kissed him on the cheek.

'Perhaps I can take your mind off things for a while,' she purred, moving to kiss him on the lips. 'Perhaps a repeat of last night?'

He kissed her back, but when she tried to climb on top of him, he held her off.

'Sorry. I can't. I'm just... I can't tonight.'

She slid back to the other side of the sofa, clearly hurt. He couldn't ever recall turning down her advances before.

The intercom buzzer sounded and Campbell nearly jumped out of his seat. His heart pounded in his chest.

This was it, he thought. Green was there to kill him. Should he call the police? The FBI?

Ryker?

He remained rooted to the spot as Kate got up and headed over.

'Hello... Dad! Come on up.'

Campbell's eyes grew wide as Kate buzzed him in. His head was in meltdown. He thought frantically about how he could escape. Run through the open door as Green walked in? Climb out the window and down the fire escape? He looked over to the kitchen. The wooden block containing six sharpened knives. Was standing and fighting, proving his worth, the best option? But he couldn't move.

'It's Dad,' Kate said, coming back into the lounge and snapping the ridiculous thoughts from his mind. 'No idea why. Not like him to visit.'

'Kate, I don't know how... I'm so sorry.'

She looked at him like he was an idiot. Which in many ways he was.

A purposeful knock on the front door.

'What is the matter with you?' she said, frowning, before plodding off to open the door.

Campbell, pacing, looked over to the knives again. He heard the door opening.

'Hey, Kate,' came a female voice.

Jackie Green? Kate's mum was there?

A moment later Green and his wife walked into the room, sombre looks on their faces.

'Hi, Scott,' Jackie said, managing a half smile.

Green glared and Campbell tried his best not to look him in the eye. Yet Campbell already realised this wasn't at all what he'd expected. Not that he would relax just yet.

'Kids,' Green said, his voice low and croaky. 'We wanted to come over because we have some bad news.'

Concern spread across Kate's face. She grabbed Campbell's arm.

'Uncle Charlie's been killed.'

As soon the words passed Green's lips, Jackie started crying. Kate went over to her mother and tried to comfort her. She was crying too.

'I knew something was wrong,' Kate said 'What happened?'

Campbell was frozen to the spot, emotionless. Green looked straight at him, betraying no emotion himself.

'We don't know yet. The police are saying it was a mugging. He wasn't far from here. Near the Lincoln Center. No idea why.'

Green gave Campbell a piercing look. Campbell put his head down.

'We've just come back from identifying him.'

Green's words were slow and monotone. Campbell's head was on fire. A mugging?

Not yet knowing if he really was off the hook, Campbell urged the Greens to sit down. For the next half hour Green and Jackie and Kate reminisced fondly about Charlie. Campbell barely said a word, though he did find it strange everyone was being so nice about the dead man. The impression he'd always got was that Kate couldn't stand him.

Kate and Jackie got up to go to the kitchen to make some coffee. Campbell and Green headed to the balcony with a tumbler of whisky each. The evening air was hot and thick and as uncomfortable to breathe as it was for Campbell to be standing drinking with Green.

'I want you to come to Evolve first thing tomorrow,' Green said, with a cold and determined look in his eye.

There was nothing unusual about the request, but it sounded anything but a friendly invitation.

'We've got a big problem, Campbell.'

Could Campbell's heart beat any faster?

'What do you mean?'

'What do I mean? I mean someone's killed my brother, you fucking idiot! And I've got a pretty good idea who.'

'The police said it was a mugging.'

Green gave him a scathing look.

'Are you actually dumb? Charlie wouldn't let that happen to him. And what was he doing around here anyway?'

'I've no—'

'The only thing that brings him up here is the ladies. I've never trusted those bitches.'

'What are you saying?'

'Someone set him up. And I'm pretty damn sure I know who. That bastard Doherty. He's fucked with me for the last time.'

'Why would Doherty kill Charlie?' Campbell blurted and immediately regretted it. Really, Green blaming Doherty was a good thing. For Campbell at least. It suggested Green had no clue as to what had really happened. But what would be the ramifications of Green's misguided vengeance?

'Look, Scott. This changes things. Charlie was a big part of my life. He was also a big part of the business. There's no way I can replace a man like that. I want you to help me out with his clubs, step up your involvement a bit more. You're family to me, kid. We need to stick closer together now more than ever.'

Campbell simply couldn't find any words. He was flattered by Green's trust in him. Under different circumstances, he would have brimmed with pride and happiness. Yet more than anything, he felt betrayal.

'Did you hear me?'
'Yeah, of course. Thanks, Henry. Thanks for everything.'

***

It was after ten o'clock when the Greens finally left. Kate was still upset, and she and Campbell hugged on the sofa, not speaking, for quite a while. Only when she'd gone to bed did Campbell see the message waiting on his phone. As he read it he whipped his head around the room, as though he half expected Green to be there watching his every move. But it wasn't Green who had eyes on Campbell at all times. It was that damn James Ryker.

We need to meet. Tonight.

Campbell stared at the message. The phone vibrated in his hand and he jumped in shock. Realised it was another message from the same withheld number.

Green's gone. You're free now. I'm waiting outside.

He shivered. Looked around again. Then thought about what he could say. Whether he should respond at all.

What choice did he have? He crept to the bedroom, made sure Kate was asleep, then headed for the front door.

Chapter thirty-two

From the cover of a parked van, Ryker spied Campbell as he stepped out into the night. He looked angry as much as anything else. He'd only made it three steps when the build-up of heat and humidity finally became too much and the heavens opened. Thick drops of warm rain drummed onto Ryker and everything around him. He stepped out from behind the van.

'This way,' Ryker said.

Campbell turned. 'Where'd you–'

'Let's take a walk.'

'In this?'

'I've been waiting for this rain for days.'

'Finally feel at home?'

Ryker said nothing to that and the two of them set off toward Amsterdam.

'All I can hear is my mum's voice in my head,' Campbell said after a few moments of silence.

'Telling you to steer well clear of the likes of Henry Green?'

'Telling me not to forget my damn raincoat.'

Ryker looked at Campbell and saw the slight smile on his face. Strange time to joke, but it was better than him moping.

'I take it you've heard about Charlie Ward?' Ryker asked.

'From Henry.'

'I don't know why he ran, but I couldn't risk letting him go.'

'I get that. But how did he wind up dead?'

'It was his own making. For whatever reason he chose to stand and fight rather than have Chan take him in.'

'That doesn't make any sense.'

'Maybe not. But he'll have had his reasons.'

'He would have gone straight to Green to tell him what he saw.'

'I know. Which I'm guessing is why the police have claimed it was a mugging. If they'd announced anything to do with the FBI it would set Green off like a rocket.'

'I think that's already happened to be honest.'

'He knows about Chan?'

'No. But he has gone off. He thinks Shaun Doherty killed Charlie.'

'Bloody hell.'

'Exactly.'

'On the plus side, given that you're still alive and kicking, I presume he knows nothing about you and Chan.'

'Me and Chan? There is no me and Chan. We talked for a few minutes. I basically told her to piss off.'

Ryker grabbed Campbell's arm to bring him to a stop.

'You seriously need to wake up. Shit just got real here. Green's brother is dead, and if he sets out for revenge you can be sure more blood will follow.'

Campbell snatched his arm away. 'It's because of you that Ward is dead. Any blood from here will be as much on you as it is on me.'

'Maybe. But are you sure *you* can live with that? I've already seen plenty in my time.'

Campbell didn't answer.

'There's only one thing you can do,' Ryker said. 'You help Chan bring them both down. Green and Doherty.'

'Are you taking the piss?'

'Not at all. You would rather Green found out the truth?'

Again Campbell didn't answer. He started walking and Ryker fell into step beside him. They continued on across Amsterdam, both silent as they passed by the bustling bars and restaurants whose pavement terraces were busy with people crammed under awnings to avoid the heavy downpour. Only when they were alone again, on the brownstone-lined 80th, the road crammed with parked cars on either side but few pedestrians, did the conversation restart.

'I know how to end this,' Ryker said.

'What does that even mean?'

'It means Green and Doherty go down and you and Kate get to walk away.'

'Why do you care so much?'

'That's irrelevant. You only need to do one thing: listen to me. You're in no bargaining position now.'

Ryker left that one hanging and he could tell from Campbell's silence that his protestations were largely over.

'Let's get back to the start. You need to tell me what you know. Who was the dead man outside Malloy's?'

'Why should I tell you? If I'm going to work with the FBI it should be them I'm speaking to.'

Ryker had had enough. He spun around and grabbed Campbell's arm, twisted it into a hammerlock and pushed the shoulder socket to bursting point. Campbell whined in pain. Ryker shoved him forward, slamming him up against a parked SUV.

'Let go! Are you crazy?'

'You'll speak to me because I'm not giving you the choice anymore.'

'You can't do this,' Campbell protested. 'How is this what my mother would want?'

'She wants you out of this life. That's what I'm trying to achieve. It doesn't mean I have to be nice to you.'

He let go of Campbell's arm. Campbell turned and cradled the stricken limb.

'Whatever you might think, I'm not the bad guy here,' Ryker said.

'And neither am I.'

'Then tell me about the body.'

Campbell sighed. Looked around as though making sure no one was in earshot. They set off again, and were soon walking past Columbus Avenue. In the distance was the traffic-heavy Central Park West and the darkness of the park beyond.

'I never met him before,' Campbell said. 'But he was one of Green's dealers.'

'Green killed him?'

'Green ordered him to be killed.'

'You saw it?'

Campbell nodded then looked away, clearly troubled by the fact.

'Why?'

'Green said he was skimming cash from him.'

'That true?'

'I really have no idea.'

'So it was nothing to do with Doherty?'

'Not that I know of. Green dumped the body there to cause Doherty grief. Those two have fallen out big time. Like I said, Green now thinks Doherty killed his brother.'

'Which could still work to our advantage.'

'How?' Campbell said with an incredulous look.

'You need to do something for me.'

Campbell scoffed. 'You mean I need to put my neck on the line for you?'

'If you do what you're told, it will all work out.'

'Says you.'

'Where does Green get his drugs from?'

'I've no idea!'

'You must know something.'

'I know where he stores and cuts it, but that's it.'

'Yeah? Where?'

Campbell sighed again, as though contemplating whether he really wanted to do this. This time Ryker gave him the time.

'Down by the docks in New Jersey. There's a warehouse. I don't know anything about his suppliers but he said it comes in both on the water and by air.'

'Can you give me the exact location?' Ryker asked. 'Have you been?'

'Yeah,' Campbell said.

'Can you get into it?'

'I guess so.'

'Then this is what you'll do. First step is for you to find out everything you can about that place: how big it is, how many rooms there are, how big the rooms are, how many workers are there, what they're armed with. Could you get pictures?'

'How the hell am I supposed to do that? Hey, Henry, I'm just heading down the drug warehouse to take a few pictures for my photo album!'

'Very funny. I can stake out the outside, but I need to know what's inside too.'

'Why? What exactly are you planning?'

'It doesn't matter. You just do your part. You're in the perfect position. You've got a phone – use that. All you need is an excuse to go there.'

'That's easy for you to say. It's me who'll be risking my life with a drug-dealing murderer.'

Ryker said nothing to that. Plenty of times in his life he'd been the one doing the dirty and dangerous work at the behest of others. Campbell's father, most often. For once the roles were reversed. For now. Ryker still wasn't afraid to get his hands dirty. In many ways he needed it.

'That place could be crucial to the FBI in breaking the case,' Ryker said. 'You do this and it's going to look pretty good for you when Green's world comes crashing down.'

Ryker could tell Campbell was afraid, and he did feel for him. Ryker was asking him to do something that was potentially extremely dangerous. On the other hand, very soon an all-consuming war could break out between Green and Doherty and there was no telling how many people could lose their lives in that. Innocent people, even. Campbell was close enough to make a difference.

'Okay,' Campbell said eventually. 'I'll do it. But you'll need to give me a few days.'

Chapter thirty-three

The humidity was worse than ever and despite the high temperature the ground remained wet from the night-time rain several hours before. The morning sky above Queens was as grey as Chan's mood as she walked along 46th Avenue back to her apartment. It had been many days since she'd been around so late in the morning that she was able to take her kids to school. But she wasn't yet feeling any positivity about having some spare time on her hands. Would McKinley get her back onto the team at all or was she done?

She turned the corner onto her street. Noticed the man across the other side of the road out of the corner of her eye, but didn't really pay him any attention until he stepped into the road, walking toward her, and spoke.

'Agent Chan,' James Ryker called.

She kept walking. 'How did you find me here?'

'It's what I'm good at,' Ryker said, catching up with her and matching her stride. 'You're suspended?' he asked.

'I don't know yet.'

'I'm sorry.'

'Really?'

'Yeah. I mean it. I never intended to cause you problems here.'

'But you seem so good at it.'

Ryker said nothing to that. Chan found she was impressed, strangely, with his ability to pop up here, there and everywhere.

'I saw Campbell again last night,' Ryker said.

Chan stopped now and glared at him. He didn't seem at all moved by the fact that the lives of people around him were in turmoil because of his actions.

'What exactly are you trying to do here?'

'Here in Queens? Or here in New York generally?'

'Good questions. Both actually.'

'I came to tell you where I'm at. Campbell's talking.'

'Talking? To you? And what good is that? Nothing he tells you is admissible evidence.'

'It doesn't need to be. You can still build the case around anything he gives me. Or you.'

Ryker looked around him. Glanced to the other side of the street where two men were walking past. He kept half an eye on them until they were out of sight.

'Come on, keep walking,' he said.

'What are you?' Chan asked, setting off with him.

'A helping hand.'

'Not what I meant.'

'I'm someone who's used to bringing down the bad guys.'

'Really? What about Charlie Ward?'

'The brother of a murdering drug dealer?'

'An FBI informant.'

That shut Ryker up.

They turned the corner, moving away from Chan's apartment, and were soon walking into the sprawling Flushing Meadows Corona Park, a massive green urban space, most famous for its Unisphere – the giant metallic globe built for the 1964 New York World's Fair. She noticed Ryker staring in awe off into the distance at the familiar structure. After walking in silence for a few minutes they settled on a bench overlooking the shimmering water of Meadow Lake.

'I take it you didn't know about Ward?' Ryker asked.

'Being an informant? No.'

'It wouldn't have made a difference if you did.'

'You don't know that.'

'He was intent on attacking me. Maybe he wanted you to shoot.'

'That's ridiculous.'

'Not really. I'd hazard he wasn't a willing FBI informant. Blackmail, right?'

Chan didn't answer.

'Perhaps he was looking for a way out. Better than having his brother find out the truth.'

Chan scoffed but didn't say anything.

'You've got no reason to trust me, but I can assure you, I'm going to get Campbell out of this life one way or another. With or without your help.'

Chan looked at Ryker. She admired his confidence. In fact, it was magnetic – she could feel the pull of his will. She should have been running a mile from this man but she wanted to know more. About him, and what he would do to help.

'What has Campbell told you?' Chan asked.

Ryker smiled. Chan grimaced. He had her.

'Green killed the guy found outside Malloy's.'

'He told you *that*?' Chan said.

Ryker nodded, looking pleased with himself.

'For god's sake, we need to get this on record.'

'No. Just hold on. There's a bigger picture here. The body was dumped there to put pressure on Doherty. In return, Green thinks Doherty killed Ward.'

Chan put her hand to her head and rubbed her temple. 'This is crazy.'

'Maybe. But it could play into our hands. Your hands. Those two are going to come to blows. Campbell can give you them both if you just play this right.'

'And you're going to tell me how you think we should play it, right?'

Ryker smiled. 'Damn right.'

***

Half an hour later Chan opened the door to her apartment, closed it behind her then let out a long sigh. What was she doing? It was true that the information Ryker had found was potentially huge.

How had he so easily broken the case open? But she was also worried. What was McKinley going to say? Should she just be straight and tell him about Ryker?

She really didn't know. But she did have to speak to her boss. She had to tell him the information Ryker had found, even if she wasn't quite sure yet how she'd say *she* found it.

Before she could talk herself out of it she took her phone from her purse and dialled the number.

Chapter thirty-four

Shaun Doherty looked up to the clock in the corner of the dingy room. It was 10am. He'd been in the private room – not the VIP room, the place was too grotty for that – in the Empire casino near Long Beach for the best part of twelve hours. What had started out as a celebration, of sorts, after hearing of Charlie Ward's demise, had soon turned into an all-night gambling bender. Doherty had stopped drinking before midnight, by which point he'd been nearly fifty grand down. He hated losing. Steadily through the night, more focused without alcohol, he'd clawed most of that back, but he still despised this croupier. Doherty was sure the guy was making him lose on purpose, just to piss him off. Every time he lost, the little bastard just stood there with a stupid smirk on his face like it was a big joke. 'Better luck next time, sir!' the guy kept on saying. *Better luck with my foot stuck up your arse more like*, Doherty thought.

While Doherty had welcomed the news of Charlie Ward's death, he did remain suspicious as to what had gone down. It certainly wasn't on his orders, so who had done it? Men like Henry Green and Charlie Ward naturally had plenty of enemies, but what he'd heard – a mugging gone wrong – just didn't ring true.

Doherty's phone, vibrating on the table, stole him from his thoughts. He picked it up and glanced at the croupier.

'Don't you even think about spinning that thing again until I'm ready.'

Doherty's tone wiped some of the smirk from the guy's face. The other two players at the table groaned but they wouldn't dare kick up a fuss.

'What is it?' Doherty said into the phone, turning around on his stool.

'It's me,' the contact said.

'And?'

'Ward's death is a cover-up.'

'Police?'

'Feds. But I can fill you in on that next time. More important is that Green thinks it was you.'

'That low life piece of…' Doherty slammed the table with his fist.

'If you ask me, this could be good for you.'

'I didn't fucking ask you, did I?'

'No, but–'

'Is that it?'

'There's more. The body was one of his dealers.'

'That was pretty bleedin' obvious.'

'Maybe. But I also got what you needed.'

'The location?'

'Yeah.'

Doherty's mood improved immediately. 'Give it to me.'

The contact recited the New Jersey address. Doherty memorised it.

'So that's it?'

'That's it,' Doherty said. 'Everything's set now.'

He hung up. Turned to the table with a wide smile on his face. It wasn't returned by any of the ugly mugs there.

'One second. I just need to make another call.'

Chapter thirty-five

Campbell could barely concentrate at work. His whole life felt like it was falling away from him. He was torn. On the one hand he still undoubtedly felt respect and loyalty for Henry Green, even though he was a criminal, a killer. And there was little he liked about Ryker and his strong-handed approach, which simply reminded him of his father, and mother, and the life he was trying to get away from. Yet Ryker was looking out for him, he truly believed, and stripping everything else away, he really didn't want to spend the best part of his adult life in jail. If betraying Green meant a life of freedom, that had to be worth it? Had to be worth doing what Ryker, and the FBI, wanted?

And then there was Kate. Although she had seemed surprisingly cut up by the death of her uncle, she'd still headed to work that morning. More than anything, Campbell had to be there for her now. She was the most important aspect of his life, and whatever trouble he or her father had coming their way, he had to do his best to make sure she was protected.

Hence he was travelling to her office near Times Square in the S-Class to pick her up from work – an impromptu visit that he hoped would put a smile back on her face. Passing by the myriad brightly coloured billboards and flashing lights and the tourists with their camera phones held aloft, Campbell turned onto the quieter West 42nd Street, alongside the quaint and bustling Bryant Park. He found a loading space near to Kate's office and pulled in, leaving the engine running.

He looked at his watch. Five twenty-eight. Kate nearly always finished work at five thirty on the dot. The truth was, she needn't have bothered with work at all. Her father was a multi-millionaire who loved to dote on his only daughter. Yet she'd always made it clear she had no intentions of being a kept lady. She had no huge ambitions as such – just wanted to prove she could make it on her own. Campbell admired her a lot for that.

He stared at the revolving glass doors of her modern office building fifty yards away. People were already filtering out. Watching the throngs of office workers – half of them dreary from a long day's work, half of them smiley at finally being free – reminded him how he'd been like that not long ago. The same routines each day: in at the same time, out at the same time, same people, same work, same petty grievances. So monotonous. Yet, given where he'd ended up, in many ways he wished he was right back there among them.

He spotted Kate coming through the doors, her hair catching in the breeze as she stepped outside. He glanced up and down the street. No traffic enforcement agents in sight. He shut the engine down then grabbed the bunch of flowers from the passenger seat and stepped out.

As he strolled toward her she still had no idea he was there. He saw her stop and turn around, and then he saw Mark Powell emerge from the building with the most ludicrous grin on his face. The two of them stopped on the pavement. Kate smiled up at Powell, who stepped forward and put his arms around her.

'No bloody way,' Campbell said out loud.

His heart raced as a rush of adrenaline hit him from nowhere, fuelling an equal mixture of anger and betrayal. He dropped the flowers and lurched toward the two of them. They let go of each other and Kate turned, sensing Campbell's approach. But before either Kate or Powell had a clue what was happening, Campbell barrelled into the prick Powell, knocking him to the ground.

'Scott! No!' Kate shouted.

Campbell jumped back to his feet. With Powell dazed on the floor Campbell launched his foot into Powell's midriff, eliciting a groan of pain. Without thinking Campbell kicked him again, even harder.

'You come near her again, I'll kill you!'

Powell tried to prop himself up and Campbell swung his foot again, smacking it into Powell's face. His lip split, his nose exploded and blood gushed down onto his shirt.

Kate grabbed Campbell and tried to pull him away. With rage consuming him he grunted and writhed. She let go. He turned to face her, snarling. When he saw the tears rolling down her face it was exactly what he needed to take the edge off.

'What are you doing?' she sobbed.

'What am I doing? What the hell are *you* doing!'

'Are you crazy! There's nothing going on, Scott! What is wrong with you?'

Campbell saw Powell trying to get to his feet.

'Not good, Campbell. You'll pay for this,' Powell said.

'Go to hell, wanker,' Campbell said. He felt like kicking him back down again but Kate grabbed his arm to stop him.

He shrugged her off, peeled away and trudged back to the car. When he got there he didn't get in, but stood looking up to the grey New York sky, his hands behind his head. What the hell had he just done?

'You've lost the plot, Scott,' Kate said, storming up behind him.

'What's going on with you two? The truth.'

'Absolutely nothing, you idiot! He's just a friend.'

'Then why the hell did you have your hands all over each other?'

'He was consoling me. That's what people do. In case you hadn't realised, my uncle was just killed. Mark was being caring.'

'Yeah, I'm sure he cares all right. Cares enough to do anything to get between your legs.'

Kate slapped him hard across the face. His cheek stung. Campbell glared at her but said nothing. He got into the car. Kate went around to the passenger side, and when she was in he put his foot down and sped out into the street, soon passing by where Powell was groggily standing by a lamp post.

'Do you know nothing at all about me?' Kate said. 'I would never do that to you.'

She broke down in tears. With Campbell's anger finally subsiding, the emotion that took over was regret. Not for hitting Powell, but for hurting Kate.

'You know, you're turning out to be just like him.' He knew exactly who she meant. Green. 'First London. Now this. It's exactly how he would act.'

Campbell didn't say anything to that. He let the words sink in.

Neither of them spoke another word on the journey home. Campbell's mind replayed over and over the moment he'd seen Powell and Kate embracing. When Powell had touched her it was like a red rag to a bull. Campbell couldn't control himself. And Kate was right, it was exactly like back in London. It was as though there was a dark side in him, normally under wraps, but just waiting to burst out. And when it came, there was simply no stopping it.

He gripped the steering wheel tightly, trying to calm himself. He was ashamed. More for hurting Kate than for what he'd done to Powell. He believed her. There was nothing between those two. However angry she'd been with Campbell for lashing out, she'd still followed Campbell straight back to the car; she hadn't stayed with Powell to check he was okay. And he knew she was right. Consumed by his new life with Green, he'd neglected her recently, and the way he'd reacted to seeing her with Powell, beating up the man without a second thought, was exactly the way Green would have reacted in that situation.

Had he really changed since being in New York under Henry Green, or had *that* side of him always been there?

Campbell parked in the underground car park beneath their apartment building and they headed up in the lift. When they were inside their home Campbell shut the door softly and put his hand on Kate's shoulder.

'I love you, Kate. I would do anything for you. Anything to protect you.'

She didn't say a word, just put her arms around him and sank her head into his chest.

That was all the answer he needed.

Chapter thirty-six

Campbell had held Kate in bed all through the night. He couldn't remember the last time he'd done that. Even though they'd hardly chatted the following morning, there was a far more relaxed, although not exactly happy, vibe between them, and Campbell was hopeful that despite his violent outburst he hadn't bollocksed things with her. Still, he remained on edge as he headed into Evolve that morning, fearful that somehow Green or one of his cronies would find out he'd been speaking with Ryker and the FBI.

That would surely be the end of him.

Since Charlie Ward's death, Green had stepped up his security across all premises and Deontay was, for now, a permanent fixture at Evolve. Deontay, as much a watchdog as anything else, Campbell had decided, was sitting blankly on the sofa across from where Campbell was trying to work when there was a buzz on the intercom from the main doors.

Deontay looked to Campbell.

'Well go then,' Campbell said. Finally something for him to do.

Deontay glared but headed out. A minute later he reappeared in the doorway, an unimpressed look on his face.

'Two cops here for you.'

Campbell's insides churned. 'About what?'

Deontay shrugged.

'Where are they?' Campbell said, looking behind Deontay.

'Left them outside, dint I? I'm not that dumb.'

Campbell wasn't so sure. He got up. Felt like saying something. But what could he say that wouldn't raise suspicion? 'Don't call Green'?

Instead he said nothing and headed down to the main doors. Opened them up to see two NYPD officers in their standard blue uniforms. Guns holstered at their hips. One man, one woman.

'Are you Scott Campbell?' the woman asked.

'Yes.'

'I'm Officer Neville, this is Rodriguez. We need to talk to you. Can we come in?'

'Do you have a warrant?'

Rodriguez scoffed and the two of them exchanged a look. Campbell felt like he'd put his foot in it, as though what he'd said was a clear indication to the police that something untoward was going on inside. But Green would flip if he knew Campbell had invited them in.

'No. This has nothing to do with the premises,' Rodriguez said. 'It's you we need to speak to.'

'We've received a complaint against you,' Neville said. 'Mark Powell alleges you assaulted him, yesterday afternoon in Midtown.' She paused, as though waiting for Campbell to admit or deny the charge. 'We only need to ask you a few questions, that's all.'

'Am I under arrest?' Campbell asked.

He tried to remain calm but he was seething inside. Powell really was a low life, getting the police involved.

'Not yet,' Rodriguez said.

'Then I've nothing to say to you. Is there anything else?'

Campbell was surprised at his own cockiness, but if they weren't going to arrest him, he figured there was little point in volunteering information.

'I'm sorry to hear that,' Neville said. 'We have a lot of witnesses who saw what happened. We believe Ms Green was there as well. She's your partner, right? We'll want to talk to her at some point too.'

Campbell wasn't sure if the officer's words were some kind of veiled threat, but he didn't take the bait.

'Sorry, but I'm really busy,' Campbell said. 'If you'd like to speak to me or my fiancée, I suggest you speak to our lawyer first.'

The two officers exchanged another look. Part exasperation, part annoyance.

Campbell pushed the door closed a few inches. Hoped they'd get the message. Rodriguez grabbed hold of the door. Glared defiantly at Campbell.

'I'm sure we'll be in touch,' he said. 'You have a good day.'

Rodriguez let go of the door and the two officers turned and headed back to their patrol car across the street. Campbell breathed a sigh of relief, but it was short-lived. As he watched the police walk off he spotted the black Mercedes pulling up. Groaned. Talk about bad timing.

Green and Steinhauser stepped from the car. Green glared at the officers. When they reached the car Rodriguez turned and seemed to lock eyes with Green for a second before he and Neville got in.

Green faced Campbell. Stormed over.

'What were those pigs doing in my club?'

'They weren't in the club. I didn't let them in.'

That took away just a little of his anger. Green brushed past, followed by Steinhauser. Campbell shut and locked the door behind them.

'So?' Green said, his face creased with annoyance.

'It's fine. Nothing serious.'

'Nothing serious? The last time I saw the cops it was to tell me my brother was dead. That's pretty fucking serious. Any time cops are swarming around one of my clubs is serious.'

Campbell hesitated. He was certain Green would hit the roof, but he had to tell him sooner or later.

'It's my fault,' Campbell said, hanging his head. 'They were here to speak to me.'

'Why the…'

'I got into a bit of a scrap last night.'

'A bit of a scrap? Which means what exactly?'

Campbell kept his eyes on his feet, as embarrassed as he was fearful of what Green would say. 'I beat the crap out of a guy. In public.'

'And why the bloody hell would you do that!'

Campbell looked back up. 'Because the tosser had his hands all over Kate!'

Green was still staring at him but looked a tad more relaxed. Perhaps even a little amused.

'But I guess I got the wrong end of the stick. I'm sorry, Henry, it was a mistake.'

Green shook his head, but he was smiling now. 'I would love to have seen that, kid. I mean, I heard what you did back in London, but… I wasn't really sure you had it in you.'

Green looked to Steinhauser who broke out into a forced smile too. Campbell breathed a sigh of relief.

'Yeah, well, he had it coming.'

Perversely, Campbell was pleased with Green's reaction. Then Green stopped smiling.

'But we don't need this kind of attention. We can't have the police sniffing around here. One thing leads to another and we're both in the shit.'

'Understood.'

'You're lucky they haven't arrested you already. But we need to take care of this situation before it goes any further.'

'What exactly does *take care of* mean?'

'We need to make sure this goes away.'

Campbell gulped at the implication of Green words. Judging by the amused look on his face, he picked up on Campbell's train of thought.

'Don't worry. We just need to gently persuade the guy to change his story.' At the word 'gently' Green used his index fingers as quotation marks.

'Great. So you'll go and beat him up again, then he comes back with another, more serious, allegation. Or am I missing the point?'

'Trust me on this one. I can be very persuasive when I want to be. Unless you have a better solution?'

Campbell sighed. 'No. Any help you can give is appreciated.'

Really he didn't even want to know what Green would do to Powell. He was just glad for the help.

'Good,' Green said. 'Just don't get yourself into anymore bother. I won't always be around to bail you out.'

***

The rest of the day went by without incident, almost worryingly so, and Campbell left the office at five thirty. Despite the mountain of things he had to do, he was determined to be home to spend time with Kate that evening. To try to banish thoughts of Ryker and Green and the FBI and the police, if only for a few hours. He had to try and close the growing distance between him and Kate.

That good intention didn't last long. Having parked up, Campbell was moving toward the lift when his phone rang. He lifted it from his pocket. Withheld number. He knew who it'd be. He really didn't want to speak to Ryker, but if he didn't, if he ignored Ryker and the FBI and simply carried on with his head in the sand as Green's skivvy, he was hardly giving himself the best chance of securing long-term happiness for him and Kate.

'What do you want?' Campbell said.

'I never believed you had it in you.'

Campbell sighed. 'No doubt that sort of thing impresses you.'

'Beating up defenceless people in the street? Not at all. I think you're a clueless idiot.'

'Yeah, thanks for that.'

'You should be keeping your head down, not giving the police reasons to arrest you.'

'How did you even know? And where the hell are you when you see all this?'

'Trade secrets.'

'Do you do anything but spy on people?'

'Sometimes I sleep.'

'Like hell you do. You're probably a bloody cyborg or something.'

'Very funny. Don't forget our deal. I still need you to get inside that warehouse.'

'Look, Ryker, I still don't get why this is so important to you, but you do realise I have an actual life to lead too?'

'You won't for much longer if you carry on like this.'

Campbell didn't have an answer to that.

'We'll do it tomorrow,' Ryker said.

'Tomorrow, but–'

'No buts.'

'I can't! Do you have any idea of the crap I've got to deal with now, what with you killing my boss's brother and all?'

'That wasn't me.'

'No?'

'And I couldn't give two shits about you keeping on top of Green laundering his money. We do it tomorrow.'

'We?'

'I'm not sending you in there on your own. I'll come too. But I'll keep my distance. I'll be there if you need me.'

Campbell had to admit, that thought did make him feel a whole lot better.

'We'll head down there separately. Keep in contact by phone. I'll see you there at 11am.'

Campbell sighed. 'Yeah. Fine.'

But he was speaking to a dial tone.

***

Campbell headed inside and did a quick tidy in the few minutes before Kate arrived home. As she walked through the door to the lounge Campbell had just sat down with two glasses of red wine ready and waiting on the coffee table. Kate looked tired and worn but she gave him a warming smile and picked up her glass and they clinked before both taking a swig. She sat down next to him.

'The police came to see me today,' Campbell said after a few minutes of catching up. It was clear that the previous evening's incident was the elephant in the room.

'Me too,' Kate said.

Campbell's guts twisted. 'At work?'

'Yeah. Why the hell would they cause trouble for me at work like that?'

'Because they're arseholes and they're trying to make me snap. Was Powell there today?'

'He didn't speak to me at all. He's got this massive bandage over his nose. He looks like a complete div.' She smiled, but it didn't last. 'I think you probably broke it. I know everyone was talking about what happened behind my back.'

'I'm sorry. For causing you bother, I mean.'

She didn't say anything to that.

'I can't believe he's pressing charges though,' Campbell said. 'Who the hell does he think he is?'

'You can hardly blame him. You beat him pretty badly.'

'I know. I'm sorry, really I am.'

'No. You're sorry about us, but I can tell you don't give a toss about what you did to him.'

Campbell wasn't sure if that upset her or not. But she was right, he couldn't care less about having hurt Powell.

'What did the police ask you?' he said.

'Just what had gone on.' She paused. Looked at him.

'And?'

'And I said I didn't see anything.'

Kate looked deep into his eyes. He could see she was hurting, but he wasn't sure how much of the hurt was due to one or a combination of recent events.

'Thanks,' he said.

'What did you expect me to say? You're my fiancé. I'm not going to get you into trouble.'

He nodded. Put his arm around her.

'You're lucky they haven't arrested you already.'

'Obviously they don't have enough to make a case. Which is why they're trying to back us into a corner. They told me they had other witnesses, but who knows?'

'We didn't need this trouble right now, Scott. We came here to *escape* trouble.'

'I know, I'm sorry. For everything.' He hugged her tightly and she let out a long sigh. 'But I'm sure it will be fine. In fact, I know it will be.'

Chapter thirty-seven

The next morning the sunshine was back, but at least another night of rain had cleared some of the humidity and Campbell managed to make it to Evolve without his shirt being sopping wet on arrival. Deontay was once again in the office, by himself, just sat on the sofa not doing anything. Campbell didn't speak to him other than to exchange a gruff 'hello'. He knew Green was tied up for most of the day with his lawyer, discussing Charlie's estate, so timing for a trip to the warehouse was about as good as he could hope for. He was back on the road again before 10am, heading out of Manhattan to New Jersey.

Campbell moved in the opposite direction to the main flow of traffic coming into the city, and with many natives already long gone from the city to escape the heatwave, he arrived at the docks in New Jersey half an hour earlier than planned. Still, as Campbell took the turn onto the road where Green's warehouse was located, he spotted Ryker's silver Toyota Corolla parked up in a lay-by, only partly surrounded by overgrown bushes.

Campbell pulled over and wound down his window.

'You ready for this?' Ryker asked through his open window.

'Not really. Are you just going to sit there?'

Ryker gave him a blank look.

'I mean, I know I was expecting to see you, but it's not exactly the most discreet location for you to stake out, is it?'

Ryker looked amused. 'Don't you worry about me. I've got your back, that's the main thing.'

Campbell looked off into the distance, to the outline of the warehouse.

'Good luck,' Ryker said, before his window slid closed.

Campbell took a deep breath then pulled back out into the road. A few seconds later the Corolla was in his rear-view mirror, the bulky form of Ryker a silhouette behind the glass.

'What the–'

Campbell tried his best to remain calm but it was an almost impossible task. What was Ryker doing? He couldn't possibly be following Campbell inside?

No. He wasn't. As Campbell reached the warehouse and pulled off the road, Ryker's car carried on past. Campbell was initially relieved by that, but then he just hoped that whatever surveillance position Ryker had found, he remained close enough to help if Campbell needed it.

He stopped at the shiny new red and white barrier next to the reinvigorated security hut.

'Can I help you?' the guard said, not exactly welcomingly, as Campbell lowered his window.

The guy was dressed in a bog-standard security uniform and had a clipboard in his hand. Campbell presumed the clipboard served little purpose other than to make the place look more like a normal business.

'Henry wanted me to come down and do some checks on the inventory. I'm Scott Campbell.'

The guard gave him a look of recognition at the name, but remained hesitant.

'No one told me you were coming.'

'Exactly. That's the idea for a random inventory check. Better to catch people off guard.'

'Yeah, except Steinhauser told me not to let anyone in unless it comes from him or Henry.'

Campbell sighed. 'Do what you've got to do. Give Steinhauser or Green a call if you want.'

The guard thought about that for a second before reaching into his pocket and taking out his phone. Campbell was surprised at how calm and in control he now felt, even though he knew his facade was on the brink of collapse.

'Go ahead and call them,' he said. 'But you do know what Green is doing today, right?'

The guard paused. Squinted in suspicion.

'You don't?' Campbell snorted and shook his head. 'He's with his lawyer, sorting his dead brother's estate.' He checked his watch. 'Actually, by now I think he'll be at the funeral parlour, going over the arrangements. But you go ahead and give him a call – perhaps he'll welcome the distraction.'

Campbell held the glare of the guard for a few seconds before the guy looked away.

'You can come in,' he then said. 'But only cos I know who you are. At least, I know who you claim to be. Let me see your ID.'

Campbell got out his driving licence. The guard looked at it then handed it back.

'Next time you get someone to tell me beforehand.'

'In future it will probably be me that calls to confirm these things anyway. I'm making some changes to how we operate around here.'

Campbell gave him a sly look. The guard looked angry but went to his booth and a moment later the barrier lifted up. Campbell drove through and parked in front of the closed warehouse doors. There were four other vehicles there: two black SUVs, a minibus and a banged-up hatchback. It was positively bustling compared to Albert Reynolds's days.

Campbell grabbed his pen, notebook and calculator and headed to the warehouse doors where another two guards were standing, wearing casual clothes rather than uniforms. They both eyeballed him suspiciously, and as Campbell reached them, one of them held out his arm, blocking Campbell's path.

'We need to search you,' he said.

'I'm here to check the inventory for Henry,' Campbell responded, hoping he could fob off these two as easily as the guard at the gates.

'Don't matter who you are. You get checked or you ain't coming in.'

'Fine,' Campbell said with a sigh. He didn't have anything on him he shouldn't have, so there was no point in carrying on the argument.

After an intimate pat-down, the guards stood aside and Campbell pushed the side door open and walked in. The inside of the warehouse was much as before: the shelving remained on one side, the partitioned rooms on the other. There was far more activity this time though. Four more guards on the inside, two stationed by the main loading doors and one at each of the doors leading to the partitioned rooms. Each of the men carried what looked like automatic weapons – not that Campbell was in any way an expert on such things. He'd never even held a gun, and his heart skipped a beat when he saw the weapons, just like the last time he'd been here.

All four guards had their eyes on Campbell as he walked toward the shelving area where he proceeded up and down the two aisles, making notes on the number of boxes and the box labels. Checking stock may only have been his front for going to the warehouse, but he wanted to make it look convincing enough, and at least have something to show if anyone asked to see his notes. Plus, he was sure Ryker would be interested in the details of what Green had stored there.

After nearly half an hour taking down the details of the boxes, Campbell decided to do a spot check. He grabbed a box from the shelf. The labelling stated it was packed with bags of nuts; for the bars, he assumed. He used the nib of his pen to break the tape sealing the box shut and peeled back the flaps. He put his hand in and pulled aside the top layer of nuts. Gasped when he saw the rest of the box was filled with bags of small white pills.

He looked around him, hoping the guards hadn't seen his startled reaction. Only one of them would be able to see him where he was crouched, and that guy was too busy chatting to someone Campbell couldn't see. He closed the box again and put it back on the shelf. Looked across the aisle. There were hundreds of boxes just like that one. Were there drugs in them all?

More anxious than before, Campbell quickly finished up then headed back across the other side to one of the two internal doors. The guard there stood his ground, halting Campbell's progress.

'You're not going in there.'

'Seriously? I'm getting a bit tired of you lot hassling me now. I need to take the inventory, then I need to get back to see Henry to give him my counts. He's waiting on me, and if I'm late, who do you think I'm going to blame?'

Despite his still-confident exterior, Campbell could feel his nerves building. How long could he keep this up for?

'Let me call my boss.'

The guard took a walkie-talkie out of his belt and turned away from Campbell as he spoke. Campbell had no clue who was on the other end of the line. He tried to steady himself, taking deep but quiet breaths. He still had the hardest part to come. Getting pictures. He looked around at the other three guards as he waited. Only one of them was now looking in his direction. The two over by the main doors were deep in conversation with each other, paying no attention to Campbell at all.

The guard by Campbell turned back to him.

'You can go in, but I'm following you every step. And you don't touch nothing. Got it?'

'Yeah, let's go,' Campbell said, trying to sound as though he couldn't care less.

The guard knocked on the door and waited for it to be opened from the other side by another armed guard. As Campbell walked into the room, he had to hold back a gasp. He'd seen similar scenes before on TV, but the sight in real life knocked him. There were four people inside: the guard who'd opened the door, plus three workers, all Hispanic females. The women were naked except for a small pair of briefs and the masks they wore over their noses and mouths. White powder was everywhere; a haze filled the air.

Campbell had no experience in the drugs trade, but it was clear what they were doing in this room. With the guard from outside the door as his chaperone, Campbell walked around, as calmly as he could, jotting down notes on his pad. He wasn't going to attempt to weigh or quantify how much powder there was out on the tables, but he scribbled down the number of sealed boxes he counted. Whenever Campbell got too close to a table or to a box, the guard jumped in the way, as though Campbell was intent on stealing some of the drugs with some sleight of hand.

'Okay, let's head to the other room,' Campbell said to his companion.

The guard gave him a reluctant look, then headed toward the connecting door. He once again knocked and waited for it to be opened from the other side. The next room was a similar size and shape, but the activity was quite different. Another guard, but just one worker this time, who was measuring out pills using some scales and packaging them up in clear plastic bags.

Campbell quickly jotted down what he saw. Then it was time for the hardest part. The part he'd been putting off. He couldn't do so any longer.

Scanning his list of scribbles, he took a few moments to compose himself before taking out his phone, pretending it was silently ringing, and answering it.

'Campbell,' he said as he put it to his ear.

The two guards in the room looked at each other before returning their attention to Campbell. But they didn't make any move to stop him. So far, so good. Campbell had practised this several times. He knew exactly which key strokes he needed to get to the phone's camera function and then it was a case of clicking away. The phone was set to silent, making sure he avoided both the fake shutter noise that accompanied the camera, plus the awkward situation of the phone ringing should someone actually be trying to call him while he was performing the stunt.

'Hello? I can't hear you very well. Can you hear me?' He took a few steps, turning and taking two photos of the room, each from a different angle. 'I said I can't hear you properly. I'm inside. I'll walk out.'

He headed in the direction of the connecting door. Just as he reached his hand out to open it, one of the guards sprung forward, blocking Campbell's path. Campbell's heart lurched, but then he realised the guard had only cut in to knock on the door.

'You don't want to get shot do you?' the guard said.

The door was opened a few seconds later by the guard on the other side, and Campbell walked back into the powder room. He took two more photos as he passed through and stopped at the outer door so the guard could open it, which gave him a few seconds to swivel and take one last photo from that angle.

'Yeah, just hang on, I'm still heading outside.'

Out in the main warehouse Campbell took a few steps, taking more photos, before again stopping and swivelling to get some images from a different angle.

'What? No. Can you still not hear me? Look, just give me a minute, yeah?' he said, feigning frustration with the imaginary caller.

It was as he was heading for the main doors, focused on just getting out and away, that his foot accidentally kicked a metal ring sticking out from the ground. Campbell nearly went flying. Only just managed to stay on his feet as he stumbled forward. He turned and glared at the offending object as he righted himself.

For a moment he forgot all about the imaginary phone call.

'Yeah, fine. I'm almost done here anyway,' he said, remembering and pulling the phone back to his ear. 'I'll call you back later.'

He stuffed the phone away and locked eyes with his chaperone.

'I'll be out of your hair in no time,' Campbell said. He looked to the metal ring on the floor. The latch to a trapdoor flush with the warehouse floor. 'But first, I need you to show me down there.'

Chapter thirty-eight

L ooking through the binoculars a hundred yards away, Ryker had been impressed at how Campbell had circumvented the security to get inside the warehouse. It was clear the guards there were naturally dubious of visitors, and had been reluctant to let Campbell through. Whatever he'd said to them had worked.

Kind of, anyway. Yes, Campbell had got inside the warehouse, but at what cost? The moment he'd stepped inside, the guard by the booth and one of those by the warehouse doors had begun a conversation on their radio handsets. As soon as that had finished the guard by the barrier had taken out his phone and made a call.

Ryker didn't like that one bit. Had immediately called Campbell. No bloody answer. He had it on silent for obvious reasons. Ryker knew something was wrong. But it was only later when he saw the black Mercedes S-Class approaching in the distance that he knew there was a problem.

When Ryker saw Henry Green and his big-ass henchman Steinhauser step from the car, Ryker knew there was a *big* problem.

Which was why he left his surveillance position and sprinted as fast as he could down the road to the warehouse.

Chapter thirty-nine

'I'm not letting you down there.'

Campbell scoffed. 'Who said I was asking your permission? Just open the door will you?'

'No.'

'Seriously?'

'You wanna go down there? Open it yourself.'

Campbell shook his head. 'I'll be feeding back how much of a dick you are to Henry.'

'Do what you gotta do. I'm only doing my job.'

Campbell tutted and moved over to the trapdoor. He bent down and grasped the ring and tugged. Nothing happened. He looked up to the guard, who smirked, his arms folded over his broad chest.

Summoning all his strength, anger spurring him on, Campbell heaved again and this time the door wheezed as suctioned air was released, and the latch opened a few inches. Grunting with effort, he hauled the heavy door up and over. Beneath it was another door: shiny metal with an electronic keypad next to it. Like a safe door, but laid into the ground rather than on a wall. He looked up to the guard who was now looking at him with a satisfied grin.

'I'm guessing you already know the code,' the guard said, 'seeing how clued in you are with Mr Green.'

This time it was Campbell's turn to look smug.

He kneeled down and typed in the four digits. There was a chance he was wrong, but a much bigger chance he was right. Green had given him access to several otherwise off-limits areas of the business's records on the computer at Evolve. His password was always the same. Kate's birthdate. Sure enough there was a click as locks released. Campbell looked back up to the guard who was now looking a lot less pleased with himself.

'Like I said, I'll be feeding back to Henry how helpful you've been with me today.'

The guard said nothing, just glared as Campbell pulled open the four-inch-thick inner door to reveal a staircase leading down.

'I'm coming with you,' the guard said.

'Suit yourself.'

Campbell headed down first, the guard two steps behind. The steps opened out into a small, dimly lit basement, about ten feet by ten feet, with shelving on three sides.

Campbell was speechless as he stared about. The guard came to a stop at his side. Campbell glanced at him, then quickly away again as he tried to compose himself. But he really had no clue what to think or how to react as his eyes flitted across the shelves, and the guns and ammunition and money stashed there.

The money was wrapped up – individual bundles ranging from ten thousand to fifty thousand dollars. There was millions. Not to mention the mini arsenal.

At least now he knew where Green kept the cash that wasn't laundered through the bars.

He had a sudden thought, remembering that he was supposed to be getting pictures for Ryker. But the idea of doing that now, with the guard standing right there next to him…

'Where the hell is he?' came a booming voice from above, putting paid to the idea of photos in an instant. It was Green.

The guard gave Campbell a cold glare. Turned on his heel and pounded up the stairs. Campbell followed, his heart racing.

What the fuck was he supposed to do now?

As he headed up the stairs he thought about turning and grabbing one of the weapons from below. But did they work? Were they loaded? Even then, could he really bring himself to open fire on Green and whoever else was up there?

No. Not a chance. He had to play this cool. Assuming, that was, that Green didn't simply put a bullet in his head the moment he stepped out onto the warehouse floor.

When Campbell emerged his eyes immediately fell upon Green, standing a few yards away with an angry snarl on his face. Steinhauser was there too. At least neither of them had a gun in their hands, though the four guards there, spaced out, all had their hands on the grips of their weapons.

'What the fuck are you doing here?' Green blasted.

Steinhauser moved over and closed the basement door, then returned to Green's side. Campbell's insides were in bits but he fought against his nerves as best he could.

'I was checking the stock.'

'I didn't ask you to do that. Steinhauser got a call from Forrest on the gate saying it was me who sent you here. Now why would you say that?'

Campbell couldn't believe his bad luck. Damn Ryker for making him do this. Then the strangest idea came into Campbell's head.

He took a step toward Green, who tensed up. Two of the guards stepped forward too but Steinhauser waved them down.

'We need to do this properly,' Campbell said quietly, as though it were just the two of them in the room. He leaned closer. 'You want to make sure everything's in order and no one's stealing, then we have to keep proper records here. Disguised records, but still, we need to follow it all through. With all the cash and goods here, you can't trust anyone.'

Campbell pulled back and held Green's eye. He seemed to mull over what Campbell had said, but the angry look on his face never faltered.

A commotion outside grabbed everyone's attention. Shouting. Banging. A moment later the side door crashed open and James Ryker stormed in.

'Where the fuck is Campbell?' Ryker shouted angrily in an American accent. 'I'm gonna break his fucking neck!'

Two steps in and Ryker halted when a guard edged forward and pressed the barrel of his weapon up against Ryker's skull.

'Not another step,' the guard said.

'What kind of idiot are you?' Green said, face like thunder.

Ryker glared, but his initial anger dissipated. 'What is this?' he said, sounding a lot less confident as his eyes darted about the place, looking at the weapons trained on him.

'I think you walked into the wrong warehouse, pal.' Green said. 'Who the hell are you?'

Ryker didn't answer. Just focused on Campbell, his anger reinvigorated slightly.

'I don't know who you lot are,' Ryker said. 'It's him I'm having words with.'

'No,' Green said, stepping in front of Campbell to block him from Ryker's view. 'You want to have words with anyone here, you have them with me.'

'He attacked my brother!' Ryker shouted, pointing a finger. 'Now he's trying to silence him. It's not right.'

Green turned to Campbell, an almost fatherly look on his face, but he also looked quite amused.

'I've never seen him before,' Campbell said, shrugging. 'Must be Powell's brother.'

Green nodded. 'Get him the hell out of my warehouse,' he said to Steinhauser.

The big man stepped forward, Green by his side. Ryker slumped down, looking more and more scared with each step they took.

'My good friend here is going to have a little chat with you,' Green said when he reached Ryker. 'Make sure you listen very carefully to what he's got to say. Or I'll bury your brother and your whole fucking family next to you.'

Steinhauser nodded to the guard by Ryker's side, who pulled back and smashed the butt of his weapon against Ryker's head. Ryker wobbled, his eyes rolled and the guard and Steinhauser grabbed him and dragged him outside, out of sight.

When Green looked back, Campbell had to quickly shut his mouth and compose himself once more.

'And you…' Green said.

Campbell sensed the other guards in the room readying themselves once more. Waiting for the order. Campbell's life was in Green's hands.

'You're coming with me.'

Campbell heaved a sigh of relief. But as Green turned for the exit, Campbell knew he was far from in the clear.

Chapter forty

Was Ryker surprised when he'd stormed into the warehouse and spotted several men with assault rifles? Not really. Was he scared when the barrel of one of those rifles was pressed up against his head? Not exactly. The situation was far from ideal, he'd admit that, but it wasn't as though he'd had much time to prepare his rampage. And while he had every confidence that under different circumstances he could have quite easily disarmed the guard who'd brought him to a stop, and turned the tables on everyone inside that place, he wasn't there as James Ryker. How would he have explained that to Green? He was there as Powell's disgruntled brother. A local thug out for familial retribution. That story was much less likely to get Campbell in the shit.

In fact, judging by the look on Green's face, the older man found the whole thing quite amusing, and even felt some pride for the position Campbell had got himself in. As such Ryker felt his sudden appearance had likely got Campbell off the hook, at least for now.

But he was still in the shit himself.

Outside in the blazing midday heat, Ryker let his body slump, making Steinhauser and the other guard work for it as they dragged him along, his feet scraping on the ground.

They pulled him away from the warehouse entrance, toward the corner. Ryker didn't believe they would kill him, just like that, but they were planning to deliver a message he wouldn't forget.

Ryker wasn't going to stand for a beating. First things first though. He had to make sure Campbell was okay.

In a sudden sharp move, Ryker pulled his body down, feigning nausea. Steinhauser and the guard let go and Ryker landed in a heap on the tarmac, his face scraping painfully on the black surface. Squinting in pain, he looked up to Steinhauser who snarled angrily.

'Get up,' he said.

Ryker paused. Behind Steinhauser, he saw Green and Campbell emerge from the warehouse together. No other guards joined them as they moved across to Green's car. They got in. The engine started up and the brake lights flicked off.

'I said get up,' Steinhauser said, before launching his foot into Ryker's stomach.

The unprotected blow took Ryker's breath and his vision blurred for a few seconds. He panted and writhed, partly a genuine reaction, but mostly for display. When the momentary fog had cleared he spotted the Mercedes moving away toward the security booth. Whatever was happening, Campbell was safe, he believed.

Once again off guard, Ryker took another kick in the gut. Coughed and spluttered and hauled himself over onto all fours.

'Get up now, or I'll finish you here, you piece of shit.'

Steinhauser reached out and tried to pull Ryker up. Ryker let him take the weight and groggily got back to his feet.

'Go back inside,' Steinhauser said to the guard. 'I've got this.'

'You sure?'

'Just do it.'

The guard stepped away. Steinhauser whipped out a handgun and pressed it up against Ryker's back.

'Walk. No more games.'

'Please… just let me go,' Ryker begged, his voice quavering. 'I don't know what this is… but I won't say anything. Not a word. Please!'

'Move. Or the first bullet is in your knee.'

Ryker got the point. He shuffled along. Steinhauser led Ryker around the back of the warehouse, toward the edge of the dock where the dark and grimy water lapped quietly below. Stacked sea containers either side screened them from the surrounding buildings.

'You picked the wrong kid to intimidate,' Steinhauser said.

He swiped Ryker's feet away and he plummeted to the ground again. He rolled over onto his back. Steinhauser, gnashing his teeth, had the gun pointed at Ryker's head.

'Please,' Ryker begged.

'Get up.'

'Don't do this.'

'Get up!'

Ryker pulled himself to his knees. Put his hands together in prayer in front of him. He was only a yard from Steinhauser.

'Please. Don't kill me. I'll do anything.'

Steinhauser looked amused by this. Ryker glanced behind the big man. No one else was coming. It was just the two of them. This had gone on long enough.

Hands still out in front of him in fake prayer, Ryker was perfectly positioned. Steinhauser had a single hand gripped on his gun – a Glock. Ryker unclasped his hands and, in a swift motion, he smashed his right wrist into Steinhauser's, pushing his arm away and to the side. At the same time he swung his left hand in the opposite direction, wrenching the gun from Steinhauser's grip.

The barrel was pointed in the wrong direction, but the gun was still the perfect weapon at such close quarters. Ryker sprung upright before Steinhauser had a chance to even think about his next move. He crashed the gun into Steinhauser's chin and his head snapped back viciously.

On his feet, Ryker twisted his right arm behind Steinhauser's neck and wrenched down while hauling up his knee. Blood erupted from Steinhauser's mouth and he grimaced in pain as his body sank to the ground. He landed in an awkward heap, conscious, but only just.

Ryker kneeled down, grabbed him by the scruff of his neck and shoved the barrel of the Glock into his blood-filled mouth.

'Don't worry,' Ryker said. 'You didn't do anything wrong. You just weren't good enough.'

Steinhauser, as surprised as he was fearful, glared at Ryker. He tried to mumble something but with half his teeth missing and the gun in his mouth it was indecipherable.

'I'm going to take out your phone,' Ryker said. 'I'm going to type a message to your boss. When you see him, this went down exactly as I say it did. Otherwise next time you don't get to walk away.'

No reaction from Steinhauser. Ryker swung his elbow down and ground it into Steinhauser's groin. The big man moaned and writhed.

'Do you understand?'

Eyes watering, Steinhauser nodded.

Ryker reached down and took Steinhauser's phone from his pocket. Stood up straight, and with one hand on the phone, the other keeping the gun trained on the big man, he typed then sent the message.

When he was done he threw the phone down and it bounced off Steinhauser's forehead and clattered onto the bloodied ground next to him.

Ryker bent down and wiped the gun on Steinhauser's shirt then stuffed it into the waistband of his jeans. He thought about saying something else to the man by his feet. No.

It was a risk to leave him alive. But it was an even bigger risk to kill him and try to cover it up. He had to hope Steinhauser would be sufficiently afraid of Green to keep quiet. After all, if he admitted to Green that he'd let Ryker get away so easily, what would his boss do to him?

Without another word, Ryker turned and walked away.

Chapter forty-one

Campbell was trembling as he and Green sat in the back of the Mercedes, heading away from the warehouse. He had no idea what they would do to Ryker. Would they kill him? Strangely, Campbell's biggest worry wasn't Ryker's fate, but whether Ryker would blurt out the truth about who he was and what he and Campbell were concocting with the FBI.

'Don't worry,' Green said, looking over. 'I said I'd take care of Powell and I will. As for his brother…'

'They've got what's coming to them,' Campbell said. 'How dare that guy barge into your warehouse like that.'

Green raised an eyebrow. Campbell looked away.

'So?'

'So what?' Campbell said.

'You were snooping.'

'I was doing my job!'

Green huffed. Held Campbell's eye.

'I meant what I said,' Campbell added. 'I honestly can't say for sure but you must have millions in merchandise stored there. How the hell can you know if someone is stealing tens of thousands, even hundreds of thousands, worth of goods from under your nose if you haven't taken a proper inventory?'

Green seemed to think about that one, but he didn't look appeased.

'Think about it. It doesn't matter whether you're talking about drugs or bottles of beer. You have to keep full records of what goes in and what goes out. I'm going to set that up for you. It'll be discreet, but it'll give you full control. You're expanding and your set-up has to change with it.'

Green nodded. 'You've got a decent head on you.'

Green's phone vibrated. He took it from his pocket. Without being too obvious Campbell did his best to glance at the screen as Green opened up the message.

The fucker tried to fight back, but he's got the message now. He won't be a problem anymore.

Green smiled then put the phone away.

'Some people learn the hard way,' he said. He returned Campbell's gaze. 'But I still don't like that you went behind my back.'

'I know. I'm sorry. You were tied up… with Charlie, and—'

'What were you doing in the basement?'

'I just wanted to know what was in there.'

'None of those men know the code.'

'I guessed it.'

Green scoffed. Campbell's brain fired off a thousand ideas to try to get Green off the subject.

Play to his ego. With Green, it was always worth a shot.

'How much is down there? I mean, it must be a couple of million.'

Green smiled. 'A lot more than that, kid.'

'And we're going to make it grow even further,' Campbell said. Green nodded. 'It's good that you haven't given the guards access to the basement. You're in charge and they need to know their place. Plus you can't be too careful. I would say you should make the entrance more discreet. Put something over the top of it so most people don't even know it exists.'

'I know. And I will. Not many of my men know about that room, and even fewer know how to get inside. But *you* need to be careful. You've got initiative to go with your balls, but turning up unannounced like that… Everyone's on high alert at the moment, and one wrong move could land you in serious trouble.'

'I get that now.'

'Do you? I'm only going to say this to you one time, Scott… You ever lie to me, and I'll kill you myself.'

Campbell gulped. There really was nothing he could say to that.

The rest of the journey carried on in near silence. Campbell wasn't off the hook exactly, but he was still in one piece and breathing. He really couldn't be sure if the same could be said of James Ryker. What had Steinhauser done to him?

They came to a stop outside Evolve. Green didn't make a move to get out.

'I've still got plenty to do elsewhere. I didn't need this distraction today.'

'I know. I'm sorry.'

'Steinhauser will bring your car back later.'

Campbell paused. Didn't really know what else to say. 'Thanks, Henry.'

He got out of the car. The Mercedes sped off down the street. Campbell headed inside and up to the office where Deontay was snoozing on the sofa. He bolted upright when Campbell walked in.

'Busy day?'

Nothing but a grunt in response.

The next few hours were among the slowest of Campbell's life. He had his phone in his hand almost the entire time but didn't make a single call or send a single message. There was no way he could try to contact Ryker. The risk of tipping off Steinhauser, and therefore Green, if the big man had taken Ryker's phone, was too great.

Instead he just stared at the small lump of glass and black plastic, thinking through all of the grim possibilities as to what had happened to Ryker and why he hadn't yet been in contact.

At quarter to five, Campbell had had enough. He packed up his things, headed out and made his way across to 7th Avenue to catch the subway to take him home. The streets in Midtown were as busy as ever with tourists snapping photos and queuing outside theatres, and Campbell, feeling more jittery than usual, was on high alert as he jostled past the throngs, his eyes sweeping around him, looking for anyone out of place. Yet he still had no clue he was being followed until he heard the voice.

'Busy day?' Ryker said.

Campbell stopped, spun around, and there was Ryker, standing right behind him, casual as could be. Not a mark or blemish visible on his face or anywhere else. What the hell?

Campbell turned and walked again. Ryker kept up by his side.

'You're alive then,' Campbell said. 'I suppose that's a good thing.'

'I was thinking the same thing about you, to be honest.'

'What happened? Green got a text… You sent it?'

Ryker shrugged. 'I didn't quite get Steinhauser's intended message. Hopefully he'll get mine in return.'

'Jesus, Ryker, you're going to get us both killed.'

'No. We're going to finish this before either of those two figure it out.'

'I admire your confidence. I wish I had some of it myself.'

'You've got plenty. You did good today.'

Campbell didn't know what to say to that.

'You got the pictures?'

'Pictures, and a whole lot more.'

'Meaning what?'

Campbell briefly explained what he'd seen. The drugs rooms. The basement filled with weapons and money. Ryker said nothing, just took it all in, though Campbell could tell he was intrigued.

They reached the subway station. Ryker stopped.

'You did good today.'

Campbell huffed.

'Send what you've got to me as soon as you can,' Ryker said.

'And then what?'

'I'll let you know.'

And with that Ryker turned and two seconds later he'd disappeared, losing himself in the crowds. Campbell shivered as though he'd just seen a ghost.

He headed into the station, his brain a jumble of conflicting thoughts. Strangely, the biggest emotion he was feeling was pride, but there was a debilitating conflict as to where it was coming from. He'd done exactly what Ryker had asked, and the ex-spy might not have been explicit, but he'd been impressed with Campbell's efforts, hadn't he? Campbell didn't like to think it, but in many ways Ryker reminded him of his dad, perhaps because it was his dad who, all those years ago, had moulded Ryker into who he now was. The feeling Campbell got from pleasing him was very similar to how he'd felt when trying to impress his father.

But then, Campbell realised, he also got the exact same sense of pride when he was around Green. Despite Campbell going to the warehouse under Green's nose, he still seemed to trust Campbell. In fact, he seemed pleased with Campbell's supposed initiative. Day by day Campbell was being sucked deeper into Green's inner circle. With every move he made to get Ryker more information to bring Green down, Campbell in fact moved a step closer to Green. Which only made his betrayal that much harder to stomach.

He just had to keep reminding himself that the key objective was to get out. To get him and Kate out. Green's kingdom would crumble, but he and Kate would be fine, would start afresh somewhere else.

Campbell winced at the thoughts. Was tearing apart his future wife's family really the right thing to do?

He really didn't know anymore. He just hoped he'd figure out the answer sooner rather than later.

Chapter forty-two

Shaun Doherty was back at home in Long Island when he got the call. He was watching golf on TV in one of the lounges, a room bigger than most apartments back in Manhattan. He liked golf – at least, playing it – but he could never understand why people got so enthralled in watching others play. For starters, he could barely see the ball most of the time. But he still watched it. In fact, he watched it whenever it was on. He liked to study the swings of the professionals, going so far as to practice his own swing standing on the rug in the middle of the room, gazing over at the mirror while the TV was on, trying to mimic how they did it. As far as he was concerned, he had the swing perfected. So how could they be that much better than him? He did it the exact same way as they did, didn't he? Perhaps he should fire his coach. He had never liked the guy much.

'Yeah?' Doherty said, taking the call. He took off his sun visor and started to undo the laces of his golf shoes. He'd had enough practice for one day.

'Are you at home?' the voice on the other end said as Doherty sat back in a leather armchair. It was Peterson, Doherty's eyes and ears in New Jersey ever since he'd learned of the location of Green's warehouse.

'Yeah. What's up?'

'I'm emailing you some pictures.'

'Pictures of what? I'm intrigued, really I am, but just spit it out will you?'

'That kid Scott Campbell turned up today. I've never seen him down here before. And there was someone else with him.'

'Who?'

'Don't know him. He was sat in his car on the edge of the street where I am. At first I wasn't sure why he was there. He arrived on his own, minutes before Campbell. Campbell was inside for ages and then Green turns up all in a rage. Minutes later Campbell's buddy goes on a bender, knocking out two of Green's guys on the outside before storming in.'

'What are you trying to tell me?' Doherty said, not yet sure whether this was good news or bad.

'I don't know. Two minutes later Steinhauser drags this other guy back out – takes him for a beating, I'm guessing. Only it was Steinhauser who got turned over.'

Doherty snorted. Steinhauser was having a bad week. Maybe Green needed a better right-hand man.

'What about Green and Campbell?'

'They went off together. Who knows what's happened there? But take a look at the pictures of this guy; maybe it'll make sense to you. Should be with you now.'

Doherty stood up and grabbed his tablet from the side and opened up his email account. He took a look at the first photo. A profile of the man in the Toyota Corolla. Doherty recognised him immediately.

'Who the fuck *are* you?' Doherty said. 'And what have you got yourself into, Scott Campbell?'

'Thought you'd like it,' Peterson said.

Chapter forty-three

Ryker received the photos of the warehouse on his phone from Campbell as he was making his way across town to Queens. Having decided to drive this time, he didn't get the chance to look at them properly until he'd parked up a few buildings down from where Jane Chan lived. He spent a couple of minutes perusing them, not exactly shocked by what he saw, more surprised that Green's operation was so brazen. If Green was operating so casually, who exactly had he paid to keep heat off him? The local police in New Jersey? The FBI? That thought worried Ryker, because he didn't yet know who he was going up against, but it wasn't going to stop him now.

He headed up the outside steps and pressed on the intercom, then stepped back to look up to Chan's apartment. The window of one of the front rooms was wide open, but he got no response to the call. He pressed the intercom again. Looked up again. Was sure he could hear the screeching voices of young kids from above. A moment later a head popped out the open window. Chan. When she saw who was outside she whipped her head away.

Ryker smiled. Pressed on the intercom one more time. This time it was answered.

'What do you want?' She sounded harried.

'I have something to show you.'

'I'm kinda busy.'

'I could take it straight to your boss, if you like?'

A pause. A sigh. The door locks clicked open.

***

Ryker wasn't sure whether to smile or shudder. He was sitting on a spongy sofa with a sheet over the top covered in all manner of stains – likely all child inflicted. Toys and clothes were strewn across the floor in front of him. The three kids tore about the place, engaged in some sort of play-fight involving dragons and a Pokémon, whatever that was. However stressed Chan appeared, watching her children play was heartening, if exhausting, to Ryker. Yet he was out of his depth. Children really were not his bag. Not because he didn't like them, but because he had zero experience of being responsible for them.

'Who *are* you?' the tallest of the two girls said as she suddenly broke from the gang and stopped right in front of Ryker, her hand on his knee.

'I work with your mummy.'

'You talk funny.'

'So do you.'

She raised an eyebrow at that. A reaction far older than her years. 'So you're an FBI agent too?'

'Not exactly. What's your name?'

'Monica.'

'That's nice. It suits you.'

A coy smile.

'And how old are you, Monica?'

'Eight.'

'Wow. I thought you were much older – you're so tall.'

Her smile widened. 'Are you my mommy's new boyfriend?'

Ryker laughed. Monica didn't seem to get the joke.

'No. I don't think she likes me like that.'

'But you like her? She's really nice… most of the time.'

Chan burst into the room and Monica took that as her chance to scarper. Looking even more frazzled than before, and just a little embarrassed, Chan scooped up a handful of clothes from the floor as she moved through.

'Your food's ready!' she shouted to the kids who'd all shot out of the room the moment she came in.

A couple of whoops of delight from out in the hall as the kids hurtled to the kitchen.

'Just give me one more minute,' Chan said before disappearing again.

Ryker nodded. Picking up his mug of coffee, he got to his feet and mooched around the room, looking at the family photos. When he reached the window he glanced out, surveying the scene on the street.

'Talk about lousy timing,' Chan said.

Ryker turned around. Chan, in sweatpants and a T-shirt, a tea towel over her shoulder, was red-cheeked from all the running around.

'I don't know how you do it,' Ryker said.

Chan seemed to know what he meant. 'Sadly most of the time I don't. Between friends and neighbours I get cover most of the time.' She smiled, but it wasn't a happy smile. 'The thing is, whenever I'm at work I can't wait to get back here to be with them. I spend all day looking forward to seeing their faces. Most nights they're already asleep when I get back. Yet today, when I'm finally around for once, I've been pissy with them the whole time.'

'Kids know which buttons to press.' He said it as though he were an expert. She nodded in agreement. 'What happened to their dad?'

Ryker indicated the photos on the bookshelf. There were several pictures of the man Ryker assumed was the father. In two he was in military uniform. He saw the slightly uncomfortable look on her face but he didn't feel bad for prying.

'He was in the army,' Chan said. 'Now he's dead.'

'On tour?'

'No. Cancer.'

Now he felt bad. Ryker really didn't know what to say to that. 'I'm sorry.'

It was lame, but it was something.

'I don't know why this couldn't wait,' Chan said, 'but tell me what you've got.'

Ryker took out his phone and Chan came over. He handed the device to her and she took a few minutes to scroll through the pictures, her face changing several times in the process: surprise, astonishment, anger, satisfaction.

She passed the phone back without a word and Ryker briefly explained what Campbell had told him, and what he'd seen himself. He left out the part about him beating the crap out of Steinhauser.

Chan turned and slumped down onto the sofa.

'I can't believe Campbell got you all of this.'

Ryker didn't respond. He could tell she was deep in thought.

'I'm impressed with your work. Jesus, I can't believe this. It's bigger than I imagined. The drugs I mean. This is some operation Green has going.'

'You're not wrong.'

'What else? You mentioned cash. There aren't any pictures?'

'Campbell said it was too difficult. Green turned up out of the blue. But yes, there's cash, hidden in a basement. Millions. Plus weapons.'

'Weapons?'

'Campbell didn't know specifics, but he said handguns, shotguns, automatics. He had no idea what type but it sounds like a lot.'

Chan thought for a few moments and Ryker gave her the time. She looked up to him, a suspicious glint in her eye.

'Why are you doing this for me?'

'For you?'

'For me, for Campbell? I still don't get why you're here.'

'Why does it matter?'

She didn't answer that.

'Take it to your boss. Maybe you'll get back in his good books now.'

'And what about you?'

'I only ask for two things from you.'

'Yeah?'

'Get protection for Campbell.'

'Witness protection? I–'

'No. Security. He needs eyes on him at all times until this is over. But more importantly, he needs immunity for what's to come.'

'You know I have no say in that–'

'But you can try.'

She sighed. 'Yes, I can try. What was the second thing?'

'Keep me up to date. I want to know what's happening.'

She scoffed at that. 'Ryker, you've been a help here, but what you're doing, what we're doing, it's against every rule I have.'

'No it's not. I'm just an asset. An informant.'

'That's not what you are at all.'

'Just let me know what's going on. Better than us crossing paths the wrong way. That's all I'm asking.' She didn't respond. 'Will you do that?'

Another sigh. 'Yeah. I'll do it.'

Ryker smiled. Walked up to her and held out his hand. She stood up and shook it, holding his gaze at the same time. When Ryker released her hand she carried on staring. He thought she was about to say something but in the end she just looked away.

'I cooked extra. You wanna eat? It's not often I get adult company at home.'

'No, I'm good, thanks. I already ate. Enjoy the rest of your evening.'

He turned and headed for the door, pretending he hadn't seen the flash of disappointment that swept across her face.

Chapter forty-four

McKinley and Trapp were already sat waiting in the office when Chan arrived the following morning.

'Better late than never, Chan,' McKinley said, not bothering to get up.

'Yeah, a good morning to you too, sir.'

She closed the door and took a seat opposite McKinley at the round table, with Trapp off to her left.

'That was one hell of a fuck-up last night, wasn't it?' McKinley said to neither Trapp nor Chan in particular.

'I'm not with you,' Chan said. The previous evening when she called McKinley after Ryker had left, her boss had seemed animated about what she'd found. This was hardly the reception she'd expected. 'Sir?'

'You know the whole point in having surveillance is so we can be on top of events when they happen. We're getting closer to a gang war here and where the hell were we?' He left that one hanging, but neither Trapp nor Chan made an attempt to answer. 'Nowhere. That's where. Green's made his move and we were completely blind to it.'

'What are you talking about? What move?' Chan felt like defending herself further by stating that the previous day she'd been off the team, officially, so any fuck-up wasn't on her. But really she was more intrigued about what had happened.

'While we were sat watching paint dry, there were five separate arson attacks in New York last night. All of them on properties owned by Shaun Doherty, including his favoured shitty bar up in the Bronx.'

Chan's mouth fell open in astonishment. 'Was anyone in them?'

'We don't know yet. The clear-up has only just started, but we've had eyes on Doherty this morning so he's fine. Do you know how much crap I'm getting from up above? I don't like to be made the fool.'

'With all due respect,' Trapp said, 'we didn't have any of those locations covered full-time.'

'And I previously pointed out we needed more surveillance,' Chan added.

'This isn't the time for finger pointing!' McKinley shouted. 'This isn't *my* investigation, or *your* investigation; we're in this together. We should have been in a position to stop this, or at the very least been somewhere near when it happened. As it was, we were all safely tucked away in bed, and that's really not good enough, is it?'

'No, it's not,' Chan said. 'Whatever you may think, nobody wants to sort this mess out more than me. Which is why you called me back here today.'

McKinley's anger came down a notch. 'Yeah. What about that? You were supposed to be off active duty. Remember our conversation? Yet you're still running Scott Campbell.'

'So you don't want this intel?'

'What I want is an agent who does as she's told!'

'No, what you should want is a successful end to this investigation!'

Silence from McKinley.

'Campbell's talking to you?' Trapp asked, surprised.

'Yes,' Chan said. 'Yesterday he went to a warehouse near Newark where he knew Green stores drugs. But turns out it's more than that. He found it's where Green cuts and packages his product. There's millions of dollars' worth of drugs there, not to mention a secret stash of money and weapons.'

Chan took out her phone, opened up the pictures and slid the device across the desk. McKinley scrolled through without saying a word.

'What does Campbell want?' Trapp asked.

'He wants out. Immunity. This guy could give us everything we need.'

'Immunity?' McKinley said. Nothing more.

'We need to arrange a raid on the warehouse when Green's there, so we can take him down for good. I say we put more bodies on this straight away. We need to know Green's plans and be ready to act.'

McKinley looked to Trapp, as though what Chan said was ridiculous. 'I'm not saying no,' he said, more calm than at any other point during the meeting. 'But I am saying wait.'

'Wait for what?' Chan said. 'For Green and Doherty to kill each other first? Who do you think was responsible for the attacks on Doherty's properties? What do you think the next move will be?'

'You're right. We have to expect retaliation. But not today.'

'Not today?'

'The *other* reason I asked you back… We're moving on Doherty tonight.'

Chan's mouth was open but she didn't know what to say.

'We've had more intel about Doherty's upcoming shipment,' Trapp chipped in. 'It's happening tonight.'

'Tonight? But–'

McKinley looked at his watch. 'You can come in on this, Chan. If you want?'

Even if she was enraged at being so out of the loop, the answer was a no-brainer.

'Yes. I want in.'

'Good. Because the final briefing is taking place in ten minutes.' McKinley got up from his chair. 'Come on, let's go.'

***

Margaret Ennis was at the briefing, alongside a dozen agents from the Special Weapons and Tactics team. Hobbs, the no-nonsense leader of the SWAT troop, led the meeting, alongside Ennis. Chan found it quite amusing that McKinley was given a back seat. He looked far less amused.

'We're working from limited intel,' Ennis said. 'So we need to be able to respond quickly if things aren't as expected. We don't know how many of them there will be, how much they're buying or what exactly they're buying. But we do know where and when. Hobbs?'

The gruff-looking Hobbs, not particularly tall but stocky, with a typical buzzcut, got to his feet and surveyed the drawing on the whiteboard behind him.

'We're going with a unit on either side of the runway here,' he said, pointing to the spot. 'The nearby fields mean we have plenty of natural cover. We can get boots on the ground as near as fifty yards. Vehicles can be positioned here, and here, about two hundred yards back. They'll have a direct route onto the runway, and can also cut off any vehicles leaving the area. Realistically, given the position of the nearest interstate, there's only one way they'll likely come in, but we'll have all exit routes covered, just in case.'

A few nods in the room from the rag-tag bunch of Rambo wannabes. Chan had plenty of experience with SWAT. They were good at their jobs, no doubt, but they were far from fun to work with. Organised chaos was the best and kindest description she could think of, based on experience.

Hobbs looked back to Ennis.

'Okay. The objective of this operation is to catch Shaun Doherty and his gang in the middle of the deal,' she said. 'But it's not just Doherty we want here. We need whoever he's buying from as well. We don't know who that is yet, but it could turn out to be a big catch for us. I can't emphasise enough that we have to wait for the exchange to take place. Given what we know about Doherty, we're expecting him and his men to be heavily armed…'

Chan looked around the room as Ennis carried on going through the plans. Although glad to be there, she had a niggling concern about the whole situation. It seemed off that the FBI had a clear idea of where Doherty would be and when, but not what he was buying and from whom. And as far as she was aware the whole sting had started with word of mouth imparted by a prostitute.

'So does anyone have any questions?' Ennis said when she'd finished. 'Okay, then that's it. Get some rest. We meet on-site at 8pm. Good luck everyone.'

***

After a quick and largely unnecessary follow-up meeting with McKinley and Trapp, Chan went outside to get some air, although it turned out the stifling city smog was no fresher than the FBI toilets upstairs. Out in the street she bought a chilled bottle of water from a hot dog seller then took out her phone. She had a message from Ryker.

All good?

She grunted. Downed half the bottle of water then found a shady spot and called him back.

'All good?' she said when he answered. 'No, it's not *all good*, Ryker.'

'Care to explain?'

'Green made a move on Doherty last night. Burned down pretty much everything he owns in New York.'

Silence for a few moments.

'I thought the FBI had surveillance?' he said eventually.

'On Green, not on Doherty!'

'So what next?'

Chan didn't answer straight away. The previous evening she'd told Ryker she would keep him up to date, but could she really divulge details of the planned raid on Doherty?

'Chan? What's the next move? Are you going after Green?'

'It's not on the cards yet.' She sighed. 'But we are going after Doherty. Tonight.'

'Doherty? How?'

'A drug deal is going down. We'll be there.'

Had she just blown everything? No. Whoever Ryker was, he wasn't working with Doherty.

'I've said enough,' she added. 'You need to figure out what Green's up to.'

'I'm not sure it's Green we should worry about after last night. The next move is Doherty's.'

'Except it looks like Doherty is gonna be tied up tonight. Just speak to Campbell. Find out what he knows, then call me back when you have something. Please?'

'I will.'

'Time is ticking, Ryker. I don't like where this is going, and I can't help but feel we're missing something.'

'I'll be in touch.'

Ryker ended the call.

Chapter forty-five

'I hope you've got a good explanation!' Doherty yelled down the phone at his contact. 'It'll take me weeks to get my businesses up and running again.'

He was at home in Long Island again. Where else did he have to go now? His businesses were little more than piles of ash and rubble. He took a bite from the sandwich on the plate on his lap. It was crap. Wholemeal bread, which he hated. And why the hell had the housekeeper put low-fat mayonnaise on it? Was he on some sort of diet that he didn't know about?

'I'm sorry. There was nothing I could do about it. Nobody knew a thing.'

'You owe me big time for this. Everything I had was in those fucking buildings. Have you any idea how much cash was lost too?'

Not to mention two of his men who'd burned alive having been beaten up and left for dead by the arsonists. Although the men, at least, were replaceable.

'I couldn't have stopped it.'

'And what the hell is going on with Scott Campbell? Since when was he an informant?'

That was the only conclusion that Doherty could come to, given Campbell's rendezvous with the mysterious man at Green's warehouse the day before, relayed to him by Peterson. Though he still didn't know exactly who James Ryker was, or who he was working for.

'Scott Campbell? How did you know about that?'

That was a yes to his deduction then. Doherty ground his teeth in anger. 'Yeah, you little prick, I'm not as stupid as you think. Why didn't you tell me?'

'I didn't tell you because Campbell isn't important. He doesn't know a thing.'

'Are you sure about that?'

'Everything is in place now. Campbell is the least of your worries. In fact, he isn't a worry at all.'

'You'd better be right. No more mistakes. I don't give a fuck who you are, I'll skin you alive. Got it?'

No answer. Doherty didn't hang up. Instead he flung the phone across the room. It hit the fridge door and split into several pieces which scattered across the floor. Two seconds later, the half-eaten sandwich and the plate it had been served on suffered a similar fate.

Chapter forty-six

Campbell hadn't woken until after ten o'clock that morning, much later than he would normally sleep in on a weekday. After the trip to the warehouse, Green had called him late the previous night to tell him to lay low for a few days. Campbell was fine with that, after the events at the warehouse.

But then Green had turned up out of the blue when Campbell was still getting dressed and told Campbell all about the arson attacks. Hence the reason he wanted Campbell to lay low. Green was on a mission and he wasn't finished with Doherty yet, even though he knew heat on him was building.

The conversation had been quite surreal to Campbell. Green had talked openly about the police and how he sensed they were watching him. Had told Campbell he thought he was being tailed, that a car had followed him over to Campbell's place that morning. Campbell wondered whether it was Ryker – he seemed to know everything all of the time – or whether in fact Green was just paranoid.

Paranoid or not, Green hadn't seemed troubled at all.

'They'll have to be at every place, all the time if they're going to stop me,' he'd said.

Did Green know about Campbell? Was everything he'd said just a ploy to get Campbell to trust him? *Keep your enemies closer* as the saying went.

The chances of Campbell coming out the other end of all this unscathed were becoming slimmer and slimmer by the day, he believed.

It was now after twelve o'clock, but Campbell still hadn't eaten. He made his way to the kitchen to fix himself some food but there was nothing in. He decided to head out for some groceries.

As he walked out of the lift on the ground floor, he was sure he saw the shadow of a person flickering across the ground to his left. His head whipped around. No one there. When he looked back the other way he jumped in shock when he saw the looming figure right in front of him. A hand wrapped around his throat. Wrenched him off his feet. He was heaved backward, into the lift.

'Going somewhere?' Ryker said, reaching back to slam the button to close the lift doors.

'Get… off me!' Campbell choked.

'I want the truth.'

'Get off!'

'The truth!'

'Okay!'

Ryker let go and Campbell slumped down against the mirrored panel, holding his aching throat. Ryker hit the button for Campbell's floor and the lift set off.

'What the hell happened last night?'

'I don't know. Did Mrs Ryker not put out?' Campbell said, agitated.

'Funny. I'm talking about Doherty. I suppose you're going to tell me you knew nothing about that.'

'Actually I didn't. Not until Green told me this morning.'

'You sure about that?'

'Yes, I'm sure!'

'For your sake you'd better be telling the truth. I'll throw you to the wolves if you lie to me.'

'I'm not lying!'

The lift arrived and Ryker grabbed Campbell's arm and dragged him over to the apartment door. Only when they were inside with the door shut did the conversation start again. Ryker remained by the closed door. Campbell hoped that meant he wasn't staying long.

'What did Green tell you?'

'Just that he wanted to get Doherty back for Charlie's death. Kind of funny, really, Doherty getting punished for what you did.'

The bitterness in Campbell's voice was clear. He'd done everything Ryker had asked of him, risking his own life in the process, yet Ryker still treated him like he was some low life.

'The point about having someone on the inside is so that we can prevent these things from happening,' Ryker said.

'We? There is no we. You're a loner. Nobody really wants you here. Not me, or the FBI.'

Ryker seemed to take offence at that but he didn't question it. 'What else has Green got planned?'

'I've no idea! I can't read his mind, and I don't think he would appreciate me badgering him all day for the intricacies of his plans for revenge and bloodshed.'

Ryker scoffed, perhaps at Campbell's nonchalance, but Campbell couldn't care less.

'What are you doing today?' Ryker asked.

'Hopefully staying alive.'

'Yeah. You do that. This is getting serious now, Campbell. If you hear about anything, you tell me. You should lay low. I don't want you getting caught in the crossfire.'

'Trust me. I don't want that either.'

Ryker glared for a second then turned, opened the door and walked out.

Chapter forty-seven

Ryker knew time was running out. Green had made the first big move against Doherty. More bloodshed would follow. He'd given Chan what she needed to set up a sting against Green, but for now the FBI were gunning for Doherty instead. Ryker's biggest fear was that Campbell would get caught in the middle, particularly after what had happened at the warehouse the day before.

There was something he still wasn't seeing clearly. What was Doherty's game exactly? All of the moves made so far seemed to be by Green: the body outside Malloy's, the arson attacks. Green felt threatened, clearly, but it was more than that. The FBI were convinced Doherty was setting up a big drug deal, and perhaps the answer was as simple as Doherty was trying to muscle in on Green's patch, but were they seeing the bigger picture?

Charlie Ward still bothered Ryker too. Chan claimed he was an FBI informant. If that was true, why had he run away like he had? And then chosen to stand and fight? There was more to that story, and with Doherty, and likely Green, following the warehouse intel, both increasingly under close surveillance, Ryker determined that Charlie Ward was an angle he could still pursue under the radar.

Which was why, since he'd spoken to Campbell earlier, he'd been visiting Ward's old haunts. Or, more specifically, visiting Ward's prostitutes – not exactly Ryker's favourite way to spend a few hours, and the first three women he'd spoken to had been entirely unhelpful. Yes, they knew Charlie, but no, they didn't know anything about him, really.

The fourth woman called herself Kitten. She was a piece of work. A master manipulator. But then, so was Ryker. Kitten had given Ryker the lead he needed. From what he could figure out, Ward had been scuppered by a classic honeytrap. Pictures of him with an underage prostitute had been enough for the FBI to put the noose around his neck. Would the FBI really be so sneaky, and immoral, as to have set that up? Or had they got the pictures from another source? If the latter, then who was the source and what was their motivation?

After leaving Kitten's luxury apartment near the Lincoln Center – possibly the reason Charlie Ward had been in that part of the city that fateful day – Ryker made his way down to the Lower East Side. A neighbourhood of clashing demographics, the area contained some of Manhattan's largest and most deprived housing projects, but other trendier parts were thriving and full of young professionals.

Ryker drove around the outskirts of Baruch Houses, the largest of the projects in Manhattan with over two thousand apartments spread across multiple 1950s high-rise buildings. He turned onto a street of downtrodden tenements in a seedy part of the neighbourhood where the buildings were mostly derelict. As he drove along a few streets, it wasn't hard to spot the prostitutes hanging around on the street corners here and there. Very few other folk were brave enough or had reason to wander about the place.

At just before 8pm, Ryker finally arrived at the building where Kitten had told him a girl called Megan worked. The girl Charlie Ward had been pictured with. He parked up, not struggling to find a space on the mostly deserted street, and looked at the building out of his window. A shabby four-storey terrace, its window frames were almost stripped bare of their lime-green paint, and the rendering of the brickwork was so eroded it looked as though it would crumble away at the slightest touch. Ryker would have thought the building was empty had it not been for the orange illumination he could see coming through the lace curtains in the downstairs front room.

He walked up to the grimy-looking door and knocked. A hard-faced woman with scraggy blonde hair opened the door.

She looked to Ryker to be in her mid-forties, though she was haggard, presumably because of too much booze and drugs. She was dressed in virtually nothing, and wore hideous thick make-up that together with the wrinkles hid what may once have been a pretty face.

'What the fuck do you want?' she snarled.

'Is Megan here?'

'You a cop?'

'Do I look like one?'

She thought about that one. Eyed him up and down. 'They got all sorts working vice these days. Wouldn't surprise me.'

'Bet you don't get many vice cops from England though?'

A flicker of suspicion still.

'I'm not here to cause trouble. In fact, I'm trying to stop it. I really need to speak to Megan.'

'Don't know her,' she said, attempting to close the door as she spoke. Ryker grabbed the edge of the wood to stop her.

'Yes, you do. And I know she's here.' Ryker took out twenty dollars and held it out. 'Please, just get her for me?'

She took the money, scowling, then stepped aside.

'Just don't try nothing funny,' she said as he walked in. 'Calvin'll be back any minute.'

'I'll be gone in no time,' Ryker said.

He certainly had no desire to have a run-in with an angry pimp.

'In the back room, down there,' the woman said, pointing the way.

Ryker headed down the narrow hallway that wasn't much of an improvement decor wise to the outside of the house, and turned into the back room. He stopped in the doorway and looked over to Megan, sat down on an old blue sofa that looked like it had been found on a scrap heap. Other than the coffee table in the middle of the floor there was no other furniture in the room.

Megan, dressed in tight denim shorts and bra, was smoking and staring at the wall in front of her, and hadn't noticed Ryker at all. She looked ill and gaunt. Probably from a combination of cigarettes, drugs, alcohol and a lack of money to buy decent food as a result of those habits. Ryker could tell she was young, but he didn't think that she looked under seventeen. Regardless, hers was a sad existence, and as he stared, Ryker felt sorry for her, for all of the people who lived like that. He even pitied the detectives whose jobs were to work the streets. A thankless and depressing task.

'Megan, this cop wants to speak to you about something,' the woman from the door said, pushing her way past Ryker.

Megan jerked and looked over. Ryker smiled at her.

'What the hell? Why'd you let him in!'

Megan sprang off the sofa. She looked frightened.

'Whoa. It's okay,' Ryker said, holding his hands up. 'You're not in trouble. I just need to talk to you.'

'Yeah? About what?'

'About Charlie Ward.'

On hearing his name the expression on her face turned to one of sorrow, and she slumped back down on the sofa.

'So you are a cop.'

'No.'

'You know Charlie?'

'I did.'

'What do you want to know?'

'How'd you meet him?'

'He came over a few times.'

'For a cup of tea?'

'What do you think?'

'How long had you known him?'

'Only a few weeks...'

'And?'

Megan looked nervously to her older companion.

'Charlie was... he was just nice.' Her eyes welled with tears. 'I heard about what happened to him. I hope they fry the scumbag who did it.'

Ryker tried not to look uncomfortable; after all, he was basically the scumbag.

'How old are you, Megan?'

'What? I'm twenty.'

'Is that the truth? Like I said, you won't get into any trouble here. You said you liked Charlie. I'm trying to help him.'

'It's true. You don't believe me?'

'She's not lying. I know her mom,' the older woman said.

Ryker shook his head, not wanting to delve further into how a twenty-year-old woman had come to work as a prostitute with her mother's friend. But he knew he was onto something now. If Megan wasn't underage, Charlie Ward had been conned into talking to the FBI. Why? And by who?

'How did you first meet Charlie?'

'I was already doing this, you know, working the streets. But some guy pays me to go and see Charlie. Says Charlie'll help me out. And he did. He was a good guy. He knew a lot of girls and they all liked working for him. He introduced me to a few of his friends. They paid good money. Much better than I'm used to here. Then…'

'Then what?'

Megan looked over to the woman by the door again.

'Tell him,' she said.

'The same guy comes back. He roughed up Celine pretty good,' she said, indicating to the woman at the door.

'He punched me in the fucking face,' Celine spat. 'Broke my lip. Knocked a tooth out.'

She opened her mouth to show Ryker the gap.

Megan hung her head. 'It wasn't my fault. He told me to stay away from Charlie. Gave me a thousand dollars, but told me if I went near Charlie again he'd come back and cut us both to pieces.'

A tear escaped her eye. Neither Celine nor Ryker went to comfort her. Ryker's mind whirred. The set-up didn't sound like the FBI at all. Yes there were lengths they'd go to in order to get informants on board, but this was beyond those lengths.

'Who was he? Do you know his name?'

'I only saw him those two times.'

'Describe him to me.'

'I don't know. He was big. Mean looking. Shaved head. Spoke kinda funny.'

'Kinda funny? Like what? Like me?'

She shrugged. 'A little, but not the same.'

'Maybe Irish,' Celine said. 'Something like that.'

And there it was.

Ryker dug his phone out and scrolled through the pictures he'd taken outside Malloy's the first time he'd scoped out the place. The two bouncers on the door. A picture of Doherty he'd got since.

'Was it this guy?' he asked, showing Megan his phone screen.

'Never seen him. But he looks kinda cute.'

Doherty, cute? Not exactly.

'What about this one?' Ryker showed her the picture of the bigger of the two bouncers.

'How'd you know?' she said, squinting in distrust.

Ryker felt a surge of adrenaline as the pieces fell into place. The picture was of Victor, Doherty's heavy.

'Thanks Megan,' Ryker said. 'You're a star. You see him again, you call me.'

He scribbled his number down on the corner of a tobacco wrapper and placed it on the coffee table. Then he turned and dashed out, past the puzzled Celine.

Outside he looked at his watch. It was already after 8pm. He only hoped he wasn't too late.

Chapter forty-eight

Chan sat in the back of the blacked-out minivan a few hundred yards down the road from the airstrip. She had no intention of being in the thick of the action tonight. She'd let the commandos do their thing. But she did want to be on the scene still. With her headset on she had access to the channel that, come the time, would link in to every member of the SWAT team as they made their assault. For now it was just the central command team online, comprising of Hobbs, Trapp and herself, plus the two plain-clothed FBI agents in a car in sight of Doherty's mansion in Long Island.

'Any action yet?' came Hobbs's voice in her ear.

So far there hadn't been a peep from the house for hours, though Doherty was definitely home. Unless there was a way off the property other than from the front. The water?

'Two black BMW X5s arriving now,' came the voice from one of the agents on the surveillance team.

Chan sat up in her chair, paying full attention. She'd never seen the property, but she had an image in her head based on what the agents had relayed. There was already a BMW 7 series and a Range Rover parked up in front of the house. That was four vehicles now. How many people were inside?

'Did you get eyes on the occupants?' Hobbs asked.

'Not properly. Two men in the front of each. Back windows tinted. They've parked now. People getting out but we don't have a full view.'

A groan from Hobbs. The surveillance team were necessarily inconspicuous, and that meant they'd had to limit their view of the sprawling house and grounds somewhat and focus on having a clear view of the electronic gates at the front of the property, to see the comings and goings.

The agents relayed the licence plates of each of the newly arrived BMWs.

'I'll check on it straight away,' Trapp said.

A few minutes of silence.

'Tell me what's happening?' Hobbs said.

No response.

'Do you read?'

'People coming out of the house now.'

'How many?'

'Five, six, seven.'

'Echo?' The code name for Doherty.

'Can't say for sure. They're huddling together, trying to cover themselves.'

Did they already know about the surveillance team?

'I've got the licence plates' results,' Trapp said. 'Neither belongs to a BMW X5.'

'Great,' Hobbs said. 'If nothing else we'll bust them for illegal plates then.'

Chan rolled her eyes, as she imagined Hobbs was doing.

'Okay, this is it. I think they're about to leave.'

'Have you seen Echo yet?' Hobbs said. 'Make sure you know which car he's in.'

'It's hard to make out. We can only see the passenger sides of the X5s. We couldn't see who got into the other two cars at all.'

'For Christ's sake. Just figure it out,' Hobbs said, clearly losing patience.

Silence again. Chan held her breath.

'Okay, the cars are all coming out now. We haven't seen Echo. Do you want us to follow?'

'Keep looking as they go past. We need to make sure Echo's there.'

'We haven't had eyes on Echo at all. All the cars are past us now. What do you want us to do?'

'Jesus Christ. Follow! But one of you get out and keep watch on the house.'

Silence.

'Did you hear me?'

'Roger. Understood.'

Chan heard the engine rev as the remaining agent sought to catch up.

'Okay, I'm en route now,' came the driver's voice. Then not a minute later: 'Crap. They're splitting up. What do I do now?'

Silence from Hobbs and Chan and Trapp.

'I said—'

'I heard what you said,' Hobbs interrupted. 'What directions are they headed in?'

'One onto the four ninety-five, the other Northern State Parkway. You need to be quick.'

'Four ninety-five,' Hobbs said.

'Roger that.'

Chan sighed. It was the same call she'd have made. The I-495 was the main route out of Long Island. It was the most obvious choice to make if they were headed across the city and out to New Jersey. But the fact the cars had split up was worrying. Where were the other two cars going?

'Can we get helicopter support on the others?' Chan asked.

Nobody responded for a few seconds. She checked her comms. Her question had definitely gone through.

'No,' Hobbs said. 'I'm not going to risk spooking them.'

Chan wanted to argue with that. They already had a car following the other two vehicles, so what was the difference really? Unfortunately, Hobbs was calling the shots.

For the next hour Chan listened without saying another word as the FBI agent stealthily followed the BMW 7 series and the X5, accompanying it across New York and into New Jersey. The fact the cars were still headed in the right direction had to be a good thing, but she remained concerned about where the other two cars had gone. If Doherty was in the latter, what did that mean for their sting?

'Where are you now?' Hobbs asked.

'I'm on the eighty. Not long past Roxbury Township.'

Chan scanned the map image on the computer screen in front of her. They were getting close. Less than twenty-five miles away and heading directly for them.

'Wait, damn it, they've just pulled a U-turn!'

'Then do the same!' Hobbs shouted. 'Keep on them.'

'I can't. I was already past the divider. They've gone past me, headed back in the other direction... I don't think they saw me, but...'

Chan had to pull the headset away from her ear for a few seconds as Hobbs launched into a deafening tirade.

'Wait. It's okay, I've turned too... but I-I can't see them. They must have turned off. I'm going over a hundred but they're nowhere.'

Chan only caught the start of Hobb's next tirade because her phone scuttled across the worktop in front of her with an incoming call. She looked at the screen. Recognised the number. She pulled off her headset, picked the phone up and looked around the van at the two analysts with her in the back. Neither was paying her any attention.

'What do you want?' she said, holding the receiver close to her mouth.

'Where are you?' Ryker said.

'I can't tell you that.'

'Are you alone?'

'Not exactly.'

'You've made a mistake. *We* made a mistake.'

'What mistake?'

'You said you're going after Doherty tonight?'

Chan sighed. She couldn't be having this conversation with Ryker now. 'Yes. We are.'

'I think it's a set-up. He's got someone on the inside at the FBI. He's been playing you the whole time.'

'What are you talking about?'

'Trust me. There's nothing going down wherever you are. I think I know what Doherty wants. It's…'

Ryker didn't finish the sentence. Or maybe he did. Chan looked at her phone. The call had gone. No signal.

'Fuck's sake,' Chan said, waving it about the place.

Then she heard Hobbs's voice and she pulled the headset back over her ear.

'Okay, we've had some drama, but this is it. They're coming from the north, not south. The comms vehicle in the north – I need you to wait for the targets to pass then follow on from a distance. Don't engage, just hold tight. We need cover that side… They'll reach the runway in under five minutes.'

Chan looked around the van. The energy levels all of a sudden ramped up several notches. Most of it was nerves. She could understand why. They were being put right in the firing line. She looked at her phone again, Ryker's words still bouncing in her mind. No signal. She couldn't do anything about that now.

Three minutes later the van's engine grumbled to life and Chan bounced this way and that as they pulled out into the pothole-ridden road.

The blacked-out windows together with the now dark night sky meant Chan could see nothing of the outside. She knew, though, that as well as the vehicles stationed strategically around the airstrip, there were twelve armed SWAT members on foot, hiding in the long grass that lined the runway on either side. Each of the men carried either an MP5 submachine gun or an M4 carbine. There were another twelve SWAT members inside the vehicles, not to mention the various plain-clothed agents here, there and everywhere, Chan included. Though she wasn't quite plain-clothed tonight. She had a thick Kevlar vest on, with 'FBI' emblazoned on it in bold yellow writing. Just in case.

The van pulled to a stop again.

'Wait for my command,' came Hobbs's voice. 'Targets are in sight. Waiting for the payload.'

'No visual on the bird yet,' came an unfamiliar voice. 'We remain black.'

Which Chan took to mean that the airstrip lights, running along each side of the runway to guide aircraft in, were currently all off. She'd never flown a plane but she certainly wouldn't fancy trying to land one not being able to see the tarmac.

The airstrip definitely was still in use though. According to official flight records, only about half a dozen recorded flights had landed there in the last year. From the satellite shots she'd seen there was a single small hangar and what looked like an even smaller control centre which wasn't much more than a pre-fabricated shed. From the outside, it didn't look as though it could fit more than one person at a time.

'Okay, three people are out of the cars,' came another male voice. 'They don't appear to be carrying anything.'

'Is it Echo?' Hobbs asked.

'No. Another man is heading to the control room... He's inside.' There was a few seconds' pause. 'Okay, the lights are on. We're close.'

Chan could now see the foggy glow of the airstrip through her window. They sat in silence for a few more seconds.

'We have a visual on the bird. Approaching now.'

'What about Echo?' Chan asked. No response. Ryker's words still rattled in her head. This didn't feel like a set-up, what with the cars and the plane approaching, yet Ryker had found something...

She looked at her phone again. No signal still.

Outside Chan could hear the engines of the small prop plane making its approach. The sound made her insides vibrate. She was about to ask the same question again, then...

'Five, four, three, two, one... Bird has landed... Taxiing now.'

Chan's heart thudded in her chest. She couldn't stay cooped up. She needed to see this.

She got up from her chair and carefully opened the back doors of the van. Facing away from the airstrip, still more than a hundred yards away, she crouched low and moved around the side of the van, her body pressed up against the metal.

She pulled night vision binoculars to her eyes. Focused. Saw the plane. Scanned across to the waiting figures. Looked over each of them. No, Doherty definitely wasn't there.

'Still just the three men we can see,' the voice in her ear said. 'Make that four. The other one is out of the control room now. There's the pilot and at least one male passenger on the plane... waiting for the steps to be lowered. Advise?'

Silence from Hobbs. What was he waiting for? Chan watched as a door on the side of the plane opened and the steps swung downward to the ground below.

'They're coming out now... Wait, what is this?'

Chan was thinking the same thing when she spotted the woman on the top step, followed directly after by a young girl with flowing hair.

'We have a–'

'I can fucking see what we have,' Hobbs blasted.

'Advise?'

'Hold.'

'They're getting into the 7 series. What do you want us to do?'

'Just keep watching!'

'Okay, a male passenger is coming out now too. He's got two large holdalls. This must be it... another man behind. Carrying the same.'

'Hold,' Hobbs said. 'We need to see Echo. We need an exchange.'

'They're getting into the cars. There is no exchange. Steps are closing. This is done.'

'Shit,' Hobbs said. 'Take them down. Go now!'

In an instant bright white spot lights blared. Chan had to tear the night vision binoculars from her eyes. The sound of shouting and guzzling diesel engines filled the air. Within seconds there were vehicles and more than a dozen armed SWAT members out in the open, closing in with weapons trained on the startled party. No one made any attempt to fight back or to escape.

Chan watched it all from a distance as the SWAT team quickly closed in. Rounded up all of the people on the ground, except for the little girl who was taken off to the side, crying and screaming.

A few moments later: 'Hobbs, you need to come see this.'

Chan wanted to see it too. She jogged over. As she approached she spotted Hobbs remonstrating with one of the SWAT guys. Trapp was there too, arms folded, not talking to anyone. The SWAT team had all four of Doherty's men, plus the men from the plane, lying face down on the ground, cable ties securing their wrists. Only the woman and the girl remained on their feet. The woman, hands secured behind her back, had a vicious snarl on her face and was shouting abuse in Hobbs's direction.

Chan went up to him.

'What's going on?' she asked.

'Doherty's not here,' Hobbs said. She could tell he was as angry as he was embarrassed.

'The other two cars…' Chan said, as much a thought to herself as anything else.

Hobbs glared at her. 'The woman claims she's Mrs Doherty. The girl is her daughter.'

Chan slumped. Ryker's words echoed again. Someone within the FBI was working with Doherty. Was that how he'd fooled them?

She couldn't let that out yet. The risk of tipping off was too big. But she did need to speak to Ryker. Urgently.

'What about the bags?' she asked.

'Clothes. No drugs, no weapons. None of the men are even armed.'

Chan said nothing. Hobbs growled and turned around to face the woman.

'What are you doing here?' he snapped.

'The hell is it to you?'

'Where's your husband?'

'Not here,' she said, a wicked smile on her face.

Hobbs turned back to his men. 'Search them all. Check the flight records. They can't have come from Ireland in that thing.

Take apart the vehicles and the plane. If there's anything there at all, bring the lot of them in.'

'Yes, sir,' the agent said.

'Are those your cars, Mrs Doherty?' Hobbs said, pointing to the X5 and 7 series.

'So what if they are?'

'Just tell me. Are they yours?'

'Yeah.'

'Then you're coming with us. The plates on that vehicle are fake,' Hobbs said, smiling as he pointed at the X5.

'You bastard! You'll pay for that!' she screamed, but Hobbs was already walking away.

Chan looked at her phone again. Still no signal. She needed to get back in touch with Ryker. And McKinley, who would likely be even more furious than Hobbs. Shaun Doherty had set the FBI up. Had set up the whole fake drug deal. Was his wife a knowing accomplice or just bait? Either way, the biggest question was why. And where the hell was he?

Chapter forty-nine

After the failed call to Chan, Ryker had tried calling back several times but with no luck. It was down to him to stop whatever Doherty had planned. First Doherty had gone to a lot of trouble to set up Charlie Ward, and now he'd faked a drug deal. What if the two were linked? Perhaps Ward, as an informant for the FBI, was supposed to feed the lies about the fake drug deal, believing he was getting one over on Doherty. Until Ward had been killed, that was.

Ryker remembered what Campbell had told him about Doherty trying to get in on Green's patch. To do that there was one very important thing he needed: a drugs supply. It made sense to Ryker, and clearly to the FBI, that Doherty was therefore in the market for a big purchase. Except he'd duped the FBI. So what was his plan?

Then Ryker got it. Kill two birds with one stone. Doherty needed drugs. But he was also in a war with Green. Doherty had been surprisingly quiet in that war so far. The next move – the big move – was Doherty's.

There was only one place that would satisfy both of the Irishman's needs.

Ryker started up the engine and headed south toward the Lincoln Tunnel, the Port Newark–Elizabeth Marine Terminal his next stop.

***

With the time past 10pm, there was little traffic and Ryker soon arrived at the docks for the second time in as many days. He switched his headlights off and headed down the road where

Green's warehouse was located and slowly drove past the entrance, surveying the area.

Everything looked quiet. There was a lone security guard in his hut. The security barrier was down. Two floodlights in the warehouse grounds were on, though they acted more like spotlights and much of the area around the warehouse was in darkness. The warehouse doors were closed, and Ryker couldn't see any men outside, but he presumed there would be 24/7 security on the inside, given the precious nature of the warehouse's contents.

No sign of Green, nor of Doherty or his men yet.

Ryker carried on and drove into a dark spot on a deserted side road. He pulled the car over, got out and took a look around at the nearby buildings. He wanted to get up high to properly survey the area. There were plenty of choices nearby, and most of the buildings appeared derelict. One, a hundred yards away, would have a perfect view over the whole area, he decided.

He headed on through the darkness and walked through one of several gaping holes in the mesh fence around the perimeter of the building, its days of being a useful security measure long gone. The brick building beyond was in a similar state of disrepair. About four storeys tall, it had what looked like a factory, or warehouse area, connected to it at the far end. The top of the brick structure had a flat roof, and that was Ryker's destination.

The doors and windows to the building were boarded up, and Ryker was standing contemplating how he would get in when he realised the boards on the main door were no longer affixed. He went over and moved the boards aside. Shining his pocket torch into the pitch-black interior, he saw no obvious signs that anyone had been there recently, but he remained cautious and alert as he walked into the building.

He found a set of stairs. Walked quietly but quickly up to the roof. As he approached the exit door, he noticed it had been prised open. Given the small mound of wood chippings in a neat pile on the ground, it looked like it had been done recently.

He slowly moved forward and peered through the doorway. Spotted a man, lying flat on his chest, near the edge of the roof. The man had no clue of Ryker's presence. He had a camera with a telephoto lens next to him, and was holding a pair of binoculars up to his face. On the other side of him, on a bipod, lay a scoped Mauser M59 sniper rifle – an old model with a battered wooden stock.

Ryker's mind raced as he thought through who the man was. It was possible he was police or FBI, seeing as Ryker had previously given Chan the location of Green's warehouse. Except he'd rarely seen professional marksmen and snipers wearing casual clothing. And the man's aged kit – the gun was probably fifty years old – was hardly of the quality required for elite law enforcement.

Most likely this was Doherty's man.

As he took another half step forward, Ryker's foot slipped, making a scraping noise on the ground. Nothing more than a tiny pebble scratching the smooth surface. But enough to give Ryker away.

The man swivelled on his belly in a flash, a handgun held out, pointed at Ryker. Quick moves.

Ryker froze. Stared straight at the man.

'It's okay,' Ryker said, calmly lifting his hands up. 'Doherty sent me. Said you might need some help.'

The guy didn't look like he was buying it. But he also didn't react to Doherty's name. No rebuttal. So he was definitely part of Doherty's crew.

'What have you seen so far?' Ryker asked. 'Any sight of Green?'

'That's a good one,' the man said. 'But I call your bluff. Who are you?'

Ryker said nothing to that. He knew the only reason he wasn't already dead was because the guy couldn't afford to make too much noise. Not yet, before the party had started.

'Should have brought your silencer,' Ryker said, nodding to the barrel.

'Yeah, I suppose you're right.'

Ryker was ready for the man's next move. He dropped the gun and sprang to his feet, a serrated hunting knife now in his hand. Ryker had the Glock he'd pilfered the day before from Steinhauser in the waistband of his jeans, but likewise he couldn't risk firing it yet.

Instead, he whipped out his pocket knife and lunged forward.

The man thrust his larger blade toward Ryker's midriff. Ryker blocked the move and slashed his knife down across the man's wrist. He yelped and took a half step back. Glanced down. The blow had cut a large hole in his shirt sleeve and a dark patch was spreading out across the torn fabric.

He looked up, snarling, and lurched forward a second time. Ryker blocked the arcing blow, pivoted, and drove his blade down into the base of the man's neck. He collapsed onto his knees, shuddering, Ryker guessed, as the nerves at the top of his spine erupted.

Ryker yanked the blade out and the man fell flat on his face. His body quivered for a few more seconds then went still. Ryker would have subdued rather than killed the guy if he could, but it was the guy's choice to have fought.

Ryker kicked the knife out of the dead man's hand. Just to be sure. Then he moved to the edge of the roof and peered over. No indication that the rooftop ruckus had alerted anyone down below. The guard remained in his hut. No one else was in sight.

He spent a couple of minutes going through the dead man's possessions. No ID of any kind, no bank card. A little over a hundred dollars in cash plus a high-end mobile phone, a small laptop, a radio set and a pair of night vision goggles.

Ryker went for the phone, interested to see who had been calling and messaging. He needed a thumbprint to unlock it. He was in luck. He moved over to the dead man, lifted up his hand and was soon inside the phone.

Several calls sent and received to the same number. Ryker hit the green button. The call was answered on the third ring. A lot of background noise. Someone driving?

'What have you got?'

An Irish accent. It was surely Doherty.

'Peterson? Are you there? I'm five minutes away.'

Ryker hung up. Looked at his watch. His own phone vibrated in his pocket. Chan.

'He set us up, Ryker.'

Given the background noise he guessed she was driving too.

'I was trying to tell you. There was no deal, was there?'

'No. He's making fools out of us all. What the hell is Doherty doing?'

'I think I know. Where are you?'

'Heading back to the city. You?'

Ryker heard the cars before he saw them. He turned to look over the rooftop and spotted two vehicles approaching. They were moving fast. Ryker threw himself down. Lay flat on his stomach, out of sight.

'Ryker? Are you there?'

'I'm at Green's warehouse. You'd better send an armed response team here pronto. Doherty's here.'

'Ryker, what the hell? Don't you dare get involved!'

'You need to find your mole. Someone set Charlie Ward up.'

Ryker ended the call. Put his phone away and looked over the edge back to Green's warehouse. The two cars sped past where he was, then slowed as they approached the gates. Ryker grabbed the binoculars. Focused on the security guard in his hut, casually reading a magazine.

'Look up, you idiot.'

He did. But by then the cars were only a few yards away. Before the guard even got up from his seat, the front vehicle careened past, rocking on its suspension as it hit a pothole, before smashing its way through the security barrier.

The guard was on his feet immediately. Reached under his desk. Pulled out a shotgun. He took a step outside, but before he could do a thing, the second vehicle rolled past, a gun barrel protruding from the back window. Multiple holes opened up in his uniform as bullets tore through him.

The whole thing, from the first vehicle approaching to the guard's demise, was over in a matter of seconds.

Ryker was on his feet and rushing for the stairs before the security guard's body hit the ground.

Chapter fifty

Ryker was out of the building and running for his car. Although the warehouse was only a short distance away, speed was of the essence, and he didn't want to waste a second. Once inside he accelerated to the end of the road, nearly losing control of the car as he turned sharply around the corner. As the warehouse came into view, he saw the two vehicles that had arrived moments earlier now parked in front of the large warehouse doors. Ryker thumped the brake to stop his car just outside the gates. Moments later he was running past the fallen guard.

He slowed his pace as he approached Doherty's vehicles. Stepped behind a skip to survey the area from cover.

Both vehicles in front of him were parked with their rears toward the warehouse. Ryker could make out a man in the driver's seat of the Range Rover. The other car was a BMW X5, but he could see no one behind the glass.

Two men came out of the warehouse, each carrying two large cardboard boxes, which they loaded into the boot of the Range Rover. Both men had large semi-automatic weapons on straps around their necks. They went back inside. Moments later two other men came out, again with boxes.

Green's drugs. But where was Green?

Ryker slunk around to the other side of the skip, where he had a better view through the open warehouse doors. He spotted two bodies on the ground inside, right by the entrance. From the light shining on the bodies, Ryker could see the numerous bullet holes in their torsos, and the large pool of blood forming underneath each man.

Ryker didn't know how many of Doherty's men were inside, but including the driver still in the car he'd counted five faces so far. Doherty was there somewhere too, so that was at least six. Ryker was vastly outnumbered, but he wasn't going to sit and wait for the police or the Feds to arrive and risk Doherty getting away.

After the next set of boxes was loaded, Ryker edged forward to the cars, keeping low. He got to within five yards. The driver hadn't spotted him. Ryker darted forward. Only when he grabbed the door handle did the guy realise Ryker was there.

Ryker flung open the door, wrenched the driver out and smashed the Glock into his head three times. The man slumped. Ryker eased him to the ground. He was going nowhere fast.

Crouched low, Ryker moved forward and reached the rear bumper of the Range Rover. He peered around the corner to see if any of the others had been alerted by him taking out the driver. He waited for almost a minute, counting the seconds.

No one came outside. Either they hadn't heard, or they were forming an ambush on the inside.

Ryker moved from his position and pressed himself up against the warehouse wall, about two yards from the open loading doors. He took a deep breath then slowly crept along and poked his head around.

Inside the warehouse four men were going through boxes by the shelving area, opening them up and discarding whatever they didn't want. From where he was, Ryker could only see about half of the space, but as he scanned, he spotted who he was looking for. Doherty and another man, Victor, were standing over two others who were on chairs, their hands tied behind their backs. The captives were wearing nothing but their underwear and were badly beaten, their faces and bodies covered in blood. They were facing Ryker, and he thought one saw him looking in. Ryker quickly moved his head back out of view.

Doherty shouted loud enough for Ryker to hear: 'Last chance. What's the code?!'

The code. Ryker had seen the open hatch for the basement beside Doherty. Doherty was there not just for the drugs, but for Green's secret stash of money and guns. He wanted to ruin Green. But how did he even know about what was down there?

The mole at the FBI, of course. Campbell's intel had been passed right through.

Ryker looked again. The men on their knees pleaded. Doherty nodded to Victor who stepped forward. Hammer in hand. He kneeled down by the man on the left. Swung the hammer up… then down onto the man's bare foot. The scream from the man was blood-curdling as the bones in his foot shattered. He writhed on the chair. Moaned and pleaded.

Victor looked to his master, who nodded again. Another hammer strike. Then another. And another. All to the same foot. The man's eyes rolled as spittle dribbled from his mouth. He was clearly delirious with pain. Even from where he was, Ryker could see the foot was nothing more than a mess of mangled flesh and bone fragments – an unrecognisable mush.

He couldn't stand there and wait any longer. But he had to be sure before he made a move…

'The code,' Doherty said, moving to the second man. 'Or it's you next.'

The moans of the first man died down. Was he unconscious? There were a few moments of serene silence. Then Doherty pulled out a handgun, casually took aim and fired. The bullet caught the first man in the head.

Ryker flinched. He stepped back into cover. Readied himself. His body jerked, as he was about to fly into action, but just then two of the men from the shelving area stepped out, each carrying a box. Ryker sprang a step further back, his heart jumping from the surprise. In the darkness the men hadn't yet seen him. They moved toward the X5, chatting away about something. They would surely spot Ryker the moment they turned to go back into the warehouse.

Ryker had a split-second decision to make.

The men finished loading the boxes. As the first one turned to head back to the warehouse, he seemed to catch a glimpse of Ryker out of the corner of his eye. His head turned sharply, surprise plastered on his face. The other man turned too...

The men never had a chance to react anymore than that. Ryker lifted the Glock and fired two shots. Two shots, both to the chest. Both collapsed to the ground.

But now Ryker's cover was blown. There was frenzied shouting from inside. Ryker hugged the warehouse wall. Gunfire rattled and holes opened up in the metal sheet wall, inches from where he was standing. He dove to the ground and scuttled across the tarmac. A moment later bullets were pinging against the ground around him and Ryker flung himself forward and rolled behind one of the shipping containers at the side of the warehouse.

The gunfire stopped. That was when Ryker heard the faint sound of police sirens. No more than a few minutes away. The shouting started again.

Ryker glanced around the corner. A bullet ricocheted right next to his face, but the momentary glance was enough for him to see two more men outside looking for him. One in front, who'd fired, and one heading around the side to try and outflank Ryker. Not a bad move, if a little predictable. And Ryker wasn't going to sit and wait for them to corner him.

He dove out into the open, firing two shots as he hurtled through the air. One hit, the other didn't, but it was enough to send the man in front of him to the ground, screaming in agony. Ryker sprang to his feet and rushed forward. Fired off three more rounds on the move. The first missed the second man, who was now hunkered behind the cars, but the next two hit as the guy momentarily bobbed up.

Ryker reached the first man. Stomped on his face to put him out of the fight. Wrestled the M16 from him and stuffed the Glock into his waistband again. He dashed back to the warehouse doors and was a couple of yards away when from nowhere something clattered into the back of his head.

Ryker skidded into a heap on the ground, dazed.

In his haste, he'd made a big mistake. He'd not spotted the third man outside at all.

'Get up,' he heard a gruff voice say.

Groggily Ryker pulled himself to his feet. Didn't need to look to know there was a rifle barrel inches from his head, a looming figure behind it.

Victor prodded Ryker forward until he was at the entrance, looking in. Doherty was standing in front of Ryker, gun in hand. Ryker's eyes flicked to the men on the chairs. Both now dead. Doherty saw where Ryker was looking and turned to them, smiling at his own handiwork.

'Yeah, shame about them. That's your fault really isn't it? I was going to let the second guy live if he gave me what I needed. Then you showed up.'

Ryker said nothing.

'You won't be so lucky. No quick death for you. You've cost me good men tonight.'

Victor took a step closer and snatched the M16 from Ryker's grip, then the Glock from his trousers.

With two guns trained on him, Ryker was in a seriously bad position. He wasn't sure how he was going to get out. He just had to hope either Victor or Doherty made a mistake.

People always did eventually.

Outside the sirens were getting louder by the second. Perhaps that would be his chance. Doherty couldn't take his time now.

Ryker looked over to the basement hatch. The inner door was still shut tight. Doherty had failed to get inside.

'I know the code,' Ryker said.

Ryker's words stumped Doherty for a second. That was good. Any delay now was good.

'Let me go and I'll give it to you.'

'How about we get the hammer out again instead?'

Go ahead, Ryker thought. The police would be there any minute.

'Bring him with us,' Doherty said to Victor. 'I'm not finished with him. Not until I know what him and that tosser Campbell have been up to.'

Ryker tried to show no reaction to that. What did Doherty know about him and Campbell? That wasn't good. It made Campbell's position all the more precarious.

Victor took a step forward. Lifted his gun to take another swipe at Ryker, trying to catch his temple with the butt.

And there was the mistake. Another predictable move. With Doherty already moving to the outside, putting his gun back into his waistband, Ryker had a chance.

At the last moment, with the butt of the rifle arcing toward his head, Ryker ducked and sprang sideways. With his right arm outstretched, he caught Victor around the neck. Sent him to the ground, like a viciously bad tackle in a game of American football. Ryker's body slammed down on top, knocking the wind from Victor. The crack Ryker heard told him he'd likely broken a rib or two of Victor's in the process. Before the big man could muster a response, Ryker hurled his head down. The contact was solid. Victor's eyes rolled.

Ryker got to his feet and turned… but Doherty was on him and caught him with a fist to the jaw. He didn't look much, but Doherty moved quickly, knew how to throw a punch. A pastime of boxing or similar. Doherty followed up with a flurry of fists to Ryker's stomach and sides. Ryker doubled over. Stumbled a step back to give himself space and the seconds he needed to recover.

Screeching tyres outside. The first of the police cars had arrived. Which explained why, when Ryker looked up, ready to counter and put Doherty down, the Irishman was already three yards away, sprinting for the X5.

Ryker gave chase. As Doherty reached the car, he opened the door, then turned back in Ryker's direction. Fired one shot from his handgun. Ryker threw himself to the ground. The hasty shot went wayward. Doherty didn't have time for another. He jumped in the car and the X5's engine growled as the beast shot toward the smashed security barrier.

On the road, two police officers were out of their car, and when the X5 lurched toward them they hunkered down, one behind the security hut, one behind the patrol car. They both had their guns drawn, and both opened fire on the X5. It made no difference.

Ryker darted to the Range Rover and jumped into the driver's seat. Started the engine and, not heeding the policemen's warnings, headed after Doherty.

As with the X5, the police could do nothing to stop the Range Rover bursting out of the warehouse grounds. Both officers fired their weapons but to no avail.

Out on the open road, Ryker was only five seconds behind Doherty. As he raced down the road in pursuit, three other police cars came hurtling around the corner toward the two fleeing vehicles. The police couldn't react quickly enough to block their paths. After passing them, Ryker glanced in his rear-view mirror. Saw the cars pull U-turns. They wouldn't be far behind.

Ryker was gaining on Doherty, but then at the next junction Doherty veered left, before taking a hard right, momentarily flummoxing Ryker, and allowing Doherty to pull ahead slightly.

At least the road, in the heavily industrialised area, was relatively quiet, meaning Ryker could push the car as much as possible. But he knew that within a couple of minutes they would be on busier streets. Not only would the tightly clustered roads give Doherty a better chance of escape, but the risk of collateral damage would increase hugely too.

Ryker made a snap decision. As Doherty slowed to take the next corner, Ryker kept his foot hard on the accelerator. Doherty was making to turn left, but as he did so, Ryker continued straight ahead. The Range Rover bulldozed into the side of the X5.

On impact Ryker shot forward in his seat. His face smashed into the deployed airbag. His belt locked, causing his head to spring back. Shards of broken glass and plastic filled the air.

For a few seconds the bulky Range Rover, front end mangled and wedged into the side of the BMW, carried on its path, sweeping the X5 with it. Both cars came to a sudden stop when the BMW crunched into a brick wall, sending another searing jolt through Ryker.

Steam rose from the crumpled front end of the Range Rover. Blood poured into Ryker's eyes, blurring his vision. The manoeuvre had been a risk. It had only partly paid off. Ryker had managed to stop Doherty. But at what cost?

Trying to move, but unable to, his legs wedged in the footwell, Ryker heard the sound of the fast approaching police cars. He tried to keep his eyes open. Tried to move his limbs. He couldn't manage either. Seconds later, his eyes closed and he was out.

Chapter fifty-one

When Chan arrived on the scene not long after, the ambulances had already left, James Ryker in the back of one, unconscious but handcuffed and with a police escort. Apparently. Chan would follow up with him as soon as she could. She needed to figure out what he knew about Doherty's plans, and who was compromised within the FBI, but she also had to help him out. Get him away from the clutches of the police. She needed him still. But first things first.

'What happened?' Chan asked, heading over to Officer Harnett of the Port Authority Police, whom she'd been told was in charge. Until the FBI had turned up, that was.

'We got multiple fatalities two miles from here at the premises of J.B. Reynolds & Son. Some kinda armed robbery. These two vehicles escaped the scene.'

'You were in pursuit?'

'My officers were. Said the Range Rover lost it and crashed into the Beemer. One dead in the first car. One got away.'

Chan shook her head in disbelief. Doherty. The one that got away. How was that even possible?

'He ran on foot?'

'We didn't have the chopper out in time. We've no clue where he's at.'

Which basically equated to a complete clusterfuck.

'Thanks,' Chan said, not really feeling grateful at all. 'My colleagues will debrief you before you leave the scene.'

Chan headed back to her car. She didn't know whether to go and survey the carnage at the warehouse or not. Was there any point?

She took out her phone. Saw McKinley had called her three times in the ten minutes she'd been on the scene. She called him back.

'Any news on Doherty?' he asked.

'No, sir.'

A sigh. 'Do you know which hospital they're taking the prisoner to?'

'Not yet,' Chan lied. And she also hadn't told McKinley that James Ryker was 'the prisoner'. As far as anyone else knew he was just one of Doherty's crew trying to escape with the others. She wanted to speak to Ryker before anyone else did.

'Well find out,' McKinley said. 'We need to get him into our hands as soon as we can, whoever the hell he is. And we need to find Doherty.'

'I know. I'm on it. Any news on the missus?'

'It stacks up. They really are Doherty's wife and daughter. Arrived in Chicago this morning from Ireland. Paperwork all in place and everything. We got nothing on them. Not even the damn licence plates as the cars aren't in the wife's name.'

'We were played,' Chan said.

'We were.'

And Chan had a good idea by who.

'Where's Trapp?' Chan asked.

'Trapp? Last I heard he was heading back to New York.'

'Doherty set up the fake deal, but who gave you the intel?'

Silence.

'We have to get eyes on him,' Chan said.

'You can't seriously be saying Trapp is—'

'I don't know yet. But I suggest we get eyes on him until we figure this out.'

'Well figure it out quickly. Doherty's laughing at us.'

'He won't be for long. Trust me.'

Chan ended the call. Made another.

'Maloney, any news on Green and Campbell?'

Doherty was on the run, and given his obvious thirst for revenge against Green, it wasn't unthinkable that Green himself was the next target, or someone close to him. The FBI was surveilling Green's wife, and Campbell and Kate, but Green himself hadn't been seen all day. Was he dead or in Doherty's hands already?

'Not a lot happening,' Maloney said. 'Campbell and Kate have headed out. They're at some swanky restaurant in Midtown. Anderson tailed them there.'

Chan sighed. It wasn't ideal that Campbell had left home, but that all sounded low-key enough. Campbell clearly had no clue about the carnage if he was out wining and dining, and Doherty surely wouldn't start something in a restaurant in Midtown, would he?

'And still nothing on Green?' she asked.

'Not a peep. Green's wife hasn't left the house in hours. Still no sign of him.'

'Does Green even know what's happened at his warehouse?' Chan said, more to herself than to Maloney.

'I have no idea.'

She sighed, her brain whirring. 'Just let me know if anything happens. Anything at all.'

'Of course.'

Chan ended the call. Thought again about whether to go to the warehouse or not.

Not. There was somewhere else she needed to be. If anyone could help pull the pieces of the mess together, then it was James Ryker.

Chapter fifty-two

Campbell was feeling quite refreshed from his day at home. Apart from Green's morning visit, it'd been a day away from *that* life. So come the evening, he and Kate were heading out for dinner at a new fine dining restaurant in Midtown he'd been meaning to take her to for weeks. For some reason she'd insisted on driving Campbell's car. Fine by him. A few drinks were exactly what he needed to help him relax further.

'You know I think we're being followed,' Kate said, glancing into the rear-view mirror as she drove them there.

Campbell groaned. That was the last thing they needed. He looked into his side mirror.

'That maroon car, about three back. It was parked outside the apartment this morning with a man in it. And it was there again when I got home tonight, the same man still inside. Now it's behind us.'

'How do you know it's not just a coincidence? It could be a neighbour,' Campbell said, but he didn't really believe that. It was the FBI, no doubt. But why now?

Campbell kept his eyes on the mirror. When they turned the next corner he got a glimpse of the driver. He'd half expected it to be Chan, or Ryker. It was neither.

'Scott, why would someone be following us?' Kate asked, her tone more stern now.

'I've no idea,' Campbell said.

'What are you not telling me?' she said, flashing a steely glare at him.

What a question to ask, Campbell thought. Where would he even start to answer that? There was so much he wasn't telling her, about her dad, Doherty, Ryker, Chan. 'It's probably the FBI. They're just keeping tabs on us.'

He chastised himself. Why the hell had he said that!

'What? The FBI? Why?'

'Just forget it, okay? Let's enjoy the night.'

'That's not good enough, Scott! What have you done?'

'Look. It's hard to explain. There's some bad blood between your dad and this guy Shaun Doherty. I think it's the Feds following us, but they're just there to keep us safe more than anything.'

'I knew you weren't telling me something. What's going on between Shaun Doherty and my dad?'

'I really don't know. Let's just forget about all that for tonight. Please?'

She huffed. He guessed that was an okay response under the circumstances.

'Fine. We'll enjoy tonight.' He could see she was upset but trying not to show it. 'After tonight, though, I want you to talk to me. Properly. I know I said I didn't want to know about what you do for my dad, but I can't live like this. You're my fiancé. We shouldn't keep secrets any longer.'

She paused. Campbell looked out of his window. Then back to the mirror. The car was still there.

'Scott, please. Promise you'll tell me everything?'

She looked at him again. Her eyes drew him in, making his heart flutter. It was a look he had fallen in love with. But he was torn about what she was asking. While in many ways he wanted to tell her everything, what if it shattered whatever image she had of her father and fiancé? Her father the murderer? Her fiancé the rat? Could she ever get over that?

And what if Green found out?

Yet Campbell would have to tell her *something*, and he wouldn't lie. The question was whether it really would be everything or not.

'I promise,' Campbell said, taking hold of Kate's hand. 'After tonight, I'll tell you everything.'

When they arrived at the restaurant, the maître d' seated them at a table by the window. They both opted for the tasting menu, much to the delight of the waiter, dollar signs flashing in his eyes at the thought of the impending generous tip. Campbell also decided to go for the rather overpriced wine pairing. As the waiter was leaving, Kate ordered each of them a glass of champagne too. Campbell looked at his fiancée, puzzled.

'I didn't know we were celebrating,' he said, smiling.

'Well, we are in a way,' Kate said. 'I know things haven't been great between us recently, but I want us to use tonight as a turning point. Uncle Charlie dying made me think about things a lot. You never know when something bad like that might happen. We need to make the most of every moment.'

The waiter came over with their champagne. They clinked glasses and took a swig.

'I love you, Scott Campbell, and I'm going to marry you and spend the rest of my life with you. I want us to move on from everything that's happened recently and just be happy again.'

'That's exactly what I want too.'

***

Two hours passed by in a blur. Campbell couldn't remember the last time he'd felt so relaxed and… happy. Kate too seemed far more like her old self. The woman he'd fallen in love with back in London. If they'd just stayed there, what would their lives be like now?

After paying in cash they headed outside, arm in arm. They got into the car and Kate was about to pull out when she stopped. She leaned over and kissed Campbell softly on the neck. The sensation caused a tingling through his body.

'Just bloody well drive,' he said. 'I need to get you back before the feeling of that kiss wears off.'

She hit his leg playfully and pulled into the road.

Yet despite the happiness in the restaurant, tension slowly built again as they carried on the journey. Kate was nervy. Looking in her mirrors every other second.

'Is it still there?' Campbell asked, looking into his own mirror.

'No. That's the thing. Where's he gone?'

They pulled up to their apartment building, but their progress was halted by another car parked up in front of the electronic gates that led to the underground car park.

'What are they doing?' Campbell said after a few seconds of no movement.

'Probably forgotten their fob,' Kate said, rolling her eyes. She took theirs from the cup holder and pressed the button and the gates slowly opened. Still the car in front didn't make any attempt to move forward into the car park. Kate honked the horn a couple of times. Nothing.

'What the hell is this guy doing? His lights aren't even on,' Campbell said.

'Is there even anyone in there?' Kate asked.

Campbell sighed. Opened his door. As he walked up to the car, he spotted the empty driver's seat through the closed window.

What idiot would just leave their car in front of the gates?

'We were wondering when you would show up,' an Irish-accented voice said from behind Campbell.

As Campbell spun around, he wasn't sure what came first: Kate's screaming, or the sweet, alcohol-scented rag that was forced in front of his face.

Either way, those were the last two things he remembered before he lost consciousness.

Chapter fifty-three

After leaving the crash scene Chan made her way into central Newark, heading for the University Hospital ER where she'd been told the ambulance was taking James Ryker. When she arrived at the gloomy-looking 1960s concrete monolith, the place was bustling, a hub of activity compared to the quiet night-time streets all around. She moved past the throngs into the ER reception area, walked to the front of the queue, much to the annoyance of the other people waiting, and showed her ID at the counter.

'I'm here for the guy the police brought in. From the marine terminal.'

'Up the stairs. Room 4B,' the frumpy woman said after checking her chart.

Chan looked to her right, saw the sign and was soon moving up the stairs to the next floor. She walked along the brightly lit, clinical corridor that was lined with closed doors. And deserted. She expected to see a police officer stationed somewhere, indicating Ryker's room, but there was no one in sight.

What she did see, when she turned a corner, was an empty chair at the far end of the corridor. She quickly moved toward it, looking at the numbered plaques on each of the doors. It quickly dawned on her which room the chair was outside. By the time she got there, she already had her gun in her hands.

She stopped outside the door. Looked up and down the corridor. She was all alone. She tried the handle of the door. Unlocked. She pushed it open.

The lights inside were off. She flicked them on. Her eyes fell to the man on the bed. Not James Ryker. But a uniformed police officer, his mouth taped over, his wrists and ankles cuffed to the bed frame. He glared at Chan. She dashed forward. Ripped the tape from the guy's mouth.

'Where is he?' she demanded.

'Who gives a… just get me off here!'

Chan's phone rang. She took it out. Half expected it to be Ryker calling. No. Maloney.

'What is it?' she snapped.

'Chan. You need to get over here. Now. It's Campbell. He's been taken.'

'You've gotta be…'

'Just get over here.'

She ended the call. Looked to the police officer. He was still glaring at her, as though him having failed miserably at his job was her fault.

'Well?' he said.

She didn't answer. Turned around and stormed out.

Chapter fifty-four

With his own car back by the crime scene at the warehouse, Ryker had had few options for travel when he'd snuck out of the hospital in Newark. He felt bad, but whoever owned the battered old Toyota Crown he'd stolen from a diner parking lot would just have to brave the night bus tonight.

He'd tried calling Campbell several times since escaping from the police. No answer. Then his phone danced on his lap. He saw who was calling.

'Where are you?' he said.

'Me? Where the hell are you?!' Chan shouted. 'Ryker, I told you not to do this. Not to go on the rampage. There're dead bodies everywhere. I–'

'Where's Doherty?'

Silence initially. 'I don't know.'

'That's the truth?'

'Yes.'

'Are Campbell and Green safe?'

'No one knows were Green is. Campbell…'

'Doherty got him?'

'Doherty. Green. Who knows? I've only just heard.'

Ryker thumped the steering wheel, then gripped it as tightly as he could as he channelled his anger and frustration.

'We have to find him,' he said through gritted teeth.

'Kate Green too.'

Ryker winced. If anyone was an innocent party in the whole mess, it was certainly her.

'Tell me where you're going,' Chan said. 'We need to meet. You said there's a mole in the FBI. I think I know who, but–'

'We need to find Campbell first.'

'Ryker, tell me! I have to know what I'm up against.'

'Charlie Ward was a set-up. There was no real dirt on him; it was bogus. It was Doherty behind the set-up.'

'That doesn't make any sense.'

'Of course it does. Doherty is taking over. But he's doing it from the inside out. Who ran Ward? Who gave you the intel for the drug deal? Most likely that's your mole.'

Silence.

'Chan? Do you know who it is?'

'Yes. But let's concentrate on Campbell. Where has Doherty taken him?'

'I've got an inkling.'

It all came down to Doherty's needs. He had to think through what Doherty would have done if Ryker hadn't showed up at the warehouse. Doherty needed somewhere to store the drugs. An equivalent place to Green's.

'Do you have a list of properties owned by Doherty?' he asked.

'We have a list of properties we *think* he owns. It's all tied up in shell companies, mostly offshore. You said so yourself.'

'Are there any in the Lower East Side?'

'I can't… I'd have to check. Is that where they're going?'

'Maybe. Doherty's crew know that area. It's where they suckered a young prostitute into duping Ward. Perhaps that means something.'

'What prostitute? Ryker, what are you talking about?'

'Just see if you can find out. We don't have much time.'

Ryker ended the call. He looked in his mirror then slammed on the brakes as he swerved the car to the side of the road. Up ahead was the entrance to the Lincoln Tunnel, beyond which the twinkling white and orange lights of the skyscrapers of Manhattan dominated the skyline over the water of the Hudson River.

Ryker navigated into the app on his phone that he'd previously set up to allow him to track Campbell's phone. The last time he'd checked, the tracker had shown Campbell was still near the Upper

West Side. Ryker had thought little of it. Had he and Kate already been snatched by that point? As Ryker looked now he saw the blinking red icon was still in Manhattan, slowly moving south, down 3rd Avenue toward the Lower East Side. It looked like his hunch was right.

After moving back onto the road, Ryker drove one-handed while he scrolled to Campbell's number. He hit 'call'.

Chapter fifty-five

Campbell came back to consciousness slowly. Not moving anything but his eyelids, it took him what felt like an age to remember what had happened, and to figure out where he was and what he was looking at.

His body jolted suddenly and his head and shoulder cracked off something hard, temporarily setting back his recovery. He fought through it. Soon felt clarity returning again.

'Kate,' he said, his voice croaky and not much more than a whisper. 'Babe, wake up.'

Lying on their sides, their bodies pushed up against each other, they were in near darkness, the only light a thin film of orange that marked the outline of the entrance to their confined space.

Another jerk, another jolt of pain. Putting together the roaring noise and the vibrations coursing through him, Campbell's foggy mind finally figured out where they were. The boot of a car.

He twisted and lifted his hands, which were wedged up by his chest. They were clasped together with plastic cable ties.

He extended his fingers and stroked Kate's cheek. 'Kate, wake up.'

Though did he really want her to wake to *this*?

He prodded her cheek more firmly. 'Kate?'

She groaned. Stirred. Opened her eyes.

'What's… happening? Where–'

'We'll be fine. I promise. Remember the FBI are out there. They'll help us.'

He wished he felt as confident as he sounded.

She didn't say anything more. Another jolt as the vehicle hit a pothole. Kate moaned in pain.

'My phone,' Campbell said. 'It's in my pocket. I can feel it. But I can't move my hands down there. Can you reach?'

He felt her fingers poking and prodding around his side.

'I can't,' she said, the distress in her voice clear.

'It's right there. You can get it.'

She cried out and writhed and he felt the phone slide up and out of his pocket. He smiled and laughed – the sense of relief for all of two seconds was almost overwhelming.

'Try to throw it up to me.'

She did so and the phone banged his upper arm and landed in the small crevice between them. He grasped it with his bound hands. Could only see part of the screen, but it was enough. He unlocked the phone with his thumbprint. Saw the list of missed calls from Ryker. One was only a minute before. He pushed the green button to call back. Tried to bring the phone to his ear but couldn't quite reach far enough.

'Campbell? Are you okay?' came Ryker's husky voice.

Campbell squeezed his eyes shut, trying to contain the hope that wanted to burst out of him.

'No. We're in a car. I don't know where we're going.'

'I do,' Ryker said. 'I'm following.'

Kate sobbed. She'd heard Ryker's words too.

But then the roar from outside died down. The rocking and jolting stopped too. A red light? Or had they already arrived?

'Ryker. Be quick. Please!'

A car door opening. Then another. Footsteps. Campbell braced himself. He was so helpless. When the boot lid opened and the bright white light blared into his eyes, screening the figures standing there, he wanted to shrink backward.

'You little bastard,' the man said. Not sounding alarmed or angry, but almost amused.

'Campbell, who is it? Who's there?' Ryker shouted.

'I don't know!'

'Tell me what you see. What you hear?'

Ryker sounded rushed. He knew what was coming.

Campbell's eyes darted about frantically. He could see nothing. What could he hear?

A gloved hand came toward Campbell. Snatched the phone from his grasp. Two other hands grabbed his body.

'Water!' he shouted. Was the call even still connected? 'A boat. I don't–'

A fist smashed into his jaw. Campbell didn't get another word out as he was wrenched from the car.

Chapter fifty-six

Back on New York soil, Chan's first stop was Campbell's apartment on the Upper West Side. Maloney was already there, in the back office of the on-site security team, sitting on a swivel chair and flicking back and forth through the security tapes.

'Anything?' Chan asked.

Maloney didn't look up from what he was doing.

'NYPD found Anderson in his car in Midtown. Shot twice.'

Chan winced. Could the night get any worse?

'Have you spoken to McKinley?' she asked. She was putting it off now. How would she explain the further downward spiral of the night to him?

'Yeah. He's on his way... Okay, this should be it.'

He hit play. Chan watched the footage, grainy with no sound. With the time stamp in the corner of the screen at just before eleven thirty, Chan saw a car park up in front of the gates. The lights went off and the driver got out. She couldn't get a good look at his face; he wore a baseball cap and kept his head down. Maloney fast forwarded a few minutes. When he hit play again, Campbell's car was pulling up. She could see the licence plate and the front portion of the bonnet but most of the car was out of the picture, and she couldn't see either Campbell or Kate.

Not long after though, Campbell came into the picture, walking toward the driver's door of the front car. Before he got there, a man appeared from behind and shoved a rag over Campbell's mouth. There was a brief struggle before Campbell went limp. The man dragged him out of the shot. Because of the camera's position, there was no sign of Kate either getting out of or being removed from the car. Not a minute later, the man with the cap got back into the front car, turned it around and drove out of the picture.

'Looks a damn professional job to me,' Maloney said.

Chan nodded. 'Are there any other cameras that would show us more? Anything from the street that might show us the vehicle they were taken away in?'

'Not that I know of,' Maloney said. 'There are some street cameras, but nothing that gets any better view of the building than this.'

'Have you checked those already?'

'Not yet, but–'

'Then do it. Please.'

Chan's phone was ringing. McKinley. She sighed. Answered.

'We'll deal with the whys and wherefores another time,' he said. 'For now, have you any idea where Doherty, Campbell or Green are?'

'I've got someone checking on Doherty's properties in the Lower East Side. We believe that's most likely where he's heading to.'

'*We?*'

'I'm gonna find Campbell, sir. I'm sure of it.'

'Use any resource you need. I want this over before dawn.'

Me too, Chan thought.

'Have you heard from Trapp at all?' Chan asked.

'No. He's not answering his phone. I've got someone looking for him.'

Chan shook her head. Another call was coming through. Ryker.

'Sorry, I've got to go…' She ended the call. Answered the other 'Ryker?'

'I've found the car.'

Chan's heart lurched. 'Campbell and Kate?'

'Nowhere to be seen. The car's dumped. They've moved them somewhere else.'

'Where are you now?'

'Heading for FDR Drive. I spoke to Campbell. He said he could hear water. A boat.'

'What? You think—'

'No, I don't think they're on a boat. But I do think they're near the water. You need to find me a location. Doherty must own something around here. A derelict building. A warehouse. Factory. Check what you know about Green too. It might be somewhere that used to be his.'

'I'm on it,' Chan said.

'And be quick.'

She just hoped they weren't already too late.

Chapter fifty-seven

When Campbell next came to, the first thing he noticed in the darkened room was Kate. The love of his life. She was on her feet now, but her wrists and ankles were tied to a metal column in the middle of the room. Her mouth was taped over. She stared teary-eyed at Campbell.

He tried to move but couldn't. Realised he was sitting on the ground, legs out in front of him. His hands were behind him, tied to something. Most likely a support column similar to Kate's. He didn't have a gag on though.

'Kate. Babe, are you okay?'

She let out a series of incoherent moans and whimpers. Tears streamed down her face but Campbell noticed she didn't look hurt physically. He scanned the rest of the room. A huge empty space, concrete floor, low ceiling, no windows. The walls were plain white, the space poorly lit by two overhead strip lights.

'Just stay calm, Kate. We'll get out of this.'

But as the words passed his lips, the expression on his fiancée's face turned to one of horror. She moaned louder, struggled against her shackles.

'Is that so, Campbell?' came a voice from behind him. A moment later Shaun Doherty walked into view.

Campbell stared defiantly but said nothing. Doherty didn't break eye contact. He was angry.

'Do you know why you're here?' Doherty asked. Campbell didn't answer. 'Do you know why you're here?!' he boomed.

'Please,' Campbell said, bowing his head. There was no point in taking a macho stand. All he wanted was for him and Kate to get out alive. 'Please don't hurt her.'

'She's here because of *you*. This is all because of you, Scott Campbell.'

Doherty moved over to Kate. Campbell saw the knife in Doherty's hand. Kate had seen it too. As Doherty moved closer to her, another man stepped into Campbell's view.

'Danny here is itching to get you, Campbell,' Doherty said, still looking at Kate. 'He wants to tear your fucking face off. Do you know how many of his friends are dead tonight? All because of you. He wants to rip you to pieces.' Doherty stopped, turned back to Campbell. 'But I told him he can't.'

Doherty paused.

Campbell didn't dare look Danny or Doherty in the eye now as he spoke. 'I don't know what you're talking about. That wasn't me.'

'No?'

'Please—'

'Shut the fuck up and listen!' Doherty snapped. He strode up to Campbell who shrivelled downward, trying to get away. 'Why are you here, Campbell?' Doherty shouted, spraying spittle on Campbell's face. 'Tell me why you're here and you might get out of this in one piece.'

'I don't know!' Campbell shouted back, finding the mental strength to lift his head. 'I haven't done anything to you!'

'You've done *everything*. Does your girl know what you are? Does Green know?' Doherty was staring at Campbell, their faces only inches apart. The anger dropped away, replaced by a crooked smile. 'He doesn't, does he? Green doesn't know a thing! You've screwed him just as much as me.'

Doherty turned back to Kate, holding the knife up and pointing it to her. 'Does wifey know?'

She murmured but kept her body still, as if she was afraid any movement would cause Doherty to launch himself at her.

'Well, do you? Do you know that your fella here is a rat piece of shit?'

Kate's eyes went wider as she stared at Campbell.

Campbell's mind raced. Did Doherty know about him and Ryker and the FBI? How could he? Even so, Campbell hadn't done anything to harm Doherty, had he?

This was down to Ryker. Whatever he'd done, Doherty was now hell-bent on revenge. It was Ryker who'd fucked everything up.

Yet, Campbell believed, Ryker was the only person who could save him and Kate now.

Chapter fifty-eight

Ryker was speeding down FDR Drive, high-rise projects to his right, the inky water of the East River shimmering under the lights of the Williamsburg Bridge to his left. Without any further updates from Chan, his immediate focus was on returning to the dump of a house where Celine and Megan lived. They knew Charlie Ward, at least a little bit. Perhaps he'd talked to them about the area, properties around there that he and Green owned. Maybe he'd even taken Megan to them. With nothing else to go on, Ryker had little alternative.

His phone vibrated. Chan.

'Please tell me you have something,' he said.

'Something, yes.'

'Better than nothing.'

'Green is a partner in a luxury high-rise down there, right opposite Sara D. Roosevelt Park. A twenty-storey skyscraper renovated and reopened last year.'

'Doesn't sound like what we're after at all. That's not where Doherty would store his goods. Nor where he'd take people he's kidnapped.'

'That's what I was thinking. On top of that, a company we believe was controlled by Charlie Ward owns two buildings in the Lower East Side. Others in Manhattan, too, but that's the immediate focus based on your... hunch.'

'Okay. Tell me about them.'

'One is a derelict apartment building off 1st Avenue–'

'1st Avenue? That's not near the water.'

'Not exactly.'

'The other?'

'An old factory and warehouse right off FDR Drive, not far from Pier 36.'

'That's the one,' Ryker said.

'I'm not so sure about that.'

'Because?'

Chan sighed. 'I've pulled out all the stops for this one. We've had a remote drone fly over the area, a heat-signature camera attached to it. The apartment building definitely has activity inside. Several bodies are visible. The factory… absolutely nothing. No one's there.'

Ryker mulled that over for a second.

'What are you telling me?' he asked.

'I've got a team going to the apartment building now. I'm on my way there too.'

'Understood,' Ryker said.

He ended the call.

***

Only two minutes later Ryker pulled up in the weed-filled parking lot of the old factory, a red-brick structure several storeys tall that had two separate corrugated iron warehouses. Ryker couldn't see any other vehicles there. As he stepped from his car he was already doubting his decision to go there rather than to the apartment building the FBI were swarming. Too late to turn back now.

With the gun he'd acquired from the policeman in New Jersey in his hand, Ryker sprinted across the barren space to the dark warehouses.

Chapter fifty-nine

'It's true!' Campbell shouted. 'I'm a rat. I've been talking to the FBI. But Kate… she has nothing to do with this.'

'How did you know about tonight?'

'Tonight?'

'The warehouse! Your goddamn hero killing half my men and stopping me getting what I wanted.'

'I don't know anything about that. I swear!'

Doherty strode over and launched his fist into Kate's stomach. She groaned, her eyes seeking Campbell's and imploring.

'No!' Campbell shouted.

'There's only one way you can make this better for yourself now, Campbell.' Doherty turned back to him. 'The code.'

'The code?'

'For Green's basement, you moron! Tell me. It's the only thing that will keep you two alive.'

That was a no-brainer. Doherty turned to hit Kate again.

'Okay!' Campbell shouted. 'I'll tell you. But please, just let Kate go.'

Campbell reeled off the simple code. Had Doherty really needed to go to such lengths? Doherty said nothing. He turned and moved to the corner of the room with his phone pressed to his ear. After a few minutes he put the phone away and turned around.

What was that look on his face? It wasn't satisfaction, that was for sure.

'I did what you asked. Please, let us go.'

'It worked,' Doherty said, more calm now, but no less menacing. 'But you cost me a lot tonight. You need to pay. An eye for an eye.'

'I didn't set you up!' Campbell screamed, his voice hoarse. 'I don't know anything about you!'

'Well you would say that, wouldn't you?'

Doherty walked to Kate, the knife once again in his hands. He moved the knife up Kate's leg. The blade pushed her dress up almost to her crotch. Tears streamed down her face. Her lips, her whole body in fact, quivered. Doherty had a manic look in his eyes. He was enjoying every moment.

The knife nicked the top of Kate's thigh, drawing a small amount of blood. The tears came harder and faster, her stare still fixed firmly on Campbell.

'Quite a pair of legs on her. Bet you've had some good times in there, haven't you?' Doherty flashed a devilish look at Campbell. 'Shame you won't get to do that anymore.'

Doherty pulled the knife away from Kate's leg. Her dress fell back down. The blood from the wound instantly soaked into the light-coloured fabric.

'An eye for an eye – that's only fair.'

'Please, you said you would let us go!'

'*You*. Not both of you. No, I'm sending you out to the wolves. Once Green knows what you did, who was responsible for his daughter's death… well, what do you think?'

'No, please!'

Danny moved over to Campbell. He grabbed Campbell's head in his hands, firmly holding it in position, pointing directly toward Kate. Doherty lifted the knife to her neck.

'Please!' Campbell begged again. Tears streamed down his face.

Doherty gave Campbell that same knowing look again. Campbell shook his head feebly. Opened his mouth to beg…

Doherty's face twisted. In a short, sharp motion, he slashed the knife across Kate's neck.

Campbell's legs went weak. For a few moments his heart stopped.

Blood gushed out of the wound on Kate's neck. Her eyes were bursting wide.

Her focus remained on Campbell the whole time.

He struggled and fought against his ties, and against Danny's hands clasped around his head, mustering every ounce of strength he had…

He could do nothing.

Campbell let out a long shout of despair as Kate gargled desperately. He could see the look of hopelessness in her eyes. Blood poured down her body, covering her skin and soaking her dress.

As the life drained out of her, her gaze never once left Campbell.

After just a few seconds more, she finally closed her eyes, and her head slumped.

Danny took his hands off Campbell's head. Campbell didn't say a word. He wasn't struggling anymore. He stared, motionless, at Kate. Even as Doherty approached him, he never took his eyes off her. Never saw the blow from Doherty coming. All he was aware of was stinging on the side of his head for a brief moment before his eyes closed.

Chapter sixty

As he rushed for the warehouses, Ryker's eyes darted around in the darkness, looking for any signs of movement within the grounds. He saw none. He moved to the front entrance of the first warehouse. To one side a thick padlock clasped the double loading doors shut. He tried the handle of the entrance door. Locked. No signs of forced entry. He moved across. The ground-floor window next to the entrance was boarded up. He prised one of the boards away, put his face up to the grimy glass behind it. This wasn't the right place.

He looked across the grounds to the next warehouse, an almost carbon copy of the first. There were no signs of life there either. He turned the other way to the red-brick factory. In the darkness its form was barely visible, but Ryker could just about make it out in the glow of the twinkling orange lights of nearby buildings.

Ryker was about to go for his phone, about to admit defeat and rush off to catch up with the FBI, when he heard the *whoomph* as a powerful car engine was started. Ryker looked over to the second warehouse. Could see nothing. He rushed forward. He couldn't move quickly enough. From an unseen nook two bright headlight beams pierced the darkness. The engine revs soared as the car accelerated. Ryker had the gun held up as the vehicle burst into view, speeding out from behind the second warehouse.

A momentary pause from Ryker. Because he recognised the car. Not Doherty, but Green. What was he doing here?

It didn't matter much. Ryker opened fire. Four shots. One hit a tyre. Three hit the back end of the car as it sped away toward FDR Drive. Ryker hadn't stopped it.

Making a snap decision, he rushed forward to the warehouse. Heaved open the unlocked loading doors. Stared into the dark space beyond.

'Campbell!' Ryker shouted out. Silence. 'Kate!'

Nothing at all. Ryker, gun in one hand, took out his pocket torch and shone it about the empty space. There were no signs anyone had been there at all. Except Green definitely had.

Ryker spotted a doorway at the far end of the open space – the entrance to a boxed-off area, roof and all. For a second Ryker stared at the shiny metallic door. He knew what he was looking at. He hadn't made a mistake at all.

'Campbell!' Ryker shouted again, sprinting for the door.

He wrenched it open. The lights were on inside the cold storage area. It was empty except for the woman tied to the pole in front of him. Her head was bowed. Blood covered her and the floor around her. Kate Green.

Ryker's heart lurched, but he knew there was nothing he could do for her now. He turned and sprinted out. He could still save Campbell. He had to.

Chapter sixty-one

Chan, hurtling down 3rd Avenue, had just seconds ago ended the call with the FBI team who'd raided the apartment building on 1st Avenue. Doherty wasn't there. Nor was Campbell or Kate or anyone else relevant to the investigation. Investigation? No, it was utter chaos. As determined by the drone, the building wasn't empty, but it was in fact being used by a group of meth-head hobos. They'd had the shocks of their lives, no doubt.

Her phone chirped again. Ryker.

'Please tell me you found them?' she said.

'Kate Green is dead.' The background noise suggested he was driving. Fast.

Chan felt a lump in her throat. 'I don't get it.'

'The warehouse had a cold storage unit. Meat storage or preparation. Lead-lined. That's why your heat signature picked up nothing.'

'I'm sorry,' she said.

'Not your fault.'

'And Campbell?'

'I'm still chasing. I think it's Green who has him now.'

'Green, but–'

'I don't know how. But I do know something. I know why Doherty took Campbell.'

'Because he's a psycho?'

'Partly. He knew Campbell was talking to us.'

'How?'

'They'd been watching Green's warehouse. Maybe for days. Earlier, when I was there, Doherty hadn't managed to get into Green's basement. He wants that money. Campbell knew the code.'

'The warehouse is crawling with police and Feds. Doherty can't go back there.'

'Exactly. Crawling with Feds. Remember your little problem?'

'Shit,' Chan said. 'I'll call you back.'

Doing her best to drive one-handed, she dialled McKinley.

'Please tell me you have good news, Chan? I'm not sure I can take this anymore.'

'Have you found Trapp yet?'

A sigh.

'Tell me!'

'We were too late. He turned up in Newark. At the warehouse. The police at the site didn't know any better.'

'They let him in?'

'In, and out. He walked off with Green's money right under the police's noses.'

'I told you to watch him!'

'Remember who you're talking to!' McKinley's bellow did the trick of shutting her up. 'We were too late. If you had still been there rather than running off after James Ryker…'

Chan gritted her teeth but didn't bite back. How did he even know?

'Get back to the warehouse,' McKinley said. 'We'll get every agent and police officer looking for Trapp. Green, Doherty and Ryker too.'

'No,' Chan said.

'No?'

New Jersey was miles away. If Trapp had already left there was no point in going back now. Ryker had claimed it was Green who now had Campbell. Quite how that had happened, she had no idea. But she did have an inkling where they might go.

'I'll call you back,' she said before ending the call.

She just prayed she was right this time.

Chapter sixty-two

"'Thanks for the money, sorry about your daughter, blame the snitch Campbell, not me." What the fuck is this?' Green snarled, holding the phone out to Campbell. 'Look at me when I'm talking to you!'

Campbell tried to lift his head but couldn't. Blood dripped from his lips and nose and the cut above his eye. The room around him – an apartment? – felt distant. One of the thick arms holding him let go. Grabbed his chin and hauled his head up. Campbell managed to focus on the phone screen for a second before his vision went blurry again.

'I'm… sorry,' Campbell said.

He looked at Green. Although angry, there was something else in the man's face too… in his eyes. Pain. He looked defeated. Exactly how Campbell felt.

Green nodded to someone Campbell couldn't see.

Campbell was wrenched off his feet – Steinhauser? – and thrust into one of the dining chairs which had been placed in the middle of the room by Deontay. Campbell's hands were tied behind his back with rope. A moment later Campbell felt a rush of blood to his brain and his heart started racing. He gasped and his head shot upright, his eyes wide. He looked to see Steinhauser by his side, a syringe in his hand.

'Adrenaline,' Green said, kneeling down in front of Campbell. 'I'm not having you pass out on me. We're going to keep this going, until *I* say you've had enough.'

'Henry… please,' Campbell begged.

Green paused. It looked like he was about to break down in tears. His hands were shaking as he looked down at his feet. Then he reached up and pulled the viper pendant from inside his shirt, turned it over in his hand for a few seconds. Campbell could see focus returning as he did so, his breathing steadying.

Green's head whipped up. A resolute determination was now plastered on his features.

'Why did they kill her?' he snapped.

'Doherty...' Campbell said, trying to find the strength. 'He told me he wouldn't.'

Green straightened up and nodded and Deontay stepped forward and thumped Campbell hard in the stomach, knocking the wind out of him. His vision blurred and danced again. With his head bowed, Campbell could see Green's foot tapping furiously. Impatience? Rage? Or was the guy on something?

'Tell me why my daughter is dead,' Green said, his voice quavering on the last few words. But anger quickly took over again. 'Tell me why her body was left like a piece of discarded meat! Do you know what it felt like to see her like that? To know I couldn't help? To know I had to leave her there too because the Feds are crawling everywhere tonight and I had to get away before they arrived.'

Green paused. Campbell could see the rage peaking. Green was struggling to contain it. His face was contorted and twisted, and when he next spoke his teeth remained gritted the whole time.

'I had to leave my daughter's body in that filthy place... Tell me why.'

'It was me. I... I've been talking... to the FBI.'

Green took a step forward and threw a fist into Campbell's face, then another into his temple. The edge of Green's ring split the skin. Blood poured. The room spun. Campbell closed his eyes, hoping it would stop, but the spinning carried on. He kept his eyes squeezed shut as he was punched again in the side, then again, followed by a flurry of punches to his face. His nose cracked and a wave of warm blood gushed down over his mouth. He could hear Green panting heavy breaths.

'I love... loved her,' Campbell said, blood spluttering from his mouth.

Despite the beating and the pain that he felt all over, Kate was the only thing he could think about. 'Do what you want. I… already lost ev-everything.'

'What do they know about me?' Green said, sounding calm again, his breathing coming under control.

Campbell couldn't even think of where to begin.

'Tell me what they know!'

'I just wanted to be with Kate.'

Green, nursing his knuckles, sent Deontay forward. He pummelled Campbell's chest and sides for what seemed like an age. Campbell began to drift again. He wasn't sure if it was into unconsciousness or to his grave.

'Give him another shot.'

'No!' Campbell slurred.

Too late. This time the surge made his heart heave uncontrollably. Campbell gasped and his lungs wrenched as he struggled to keep his breathing under control.

'I said, tell me what they know,' Green said, still measured.

'The warehouse, the drugs… the money,' Campbell said.

'What have you done?' Green shook his head in dismay. 'This is my whole life. What have you done?!'

'I did it for… Kate.'

Green looked about ready to explode. Somehow he brought himself down again.

'What about Doherty?'

It was a struggle for Campbell to even say a word now; his speech was slow and garbled. 'I… don't know how… he found out. He wanted… the money. He said… he'd let us… go.'

Green glared at Campbell, the pained look returning to his eyes. 'How did Doherty know? About the warehouse? About you?'

'I… don't know.' Campbell broke down in tears. Then he found a surge of strength. 'He only let me go so you'd kill me! This is what he wants you to do.'

The words had an effect. Green's hatred for Doherty was so severe that as much as he clearly wanted to punish Campbell, the thought that it was what Doherty had intended was causing him to rethink.

'Doherty killed my daughter because of you.'

Green stepped forward and punched Campbell hard in the face, opening up a fresh wound. Campbell tried to spit out a mouthful of blood, but he was so weak now that the liquid dribbled down his chin and onto his already bloodied clothes.

'I told you, if you ever hurt her…'

He didn't need to finish the sentence.

Campbell knew he was dead.

'You were never good enough for her.' Green turned and took two steps away, then stopped and said to Deontay, 'Finish it. Let's see what he looks like when he's inside out. No need to clean up after. I'll see you at the car.'

'Henry!' Campbell managed to shout before Green moved out of the room. Green stopped again but didn't turn around. 'I loved her.'

Green shook his head, then left without saying another word.

Chapter sixty-three

Ryker was operating on pure instinct. There simply wasn't the time for anything else. As he turned right onto Chrystie Street, the thin strip of Sara D. Roosevelt Park a black space off to his right, he glanced up at the tall apartment building on his left. The one Chan had mentioned Green owned. This had to be it. Green couldn't afford to travel far with the police and FBI swarming the area.

He found a spot to park by the side of the road, couldn't care less if it was legal or not. He rushed out. As he was running, he saw the black Mercedes further down the street. Green. Ryker looked to the top of the apartment block. It was so late at night, nearly all of the windows were black. So the strip of lights on the penthouse level, several windows across, immediately drew his eye. A balcony, beyond which patio doors were wide open.

Ryker reached the large glass-fronted main entrance to the building and scanned the intercom for the button that would put him through to the night-time concierge or security guard. Then he caught a glimpse of someone approaching the doors on the inside. Henry Green. He was alone. Ryker's head raced.

As Green opened the door to step out into the night, his eyes met Ryker's for a brief moment. Green didn't show any sign of recognition as he carried on out into the night.

Ryker stepped inside the building and looked back. Green was walking away down the street. Ryker ran to the elevator bank. He had to hit the buttons several times before one of the lifts chimed to indicate its arrival. Ryker got in and pressed the button for the top floor.

'Come on, come on!' he said. The lift doors were taking an age to close.

Once it got on its way, the lift seemed to move ever so slowly up to the top floor. Ryker quickly readied himself. Letting Green past had been a split-second decision. Green hadn't reacted at seeing Ryker because Green had never seen his face before. There was no need to stop Green there and then. Ryker believed Campbell was inside still. Ryker or the FBI would catch up with Green eventually. The priority was saving Campbell.

Gun in hand, Ryker stepped out onto the top floor, looking left and right. All clear. There were only two apartments up here, and he knew from the orientation which door he was looking for.

Ryker dashed over. Tried the handle, turning it inch by inch, waiting for the feel of the latch releasing. And there it was – the door wasn't locked. He took a deep breath and pushed on the door with his shoulder, causing it to swing wide open and crash back on its hinges.

Ryker saw the scene in front of him in slow motion: the trail of blood leading from the chair in the middle of the room to the two hulking men standing thirty feet beyond, past the open balcony doors. They were holding another man, whose upper body was dangling over the metal railing of the balcony edge.

Campbell.

The two men – Steinhauser and Deontay – turned their heads to Ryker. They released their grip on the captive. Their hands moved toward their waistbands. With no support, Campbell's body began wobbled, began to topple forward, over the balcony...

Ryker raced toward them. He was directly in the firing line of the thugs, but he had to try to save Campbell.

He fired four times – twice at each man – as he burst forward.

All four shots were direct hits.

The two big men fell, their bodies taking an eternity to hit the floor. By the time they did, Ryker was only a few feet away.

He lunged forward, reaching out in front of him, a yell of defiance screaming from his lips.

Campbell's feet were already off the ground. His somersault over the edge almost complete. Ryker grabbed hold of Campbell's left trouser leg with one hand. Dropped his gun. Threw his other hand out...

Grasped hold of Campbell's belt.

Heaving with everything he had, Ryker hoisted Campbell back over the railing. They fell back into a heap on the polished balcony tiles.

The world returned to normal speed. Ryker got to his knees, his heart thumping.

'Campbell. Are you okay?'

No response. Campbell was in a bad way.

'Say something to me.'

He didn't answer, just lay there. But the slight movement in his chest told Ryker he was still alive.

Ryker looked over to Green's fallen men. Steinhauser had been shot in the head; he was dead. He wasn't sure where Deontay had been hit – somewhere around the shoulder or chest, Ryker thought – but he was definitely still alive. He had crawled three yards back into the apartment, a trail of blood behind him.

Picking up his gun from the tiles, Ryker got to his feet and went over to Deontay. He flipped him over. The wounded man yelled in pain. One bullet had hit Deontay in the stomach, one in the shoulder. He was bleeding badly from the gut. Would probably bleed to death without medical intervention.

Ryker pressed the muzzle of his gun into the shoulder wound. Deontay's body shook with pain and he let out a long agonising cry.

'Where's Green gone?' Ryker said.

'I... don't know!'

Ryker pressed harder, eliciting an even louder shriek.

'Where is he?!'

'Outside! Waiting... Doherty. We were going after Doherty.'

Ryker got up, leaving the injured man where he lay. Ryker couldn't care less if he died. He rushed back over to Campbell.

'Come on, we need to get you out of here.'

This time Campbell responded to Ryker's words, but his body was a dead weight. Ryker didn't have time. He had to get to Green. Outside the balcony doors, the echo of sirens cut through the night air. Help was on its way. Campbell would be okay.

Ryker put him back down and raced for the door, phone pressed to his ear.

'Ryker, have you got him?' Chan asked.

'The apartment building on Chrystie Street. Campbell's here. He's alive.'

'Okay, okay. Ryker, just stay put, we're on our way.'

'No. I'm leaving. I'm going to end this. This is all going to end tonight.'

Chapter sixty-four

Ryker darted through the building's main doors into the cool night air. Over to his right, the direction he'd come from minutes earlier, he could see the pulse of blue and red light as law enforcement closed in. Ryker turned in the opposite direction. Saw Green's car was still there. More fool him.

Casually, so as not to spook Green, Ryker walked toward the car, his body half turned so that his right hand, carrying the gun, was out of sight should Green be looking in his direction. The car was parked facing Ryker, giving him a head-on view of the windscreen. Both of the front seats were empty. When he was about five yards away, he spotted Henry Green sitting on the back seat.

Green looked up just at the moment Ryker raised his gun.

Ryker's finger twitched on the trigger, but Green was already moving. Ryker dashed forward as Green threw open the back door on the driver's side. He fired several potshots at Ryker, who ducked behind the nearest car for cover. Ryker bobbed up to see Green hurtling off down the street.

Ryker gave chase. Thought about shooting. But shooting someone in the back? Plus, Green had too much to answer for.

Green hurdled the low fence into the park. Ryker followed his path. The park was dark, the only illumination coming from streetlights beyond, partially blocked by thick trees. Ryker slowed to a walk. There was no sign of Green up ahead. Ryker strained his eyes for a glimpse of a shape or movement which would give away Green's location. He took a few more steps forward, into the darkest area of the park. He knew Green would have trouble seeing him.

Ryker stopped moving. Slowed his breathing to a minimum. Intent on not making any sound that would give away his location. Nearby the sirens were louder still. Ryker heard car doors opening and closing. People shouting. The FBI or the police or both had arrived.

Ryker heard a crunch. Like someone stepping on a branch. Then he caught movement. A shadowy figure running out from behind a tree. Ryker raised his gun and fired once. The gunshot echoed across the open space.

The figure fell to the ground. Ryker ran up to the body, his gun still pointed. When he was a couple of yards away he was relieved to see it was Green that he'd hit, and not some unfortunate bum or late-night dog walker.

Green was on his back, propping himself up on his elbows. His gun lay out of reach. He was breathing, but his breaths were wheezy and strained. Given the sounds coming from him, the bullet, hitting Green's side, had likely punctured a lung. He needed medical help, and quick.

'It's over for you, Green,' Ryker said.

'Was it you?' Green asked in a rasping voice. Each breath he took required an enormous effort.

'Me what?'

'That turned Campbell?'

Ryker huffed. 'Yeah. That was me. You shouldn't have gone after him.'

'What choice did I have? Kate's dead because of him.'

'No, Kate's dead because of *you*. How would she feel, knowing what you've done?'

Green sucked in a deep breath. For all the man's failings, and there were many, Ryker knew Green had lost a lot tonight.

Green's face changed. 'Is he alive?'

'Campbell? Yeah.'

Green almost smiled.

'You played right into Doherty's hands.'

Now Green's face darkened. 'I need you… to get him for me.'

'Me?'

'Get him. For Kate.'

Ryker's eyes narrowed. Green tried to lift himself further, propping himself up on his hands. His arms gave way and he fell down on his back, letting out a painful moan. He took a few seconds to regain himself, breathing heavily, his face screwed up while he summoned the strength to speak.

'The money Doherty stole,' Green said, lifting his head to look at Ryker. 'There was a tracker. There's an app… on my phone.'

Ryker looked down at the stricken man. Green was bad. He had hurt people and he had killed people. Some of them had been good people. Ryker hated him. He despised him. And yet in that moment Ryker wanted to thank him.

Ryker kneeled down. Fished the phone from Green's pocket and opened it up with Green's thumbprint. He whispered, 'I'll get Doherty.'

'Ryker, drop the gun!'

A shout from somewhere behind. Recognising the voice, Ryker slowly rose to his feet.

'Please, Ryker.'

Ryker lowered the weapon. Didn't drop it. Slowly turned to see Chan was alone, a few yards away.

'He's bleeding out,' Ryker said to her.

She rushed over, holstered her gun as she ran. Pulled out her phone.

'You need to tell me what's happening,' she said.

Ryker assumed she was talking to him. He didn't answer. Chan could try to save Green if she wanted to. Even if a paramedic arrived now, chances were slim. Either way, Green wasn't Ryker's concern anymore.

When she began speaking into her phone a moment later, urgently requesting an ambulance, Ryker turned and disappeared into the darkness without her even noticing.

He had one last stop to make. This was almost over now.

Chapter sixty-five

As Ryker bombed up Manhattan, heading for the Bronx, he couldn't decide whether Doherty, hiding in plain sight, was spectacularly dumb or a genius.

The journey was swift and trouble free. Ryker parked the car under the subway line, directly across the road from the burned-out shell of Malloy's. Quite why Doherty had gone there, Ryker didn't know, but there was no doubt that was where the tracker was. Which meant that was where Green's money was.

He was about to step out of the car when his phone rang for the tenth time since he'd left Chan with Green. This time he answered.

'Please, just tell me where you are,' Chan said.

'Is Campbell…?'

'Yes.'

'Green?'

'Yes, but–'

'I'll call you when it's done.'

'Ryker, the FBI agent who stole the money for Doherty – his name's Trapp. If he's there–'

Ryker ended the call. Walked across the road. Despite the fire set by Green, Malloy's appeared more or less intact from the outside, its walls and roof remaining. Yet the signs of the blaze were unmistakable, the building permanently scarred with large black patches that surrounded the doors and window frames. From the front there was no indication that anyone was inside, and Ryker looked down at the receiver app on Green's phone to make sure it was still showing this as the location. It was.

Ryker walked past the boarded-up front entrance and around to the alley at the back where Green had dumped a dead body days before. A regretful move in hindsight. Would Kate still be alive if that tit-for-tat quarrel hadn't started?

Ryker stopped at the head of the alley. Pressed himself against the wall. He stole a glance around the corner. Sure enough, Danny, Doherty's little bulldog, was standing by the back door, smoking a cigarette.

A confrontation was the only way past, but using his gun would alert whoever was inside, so Ryker would have to make do without it. For now.

He waited until Danny had half turned, and then quickly but silently ran up behind the bins, about halfway between the alley entrance and Danny. Ryker barely made a sound as he moved. He reached the bins just as Danny turned back around.

Ryker waited a few seconds, listening to the sound of Danny's shuffling feet. He was going back inside. Without hesitating, Ryker jumped out, moving quickly but silently behind Danny.

Ryker was within a yard of him when Danny turned suddenly, a combat knife in his hand, an evil grin across his face.

Danny thrust the knife out but Ryker threw his body to his right, rolling away. But Danny was quick to adjust, and the knife caught Ryker's left arm. The blade tore through his unprotected flesh. He winced and glimpsed down to see a four-inch gash across the muscle. A debilitating wound, but he wasn't going to stop now.

'Quite the little ninja, aren't you? Creeping up on me like that.' Danny sniggered, circling his prey. 'Not quite good enough though.'

Ryker leaped forward and grabbed Danny's knife arm, aiming to twist him into a hammerlock. But Danny was wily and strong, and clearly no slouch at close combat. It wasn't often Ryker met his match…

Danny gritted his teeth and hauled Ryker off, throwing his left arm into Ryker's side. As Ryker tried to counter, Danny swung wildly with the blade, and it was only because Ryker decided to throw himself backward, to the ground, that he avoided the potentially fatal blow.

Blood dripping from his arm, Ryker quickly rose to his feet. The two men squared off again, both waiting for the next move. Danny, full of confidence and anger, dealt his hand first, just as Ryker hoped he would. He came in low, then at the last second swivelled away from Ryker's defence, arcing the knife around to plunge it into Ryker's back.

Smart moves, but Ryker had seen them coming. Ryker stepped forward, lifted his knee and crashed his foot down onto the side of Danny's leg. Danny shouted in pain as his leg caved inward. He slumped to his knee, but was soon back on his feet.

Ryker had expected the blow to snap Danny's tibia and fibula, but the guy was a machine, the thick muscle in his leg shielding the full force of the hit.

But he had dropped the knife. It was lying on the ground, directly between them.

Both men lunged forward, but Ryker was quicker now. Perhaps it was the blow to the leg which made the difference after all. Danny seemed to realise this, and rather than focus on the blade, at the last second, as Ryker grasped the knife, he hurled an uppercut toward Ryker's chin.

Ryker saw it late, but still had enough time to move a few inches to the side – not much, but enough to dodge the fist. With Danny's midriff exposed, Ryker plunged the knife into Danny's abdomen. The blade sank deep into his flesh. Danny let out a sound like the wind had been knocked out of him. He pulled away from the outthrust knife and stumbled back, looking down at his wound. Ryker continued to hold the knife out, ready for another attack wave.

It didn't come.

Danny fell to the ground, flat on his back, his hand clutching the hole in his stomach. He wasn't dead, yet, but he wasn't fighting again tonight. Ryker put the knife into his pocket. Glanced at the wound on his arm again. He was losing blood. But he had nothing to help stem the flow. And he wasn't going to stop now for first aid.

He took out his gun, then opened the door to the bar.

The room he stepped into was a storage area. The fire had barely reached here; some areas of the room, toward the outer wall, looked more or less untouched. Toward the doorway at the far end, however, which Ryker presumed led out into the main bar, were more obvious signs of damage, and the floor had a thick layer of sludge over it from the combination of fire debris and the water used by the fire brigade to put the flames out.

Ryker moved through the store room, partially lit by the light coming from inside the bar area. He stopped by the doorway, saw the lighting was coming from hastily erected mobile equipment. The bar was mostly still intact, but it was badly burned and areas of it looked like they were crumbling away, the fire leaving nothing but a hollow shell of ash.

At first, Ryker couldn't see anyone there, but as he moved out, he spotted a figure off to his left, across the other side of the bar. A man, standing with his back to Ryker. Shaun Doherty.

Ryker stepped forward slowly, bringing his gun up so that it was pointed at the back of Doherty's head. Doherty was in his sights now; there was no getting away this time.

Movement to Ryker's right.

'Where's Danny gone–'

Ryker spun to the man who'd spoken, gun held out. The man pulled a gun too. Stalemate.

Calmly, Shaun Doherty turned. He, at least, was unarmed.

'You again?' he said, with a mixture of disbelief and contempt. 'Pleased to see me?'

'Drop it,' the man with the gun said. 'Or I'll blow your head off.'

'Agent Trapp, I presume?' Ryker said.

'James Ryker, I'm guessing,' Trapp said.

'What the fuck are you doing here?' Doherty said. 'Where's Green?'

Hiding in plain sight. Made a bit more sense now, Ryker guessed. This was all a game to Doherty. He'd killed Kate, taunted Green with it and set Green off against Campbell. Then he'd sat in wait for Green to show up to retrieve his lost money. Well, Ryker was about to spoil his fun once more.

'I shot Green,' Ryker said. 'Right before coming here. Half a dozen FBI agents are outside. It's over for you two.'

The look of confusion on Doherty's face was priceless.

'Bullshit,' Trapp said.

'You want to play the odds? Drop your gun. We'll take you both in.'

'*We?*' Trapp sneered. 'Except you're not FBI.' He glanced to Doherty. 'He's alone.'

'Drop the gun,' Doherty said.

'No,' Ryker said. He flicked his gaze to Trapp. 'You think you can get a shot off before I can?'

Trapp glared but said nothing.

'Why did you do it?' Ryker asked Trapp. He was buying time. Not hoping the FBI would arrive, but looking for his chance to move.

'Do what?'

'How much is Doherty paying you?'

'Enough.'

'Can you really live with all the blood on your hands? For what? A bit of money?'

'Way I see it, you've killed more people tonight than anyone else.'

Doherty laughed. 'Touché.'

'What does that say about you?' Trapp asked.

'Indeed. Yet you're willing to hold a gun to my head.'

'Just shoot him will you!' Doherty blasted.

Trapp's eyes flicked to his master. That was the momentary distraction Ryker needed.

Ryker ducked and dove left, aiming for Doherty. As expected, the move caused Trapp to pause. Ryker fired once. The bullet hit Trapp's gun hand and he screamed and opened his palm. Ryker fired again. The second shot hit Trapp in his thigh and he collapsed onto his knees.

Ryker barrelled into Doherty. Swung his elbow out as they crashed to the soggy ground. The pointed joint caught Doherty's nose. Ryker pulled the gun down, fired two more shots. Both hit Doherty in the leg.

Doherty and Trapp were both screaming and shouting in anger. Grimacing from the pain in his arm, Ryker hauled himself back to his feet. Looked down at the two sorry messes below him, both glaring defiantly. They were done for. And they knew it.

Ryker pulled the gun up. Aimed it at Trapp's head. In the past, there was no doubt Ryker would have pulled the trigger with barely a second thought. Both of these men had caused death and misery for others. As far as Ryker was concerned they didn't deserve to live.

'Just kill me,' Trapp said.

It wasn't Ryker's call to make. He didn't have to be that man anymore.

'I said shoot me!' Trapp screamed.

'I already did,' Ryker said.

He lowered the gun. Took a step back, then plonked himself down onto a charred bar stool.

Gun in hand, his eyes flitting between Doherty and Trapp, he made the call to Chan, then sat back and waited for the cavalry to arrive.

Chapter sixty-six

The break in the weather had brought cool winds from the north, and bouts of heavy rain with it. A relief, in a way, though the dark skies were hardly a comfort to Chan, given the sharp turn in her career path over the last few weeks.

The extra time with the kids was at least proving a welcome distraction.

She was walking along 46th Avenue when she saw him. It was almost a carbon copy of the last time he'd collared her on the school run, except for the weather.

'Don't you ever call in advance?' Chan said as Ryker, one arm still heavily bandaged, crossed the road and caught up with her.

'Why give people the chance to say no?'

'I can still say no.'

'Most people don't.'

They walked on in silence for a few steps. Chan wouldn't admit it to him but she was intrigued that he'd showed up. Also a little pleased too. They hadn't seen each other since that fateful night five days ago when Ryker had single-handedly brought down two criminal empires. She was grateful and in many ways impressed with his actions, even if no one else at the FBI was.

'So are you officially suspended this time or just taking a break?' Ryker asked.

'Officially suspended.'

'You could still get your job back then.'

'If they really want me there.'

'And what do you want?'

She glanced over at him and held his eye for a moment. 'I'm not sure anymore.'

'Why don't we go and get a coffee?' Ryker said.

Chan sighed. Looked at her watch.

'Come on. It's not like you've got a busy day ahead of you,' he said.

'Says who?'

He raised an eyebrow. Gave her a cheeky smile.

'Fine,' she said.

***

In the coffee shop a long queue of office workers were getting their morning fix in takeout cups. Ryker and Chan were the only customers who had bothered to take their drinks to a table. Chan had keenly observed Ryker as they waited for their drinks and as they headed over to their table. It struck her that Ryker was a man of few words, and that his mind was never at rest. The way he was always busy looking at everything and everyone around him… it was exhausting just watching him. Was it some inbuilt paranoia inside him or did he enjoy being all-seeing?

'I went to the hospital to visit him,' Ryker said after taking a short sip of his double espresso.

'Campbell?' she asked, hoping Ryker meant him rather than Green or Trapp or Doherty, who were all still alive and recuperating.

Ryker nodded.

'You got to speak to him? I thought he was under twenty-four-hour watch?'

'He is.' That look again. 'I didn't speak to him. I wanted to, but…'

'He's alive,' Chan said. 'You have to be thankful for that.'

'I can imagine he might not look so kindly on me when he recovers.'

Chan didn't say anything.

'What will you do now?' he asked.

'I'll wait it out. I'm in no rush. Perhaps the break will do me good. Give me a chance to get my priorities straight.'

'You're too good an agent to walk away.'

That he thought so made her glow. 'Perhaps the choice won't be mine.'

'Have you told your boss the truth?' he asked. 'About me?'

Chan screwed up her face. 'I've got nothing to hide. Everything I did was to further the investigation into Green. And it paid off. The way I see it, my actions, *your* actions, saved a lot of lives that would otherwise have been lost if Green and Doherty had gone at each other no holds barred.'

Ryker put his hands up. 'You don't need to convince me.'

Chan snorted. 'I will say this though. You're lucky you've got your protection. Whoever is looking out for you… I wish I had a guardian angel like that.'

'That's not how I'd describe it,' Ryker said.

'You killed people on American soil. Bad people, yes, but still. The FBI can't even question you… whereas I was only doing my job and…'

She trailed off. She hadn't intended her bitterness to be aimed at Ryker. It wasn't his fault he was who he was, and it wasn't his fault that her superiors had to go through the motions with an official disciplinary investigation. She'd broken protocol. She had to face the consequences, whatever they might be.

Ryker picked up his cup. Looked at it for a second, then downed the rest of his coffee.

'I enjoyed working with you,' Ryker said.

Chan didn't know what to say to that.

'You're good at what you do. And I like that you see the end goal rather than a set of rules.'

'We all need rules, Ryker.'

'But it's our choice whether to follow them or not.'

They sat through a few moments of awkward silence. Ryker began to fidget.

'What will *you* do now?' Chan asked.

'I've done what I came to do.'

'You're going back to England?'

'Today.'

She felt disappointed about that. 'If you're ever back in town…'

'Don't you worry. I'll check in on you. And if you ever decide to break free from the FBI…'

He got up from his chair. Didn't finish his sentence. Just held her stare for a few seconds. He put his hand on her shoulder, then turned and walked away.

Chapter sixty-seven

Ryker wasn't in the least surprised when he stepped out of the arrivals hall at Heathrow to see Peter Winter, coffee cup in hand, waiting by the railing next to the chauffeurs and taxi drivers and eager relatives.

Ryker headed up to him. Took the coffee.

'Welcome home,' Winter said.

'Best welcome I've ever had.'

They found an empty bench. Winter had come to say his piece. Ryker would hear him out, then he'd head on his way and spend some much-needed alone time recuperating.

'Thank you,' Ryker said.

Winter seemed to understand what he meant.

'Someone had to do it,' he said. 'What use are you to me if you're locked up in America for the next who knows how many years?'

Ryker wanted to bite back at that but held his tongue.

'Was it worth it?' Winter asked.

That was the big question. Ryker really wasn't sure he knew the answer. Campbell was still alive, and he was certainly out from under the control of Henry Green. That was what Ryker had gone to America to achieve. But at what cost?

'Have you spoken to her?' Ryker asked.

'Yes.'

'And?'

'And she's at death's door. She's barely coherent. But she wanted me to pass on her thanks. She's grateful for your help.'

'I don't think I got her son back exactly.'

'Who knows? But don't forget it was Campbell who put himself into that life in the first place.'

'My actions got Kate Green killed.'

'You don't know how events would have turned out without you there. Perhaps Kate and Campbell would both be dead by now.'

'Still doesn't feel like much of a victory to me. Campbell may never fully recover. Brain damage, spinal damage. Meanwhile Green and Doherty and that piece of shit from the FBI are all still walking.'

'They'll all spend the rest of their lives in prison,' Winter said.

'Best case. But it'll be years before they're even convicted.'

Winter stared. Ryker wondered what he was thinking.

'I get it,' Winter said.

'Get what?'

'I see what's got under your skin.'

'Humour me.'

'You hate that the bad guys got away.'

'Got away?'

'From you.'

'I could have killed them all if I'd wanted to. I had the chance.'

'Then why didn't you?'

'Because I didn't have to.'

'No? If you'd had an order to kill them, would you have done it?'

'An order from who? You?'

'Does it matter?'

Ryker sighed. 'They ruined so many people's lives. They don't deserve to keep their own.'

'According to your moral code, but not according to the laws of the United States, or most other countries in the world for that matter.'

Ryker went silent and looked off into the distance, his brain whirring.

'I can't stop thinking about them,' he said. 'It's just not right.'

'There is a solution,' Winter said.

Ryker huffed.

'I'm not talking about Green and Doherty, I'm talking about you. What life have you got now, Ryker? I've looked out for you these last few days, before that too, but my loyalty to you will last only so long if I get nothing in return. You're good at what you do. Hell, you're great. But you need people like me behind you.'

'Here we go again.'

'Yes. Here we go again. Come and work for me. It doesn't have to be on the books. Only between you and me and the people who need to know. We'll find the bad guys. Put them down for good. No escape, no prison.'

'Like the old days.'

'No. Not like the old days. Better than that. What do you say, are you in?'

Ryker finished the coffee, looked away from Winter. He had to clench his teeth hard to keep his brain focused. It kept on flashing with images of the people he'd failed recently, Campbell and Kate the most prominent. He couldn't go through something like that again. He couldn't let the likes of Green and Doherty cause carnage and come out the other end so lightly.

And what else was he really doing to do?

Ryker looked back to Winter. The Commander was already smiling.

'Just say it,' Winter said. 'For me. It'll make my day.'

Ryker smiled too. Got to his feet.

'Yes,' he said. 'I'm in.'

Lightning Source UK Ltd.
Milton Keynes UK
UKHW041633071220
374769UK00001B/227